SAM GUNN, UNLIMITED

Thief, CIA spy, blackmailer, womanizing SOB, free spirit, underdog, little so-and-so, loose cannon, Huckleberry Finn. And now ... MAROONED

Those bastards at Rockledge have shown their hand at last. They're going to kill me and my partners and steal my claim to Pittsburgh asteroid and the metals we've mined.

Raising one clenched fist over my head I yelled into my suit radio's microphone, "I'll see you—all of you—hanging from the highest yardarm in the British fleet!"

It was the only damned thing I could think of.

A blazing flare of light bellowed from the *Argo*'s rocket nozzles and the ship—*my* ship—suddenly leaped away and dwindled in the dark sky until I couldn't see it any more.

Fiction by Ben Bova

MARS
THE TRIKON DECEPTION *(with Bill Pogue)*
ORION IN THE DYING TIME
FUTURE CRIME*
VOYAGERS III: STAR BROTHERS
CYBERBOOKS
PEACEKEEPERS
VENGEANCE OF ORION
THE KINSMAN SAGA
BATTLE STATION*
VOYAGERS II: THE ALIEN WITHIN
PROMETHEANS*
PRIVATEERS
THE ASTRAL MIRROR*
ORION
ESCAPE PLUS*
THE WINDS OF ALTAIR
TEST OF FIRE
VOYAGERS
THE EXILES TRILOGY
KINSMAN
MAXWELL'S DEMONS*
COLONY
THE MULTIPLE MAN
MILLENNIUM
CITY OF DARKNESS
THE STARCROSSED
GREMLINS, GO HOME! *(with Gordon R. Dickson)*
FORWARD IN TIME*
WHEN THE SKY BURNED
AS ON A DARKLING PLAIN
THX 1138 *(with George Lucas)*
ESCAPE!
THE DUELING MACHINE
OUT OF THE SUN
THE WEATHERMAKERS
STAR WATCHMAN
THE STAR CONQUERORS
TO SAVE THE SUN *(with A. J. Austin)*

*collection

Sam Gunn, Unlimited

Ben Bova

BANTAM BOOKS
NEW YORK • TORONTO • LONDON • SYDNEY • AUCKLAND

SAM GUNN, UNLIMITED
A Bantam Spectra Book / October 1993

ISBN 0-553-56289-4

Published simultaneously in the United States and Canada

PRINTED IN THE UNITED STATES OF AMERICA

RAD   0 9 8 7 6 5 4 3 2 1

To Audrey and Edward L. Ferman

Sam Gunn, Unlimited

1

●━●■●━●■●━●■●━●■●━●■●━●■●━●

Selene City

SHE LIKES TO be called Jade, although her name is actually
Jane. Jane Avril Inconnu. Sometimes new acquaintances
mistake that last name for Romanian, although her flame-
red hair and dazzling green eyes speak of more northern
and flamboyant lands. She will tolerate such misunder-
standings—when there is some advantage to being toler-
ant.

She received her name from the Quebecoise surgeon
who adopted her as a foundling at the old original
Moonbase back when that was civilization's rugged frontier. There were no pediatricians on the Moon; the surgeon happened to be on duty when the female infant,
red-faced and squalling, was discovered in the corridor
just outside the base's small hospital. No more than a few
days old, the infant had been placed in a plastic shipping
container, neatly bundled and warmly blanketed. And
abandoned. Who the baby's mother might be remained a
mystery, even though Moonbase hardly supported more
than two hundred men and women in those days, plus a
handful of visitors.

Her adopted mother's name was Jane, the month

was April, and *inconnu* is the French word for "unknown." So the orphaned baby girl became Jane Avril Inconnu, raised alone by the surgeon for the first four years of her life.

By the time the surgeon's five-year contract with Moonbase was completed and she was due to return to Montreal, the medical staff—which doted on the little girl—had discovered that Jane Avril suffered from a congenital bone defect, a rare inability to manufacture sufficient amounts of calcium. Neither exercise nor medicine could help. Although she could walk and run and play normally in the gentle gravity of the Moon, on Earth she would be a helpless cripple, confined to a wheelchair or a mechanical exoskeleton, in constant danger of snapping her brittle, fragile bones.

Her adopted mother bravely decided to remain with the child, but then the news came from Montreal that her own mother was gravely ill, dying. Torn between the generations, the woman returned to Earth, promising to return soon, soon. She never did. There were family obligations on Earth, and later a husband who wanted children of his own.

Jane Avril remained at Moonbase, orphaned once again, raised by a succession of medical personnel at the hospital. Some were warm and loving; some were distant and uncaring. A few were actually abusive now and then.

Moonbase grew, over those years, into the city called Selene. The frontier of civilization crept across the battered old face of the Moon and expanded into cislunar space, where great habitats were built in the dark emptiness to house hundreds of thousands of people. Explorers reached out to Mars, and then farther. Entrepreneurs, some wildly reckless, some patient and cautious, began to reap the wealth of space. Fortunes were built on lunar mining, on power satellites to feed the energy hungers of Earth, on prospecting the metals and minerals of the asteroids.

Of all those daring and dashing fortune-seekers, the first, the most adventurous, the best known of them all was Sam Gunn. As she grew into young womanhood, Jane Avril heard endless stories about Sam Gunn and the fortunes he had found in space. Found and lost. For Sam was more impetuous and unpredictable than a solar storm. Long before Jane Avril acquired the nickname Jade, Sam Gunn was already a living legend.

She could not consider herself beautiful, despite the gorgeous red hair and those dazzling green eyes that gave her the sobriquet. She was small, just a shade over 165 centimeters tall. Her figure was slim, elfin, almost child-like. Her face was just a trifle too long and narrow to suit her, although she could smile very prettily when she wanted to. She seldom did.

Being raised as an orphan had built a hard shell of distrust around her. She knew from painful experience that no relationship ever lasted long, and it was foolish to open her heart to anyone.

Yet that heart of hers was a romantic one. Inside her protective crust was a yearning for adventure and love that would not die, no matter how sternly she tried to repress it. She dreamed of tall handsome men, bold heroes with whom she would travel to the ends of the solar system. She wanted with all her heart to get free of the dreary monotony of Selene, with its gray underground corridors and its unending sameness every day, year after year.

She knew that she was forever barred from Earth, even though she could see its blue, beautiful glory shining at her in the dark lunar sky. Earth, with all its teeming billions of people and its magnificent cities and oceans of water so deep and blue and raging wild. Selene was a cemetery by comparison. She had to get away, to fly free, anywhere. If she could never set foot on Earth, there were still the great habitats at the Lagrangian points, and the bridge ships plying out toward Mars, the rugged frontier of the Asteroid Belt and beyond, to the deadly beautiful dangers of the gas giant worlds.

Such were her dreams. The best she could do, though, was to get a job as a truck driver up on the dusty dead lunar surface.

But still she dreamed. And waited for her opportunity.

2

━•━•━•━•━•━•━•━•━•━•━•━•━•━•━•━

The Sea of Clouds

THE SPRING-WHEELED truck rolled to a silent stop on the Mare Nubium. The fine dust kicked up by its six wheels floated lazily back to the *mare*'s soil. The hatch to the truck cab swung upward, and a space-suited figure climbed slowly down to the lunar surface, clumped a dozen ponderously careful steps, then turned back toward the truck.

"Yeah, this is the spot. The transponder's beeping away, all right."

At first Jade had been excited by her work as a truck driver. Even inside a space suit, being out on the wide-open surface of the Moon, beneath the solemn eyes of the unblinking stars, was almost like being able to run wild and free in comparison to the dreariness of Selene's underground corridors. But now she had been at the job for nearly a year. The excitement had worn away, eroded as inevitably as the meteor-pitted rocks of the Sea of Clouds.

And always in that dead-black sky there hung the glowing jewel of Earth, tantalizing, beautiful, forever out of her reach.

She and the hoist operator (male and married) clambered down from the cab, bulbous and awkward-looking in their bulky space suits. Jade turned a full 360 degrees, scanning the scene through the gold-tinted visor of her suit's bubble helmet. There was nothing to be seen except the monotonous gray plain, pockmarked by craters like an ancient, savage battlefield that had been petrified into solid stone long eons ago.

"*Merde*, you can't even see the ringwall from here!" she exclaimed.

"That's what he wanted," came the voice of their supervisor through her helmet earphones. "To be out in the open, without a sign of civilization in sight. He picked this spot himself, you know."

"Helluva place to want to be buried," said the hoist operator.

"That's what he specified in his will. Come on, let's get to work. I want to get back to Selene City before the Sun goes down."

It was a local joke: the three space-suited workers had more than two hundred hours before sunset.

Grunting even in the gentle lunar gravity, they slid the gleaming sarcophagus from the back of the truck and placed it softly on the roiled, dusty ground. It was made of stainless steel, delicately inscribed in gold by the solar system's most famous sculptress. At one end, in tastefully small lettering, was a logo: S. GUNN ENTERPRISES, UNLIMITED.

The supervisor carefully paced to the exact spot where the tiny transponder lay blinking and used a hand laser to draw an exact circle around it. Then he sprayed the stony ground inside the circle with the blue-white flame of a plasma torch. Meanwhile, Jade helped the hoist operator swing the four-meter-high crate down from the truck bed to the ground next to the sarcophagus.

"Ready for the statue?" Jade asked.

The supervisor said nothing as he inspected his own work. The hot plasma had polished the stony ground. Jade and the hoist operator heard him muttering over their helmet earphones as he used the hand laser to check the polished ground's dimensions. Satisfied, he helped them drag the gold-filigreed sarcophagus to its center and slide it into place over the transponder.

"A lot of work to do for a dead man."

"He wasn't just any ordinary man."

"It's still a lot of work. Why in hell couldn't he be recycled like everybody else?" the hoist operator complained.

"He's not in the sarcophagus, dumbskull," snapped the supervisor. "Don't you know any goddamned thing?"

"He's not . . . ?"

Jade had known that the sarcophagus was empty, symbolic. She was surprised that her coworker didn't. Some people pay no attention to anything, she told herself. I'll bet he doesn't know anything at all about Sam Gunn.

"Sam Gunn," said the supervisor, "never did things like everybody else. Not in his whole cussed life. Why should he be like the rest of us in death?"

They chattered back and forth through their suit radios as they uncrated the big package. Once they had removed all the plastic and the bigger-than-life statue stood sparkling in the sunlight, they stepped back and gaped at it.

"It's glass!"

"Christ, I never saw any statue so damned big."

"Must have cost a fortune to get it here. Two fortunes!"

"Sam's company had it done at Island One, I heard. Brought the sculptress in from the Belt and paid her enough to keep her at L4 for two whole years. Drove 'em bankrupt, I hear. God knows how many times she tried to cast a statue this big and failed, even in low gee."

"I didn't know you could make a glass statue this big."

"In microgee you can. It's hollow. If we were in air, I could ping it with my finger and you'd hear it ring."

"Crystal."

"That's right."

Jade laughed softly.

"What's so funny?" the supervisor asked.

"Who else but Sam Gunn would have the gall to erect a crystal statue to himself and then have it put out in the middle of this godforsaken emptiness, where nobody's ever going to see it? It's a monument to himself, for himself. What ego! What monumental ego."

The supervisor chuckled, too. "Yeah. Sam had an ego, all right. But he was a smart little SOB, too."

"You knew him?" Jade asked.

"Sure. Knew him well enough to tell you that he didn't pick this spot for his tomb just for the sake of his ego. He was smarter than that."

"What was he like?"

"When did you know him?" the hoist operator asked.

"Come on, we've still got work to do. He wants the statue positioned exactly as he stated in his will, with its back toward Selene and the face looking up toward Earth."

"Yeah, okay, but when did you know him, huh?"

"Oh, golly, years ago. Decades ago. When the two of us were just young pups. The first time either of us came here, back in—Lord, it's thirty years ago. More."

"Tell us about it. Was he really the rogue that the history tapes say he was? Did he really do all the things they say?" Jade found to her surprise that she was eager to know.

"He was a phony!" the hoist operator snapped. "Everybody knows that. A helluva showman, sure, but he never did half the stuff he took credit for. Nobody could have, not in one lifetime."

"He lived a pretty intense life," said the supervisor. "If it hadn't been for that black hole he'd still be running his show from here to Titan."

"A showman. That's what he was."

"What was he like?" Jade asked again.

So, while the two young workers struggled with the huge, fragile crystal statue, the older man sat himself on the lip of the truck's hatch and told them what he knew about the first time Sam Gunn had come to the Moon.

3

The Supervisor's Tale

THE SKIPPER USED the time-honored cliché. He said, "Houston, we have a problem here."

There were eight of us, the whole crew of Artemis IV, huddled together in the command module. After six weeks of living on the Moon, the module smelled like a pair of unwashed gym socks. With a woman president, the space agency figured it would be smart to name the second round of lunar exploration after a female: Artemis was Apollo's sister. Get it?

But it had just happened that the computer that picked the crew selections for Artemis IV picked all men. Six weeks without even the sight of a woman, and now our blessed-be-to-God return module refused to light up. We were stranded. No way to get back home.

As usual, Capcom in Houston was the soul of tranquility. "Ah, A-IV, we read you and copy that the return module is no-go. The analysis team is checking the telemetry. We will get back to you soonest."

It didn't help that Capcom, that shift, was Sandi Hemmings, the woman we all lusted after. Among the eight of us, we must have spent enough energy dreaming about cornering Sandi in zero gravity to propel each of us right back to Houston. Unfortunately, dreams have a very low specific impulse, and we were still stuck on the Moon, a quarter-million miles from the nearest woman.

Sandi played her Capcom duties strictly by the book, especially since all our transmissions were taped for later review. She kept the traditional Houston poker face, but she managed to say, "Don't worry, boys. We'll figure it out and get you home."

Praise God for small favors.

We had spent hours checking and rechecking the cursed return module. It was engineer's hell: everything checked but nothing worked. The thing just sat there like a lump of dead metal. No electrical power. None. Zero. The control board just stared at us cold and glassy-eyed as a banker listening to your request for an unsecured loan. We had pounded it. We had kicked it. In our desperation we had even gone through the instruction manual, page by page, line by line. Zip. Zilch. The bird was dead.

When Houston got back to us, six hours after the skipper's call, it was the stony, unsmiling image of the mission coordinator glowering at us as if we had deliberately screwed up the return module. He told us: "We have identified the problem, Artemis IV. The return module's main electrical power supply has malfunctioned."

That was like telling Othello that he was a Moor.

"We're checking out bypasses and other possible fixes," Old Stone Face went on. "Sit tight, we'll get back to you."

The skipper gave a patient sigh. "Yes, sir."

"We ain't going anyplace," said a whispered voice, just loud enough to be heard. Sam's.

The problem, we finally discovered, was caused by a micrometeoroid, no less. A little grain of sand that just happened to roam through the solar system for four and a half billion years and then decided to crash-dive itself into the main fuel cell of our return module's power supply. It was so tiny that it didn't do any visible damage to the fuel cell; just hurt it enough to let it discharge electrically for most of the six weeks we had been on the Moon. And the two other fuel cells, sensing the discharge through the module's idiot computer, tried to recharge their partner for

six weeks. The result: all three of them were dead and
gone by the time we needed them.

It was Sam who discovered the pinhole in the fuel
cell, the eighteenth time we checked out the power supply. I can remember his exact words, once he realized
what had happened: "Shit!"

Sam was a feisty little guy who would have been too
short for astronaut duty if the agency hadn't lowered the
height requirements so that women could join the corps.
He was a good man, a whiz with a computer and a born
tinkerer who liked to rebuild old automobiles and then
race them on abandoned freeways whenever he could
scrounge up enough old-fashioned petrol to run them. The
Terror of Clear Lake, we used to call him. The Texas Highway Patrol had other names for him. So did the agency administrators; they cussed near threw him out of the
astronaut corps at least half a dozen times.

But we all liked Sam, back in those days, as we went
through training and then blasted off for our first mission
on the Moon. He was funny, he kept us laughing. And he
did the things and said the things that none of the rest of
us had the guts to do or say.

The skipper loved Sam a little less than the rest of us,
especially after six weeks of living in each other's dirty
laundry. Sam had a way of *almost* defying any order he received. He reacted very poorly to authority figures. Our
skipper, Lord love him, was as stiff-backed an old-school
authority figure as any of them. He was basically a good
Joe, and I'm cursed if I can remember his real name. But
his big problem was that he had memorized the rule book
and tried never to deviate from it.

Well, anyway, there we were, stranded on the lunar
surface after six weeks of hard work. Our task had been to
make a semipermanent underground base out of prefabricated modules that had been, as the agency quaintly
phrased it, "landed remotely on the lunar regolith in a series of carefully coordinated unmanned logistics missions."
In other words, they had dropped nine different module
packages over a fifty-square-kilometer area of Mare
Nubium and we had to find them all, drag them to the site
that Houston had picked for Base Gamma, set them up

properly, scoop up enough of the top layers of soil to cover each module and the connecting tunnels to a depth of 0.9144 meter (that's three feet, in English), and then link all the wiring, plumbing, heating, and air circulation units. Which we had done, adroitly and efficiently, and now that our labors were finished and we were ready to leave— no-go. Too bad we hadn't covered the return module with 0.9144 meter of lunar soil; that would have protected the fuel cells from that sharpshooting micrometeoroid.

The skipper decided it would be bad procedure to let us mope around and brood.

"I want each of you to run a thorough inventory of all your personal supplies: the special foods you've brought with you, your spare clothing, entertainment kits, everything."

"That'll take four minutes," Sam muttered, loud enough for us all to hear him. The eight of us were crammed into the command module again, eight guys squeezed into a space built for three. It was barely high enough to stand in, and the metal walls and ceiling always felt cold to the touch. Sam was pressed in with the guys behind me; I was practically touching noses with the skipper. The guys in back giggled at Sam's wisecrack. The skipper scowled.

"Goddammit, Gunn, can't you behave seriously for even a minute? We've got a real problem here."

"Yessir," Sam replied. If he hadn't been squeezed in so tightly I'm sure he would have made a snappy salute. "I'm merely attempting to keep morale high, sir."

The skipper made an unhappy snorting noise, and then told us that we would spend the rest of the shift checking out *all* the supplies that were left: not just our personal stuff, but the mission's supplies of food, the nuclear reactor, the water recycling system, equipment of all sorts, air . . .

We knew it was busywork, but we had nothing else to do. So we wormed our way out of the command module and crawled through the tunnels toward the other modules that we had laid out and then covered with bulldozed soil. It was a neat little buried base we had set up, for later explorers to use. I got a sort of claustrophobic feeling, just then, that this buried base might turn into a mass grave for eight astronauts.

I was dutifully heading back for barracks module A, where four of us had our bunks and personal gear, to check out my supplies, as the skipper had ordered. Sam snaked up beside me. Those tunnels, back in those days, were prefabricated Earthside to be laid out once we got to the construction site. I think they were designed by midgets. You couldn't stand up in them, they were too low. You had to really crawl along on hands and knees if you were normal size. Sam was able to shuffle through them on bent knees, knuckle-walking like a young chimpanzee. He loved those tunnels.

"Hey, wait up," he hissed to me.

I stopped.

"Whattaya think will get us first, the air giving out or we starve to death?"

He was grinning cheerfully. I said, "I think we're going to poison the air with methane. We'll fart ourselves to death in another couple of days."

Sam's grin widened. "C'mon ... I'm setting up a pool on the computer. I hadn't thought of air pollution. You wanna make a bet on that?" He started to King-Kong down the shaft to the right, toward the computer and life-support module. If I had had the space I would have shrugged. Instead, I followed him there.

Three of the other guys were in the computer module, huddled around the display screen like Boy Scouts around a campfire.

"Why aren't you checking out the base's supplies, like the skipper said," I asked them.

"We are, Straight Arrow," replied Mickey Lee, our refugee from Chinatown. He tapped the computer screen. "Why go sorting through all that junk when the computer already has it listed in alphabetical order for us?"

That wasn't what the skipper wanted and we all knew it. But Mickey was right. Why bother with busywork? We wrote down lists that would make the skippy happy. By hand. If we had let the computer print out the lists, Skip would have gotten wise right away.

While we scribbled away, copying what was on the screen, we talked over our basic situation.

"Why the hell can't we use the nuke to recharge the fuel cells?" Julio Marx asked. He was our token Puerto Rican Jew, a tribute to the space agency's Equal Opportunity employment policy. Julio was also a crackerjack structural engineer who had saved my life the day I had started to unfasten my helmet just when one of those blessed prefab tunnels had cracked its airlock seal. But that's another story.

Sam gave Julio a sorrowful stare. "The two systems are incompatible, Jules. Two separate teams of engineers designed them and none of the geniuses in the labs ever thought we might have to run one off the other in an emergency."

Julio cast an unbelieving glance at Sam. So Sam grinned and launched into the phoniest Latino accent you ever heard. "The nuclear theeng, man, it got too many volts for the fuel cells. Like, you plug the nukie to the fuel cells, man, you make a beeg boom an' we all go to dat beeg San Juan in thee sky. You better steek to pluckin' chickens, man, an' leave the eelectreecity alone."

Julio, who towered a good inch and a half over Sam, laughed good-naturedly and answered, "Okay, Shorty, I dig."

"Shorty! Shorty?" Sam's face went red. "All right, that's it. The hell with the betting pool. I'm gonna let you guys die of boredom. Serve you right."

We made a big fuss and soothed his feathers and cajoled him into setting up the pool. With a great show of hurt feelings and reluctant but utterly selfless nobility, Sam pushed Mickey Lee out of the chair in front of the computer terminal and began playing the keyboard like a virtuoso pianist. Within a few minutes the screen was displaying a list of the possible ways for us to die, with Sam's swiftly calculated odds next to each entry. At the touch of a button the screen displayed a graph showing how the odds for each mode of dying changed as time went on.

Suffocation, for example, started off as less than a one percent probability. But within a month the chances began to rise fairly steeply. "The air scrubbers need replacement filters," Sam explained, "and we'll be out of 'em inside of two more weeks."

"They'll have us out of here in two weeks, for Christ's sake," Julio said.

"Or drop fresh supplies for us," said Ron Avery, the taciturn pilot we called Cowboy because of his lean, lanky build and slow western drawl.

"Those are the odds," Sam snapped. "The computer does not lie. Pick your poison and place your bets."

I put fifty bucks down on Air Contamination, not telling the other guys about my earlier conversation with Sam. Julio took Starvation, Mickey settled on Dehydration (Lack of Water), and Cowboy picked Murder—which made me shudder.

"What about you, Sam?" I asked.

"I'll wait'ill the other guys have a chance," he said.

"You gonna let the skipper in on this?" asked Julio.

Sam shook his head. "If I tell him . . ."

"I'll tell him," Cowboy volunteered with a grim smile. "I'll even let him have Murder, if he wants it. I can always switch to Suicide."

"Droll fellow," said Sam.

"Well, hell," Cowboy insisted, "if a feller takes Suicide he can always made sure he wins just by killing himself, can't he now?"

It was one of those rare occasions when Sam had no reply. He simply stared at Cowboy in silence.

Well, you probably read about the mission in your history classes. Houston was supporting three separate operations on the Moon at the same time and they were stretched to the limit down there. Old Stone Face promised us a rescue flight in a week. But they had a problem with the booster when they tried to rush things on the launch pad too much and the blessed launch had to be put back a week, then another week. They sent an unmanned supply craft to us, of course, but the descent stage got gummed up. Our fresh food, air filters, and water supply wound up orbiting the Moon, fifty miles over our heads.

Sam calculated the odds against all these foul-ups and came to the conclusion that Houston was working overtime to kill us. "Must be some kind of an experiment," he told us. "Maybe they need some martyrs to make people more aware of the space program."

Cowboy immediately asked if that fell under the category of Murder. He was intent on winning the pool, even if it killed him.

We learned afterward that Houston was deep in trouble because of us. The White House was firing people right and left, congressional committees were gearing up to investigate the fiasco, and the CIA was checking out somebody's crack-brained idea that the Japanese were behind all our troubles. Or maybe the Arianespace, the European space company.

Meanwhile, we were stranded on the Mare Nubium with nothing much to do but let our beards grow and hope for sinus troubles that would cut off our ability to sense odors.

Old Stone Face was magnificent, in his unflinching way. He was on the line to us every day, despite the fact that his superiors in Houston and Washington were either being fired directly by the president herself or roasted over the simmering fires of media criticism. There must have been a zillion reporters at mission control by the second week of our marooning. We could *feel* the hubbub and tension whenever we talked with Stony.

"The countdown for your rescue flight is proceeding on an accelerated schedule," he told us. It would never occur to him to say, *We're hurrying as fast as we can.* "Liftoff is now scheduled for 0700 hours on the twenty-fifth."

None of us needed to look at a calendar to know that the twenty-fifth was seventeen days away. Sam's betting pool was looking more serious by the hour. Even the skipper had finally taken the plunge: Suffocation.

If it weren't for Sandi Hemmings we might all have gone crazy. She took over as Capcom during the night shift, when most of the reporters and the agency brass were either asleep or drinking away their troubles. She gave us the courage and desire to pull through, partly by just smiling at us and looking female enough to *make* us want to survive, but mainly by giving us the straight info with no nonsense.

"They're in deep trouble over at Kennedy," she would

tell us. "They've had to go on triple shifts and call up
boosters that they didn't think they would need until next
year. Some senator in Washington is yelling that we ought
to ask the Russians or the Japanese to help us out."

"As if either of them had upper stages that could make
it to the Moon without six months worth of modification
work," one of our guys grumbled.

"Well," Sandi said with her brightest smile, "you'll all
be heroes when you finally get back here. The women will
be standing in line to admire you."

"You won't have to stand in line, Sandi," Cowboy answered, in a rare burst of words. "You'll always be number
one with us."

The others crowded into the command module added
their heartfelt agreement.

Sandi laughed, undaunted by the prospect of having
the eight of us grabbing for her. "I hope you shave first,"
she said.

Remember, she could see us but she couldn't smell us.

A night or two later she spent hours reading to us the
suggestions made by the Houston medical team on how to
stretch out our dwindling supplies of food, water, and air.
They boiled down to one basic rule: lie down and don't ex-
ert yourselves. Great advice, especially when you're beginning to really worry that you're not going to make it
through this mess. Just what we needed to do, lie back in
our bunks and do nothing but think.

I caught a gleam in Sam's eye, though, as Sandi
waded through the medics' recommendations. The skipper
asked her to send the whole report through our computer.
She did, and he spent the whole next day poring over it.
Sam spent the day—well, I couldn't figure out where he'd
gotten to. I didn't see him all day long, and Base Gamma
really wasn't big enough to hide in, even for somebody as
small as Sam.

After going through all the medics' gobbledygook the
skipper ordered us to take tranquilizers. We had a small
supply of downers in the base pharmaceutical stores, and
Skip divided them equally among us. At the rate of three
a day they would last just four days, with four pills left
over. About as useful as a cigarette lighter in hell, but the

skipper played it by the book and ordered us to start swallowing the tranquilizers.

"Just the thing for the tension that arises from predeath syndrome," Sam muttered. Loud enough for Skip to hear, of course.

"The medics say the pills will ease our anxieties and help us to remain as quiet as possible while we wait for the rescue mission," Skip said, glowering in Sam's direction.

He didn't bother to remind us that the rescue mission was still twelve days off. We would be out of food in three more days, and the recycled water was starting to taste as if it hadn't been recycled, if you know what I mean. The air was getting foul, too, but that was probably just our imaginations.

Sam appeared blithely unconcerned, even happy. He whistled cheerfully as Skip rationed out the tranquilizers, then gave his pills to me and scuttled off down the tunnel that led toward our barracks module. By the time I got to my bunk Sam was nowhere in sight. His whistling was gone. So was his pressure suit.

I put his pills under his mattress, wondering where he could have gone. Outside? For what? To increase his radiation dose? To get away from the rest of us? That was probably it. Underneath his wiseguy shell Sam was probably just as worried and tense as any of us, and he simply didn't want us to know it. He needed some solitude, not chemical tranquility. What better place to find solitude than the airless rocky waste of Mare Nubium?

That's what I thought. That's why I didn't go out after him.

The same thing happened the next "morning" (by which I mean the time immediately after our sleep shift). And the next. The skipper would gather us together in the command module, we would each take our ceremonial tranquilizer pill and a sip of increasingly bad water, and then we would crawl back to our bunks and try to do nothing that would use up body energy or burn air. All of us except Sam. He faked swallowing his pill, handed it to me when Skip wasn't watching, and then disappeared with his pressure suit.

All of us were getting grumpier, surlier. I knew I

found myself resenting it whenever I had to use the toilet.
I kept imagining my urine flowing straight back into our
water tank without reprocessing. I guess I was starting to
go crazy.

But Sam was happy as could be: chipper, joking,
laughing it up. He would disappear each morning for several hours and then show up with a lopsided grin on his
round face, telling jokes and making us all feel a little better.

Until the day Julio suddenly sat bolt upright on his
bunk, the second or third morning after we had run out of
tranquilizers, and yelled:

"Booze!"

Sam had been sitting on the edge of Julio's bunk, telling an outrageous story of what he planned to do with
Sandi once we got back to Houston.

"Booze!" Julio repeated. "I smell booze! I'm cracking
up. I must be loosing my marbles. I smell *booze!*"

For once in his life Sam looked apologetic, almost
ashamed.

"You're not cracking up," he said in as quiet a voice
as I've ever heard Sam use. "I was going to tell you about
it tomorrow—the stuff is almost ready for human consumption."

You never saw three grown men so suddenly atten-
tive.

With a self-deprecating little grin Sam explained,
"I've been tinkering with the propellants and other junk
out in the return module. They're not doing us any good
just sitting there. So I tinkered up a small still. Seems to
be working okay. I tasted a couple sips today. It'll take the
enamel off your teeth, but it's not all that bad. By
tomorrow . . ."

He never got any further. We did a Keystone Kops
routine, rushing for our pressure suits, jamming ourselves
through the airlock, and running out to the inert, idle,
cussedly useless return module.

Sam was not kidding us. He had jury-rigged an
honest-to-backwoods still inside the return module, fueling
it with propellants from the module's tanks. The basic alcohol also came from the propellant, with water from the

fuel cells and a few other ingredients that Sam had scrounged from Base Gamma's medical supplies.

We took turns at the still's business end, sticking its little copper tube into the water nipple of our helmets to sample Sam's concoction. It was *terrible*. We loved it.

By the time we had staggered back to our barracks module, laughing and belching, we had made up our minds to let the other three guys in barracks B share in Sam's juice. But the skipper was a problem. If we told him about it he'd have Sam up on charges and drummed out of the agency even before the rescue mission reached us. I figured if Old Stone Face found out he'd order the rescue mission to leave Sam behind.

"Have no fear," Sam told us with a giggle. "I myself will reveal my activities to our noble skipper."

And before we could stop him he had tottered off toward the command module, whistling through the tunnel in a horribly sour off-key way.

An hour went by. Then two. We could hear Skip's voice yelling from the command module, although we couldn't make out the words. None of us had the guts to go down the tunnel and try to help Sam. After a while the tumult and the shouting died. Mickey Lee gave me a questioning glance. Silence. Ominous silence.

"You think Skip's killed him?" Mickey asked.

"More likely Sam's talked the skipper to death," Julio replied.

Timidly we slunk down the tunnel to the command module. The three other guys were in there with Sam and the skipper. They were all quaffing Sam's rocket juice and giggling at each other.

We were shocked, but we joined right in. Six days later, when the guys from Base Alpha landed their return module crammed with emergency food and fresh water for us, we invited them to join the party. A week after that, when the rescue mission from Kennedy finally showed up, we had been under the influence for so long that we told them to go away.

I had never realized before then what a lawyer Sam was. He had convinced the skipper to read the medics' report carefully, especially the part where they recom-

mended using tranquilizers to keep us calm and minimize
our energy consumption. Sam had then gotten the skipper
to punch up the medical definition of alcohol's effects on
the body, out of Houston's medical files. Sure enough, if
you squinted the right way, you could claim that alcohol
was a sort of a tranquilizer. That was enough justification
for the skipper, and we just about pickled ourselves in
rocket juice until we got rescued.

The crystal statue glittered under the harsh rays of
the unfiltered sun. The supervisor, still sitting on the lip of
the truck's hatch, said, "He looks beautiful. You guys did
a good job. Is the epoxy set?"

"Needs another few minutes, just to be sure," said the
hoist operator, tapping the toe of his boot against the base
that they had poured on the lunar plain.

"What happened when you got back to Houston?"
asked Jade. "Didn't they get angry at you for being
drunk?"

"Sure," laughed the supervisor. "But what could they
do? Sam's booze pulled us through, and we could show
that we were merely following the recommendations of
the medics. Old Stone Face hushed it all up and we became heroes, just like Sandi told us we'd be—for about a
week."

"And Sam?"

"Oh, after a while he left the agency and started his
own business: S. Gunn Enterprises, Unlimited. The rest
you know about from the history tapes. Entrepreneur,
showman, scoundrel, trail-blazer. It's all true. He was all
those things."

"Did he and Sandi ever, uh, get together?" the hoist
operator asked.

"She was too smart to let him corner her. Sandi used
one of the other guys to protect her; married him, finally.
Cowboy, if I remember right. They eloped and spent their
honeymoon in orbit. Zero gee and all that. Sam pretended
to be very upset by it, but by that time he was surrounded
by women, all of them taller than he was."

The three of them walked slowly around the gleaming
statue.

"Look at the rainbows it makes where the Sun hits it," said Jade. "It's marvelous."

"But if he was so smart," the hoist operator said, "why'd he pick this spot 'way out here for his grave? It's kilometers from Selene City. You can't even see the statue from the City."

"*Imbecile,*" Jade said. "This is the place where Base Gamma was located. Isn't that right?"

"Nope," the supervisor said. "Gamma was all the way over on the other side of Nubium. It's still there. Abandoned, but still there. Even the blasted return module is still sitting there, dumb as ever."

"Then why put the statue here?"

The supervisor chuckled. "Sam was a pretty shrewd guy. In his will he set up a tourist agency that'll guide people to the important sites on the Moon. They'll start at Selene and go along the surface in those big cruisers they've got back at the city. Sam's tomb is going to be a major tourist attraction, and he wanted it to be far enough out on the *mare* so that people won't be able to see it from Selene; they have to buy tickets and take the bus."

Both the young people laughed tolerantly.

"I guess he was pretty smart, at that," the hoist operator admitted.

"And he had a long memory, too," said the supervisor. "He left this tourist agency to me and the other guys from Artemis IV, in his will. We own it. I figure it'll keep us comfortable for the rest of our lives."

"Why did he do that?"

The supervisor shrugged inside his cumbersome suit. "Why did he built that still? Sam always did what he darned well felt like doing. And no matter what you think of him, he always remembered his friends."

The three of them gave the crystal statue a final admiring glance, then clumped back to the truck and started the hour-long drive to Selene City.

But as she drove across the empty pitted plain, Jade thought of Sam Gunn. She could not escape the feeling that somehow, in some unexplainable way, her future was intimately tied to Sam Gunn's past.

4

The Hospital and the Bar

JADE'S FIRST MEMORIES were not of people, but of the bare-walled rooms and wards of the hospital. The hushed voices. The faintly tangy smell of disinfectant. The hospital had seemed so snug and safe when she had been a child. Even though she had never had a room of her own, and had spent most of her childhood nights sleeping in the main ward, the hospital was the closest thing to a home that Jade had ever had.

She was an adult now, with a job and an apartment of her own. A single room carved deep into the lunar rock, two levels below the hospital, four levels below Selene City's main plaza and the surface. Still, returning to the hospital was like returning to the warmth of home. Almost.

"It would be a really good thing to do," said Dr. Dinant. She was a Belgian, and even though her native language was French, between her Walloon accent and Jade's fragmentary Quebecoise, they found it easier to converse in English.

"You mean it would be good for science," Jade replied softly.

"Yes. Of course. For science. And for yourself, as well."

22

Dr. Dinant was quite young, almost Jade's own age. Yet she reminded Jade of the blurry memory of her adoptive mother. She felt as if she wanted this woman to love her, to take her to her heart as no one ever had since her mother had gone away from her.

But what Dr. Dinant was asking was more than Jade could give.

"All you have to do is donate a few of your egg cells. It's quite a simple procedure. I can do it for you right here in the clinic in just a few minutes."

Dinant's skin was deeply tanned. She must spend hours under the sun lamps, Jade thought. The physician was not a particularly handsome woman: her mousy hair was clipped quite short and her clothes showed that she paid scant attention to her appearance. But she had an air of self-assurance that Jade sorely envied.

"Let me explain it again," Dr. Dinant said gently. Even though the chairs they were sitting in were close enough to touch one another, she kept a distinct separation from the younger woman.

"I understand what you want," Jade said. "You want to make a baby from my eggs so that you can test it for the bone disease I carry in my genes."

"Osteopetrosis," said Dr. Dinant, "is not a disease . . ."

"It prevents me from living on Earth."

The doctor smiled at her kindly. "We would like to be able to see to it that your children will not be so afflicted."

"You can cure it?"

Dr. Dinant nodded. "We believe so. With gene therapy. We can remove the defective gene from your egg cell and replace it with a healthy one, then fertilize the cell, implant it in a host mother, and bring the fetus to term."

"My—the baby won't have the disease?"

"We believe we can eliminate the condition, yes."

"But not for me," Jade said.

"No, I'm afraid it must be done in the fetal or prefetal stage."

"It's too late for me. It was too late when I was born."

"Yes, but your children needn't be so afflicted."

My children? Jade pulled her gaze away from the eager-eyed doctor and glanced around the room. A bare little cell, like all the other offices in the hospital. Like all of Selene City. Buried underground, gray and lifeless, like living in a crypt.

"You must make a decision," insisted the doctor.

"Why? Why now? I'll marry someday. Why shouldn't I have my own children myself?"

An uncomfortable expression crossed Dr. Dinant's face. "Your job, up on the surface. I know they keep the radiation exposure down to acceptable levels, but . . ."

Jade nodded, understanding. She had heard tales about what long-term exposure to the radiation levels up on the surface can do. Even inside the armored space suits the radiation effects build up, over time. That's why they pay a bonus for working up on the surface. She wondered if that was how she acquired the bone disease in the first place. Was her father a worker on the surface? Her mother?

Osteopetrosis. Marble bones, it was called. Jade remembered pictures of marble statues from ancient Greece and Rome, arms broken off, fingers gone, noses missing. That's what my bones are like; too brittle for Earth's gravity. That's what would happen to me.

Dr. Dinant forced a smile. "I realize that this is a difficult decision for you to make."

"Yes."

"But you must decide, and soon. Otherwise . . ."

Otherwise, Jade told herself, the radiation buildup will end her chances of ever becoming a mother.

"Perhaps you should discuss the matter with your family," the doctor suggested.

"I have no family."

"Your mother—the woman who adopted you, she is still alive, is she not?"

Jade felt a block of ice congealing around her. "I have not spoken to my mother in many years. She doesn't call me and I don't call her."

"Oh." Dr. Dinant looked pained, defeated. "I see."

A long silence stretched between the two women.

Finally Dr. Dinant shifted uncomfortably in her chair and said, "You needn't make your decision at just this mo-

ment. Go home, think about it. Sleep on it. Call me in a
few days."

Slowly, carefully, Jade got to her feet. "Yes. Thank
you. I'll call you in a few days."

"Good," said the doctor, without moving from her
chair. She seemed relieved to see Jade leave her office.

Jade walked blindly down the corridors of the underground city. Men and women passed her, some nodding or
smiling a hello, most staring blankly ahead. Children were
still rare in Selene and if she saw any, she paid them no
mind. It was too painful. The whole subject tore at her
heart, reminding her again of the mother who had abandoned her, of the cold and empty life she was leading.

There were only two bars in Selene City, one fre-
quented by management types and tourists, the other the
haunt of the workers. Jade found herself pushing through
the crowd at the incongruously named Pelican Bar.

Friends called to her; strangers smiled at the diminu-
tive redhead. But Jade saw and heard them only dimly.

The Pelican's owner tended the bar himself, leaving
the robots to handle anyone too much in a hurry for a joke
or a story. He was a paunchy, middle-aged man, gleam-
ingly bald beneath the overhead fluorescents. He seemed
to smile all the time. At least, every time Jade had seen
him his face was beaming happily.

"Hey there, Green Eyes! Haven't seen you since your
birthday bash."

Her coworkers had surprised her with a party to cel-
ebrate her twentieth birthday, several weeks earlier. Jade
sat on the last stool in the farthest corner of the bar, as distant from everyone else as she could manage.

"Want your usual?"

She hadn't been to the Pelican—or anywhere else, for
that matter—often enough to know what her "usual" might
be. But she nodded glumly.

"Comin' right up."

A guy in a tan leather vest and turquoise-cinched
bolo tie pulled up the stool next to Jade's, drink already in
his hand. He smiled handsomely at her.

"Hi, Red. Haven't I seen you up at the landing port?"
Jade shook her head. "Not me."

"Must be someplace else. I'm new here, just arrived last week for a year's contract."

Jade said nothing. The newcomer tried a few more ploys, but when they failed to get a response from her he shrugged and moved away.

The bartender returned with a tall frosted glass filled with a dark bubbling liquid and tinkling with real ice cubes.

"Here you go! Genuine Coca-Cola!"

Jade said, "Thanks," as she took the cold sweating glass in her hand.

"You're never gonna win the Miss Popularity contest if you keep givin' guys the cold shoulder, y'know."

"I'm not interested in any contests."

The bartender shrugged. "H'm, yeah, well maybe. But there's somebody over there"—he jabbed a thumb back toward the crowd at the other end of the bar—"that you oughtta meet."

"Why?"

"You were askin' about Sam Gunn, weren't you? Zach Bonner said you were."

Her supervisor. "Is Zach here?" she asked.

"Naw, too early for him. But this guy here now, he was a buddy of Sam's, back in the early days."

"Really?"

"Yeah. You'll see."

The bartender waddled away, toward the crowd. When he came back, Jade saw that a compactly built, gray-haired man was coming down the other side of the bar toward her, holding a pilsner glass half filled with beer in his left hand.

"Jade, meet Felix Sanchez. Felix, this is Jade. I dunno what her last name is 'cause she never told me."

Sanchez was a round-faced Latino with a thick, dark mustache. He smiled at Jade and extended his hand. She let him take hers, and for a wild moment she thought he was going to bring it to his lips. But he merely held it for several seconds. His hand felt warm. It engulfed her own.

"Such beautiful eyes," Sanchez said, his voice so low that she had to strain to hear it over the buzz of the crowd. "No wonder you are called Jade."

She felt herself smiling back at him. Sanchez must have been more than fifty years old, she guessed. But he seemed to be in good athletic shape beneath his casual pullover and slacks.

"You knew Sam Gunn?" Jade asked.

"Knew him? I was nearly killed by him!" And Sanchez laughed heartily while the bartender gave up all pretense of working and planted both his elbows on the plastic surface of his bar.

5

The Long Fall

EVERYBODY BLAMED SAM for what happened—Sanchez said—but if you ask me it never would've happened if the skipper hadn't gone a little crazy.

Space station Freedom was a purely government project, ten years behind schedule and a billion bucks or so over budget. Nothing unusual about that. The agency's best team of astronauts and mission specialists were picked to be the first crew. Nothing unusual about that, either.

What was weird was that somehow Sam Gunn was included in that first crew. And John J. Johnson was named commander. See, Sam and Commander Johnson got along like hydrazine and nitric acid—hypergolic. Put them in contact and they explode.

You've got to see the picture. John J. Johnson was a little over six feet tall, lean as a contrail, and the straightest straight arrow in an agency full of stiff old graybeards. He had the distinguished white hair and the elegant good looks of an airline pilot in a TV commercial.

But inside that handsome head was a brain that had a nasty streak in it. "Jay-Cubed," as we called him, always

28

went by the rule book, even when it hurt. Especially when it hurt, if you ask me.

Until the day we learned that Gloria Lamour was coming to space station Freedom. That changed everything, of course.

Sam, you know, was the opposite of the commander in every way possible. Sam was short and stubby where Johnson was tall and rangy. Hair like rusty Brillo. Funny color eyes; I could never tell if they were blue or green. Sam was gregarious, noisy, crackling with nervous energy; Johnson was calm, reserved, detached. Sam wanted to be everybody's pal; Johnson wanted respect, admiration, but most of all he wanted obedience.

Sam was definitely not handsome. His round face was bright as a penny, and sometimes he sort of looked like Huckleberry Finn or maybe even that old-time child star Mickey Rooney. But handsome he was not. Still, Sam had a way with women. I know this is true because he would tell me about it all the time. Me, and anybody else who would be within earshot. Also, I saw him in action, back at the Cape and during our training sessions in Houston. The little guy could be charming and downright courtly when he wanted to be.

Ninety days on a space station with Sam and Commander Johnson. It was sort of like a shakedown cruise; our job was to make sure all the station's systems were working as they ought to. I knew it wouldn't be easy. The station wasn't big enough to hide in.

There were only six of us on that first mission, but we kept getting in each other's way—and on each other's nerves. It was like a ninety-day jail sentence. We couldn't get out. We had nothing to do but work. There were no women. I think we would've all gone batty if it weren't for Sam. He was our one-man entertainment committee.

He was full of jokes, full of fun. He organized the scavenger hunt that kept us busy every night for two solid weeks trying to find the odd bits of junk that he had hidden away in empty oxygen cylinders, behind sleep cocoons, even floating up on the ceiling of the station's one and only working head. He set up the darts tournament, where the "darts" were really spitballs made of wadded

Velcro and the reverse side of the improvised target was a blowup photo of Commander Johnson.

Sam was a beehive of energy. He kept us laughing. All except the commander, who had never smiled in his life, so far as any of us knew.

And it was all in zero gee. Or almost. So close it didn't make any real difference. The scientists called it microgravity. We called it weightlessness, zero gee, whatever. We floated. Everything floated if it wasn't nailed down. Sam loved zero gee. Johnson always looked like he was about to puke.

Johnson ruled with an aluminum fist. No matter how many tasks mission control loaded on us, Johnson never argued with them. He pushed us to do everything those clowns on the ground could think of, and to do it on time and according to regulations. No shortcuts, no flimflams. Naturally, the more we accomplished the more mission control thought up for us to do. Worse, Johnson *asked* mission control for more tasks. He *volunteered* for more jobs for us to do. We were working, working, working all the time, every day, without a break.

"He's gonna kill us with overwork," grumbled Roger Cranston, our structural specialist.

"The way I figure it," Sam said, "is that Jay-Cubed wants us to do all the tasks that the next crew is supposed to do. That way the agency can cut the next mission and save seventy million bucks or so."

Al Dupres agreed sourly. "He works us to death and then he gets a big kiss on the cheek from Washington." Al was French-Canadian; the agency's token international representative.

Sam started muttering about Captain Bligh and the good ship *Bounty*.

They were right. Johnson was so eager to look good to the agency that he was starting to go a little whacko. Some of it was Sam's fault, of course. But I really think zero gee affected the flow of blood to his brain. That, and the news about Gloria Lamour, which affected his blood flow elsewhere.

We were six weeks into the mission. Sam had kept his nose pretty clean, stuck to his duties as logistics officer and all the other jobs the skipper thought up for him, kept out of Johnson's silver-fox hair as much as he could.

Oh, he had loosened the screw top on the commander's coffee squeezebulb one morning, so that Johnson splashed the stuff all over the command module. Imagine ten thousand little bubbles of coffee (heavy on the cream) spattering all over, floating and scattering like ten thousand teeny fireflies. Johnson sputtered and cursed and glowered at Sam, his coveralls soaked from collar to crotch.

I nearly choked, trying not to laugh. Sam put on a look of innocence that would have made the angels sigh. He offered to chase down each and every bubble and clean up the mess. Johnson just glowered at him while the bubbles slowly wafted into the air vent above the command console.

Then there was the water bag in the commander's sleep cocoon. And the gremlin in the computer system that printed out random graffiti like: *Resistance to tyranny is obedience to God.* Or: *Where is Fletcher Christian when we really need him?*

Commander Johnson started muttering to himself a lot, and staring at Sam when the little guy's back was to him. It was an evil, red-eyed stare. Sent chills up my spine.

Then I found out about the CERV test.

Crew emergency reentry vehicle, CERV. Lifeboats for the space station. We called them "capsules." Suppose something goes really wrong on the station, like we're hit by a meteor. (More likely, we would've been hit by a piece of man-made junk. There were millions of bits of debris floating around out there in those days.) If the station's so badly damaged we have to abandon ship, we jump into the capsules and ride back down to Earth.

Nobody'd done it, up to then. The lifeboats had been tested with dummies inside them, but not real live human beings. Not yet.

I was on duty at the communications console in the command module that morning when Commander Johnson was on the horn with Houston. All of a sudden my screen breaks up into fuzz and crackles.

"This is a scrambled transmission," the commander said in his monotone, from his station at the command console, three feet to my right. He plugged in a headset and clipped the earphone on. And he *smiled* at me.

I took the hint and made my way to the galley for a squeeze of coffee, more stunned by that smile than curious about his scrambled conversation with mission control. When I got back Johnson was humming tunelessly to himself. The headset was off and he was still smiling. It was a ghastly smile.

Although we put in a lot of overtime hours to finish the tasks our commander so obligingly piled on us, Johnson himself left the command module precisely at seven each evening, ate a solitary meal in the wardroom, and then got eight full hours of sleep. His conscience was perfectly at ease, and he apparently had no idea whose face was on the reverse of the darts target.

As soon as he left that evening I pecked out the subroutine I had put into the comm computer and reviewed his scrambled transmission to Houston. He may be the skipper, but I'm the comm officer and *nothing* goes in or out without me seeing it.

The breath gushed out of me when I read the file. No wonder the skipper had smiled.

I called Sam and got him to meet me in the wardroom. The commander had assigned him to getting the toilet in the unoccupied laboratory module to work, so that the scientists who'd be coming up eventually could crap in their own territory. In addition to all his regular duties, of course.

"A CERV test, huh," Sam said when I told him. "We don't have enough to do; he's gonna throw a lifeboat drill at us."

"Worse than that," I said.

"What do you mean?" Sam was hovering a few inches off the floor. He liked to do that; made him feel taller.

Chairs are useless in zero gee. I had my feet firmly anchored in the foot loops set into the floor around the wardroom table. Otherwise a weightless body would drift all over the place. Except for Sam, who somehow managed to keep himself put.

Leaning closer toward Sam, I whispered, "It won't be just a drill. He's going to pop one of the lifeboats and send it into a real reentry trajectory."

"No shit?"

"No shit. He got permission from Houston this morning for a full balls-out test."

Sam grabbed the edge of the galley table and pulled himself so close to me I could count the pale freckles on his snub of a nose. Sudden understanding lit up those blue-green eyes of his.

"I'll bet I know who's going to be on the lifeboat that gets to take the long fall," he whispered back at me.

I nodded.

"That's why he smiled at me this evening."

"He's been working out every detail in the computer," I said, my voice as low as a guy planning a bank heist, even though we were alone in the wardroom. "He's going to make certain you're in the lab module by yourself so you'll be the only one in the lifeboat there. Then he's going to pop it off."

The thought of riding one of those uncontrolled little capsules through the blazing heat of reentry and then landing God knows where—maybe the middle of the ocean, maybe the middle of the Gobi Desert—it scared the hell out of me. Strangely, Sam grinned.

"You *want* to be the first guy who tries out one of those capsules?" I asked.

"Hell no," he said. "But suppose our noble liege lord happens to make a small mistake and *he's* the one to take the ride back home?"

I felt my jaw drop open. "How're you going to . . ."

Sam grinned his widest. "Wouldn't it be poetic if we could arrange things so that ol' Cap'n Bligh himself gets to take the fall?"

I stared at him. "You're crazy."

"That's what they said about Orville and Wilbur, pal."

The next week was very intense. Sam didn't say another word to me about it, but I knew he was hacking into the commander's comm link each night and trying to ferret out every last detail of the upcoming lifeboat drill. Commander Johnson played everything close to the ve⹀

though. He never let on, except that he smiled whenever he saw Sam, the sort of smile that a homicidal maniac might give his next victim. I even thought I heard him cackling to himself, once or twice.

The other three men in the crew began to sense the tension. Even Sam became kind of quiet, almost.

Then we got word that Gloria Lamour was coming up to the station.

Maybe you don't remember her, because her career was so tragically short. She was the sexiest, slinkiest, most gorgeous hunk of redheaded femininity ever to grace the video screen. A mixture of Rita Hayworth, Marilyn Monroe, and Michelle Pfeiffer. With some Kathryn Hepburn thrown in for brains and even a flash of Bette Midler's sass.

The skipper called us together into the command module for the news. Just as calmly as if he were announcing a weather report from Tibet he told us: "There will be a special shuttle mission to the station three days from this morning. We will be visited for an unspecified length of time by a video crew from Hollywood. Gloria Lamour, the video star, will apparently be among them."

It hit us like a shock wave, but Commander Johnson spelled it out just as if we were going to get nothing more than a new supply of aspirin.

"Miss Lamour will be here to tape the first video drama ever filmed in space," he told us. "She and her crew have received clearance from the highest levels of the White House."

"Three cheers for President Heston," Sam piped.

Commander Johnson started to glare at him, but his expression turned into a wintry smile. A smile that said, *You'll get yours, mister.* None of the rest of us moved from where we stood anchored in our foot restraints.

The commander went on. "The video crew will be using the laboratory module for their taping. They will use the unoccupied scientists' privacy cubicles for their sleeping quarters. There should be practically no interference with your task schedules, although I expect you to extend every courtesy and assistance to our visitors."

The five of us grinned and nodded eagerly.

"It will be necessary to appoint a crew member to act as liaison between the video team and ourselves," said the commander.

Five hands shot up to volunteer so hard that all five of us would have gone careening into the overhead if we hadn't been anchored to the floor by the foot restraints.

"I will take on that extra duty myself," the skipper said, smiling enough now to show his teeth, "so that you can continue with your work without any extra burdens being placed on you."

"Son of a bitch," Sam muttered. If the commander heard him, he ignored it.

Gloria Lamour on space station *Freedom*! The six of us had been living in this orbital monastery for almost two months. We were practically drooling with anticipation. I found it hard to sleep, and when I did my dreams were so vivid they were embarrassing. The other guys floated through their duties grinning and joking. We started making bets about who would be first to do what.

But Sam, normally the cheerful one, turned glum. "Old Jay-Cubed is gonna hover around her like a satellite. He's gonna keep her in the lab module and away from us. He won't let any of us get close enough for an autograph, even."

That took the starch out of us, so to speak.

The big day arrived. The orbiter *Reagan* made rendezvous with the station and docked at our main airlock. The five of us were supposed to be going about our regular tasks. Only the commander's anointed liaison man—himself—went to the airlock to greet our visitors.

Yet somehow all five of us managed to be in the command module, where all three monitor screens on the main console were focused on the airlock.

Commander Johnson stood with his back to the camera, decked out in crisp new sky-blue coveralls, standing as straight as a man can in zero gee.

"I'll cut off the oxygen to his sleeping cubicle," muttered Larry Minetti, our life-support specialist. "I'll fix the bastard, you watch and see."

We ignored Larry.

"She come through the hatch yet?" Sam called. He

was at my regular station, the communications console, instead of up front with us watching the screens.

"What're you doing back there?" I asked him, not taking my eyes off the screens. The hatch's locking wheel was
starting to turn.

"Checking into Cap'n Bligh's files, what else?"

"Come on, you're gonna miss it! The hatch is opening."

Sam shot over to us like a stubby missile and stopped
his momentum by grabbing Larry and me by the shoulders. He stuck his head between us.

The hatch was swung all the way open by a grinning
shuttle astronaut. Two mission specialists—male—pushed
a pallet loaded with equipment past the still-erect Commander Johnson. We were all erect, too, with anticipation.

A nondescript woman floated through the hatch behind the mission specialists and the pallet. She was in gray
coveralls. As short as Sam. Kind of a long, sour face. Not
sour, exactly. Sad. Unhappy. Mousy dull brown hair plastered against her skull with a zero-gee net. Definitely not
a glamorous video star.

"Must be her assistant," Al Dupres muttered.

"Her director."

"Her dog."

We stared at those screens so hard you'd think that
Gloria Lamour would have appeared just out of the energy
of our five palpitating, concentrating brain waves.

No such luck. The un-beautiful woman floated right
up to Commander Johnson and took his hand in a firm, almost manly grip.

"Hello," she said in a nasal Bronx accent. "Gloria
Lamour is not on this trip, so don't get your hopes up."

I wish I could have seen the commander's face. But,
come to think of it, he probably didn't blink an eye. Sam
gagged and went over backward into a zero-gee loop. The
rest of us moaned, booed, and hollered obscenities at the
screens.

Through it all I clearly heard the commander speak
the little speech he had obviously rehearsed for days:
"Welcome aboard space station Freedom, Miss Lamour. *Mi
casa es su casa.*"

Big frigging deal!

What it worked out to was this: The crab apple's name was Arlene Gold. She was a technician for the video company. In face, she was the entire video crew, all by herself. And her palletful of equipment. She was here to shoot background footage. Was Gloria Lamour coming up later? She got very cagey about answering that one.

We got to know her pretty well over the next several days. Commander Johnson lost interest in her immediately, but although he still wouldn't let any of us go into the lab module, she had to come into the wardroom for meals. She was a New Yorker, which she pronounced "Noo Yawkeh." Testy, suspicious, always on guard. Guess I can't blame her, stuck several hundred miles up in orbit with five drooling maniacs and a commander who behaved like a robot.

But God, was she a sourpuss.

Larry approached her. "You handle zero gee very well. Most of us got sick the first couple of days."

"What'd ya expect," she almost snarled, "screaming and fainting?"

A day or so later Rog Cranston worked up the courage to ask, "Have you done much flying?"

"Whatsit to ya?" she snapped back at him.

It only took a few days of that kind of treatment for us to shun her almost completely. When she came into the wardroom for meals we backed away and gave her the run of the galley's freezers and microwave. We made certain there was an empty table for her.

Except that Sam kept trying to strike up a conversation with her. Kept trying to make her laugh, or even smile, no matter how many times she rebuffed him. He even started doing short jokes for her, playing the buffoon, telling her how much he admired taller women. (She might have been half a centimeter taller than he was on the ground; it was hard to tell in zero gee.)

Her responses ranged from "Get lost" to "Don't be such a jerk."

I pulled Sam aside after a few evenings of this and asked him when he had turned into a masochist.

Sam gave me a knowing grin. "My old pappy always

told me, 'When they hand you a lemon, son, make lemon-ade.' "

"With *her*?"

"You see any other women up here?"

I didn't answer, but I had to admit that Larry Minetti was starting to look awfully good to me.

"Besides," Sam said, his grin turning sly, "when Gloria Lamour finally gets here, Arlene will be her guardian, won't she?"

I got it. Get close to the sourpuss and she'll let you get close to the sex goddess. There was method in Sam's madness. He seemed to spend all his spare time trying to melt Arlene's heart of steel. I thought he had even lost interest in rigging the skipper's CERV test so that it would be John J. Johnson who got fired off the station, not Sam Gunn.

Sam practically turned himself inside out for Arlene. He became elfin, a pixie, a leprechaun whenever she came to the galley or wardroom.

And it seemed to be working. She let him eat dinner at the same table with her one night.

"After all," I overheard Sam tell her, "we little people have to stick together."

"Don't get ideas," Arlene replied. But her voice had lost some of its sharp edge. She damned near smiled at Sam.

The next morning Johnson called Sam to his command console. "You are relieved of your normal duties for the next few days," the skipper said. "You will report to the lab module and assist Ms. Gold in testing her equipment."

I shot a surprised glance at Larry, who was at his console, next to mine. His eyebrows were rising up to his scalp. Sam just grinned and launched himself toward the hatch. The commander smiled crookedly at his departing back.

"So what's with you two?" I asked him a couple nights later. He had just spent eighteen hours straight in the lab module with Arlene and her video gear.

"What two?"

"You and Arlene."

Sam cocked his head to one side. "With us? Nothing. She needs a lot of help with all that video gear. Damned studio sent her here by herself. They expect her to muscle those lasers and camera rigs around. Hell, even in zero gee that's a job."

I got the picture. "So when Gloria Lamour finally shows up you'll be practically part of the family."

I expected Sam to leer, or at least grin. Instead he looked kind of puzzled. "I don't know if she's coming up here at all. Arlene's pretty touchy about the subject."

Just how touchy we found out a couple nights later.

Larry and I were in the wardroom replaying Super Bowl XXIV on the computer simulator. I had lost the coin flip and gotten stuck with the Broncos. We had the sound turned way down so we wouldn't annoy the commander, who was staying up late, watching a video drama over in his corner: *Halloween XXXIX*.

Anyway, I had programmed an old Minnesota Vikings defense into the game, and we had sacked Montana four times already in the first quarter. The disgusted look on his face when he climbed up from the fourth burial was so real you'd think we were watching an actual game instead of creating a simulation. The crowd was going wild.

Elway was just starting to get hot, completing three straight passes, when Arlene sailed into the wardroom, looking red in the face, really pissed off. Sam was right behind her, talking his usual blue streak.

"So what'd I say that made you so sore? How could I hurt your feelings talking about the special-effects computer? What'd I do, what'd I say? For chrissakes, you're breaking the Fifth Amendment! The accused has got a right to be told what he did wrong. It's in the Constitution!"

Arlene whirled in midair and gave him a look that would have scorched a rhinoceros. "It's not the Fifth Amendment, stupid."

Sam shrugged so hard he propelled himself toward the ceiling. "So I'm not a lawyer. Sue me!"

Larry and I both reached for the Hold button on our tabletop keyboard. I got there first. The game stopped with the football in midair and Denver's wide receiver on the ten-yard line behind the Forty-Niners' free safety.

Arlene pushed herself to the galley while Sam hovered up near the ceiling, anchoring himself there by pressing the fingertips of one hand against the overhead panels. Commander Johnson did not stir from his corner, but I thought his eyes flicked from Arlene to Sam and then back to his video screen.

Before Larry and I got a chance to restart our game, Arlene squirted some hot coffee into a squeezebulb and went to the only other table in the wardroom, sailing right past Sam's dangling feet. The commander watched her. As she slipped her feet into the floor restraints he turned off his video screen and straightened up to his full height.

"Ms. Gold . . ." he began to say.

She ignored Johnson and pointed up at Sam with her free hand. "You're hanging around with your tail wagging, waiting for Gloria Lamour to get here."

"Ms. Gold," the commander said, a little louder.

Sam pushed off the ceiling. "Sure. We all are."

"Sure," Arlene mimicked. "We all are." She gave Larry and me a nasty stare.

Sam stopped himself about six inches off the floor. How he did that was always beyond me. Somehow he seemed able to break Newton's First Law, or at least bend it a little to make himself feel taller.

Johnson disengaged himself from his foot restraints and came out from behind his video set. He was staring at Arlene, his own face pinched and narrow-eyed.

"Ms. Gold," he repeated, firmly.

Arlene ignored him. She was too busy yowling at Sam, "You're so goddamned transparent it's pathetic! You think Gloria Lamour would even bother to *glance* at a little snot like you? You think if she came up here she'd let you wipe her ass? Ha!"

"Ms. Gold, I believe you are drunk," said our fearless skipper. The look on his face was weird: disapproval, disgust, disappointment, and a little bit of disbelief.

"You're damned right I'm drunk, *mon capitaine*. What th' fuck are you gonna do about it?"

Instead of exploding like a normal skipper would, the

commander surprised us all by replying with great dignity, "I will escort you to your quarters."

But he turned his beady-eyed gaze toward Sam.

Sam drifted slowly toward the skipper, bobbing along high enough to be eye-to-eye with Johnson.

"Yes, sir, she has been drinking. Vodka, I believe. I tried to stop her but she wouldn't stop," Sam said.

The commander looked utterly unconvinced.

"I have not touched a drop," Sam added. And he exhaled right into Commander Johnson's face hard enough to push himself backward like a punctured balloon.

Johnson blinked, grimaced, and looked for a moment like he was going to throw up. "I will deal with you later, Mr. Gunn," he muttered. Then he turned to Arlene again and took her by the arm. "This way, Ms. Gold."

She made a little zero-gee curtsy. "Thank you, Commander Johnson. I'm glad that there is at least one gentleman aboard this station." And she shot Sam a killer stare.

"Not at all," said the commander, patting her hand as it rested on his arm. He looked down at her in an almost grandfatherly way. Arlene smiled up at him and allowed Commander Johnson to tow her toward the hatch.

Then he made his big mistake.

"And tell me, Ms. Gold," said the skipper, "just when will Gloria Lamour arrive here?"

Arlene's face twisted into something awful. "You too? You too! That's all you bastards are thinking about, isn't it? When's your favorite wet dream going to get here."

The commander sputtered, "Ms. Gold, I assure you . . ."

She pulled free of his arm, sending herself spinning across the wardroom. She grabbed a table and yelled at all of us: "Lemme tell you something, lover boys. Gloria Lamour ain't comin' up here at all. Never! This is as good as it gets, studs. What you see is what you got!"

The commander had to haul her through the hatch. We could hear her yelling and raving all the way down the connecting passageway to the lab module.

"Where'd she get the booze?" Larry asked.

"Brought it up with her," said Sam. "She's been drinking since five o'clock. Something I said ticked her off."

"Never mind that." I got straight to the real problem. "Is she serious about Gloria Lamour not coming up here?"

Sam nodded glumly.

"Aw shit," moaned Larry.

I felt like somebody had shot Santa Claus.

"There isn't any Gloria Lamour," Sam said, his voice so low that I thought maybe I hadn't heard him right.

"No Gloria Lamour?"

"Whattaya mean?"

Sam steadied himself with a hand on the edge of our table. "Just what I said. There isn't any such person as Gloria Lamour."

"That's her show-business name."

"She's not real!" Sam snapped. "She's a simulation. Computer graphics, just like your damned football game."

"But . . ."

"All the publicity about her . . ."

"All faked. Gloria Lamour is the creation of a Hollywood talent agency and some bright computer kids. It's supposed to be a secret, but Arlene spilled it to me after she'd had a few drinks."

"A simulation?" Larry looked crushed. "Computer graphics can do that? She looked so . . . so *real*."

"She's just a bunch of algorithms, pal." Sam seemed more sober than I had ever seen him. "Arlene's her 'director.' She programs in all her moves."

"The damned bitch," Larry growled. "She could've let us know. Instead of building up our expectations like this."

"It's supposed to be a secret," Sam repeated.

"Yeah, but she should've let us in on it. It's not fair! It's just not fair!"

Sam gave him a quizzical little half smile. "Imagine how she's been feeling, watching the six of us—even old Jay-Cubed—waiting here with our tongues hanging out and full erections. Not paying any attention to her; just waiting for this dream—this computerized doll. No wonder she got sore."

I shook my head. The whole thing was too weird for me.

Sam was muttering, "I tried to tell her that I liked her, that I was interested in her for her own sake."

"She saw through that," Larry said.

"Yeah . . ." Sam looked toward the hatch. Everything was quiet now. "Funny thing is, I was getting to like her. I really was."

"Her? The Bronx Ball-Breaker?"

"She's not that bad once she lets herself relax a little."

"She sure didn't look relaxed tonight," I said.

Sam agreed with a small nod. "She never got over the idea that I was after Gloria Lamour, not her."

"Well, weren't you?"

"At first, yeah, sure. But . . ."

Larry made a sour face. "But once she told you there wasn't any Gloria Lamour you were willing to settle for her, right?"

I chimed in, "You were ready to make lemonade."

Sam fell silent. Almost. "I don't know," he mumbled. "I don't think so."

The skipper came back into the wardroom, fixed Sam with a firing-squad stare.

"Lights out, gentlemen. Gunn, you return to your normal duties tomorrow. Ms. Gold will finish her work here by herself and depart in two days."

Sam's only reply was a glum "Yes, sir."

The next morning when we started our shift in the command module Sam looked terrible. As if he hadn't slept all night. Yet there was a hint of a twinkle in his eye. He kept his face straight, because the skipper was watching him like a hawk. But he gave me a quick wink at precisely ten o'clock.

I know the exact time for two reasons.

First, Commander Johnson punched up the interior camera view of the lab module and muttered, "Ten in the morning and she's not at work yet."

"She must be under the weather, sir," Sam said in a funny kind of stiff military way of talking. Like he was rehearsing for a role in a war video or trying to get on the skipper's good side. (Assuming he had one.)

"She must be hung over as hell," Al Dupres muttered to me.

"I suppose I should call her on the intercom and

wake her up," the commander said. "After all, if she's only got two more days . . ."

"Emergency! Emergency!" called the computer's synthesized female voice. "Prepare to abandon the station. All personnel to crew emergency reentry vehicles. All personnel to crew emergency reentry vehicles. Prepare to abandon the station."

Bells and Klaxons started going off all over the place. The emergency siren was wailing so loud you could barely hear yourself think. Through it all the computer kept repeating the abandon ship message. The computer's voice was calm but urgent. The six of us were urgent, but definitely not calm.

"But I postponed the test!" Commander Johnson yelled at his computer screen. It was filled with big block letters in red, spelling out what the synthesizer was saying.

Larry and the others were already diving for the hatch that led to the nearest CERV. They had no idea that this was supposed to be a drill.

I hesitated only a moment. Then I remembered Sam's wink a minute earlier. And the little sonofagun was already flying down the connecting passageway toward the lab module like a red-topped torpedo.

"I postponed the goddamned test!" Johnson still roared at his command console, over the noise of all the warning hoots and wails. Sure he did. But Sam had spent the night rerigging it.

The station had four CERVs, each of them big enough to hold six people. Typical agency overdesign, you might think. But the lifeboats were spotted at four different locations, so no matter where on the station you might be, there was a CERV close enough to save your neck and big enough to take the whole crew with you, if necessary.

They were round unglamorous spheres, sort of like the early Russian manned reentry vehicles. Nothing inside except a lot of padding and safety harnesses. The idea was you belted off the station, propelled by cold gas jets, then the CERV's on-board computer automatically fired a set of retro rockets and started beeping out an emergency signal so the people on the ground could track where you landed.

The sphere was covered with ablative heat shielding. After reentry it popped parachutes to plop you gently on the ocean or the ground, wherever. There was also a final descent rocket to slow your fall down to almost zero.

I caught up with Larry and the other guys inside the CERV and told them to take it easy.

"This is just a drill," I said, laughing.

Rog Cranston's face was dead white. "A drill?" He had already buckled himself into his harness.

"You sure?" Larry asked. He was buckled in, too. So was Al.

"Do you see the skipper in here?" I asked, hovering nonchalantly in the middle of the capsule.

Al said, "Yeah. We're all buttoned up but we haven't been fired off the station."

Just at that moment we felt a jolt like somebody had whanged the capsule with the world's biggest hammer. I went slamming face first into the padded bulkhead, just missing a head-on collision with Larry by about an inch.

"Holy shit!" somebody yelled.

I was plastered flat against the padding, my nose bleeding and my body feeling like it weighed ten tons.

"My ass, a drill!"

It was like going over Niagara Falls in a barrel, only worse. After half a minute that seemed like half a year the gee force let up and we were weightless again. I fumbled with shaking hands into one of the empty harnesses. My nose was stuffed up with blood that couldn't run out in zero gee and I thought I was going to strangle to death. Then we started feeling heavy again. The whole damned capsule started to shake like we were inside a food processor and blood sprayed from my aching nose like a garden sprinkler.

And through it all I had this crazy notion in my head that I could still hear Commander Johnson's voice wailing, "But I postponed the drill!"

We were shaken, rattled, and frazzled all the way down. The worst part of it, of course, was that the flight was totally beyond our control. We just hung in those harnesses like four sides of beef while the capsule automatically went through reentry and parachuted us into the middle of a soccer field in Brazil. There was a game going on at the time, although we could see nothing because the capsule had neither windows nor exterior TV cameras.

Apparently our final retro rocket blast singed the referee, much to the delight of the crowd.

Sam's CERV had been shot off the station, too, we found out later. With the Gold woman aboard. Only the skipper remained aboard the space station, still yelling that he had postponed the test.

Sam's long ride back to Earth must have been even tougher than ours. He wound up in the hospital with a wrenched back and dislocated shoulder. He landed in the Australian outback, no less, but it took the Aussies only a couple of hours to reach him in their rescue VTOLs, once the agency gave them the exact tracking data.

Sure enough, Arlene Gold was in the capsule with him, shaken up a bit but otherwise unhurt.

The agency had no choice but to abort our mission and bring Commander Johnson back home at once. Popping the two CERVs was grounds for six months worth of intense investigation. Three congressional committees, OSHA, and even the EPA eventually got into the act. Thank God for Sam's ingenuity, though. Nobody was able to find anything except an unexplained malfunction of the CERV ejection thrusters. The agency wound up spending seventeen million dollars redesigning the damned thing.

As soon as we finished our debriefings, I took a few days leave and hustled over to the hospital outside San Antonio where they were keeping Sam.

I could hear that he was okay before I ever saw him. At the nurses' station half a block away from his room I could hear him yammering. Nurses were scurrying down the hall, some looking frightened, most sort of grinning to themselves.

Sam was flat on his back, his left arm in a cast that stuck straight up toward the ceiling. "... and I want a pizza, with extra pepperoni!" he was yelling at a nurse who was leaving the room just as I tried to come in. We bumped in the doorway. She was young, kind of pretty.

"He can't eat solid foods while he's strapped to the board," she said to me. As if I had anything to do with it.

The refreshment I was smuggling in for Sam was liquid, hidden under my flight jacket.

Sam took one look at me and said, "I thought your nose was broken."

"Naw, just bloodied a little."

Then he quickly launched into a catalogue of the hospital's faults: bedpans kept in the freezer, square needles, liquid foods, unsympathetic nurses.

"They keep the young ones buzzing around here all day," he complained, "but when it comes time for my sponge bath they send in Dracula's mother-in-law."

I pulled up the room's only chair. "So how the hell are you?"

"I'll be okay. If this damned hospital doesn't kill me first."

"You rigged the CERVs, didn't you?" I asked, dropping my voice low.

Sam grinned. "How'd our noble skipper like being left all alone up there?"

"The agency had to send a shuttle to pick him up, all by himself."

"The cost accountants must love him."

"The word is he's going to be reassigned to the tracking station at Ascension Island."

Sam chuckled. "It's not exactly Pitcairn, but it's kind of poetic anyway."

I worked up the nerve to ask him, "What happened?"

"What happened?" he repeated.

"In the CERV. How rugged was the flight? How'd you get hurt? What happened with Arlene?"

Sam's face clouded. "She's back in L.A. Didn't even wait around long enough to see if I would live or die."

"Must've been a punishing flight," I said.

"I wouldn't know," Sam muttered.

"What do you mean?"

Sam blew an exasperated sigh toward the ceiling. "We were screwing all the way down to the ground! How do you think I threw my back out?"

"You and Arlene? The Bronx Ball-Breaker made out with you?"

"Yeah," he said. Then, "No."

I felt kind of stunned, surprised, confused.

"You know the helmets we use in flight simulations?" Sam asked. "The kind that flash computer graphic visuals on your visor so you're seeing the situation the computer is cooking up?"

I must have nodded.

Staring at the ceiling, he continued, "Arlene brought two of them into the lifeboat with us. And her Gloria Lamour tapes."

"You were seeing Gloria Lamour . . . ?"

"It was like being with Gloria Lamour," Sam said, his voice almost shaking, kind of hollow. "Just like being with her. I could touch her. I could even taste her."

"No shit?"

"It was like nothing else in the world, man. She was fantastic. And it was all in zero gee. Most of it, anyway. The landing was rough. That's when I popped my damned shoulder."

"God almighty, Sam. She must have fallen for you after all. For her to do that for you . . ."

His face went sour. "Yeah, she fell for me so hard she took the first flight from Sydney to L.A. I'll never hear from her again."

"But—jeez, if she gave you Gloria Lamour . . ."

"Yeah. Sure," he said. I had never seen Sam so bitter. "I just wonder who the hell was programmed in *her* helmet. Who was she making out with while she was fucking me?"

6

The Pelican Bar

"YOU MEAN *SHE* was simulating it with someone else, too?"
Jade asked.

"You betcha."

"Like a V.R. parlor," said the bartender.

"Those helmets were an early version of the V.R.s,"
Sanchez said.

"V.R.?" Jade asked. "What's that?"

The bartender eyed Sanchez, then when he saw that
the man was blushing slightly, he turned back to Jade.

"Virtual reality," he said. "Simulating the full sensory
spectrum. You know, visual, audial, tactile . . ."

"Smell and taste, too?"

Sanchez coughed into his beer, sending up a small
spray of suds.

The bartender nodded. "Yep, the whole nine yards. For
a while back then, some of the wise guys in the video business figured they'd be able to do away with actors altogether.
Gloria Lamour was their first experimental test, I guess."

"But the public preferred real people," Sanchez said.
"Not that it made much difference in the videos, but with
real people they had better gossip."

Jade thought she understood. But, "So what's a V.R. parlor? And where are they? I've never seen one."

"Over at the joints in Hell Crater," the bartender said. "Guys go there and they can get any woman they want, whole harem full, if they can afford it."

"And it's all simulated," Jade prompted.

"Yeah." The bartender grinned. "But it's still a helluva lot of fun, eh, Felix?"

"I prefer real women."

"Do women go to the V.R. parlors?" Jade asked. "I mean, do they have programs of men?"

"Every male heartthrob from Hercules to President Pastoza," said the bartender.

Jade grinned. "Gee, maybe I ought to check it out."

"A nice young lady such as yourself should not go to Hell Crater," Sanchez said firmly.

"Besides, you wouldn't be able to afford it on your salary," the bartender added.

Jade saw that they were slightly embarrassed. She allowed the subject to drop.

Sanchez finished his latest beer and put the pilsner glass on the bar a trifle unsteadily. One of the robot bartenders trundled to it and replaced it with a filled glass, as it had been doing all during his narrative.

"Poor old Sam prob'ly thought that Bronx Ball-Breaker was falling for him, didn't he?" the bartender asked, watching the robot roll smoothly toward the knot of customers farther down the bar.

Sanchez seemed happy to return to Sam's story. "I suppose he did, at first. Funny thing is, I think he was actually starting to fall for her. At least a little. Maybe more sympathy than anything else, but Sam was a very empathetic guy, you know."

"Did he ever see her again?" Jade asked.

"No, not her. He tried to call her a few times but she never responded. Not a peep."

"Poor Sam."

"Oh, don't feel so bad about him. Sam had plenty of other fish to fry. He was never down for long. Not Sam."

The bartender gave a hand signal to the nearer of the two robots and it quickly brought a fresh Coke for Jade and a thimble-sized glass of amber-colored liquid for the bartender himself.

He raised his glass and said with utter seriousness, "To Sam Gunn, the best sonofabitch in the whole goddamned solar system."

Jade felt a little foolish repeating the words, but she did it, as did Sanchez, and then sipped at her new drink.

"Y'know," Sanchez said, after smacking his lips over the beer, "nobody gives a damn about Sam anymore. Here he is, dead and gone, and just about everybody's forgotten him."

"Damn' shame," the bartender agreed.

"I wouldn't have my business if it wasn't for Sam," Sanchez said. "He set me up when I needed the money to get started. Nobody else would even look at me! The banks—hah!"

"I was helping my daddy at his bar down in Florida when I first met Sam," said the bartender. "He's the one who first gave me the idea of opening a joint up here. It was still called Moonbase when I started this place. He had to argue a blue streak to get the base administrators to okay a saloon."

Jade, her own troubles pushed to the back of her mind, told them, "You two guys—and Zach, my boss—you're the first I've ever heard say a decent word about Sam. Everything I ever heard from the time I was a kid has been . . . well, not very flattering."

"That's because the stories about him have mostly been spread by the guys who tangled with him," said the bartender.

"The big corporations," Sanchez agreed.

"And the government."

"They hated Sam's guts. All those guys with suits and ties."

"Why?" asked Jade.

The bartender made a sound halfway between a grunt and a snort. "Why? Because Sam was always fighting against them. He was the little guy, trying to get ahead, always bucking the big boys."

Sanchez smiled again. "Don't get the idea that he was some kind of Robin Hood," he said, glancing at the bartender, then fixing his gaze once again on Jade's lustrous green eyes.

The bartender guffawed. "Robin Hood? Sam? Hell no! All he wanted to do was to get rich."

"Which he did. Many times."

"And threw it all away, just as often."

"*And* helped a lot of little guys like us, along the way."

The bartender wiped at his eyes. "Hey, Felix, you remember the time . . ."

Jade did not think it was possible to get drunk on Coca-Cola, so the exhilarated feeling she was experiencing an hour or so later must be from the two men's tales of Sam Gunn.

"Why doesn't somebody do a biography of him?" she blurted. "I mean, the networks would love it, wouldn't they?"

Both men stopped the reminiscences in midsentence. The bartender looked surprised. Sanchez inexplicably turned glum.

"The networks? Pah!" Sanchez spat.

"They'd never do it," said the bartender, turning sad.

"Why not?"

"Two reasons. One: the big corporations run the networks and they still hate Sam, even though he's dead. They won't want to see him glorified. And two: guys like us will tell you stories about Sam, but do you think we'd trust some smart-ass reporter from one of the networks?"

"Oh," said Jade. "I see—I guess."

The men resumed their tales of their younger days. Jade half listened as she sipped on her Coke, thinking to herself, But they're talking to me about Sam. Why couldn't I get other people who knew him to talk to me?

7

The Audition

It took Jade three months to get herself hired as an assistant tape editor for the Selene office of the Solar News Network. She took crash courses in Videotape Editing and News Writing from the electronic university, working long into the nights in front of her interactive TV set, catching a few winks of sleep, and then going to the garage to put in her hours on the surface driving a truck.

At first Zach Bonner, her supervisor, scowled angrily at her baggy eyes and slowed reflexes.

"Tell your boyfriend to let you get more sleep, little girl," he growled at her. "Otherwise you're going to make a mistake out there and kill yourself—maybe kill me, too."

Shocked with surprise, Jade blurted the truth. "I don't have a boyfriend, Zach. I'm studying."

Bonner had three daughters of his own. As swiftly as he could, he transferred Jade to a maintenance job indoors. She gratefully accepted.

"Just remember," he said gruffly, "what you're doing now is holding other guys' lives in your hands. Don't mess up."

Jade did her work carefully, both day and night, until her certificates of course completion arrived in her fax. Then she tackled the three network news offices at Selene. Minolta/Bell, the largest, turned her down cold; they had no job openings at the moment, they said, and they only hired people with experience. BBC accepted her application with a polite version of the classic "Don't call us; we'll call you."

Solar News, the smallest of the three and the youngest, was an all-news network. They paid much less than Jade was making as a truck driver. But they had an opening for an assistant tape editor. Jade took the job without thinking twice about it.

Zach Bonner shook his head warily when she told him she was quitting. "You sure you want to do this?"

"Yes," Jade said. "I'm sure."

He gave a sigh that was almost an exasperated snort. "Okay, kid. If things don't work out for you, come on back here and I'll see what I can do for you."

She had more than half expected him to say that, but still his words warmed her. She stood up on tiptoes and pecked a kiss on his cheek. He sputtered with mixed embarrassment and happiness.

Dr. Dinant was pleased that Jade was moving to a job below-ground. "I still would like to do the procedure on you," she said, "before I finish my tour here and return home."

Jade put her off, hoping she would return to Earth and forget about her. Just as her adoptive mother had.

She started her new job, surprised that there were only six people in the entire Selene office of Solar News. Two of them were reporters, one male and one female, who went to the same hairdressing salon and actually appeared on screen now and then, when the network executives permitted such glory. Otherwise, their stories were "reported" by anchorpersons in Orlando who had never been to the Moon.

It took her nearly a year to work up the courage to tell her new boss about her idea of doing a biography of Sam Gunn.

"I've heard of him," said her boss, a middle-aged

woman named Monica Bianco. "Some sort of a con man, wasn't he? A robber baron?"

Although Monica affected a veneer of newsroom cynicism, she could not hide her basic good nature from Jade for very long. The two women had much in common in addition to their jobs. Monica had come to Selene to escape pollution allergies that left her gasping helplessly more than half the year on Earth. When Jade confided that she could never go to Earth, her boss broke into tears at the memory of all she had been forced to leave behind. The two of them became true friends after that.

Monica was good-looking despite her years, Jade thought. She admitted to being over forty, and Jade wondered just how much beyond the Big Four-Oh she really was. Not that it mattered much. Especially in Selene, where men still outnumbered women by roughly three to one. Monica was a bit heavier than she ought to be, but her ample bosom and cheerful disposition kept lots of men after her. She confessed to Jade that she had been married twice. "I buried one and dumped the other," she said, without a trace of remorse. "Both bastards. I just seem to pick rotten SOBs for myself."

Jade had nothing to confess beyond the usual teenager's flings. So she told Monica what she knew of Sam Gunn and asked how she might get the decision-makers of Solar News to assign her to do a biography.

"Forget it, honey," advised Monica. "The only ideas they go for are the ones they think up for themselves—or steal from somebody they envy. Besides, they'd never let an inexperienced pup like you tackle an assignment like that."

Jade felt her heart sink. But then Monica added, "Unless . . ."

So several weeks later Jade found herself at dinner with Monica and Jim Gradowsky, the Solar News office chief. They sat at a cozy round table in a quiet corner of the Ristorante de la Luna. Of Selene's five eating establishments, the Ristorante was acknowledged to be the best bargain: lots of good food at modest prices. It was Jumbo Jim Gradowsky's favorite eatery.

Monica wore a black skirt and blouse with a scooped

neckline. At Monica's insistence, Jade had spent a week's salary on a glittering green sheath that complemented her eyes. Now that she saw the checkered tablecloths and dripping candles, though, she thought that Monica had overdressed them both.

Gradowsky, who showed up in a wrinkled short-sleeved shirt and baggy slacks, did not seem to notice what they were wearing. He was called Jumbo Jim because of his girth. But never to his face.

"So you can never go Earthside," Gradowsky was saying through a mouthful of *coniglio cacciatore*. His open-collared shirt was already stained and sprinkled with the soup and salad courses.

"It's a bone condition," Jade replied. "Osteopetrosis."

Gradowsky took a tiny roasted rabbit leg in one big hand. Red gravy dripped onto his lap. "Isn't that what little old ladies get? Makes 'em stoop over?"

"That's osteo*porosis*," Jade corrected. "The bones get soft with age. I've got just the opposite problem. My bones are too brittle. They'd snap under a full Earth gravity. They call it Marble Bones."

He shook his head and dabbed at the grease around his mouth with a checkered napkin. "Gee, that's too bad. I could go back Earthside if I wanted to, but the medics say I'd hafta lose forty–fifty pounds first."

Jade made a sympathetic noise.

"You know, Jim," said Monica, sitting on his other side, "Jade here's got a terrific idea for a special. If you could sell it back in Orlando it'd be quite a feather in your cap."

"Yeah? Really?"

Jade explained her hope to do a biography of Sam Gunn. Gradowsky was obviously cool to the idea, but Monica slid her chair closer to his and insisted that it was the kind of idea that Solar's upper echelons would go for.

"It could mean a boost for you," Monica said, leaning so close to Gradowsky that Jade could see her cleavage from across the table. "A big boost."

The two women went to the ladies' room together as the waiter cleared their table in preparation for dessert.

Jade saw that there were greasy paw stains on Monica's shirt.

"You're not throwing yourself at him for me?" Jade asked.

Monica smiled. "Don't worry about it, honey. Jumbo's kind of cute, if you don't mind his table manners."

"Cute?"

"After three bottles of wine."

"Monica, I can't let you . . ."

The older woman smiled sweetly at Jade. "Don't give it another thought, child. Who knows, I might marry the bum and try to civilize him."

Thus it came to pass that Jim Gradowsky sold his idea of doing a biography of Sam Gunn to the top brass of the Solar News Network. He even won the responsibility of picking the reporter to handle the interviews.

Jade faced him alone in his office, a minuscule cubbyhole crammed with a desk, two computer terminals, a battered pseudo-leather couch, and a whole wall full of TV screens.

"Monica says you oughtta get the job of doing the Sam Gunn interviews," Gradowsky said, his eyes narrowing as Jade sat demurely on the couch.

She thought to herself, If he gets up from behind that desk I'll run out of here and to hell with the interviews. Or will I?

Gradowsky stayed in his creaking desk chair. "Well, I'm not sure that somebody with no real experience can handle the assignment. You're awfully young . . ."

Jade made herself smile at him. "That's just the point. Most of Sam's friends—even his enemies—wouldn't talk to a regular news reporter. But they'll talk to me."

"Why's that?" Gradowsky seemed all business, thank goodness.

"I don't come across as a reporter. I'm a lunar worker, one of the guys."

"Hardly one of the *guys*." Gradowsky smirked.

The phone built into one of the computers chirped. Grunting, he leaned forward and punched a button on its keyboard.

Monica's face took form on a wall screen. "How's it going?" she asked cheerfully.

Gradowsky raised both hands, palms out, as if to show he was unarmed. "Okay so far. We're talkin'."

"Are we set for dinner tonight?"

"Yeah, sure. Where d'you wanna go?"

"I thought I'd cook for you tonight. How about my place at seven-thirty. You bring the wine."

Gradowsky grinned. "Great!"

"See you then."

When he turned back to Jade he was still grinning.

"Okay, listen up, kid. Here's what I'm prepared to do. There's a Russian living over at the retirement center next to Lunagrad. From what my contacts tell me, he knew Sam Gunn back in the old days, when Gunn was still a NASA astronaut. But he's never talked to anybody about it."

"Has anyone tried to interview him?" Jade asked.

"Yeah—BBC was after him for years but he always turned them down."

Jade clasped her hands together tightly, surprised to find that her palms were sweating.

"You get the Russkie to talk and the assignment's yours. Fair enough?"

She nodded, almost breathless. "Fair enough," she managed to say.

8

Diamond Sam

"A THIEF," SAID Grigori Aleksandrovich Prokov. "A thief and a blackmailer."

He said it flatly, without emotion, the way a man might observe that the sky is blue or that grass is green. A fact of life. He said it in excellent English, marred only slightly by the faint trace of a Russian accent.

Jade wrinkled her nose slightly. There was neither blue sky nor green grass here in the Leonov Center for Retired Heroes of the Russian Federation, although there was a distinctly earthy odor to the place.

"Sam Gunn," Prokov muttered. His voice seemed weak, almost quavering. The weakening voice of a dying old man. Then he gave a disdainful snort. "Not even the other capitalists liked him!"

They were sitting on a bench made of native lunar stone near the edge of the surface dome, as far away from the yawning entrance to the underground retirement center as possible. To Jade, that dark entrance looked like the opening of a crypt.

The floor of the dome was bare lunar rock that had been glazed by plasma torches and smoothed to a glassy

59

finish. She wondered how many elderly Heroes of the Russian Federation slipped and broke their necks. Was that their government's ultimate retirement benefit?

The wide curving window in front of the bench looked out on absolute desolation: the barren expanse of the Ocean of Storms, a pockmarked, undulating surface without a sign of life as far as the eye could see. Nothing but rocks and bare lunar regolith broiling in the harsh sunlight. The sky remained black, though, and above the strangely close horizon hung the tantalizing blue and white-streaked globe of Earth, a lonely haven of color and life in the stark, cold darkness of space.

For the tenth time in the past ten minutes Jade fumbled with the heater control of her electrified jumpsuit. She felt the chill of that merciless vacuum seeping through the tinted glassteel of the big window. She strained her ears for the telltale hiss of an air leak. There were rumors that maintenance at the Leonov Center was far from top-rate.

Prokov seemed impervious to the cold. Or perhaps, rather, he was so accustomed to it that he never noticed it anymore. He was very old, his face sunken in like a rotting jack-o'-lantern, wrinkled even across his utterly bald pate. The salmon-pink coveralls he wore seemed brand-new, as if he had put them on just for this visit from a stranger. Or had the managers of the Center insisted that he wear new clothes whenever a visitor called? Whichever, she saw that the outfit was at least a full size too big for the man. He seemed to be shrinking, withering away before her eyes.

But his eyes glittered at her balefully. "Why do you ask about Sam Gunn? I was given to understand that you were only a student doing a thesis on the history of early spaceflight."

"That was a bit of a white lie," Jade said, trying to keep the tremble of fear out of her voice. "I—I'm actually trying to do a biography of Sam Gunn."

"That despicable money-grubber," Prokov muttered.

"Would you help me? Please?"

"Why should I?" the old man snapped.

Jade made a little shrug.

"I have never spoken to anyone about Sam Gunn. Not in more than thirty years."

"I know," Jade said.

Frowning, Prokov examined her intently. A little elf, he thought. A child-woman in a pale green jumpsuit. How frightened she looks! Such beautiful red hair. Such entrancing green eyes.

"Ah," he sighed. "If I were a younger man . . ."

Jade smiled kindly at him. "You were a hero then, weren't you? A cosmonaut and a Hero of the Russian Federation."

His eyes glimmered with distant memories.

"Sam Gunn," he repeated. "Thief. Liar. Warmonger. He almost caused World War III, did you know that?"

"No," said Jade, truly surprised. She checked the recorder in her belt buckle and slid a few centimeters closer to the old man, to make certain that the miniaturized device did not miss any of his words.

There was hardly any other noise in the big, dark, gloomy dome. Far off in the shadows sat a couple of other old people, as still as mummies, as if frozen by time and the indifference that comes from having outlived everyone you loved.

"A nuclear holocaust, that's what your Sam Gunn would have started. If not for *me*"—Prokov tapped the folds of cloth that covered his sunken chest—"the whole world might have gone up in radioactive smoke thirty years ago."

"I never knew," said Jade.

Without any further encouragement Prokov began to speak in his whispery, trembling voice.

I was commander of Mir 5, the largest Russian space station. My rank was full colonel. My crew had been in space for 638 days and it was my goal to make it two full years—730 days. It would be a new record, fourteen men in orbit for two full years. I would be picked to command the Mars mission if I could get my men to the two-year mark. A big if.

Sam Gunn, as you know, was an American astronaut at that time. Officially he was a crew member of the NASA space station. Secretly he worked for the CIA, I am certain. No other explanation fits the facts.

You must understand that despite all the comforts that Russian technology could provide, life aboard Mir 5 was, well, Spartan. We worked in shifts and slept in hot beds. You know, when one man finished his sleep shift he got out of his zipper bag and a man who had just finished his work shift would get into the bag to sleep. Sixteen hours of work, eight of sleep. Four bunks for twelve crewmen. It was all strictly controlled by ground command.

Naturally, as colonel in command I had my own bunk and my own private cubicle. This was not a deviation from comradely equality; it was necessary and all the crew recognized that fact. My political officer also had his own private cubicle, as well.

Believe me, after the first eighteen months of living under such stringencies life became very tense inside Mir 5. Fourteen men cooped up inside a set of aluminum cans with nothing but work, no way to relieve their tedium, forced to exercise when there were no other tasks to do—the tension was becoming dangerously high. Sam must have known that. I was told that the CIA employed thousands of psychologists in those days.

You must realize that we were then in the grip of what the media journalists now call the Neo-Cold War. When the old Soviet Union broke up, back in the last century, Russia nearly disappeared in chaos and anarchy. But new leaders arose, strong and determined to bring Russia back to its rightful position as one of the world's leading powers. We were proud to be part of that rebirth of Russian strength and courage. *I* was proud to be part of it myself.

Sam's first visit to our station was made to look like an accident. He waited until I was asleep to call us.

My second-in-command, a thick-headed Estonian named Korolev, shook me awake none too gently.

"Sir!" he said, pummeling my zippered bag. "There's an American asking us for help!"

It was like being the toothpaste in a tube while some big oaf tries to squeeze you out.

"An Ameri—stop that! I'm awake! Get your hands off me!"

Fortunately, I slept in my coveralls. I simply unzippered the bag and followed Korolev toward the command center. He was a bulky fellow, a wrestler back at home and a decent electronics technician up here. But he had been made second-in-command by seniority only. His brain was not swift enough for such responsibilities.

The station was composed of nine modules—nine aluminum cylinders joined together by airlocks. It was all under zero gravity. The Americans had not even started to build their fancy rotating stations yet.

We floated through the hatch of the command center, where four more of my men were hovering by the communications console. It was cramped and hot; six men in the center were at least two too many.

I immediately heard why they had awakened me.

"Hey, are you guys gonna help me out or let me die?" a sharp-edged voice was rasping on our radio receiver. "I got a dead friggin' OTV here and I'm gonna drift right past you and out into the Van Allen Belt and fry my *cojones* if you don't come and get me."

That was my introduction to Sam Gunn.

Zworkin, my political officer, was already in contact with ground control, reporting on the incident. On my own authority—and citing the reciprocal rescue treaty that had been in effect for more than two decades—I sent one of our orbital transfer vehicles with two of my best men to rescue the American.

His vehicle's rocket propellant line had ruptured, with the same effect as if your automobile fuel line had split apart. His rocket engine died and he was drifting without propulsion power.

"Goddamn cheap Hong Kong parts." Sam kept up a running monologue all through our rescue flight. "Bad enough we gotta fly birds built by the lowest goddamn bidders, but now they're buying parts from friggin' toy manufacturers! Whole goddamn vehicle works like something put together from a Mattel kit by a brain-damaged chimpanzee. Those mother-humpers in Washington don't

give a shit whose neck they put on the mother-humpin'
line as long as it ain't theirs."

And so on, through the entire three hours it took for
us to send out our transfer vehicle, take him aboard it, and
bring him safely to the station.

Once he came through the airlock and actually set
foot inside Mir 5 his tone changed. I should say that "set
foot" is an euphemism. We were all weightless, and Sam
floated into the docking chamber, turned himself a full 360
degrees around, and grinned at us.

All fourteen of us had crowded into the docking
chamber to see him. This was the most excitement we had
had since Boris Malenovsky's diarrhea, six months earlier.

"Hey!" said Sam. "You guys are as short as me!"

No word of thanks. No formal greetings or offers of
international friendship. His first words upon being rescued dealt with our heights.

He was no taller than my own 160 centimeters, although he claimed to be 165. He pushed himself next to
Korolev, the biggest man of our crew, who stood almost
173 centimeters, according to the medical files. Naturally,
under zero-gravity conditions Korolev—and all of us—had
grown an extra two or three centimeters.

"I'm just about as tall as you are!" Sam exulted.

He flitted from one member of our crew to another
comparing heights. It was difficult to make an accurate
measurement because he kept bobbing up slightly, thanks
to the zero gravity. In other words, he cheated. I should
have recognized this as the key to his character immediately. Unfortunately, I did not.

Neither did Zworkin, although he later claimed that
he knew all along that Sam was a spy.

All in all, Sam was not unpleasant. He was friendly.
He was noisy. I remember thinking, in those first few moments he was aboard our station, that it was like having a
pet monkey visit us. Amusing. Diverting. He made us
laugh, which was something we had not done in many
weeks.

Sam's face was almost handsome, but not quite. His
lips were a bit too thin and his jaw a little too round. His
eyes were bright and glowing like a fanatic's. His hair bris-

tled like a thicket of wires, brownish-red. His tongue was never still.

Most of my crew understood English well enough so that Sam had little trouble expressing himself to us. Which he did incessantly. Sam kept up a constant chatter about the shoddy construction of his orbital transfer vehicle, the solid workmanship of our station, the lack of esthetics in spacecraft design, the tyranny of ground controllers who forbade alcoholic beverages aboard space stations, this, that, and the other. He even managed to say a few words that sounded almost like gratitude.

"I guess giving you guys a chance to save my neck makes a nice break in the routine for you, huh? Not much else exciting going on around here, is there?"

He talked so much and so fast that it never occurred to any of us, not even to Zworkin, to ask why he had been flying so near to us. As far as I knew, there were no Western satellites in orbits this close to our station. Or there should not have been.

Next to his machine-gun dialogue the thing that impressed my men most about this American astronaut was his uniform. Like ours, it was basically a one-piece coverall, quite utilitarian. Like us, he bore a name patch sewn over his left chest pocket. There the similarities ended.

Sam's coveralls were festooned with all sorts of fancy patches and buttons. Not merely one shoulder patch with his mission insignia. He had patches and insignia running down both sleeves and across his torso, front and back, like the tattooed man in the circus. Dragons, comic-book rocket ships, silhouettes of naked women, buttons that bore pictures of video stars, strange symbols and slogans that made no sense to me, such as "Beam me up, Scotty, there's no intelligent life down here" and "King Kong died for our sins."

Finally I ordered my men back to their duties and told Sam to accompany me to the control center.

Zworkin objected. "It is not wise to allow him to see the control center," he said in Russian.

"Would you prefer," I countered, "that he be allowed to roam through the laboratories? Or perhaps the laser module?"

Most of my own crew were not allowed to enter the laser module. Only men with specific military clearance were permitted there. And most of the laboratories, you see, were testing systems that would one day be the heart of our Red Shield antimissile system. Even the diamond manufacturing experiment was a Red Shield program, according to my mission orders.

Zworkin did not reply to my question. He merely stared at me sullenly. He had a sallow, pinched face that was blemished with acne—unusual for a man of his age. The crew joked behind his back that he was still a virgin.

"The visitor stays with me, Nikolai Nikolaivich," I told him. "Where I can watch him."

Unfortunately, I had to listen to Sam as well as watch him.

I ordered my communications technician to contact the NASA space station and allow Sam to tell them what had happened. Meanwhile Zworkin reported again to ground control. It was not a simple matter to transfer Sam back to the NASA station. First we had to apprise ground control of the situation, and they had to inform Moscow, where the American embassy and the International Astronautical Council were duly briefed. Hours dragged by and our work schedule became hopelessly snarled.

I must admit, however, that Sam was a good guest. He handed out trinkets that he fished from the deep pockets of his coveralls. A miniature penknife to one of the men who had rescued him. A pocket computer to the other, programmed to play a dozen different games when it was connected to a display screen. A small flat tin of rock candy. A Russian-English dictionary the size of your thumb.

That dictionary should have alerted my suspicions. But I confess that I was more concerned with getting this noisy intrusion off my station and back where he belonged.

Sam stayed a day. Two days. Teleconferences crackled between Washington and Moscow, Moscow and Geneva, Washington and Geneva, ground control to our station, our station to the NASA station. Meanwhile Sam had made himself at home and even started to learn how to tell jokes in Russian. He was particularly interested in dirty jokes, of course, being the kind of man he was. He began to peel off some of the patches and buttons that adorned his coveralls and hand them out as presents. My crewmen especially lusted after the pictures of beautiful video stars.

He had taken over the galley, where he was teaching my men how to play dice in zero gravity, when I at last received permission to send him back to the American station. Not an instant too soon, I thought.

Still, dear old Mir 5 became suddenly very quiet and dreary once we had packed him off in one of our own reliable transfer craft. We returned to our tedious tasks and the damnable exercise machines. The men growled and sulked at each other. Months of boredom and hard work stretched ahead of us. I could feel the tension pulling at my crew. I felt it myself.

But not for long.

Less than a week later Korolev again rousted me from my zipper bunk.

"He's back! The American!"

This time Sam did not pretend to need an emergency rescue. He had flown an orbital transfer vehicle to our station and matched orbit. His OTV was hovering a few hundred meters alongside us.

"Permission to come aboard?" His voice was unmistakable. "Unofficially?"

I glanced at Zworkin, who was of course right beside me in the command center. Strangely, Nikolai Nikolaivich nodded. Nothing is unofficial with him, I knew. Yet he did not object to the American making an "unofficial" visit.

I went to the docking chamber while Sam floated over to us. The airlock of his craft would not fit our docking mechanism, so he went EVA in his pressure suit and jetted across to us using his backpack maneuvering unit.

"I was in the neighborhood so I thought I'd drop by for a minute," Sam wisecracked once he got through our airlock and slid up the visor of his helmet.

"Why are you in this area?" Zworkin asked, eyes slitted in his pimpled face.

"To observe your laser tests," replied Sam, grinning. "You guys don't think our intelligence people don't know what you're up to, do you?"

"We are not testing lasers!"

"Not today, I know. Don't worry about it, Ivan, I'm not spying on you, for chrissakes."

"My name is not Ivan!"

"I just came over to thank you guys for saving my ass." Sam turned slightly, his entire body pivoting weightlessly toward me. He reached into the pouches on the legs of his suit. "A couple of small tokens of my gratitude."

He pulled out two black oblong boxes and handed them to me. Videocassettes.

"Latest Hollywood releases," Sam explained. "With my thanks."

In a few minutes he was gone. Zworkin insisted on looking at the videos before anyone else could see them. "Probably Western propaganda," he grumbled.

I insisted on seeing them with him. I was not going to let him keep them all for himself.

One of the videos was the very popular film *Rocky XVIII,* in which the geriatric former prizefighter is rejuvenated and gets out of his wheelchair to defeat a nine-foot-tall robot for the heavyweight championship of the solar system.

"Disgusting," spat Zworkin.

"But it will be good to show the crew how low the Americans sink in their pursuit of money," I said.

He gave me a sour look but did not argue.

The second video was a rock musical that featured decadent music at extreme decibel levels, decadent youths wearing outlandish clothes and weird hairdos, and decadent young women wearing hardly any clothes at all. Their gyrations were especially disturbing, no matter from which point of view you looked at them.

"Definitely not for the crew to see," said Zworkin. None of us ever saw that video again. He kept it. But now and then I heard the music, faintly, from his private cubicle during the shifts when he was supposed to be sleeping. Mysteriously, his acne began to clear up.

Almost two weeks afterward Sam popped up again. Again he asked permission to come aboard, claiming this time he was on a routine inspection mission of a commsat in geosynchronous orbit and had planned his return to the

NASA station to take him close to us. He was a remarkable pilot, that much I must admit.

"Got a couple more videos for you," he added, almost as an afterthought.

Zworkin immediately okayed his visit. The rest of my crew, who had cheered the rejuvenated Rocky in his proletarian struggle against the stainless-steel symbol of Western imperialism (as we saw it), welcomed him aboard.

Sam stayed for a couple of hours. We fed him a meal of borscht, soysteak, and ice cream. With plenty of hot tea.

"That's the best ice cream I've ever had!" Sam told me as we made our weightless way from the galley back to the docking chamber, where he had left his pressure suit.

"We get fresh supplies every week," I said. "Our only luxury."

"I never knew you guys had such great ice cream." He was really marveling over it.

"Moscow is famous for its ice cream," I replied.

With a shake of his head that made his whole body sway slightly, Sam admitted, "Boy, we got nothing like that back at the NASA station."

"Would you like to bring some back to your station?" I asked. Innocent fool that I am, I did not realize that he had maneuvered me into making the offer.

"Gee, yeah," he said, like a little boy.

I had one of the men pack him a container of ice cream while he struggled into his pressure suit. Zworkin was off screening the two new videos Sam had brought, so I did not bother him with the political question of offering a gift in return for Sam's gift.

As he put his helmet over his head, Sam said to me in a low voice, "Each of those videos is a double feature."

"A what?"

Leaning close to me, so that the technician in charge of the docking airlock could not hear, he whispered, "Play the tapes backward at half speed and you'll see another whole video. But *you* look at them yourself first. Don't let that sourball of a political officer see it or he'll confiscate them both."

I felt puzzled, and my face must have shown it. Sam

merely grinned, patted me on the shoulder, and said, "Thanks for the ice cream."

Then he left.

It took a bit of ingenuity to figure out how to play the videos backward at half speed. It took even more cleverness to arrange to look at them in private, without Zworkin or any of the other crew members hanging over my shoulders. But I did it.

The "second feature" on each of the tapes was pornographic filth. Disgusting sexual acrobatics featuring beautiful women with large breasts and apparently insatiable appetites. I watched the degrading spectacles several times, despite stern warnings from my conscience. If I had been cursed with acne these videos would undoubtedly have solved the problem overnight. Especially the one with the trapeze.

For the first time since I had been a teenager buying contraband blue jeans I faced a moral dilemma. Should I tell Zworkin about these secret pornographic films? He had seen only the normal, "regular" features on each tape: an ancient John Wayne western and a brand-new comedy about a computer that takes over Wall Street.

In my own defense I say only that I was thinking of the good of my crew when I made my decision. The men had been in orbit for nearly 650 days with almost two full months to go before we could return to our loved ones. The pornographic films might help them to bear their loneliness and perform better at their tasks, I reasoned.

But only if Zworkin did not know about them.

I decided to chance it. One by one I let the crew in on the little secret. Morale improved six hundred percent. Performance and productivity rose equally. The men smiled and laughed a lot more. I told myself it was just as much because they were pulling one over on the puritanical Zworkin as because they were watching the buxom Oral Roberta and her insatiable girlfriend Electric (AC/DC) Edna.

Sam returned twice more, swapping tapes for ice cream. He was our friend. He apparently had an inexhaustible supply of videos, each of them a "double feature." While Zworkin spent the next several weeks happily watching the regular features on each tape and perspiring every time he saw a girl in a bikini, the rest of us watched the erotic adventures of airline stewardesses, movie starlets, models, housewife-hookers, and other assorted and sordid specimens of female depravity.

The days flew by with each man counting the hours until Sam showed up with another few videos. We stopped eating ice cream so that we would have plenty to give him in return.

Then Sam sprang his trap on us. On me.

"Listen," he said as he was suiting up in the docking chamber, preparing to leave, "next time, how about sticking a couple of those diamonds you're making into the ice cream."

I flinched with surprise and automatically looked over my shoulder at the technician standing by to operate the airlock. He was busy admiring the four new videocassettes Sam had brought, wondering what was in them as he studied their labels.

"What are you talking about?" I meant to say it out loud but it came out as a whispered croak.

Sam flashed a cocky grin at me. "Come on, everybody knows you guys are making gem-quality diamonds out of methane gas in your zero-gee facility. Pump a little extra methane in and make me a couple to sell Earthside. I'll split the profits with you fifty-fifty."

"Impossible," I snapped. Softly.

His smile became shrewd. "Look, Greg old pal, I'm not asking for any military secrets. Just a couple of stones I can peddle back on Earth. We can both make a nice wad of money."

"The diamonds we manufacture are not of gemstone quality," I lied.

"Let my friends on Forty-seventh Street decide what quality they are," Sam whispered.

"No."

He puffed out a sad sigh. "This has nothing to do with politics, Greg. It's business. Capitalism."

I shook my head hard enough to sway my entire body.

Sam seemed to accept defeat. "Okay. It's a shame, though. Hell, even your leaders in the Kremlin are making money selling their biographies to Western publishers. Capitalism is swooping in on you."

I said nothing.

He pulled the helmet over his head, fastened the neck seal. But before sliding down his visor he asked, quite casually, "What happens if Zworkin finds out what's on the videos you guys have been watching?"

My face went red. I could feel the heat flaming my cheeks.

"Just a couple of little diamonds, pal. A couple of carats. That's not so much to ask for, is it?"

He went through the airlock and jetted back to his own craft. I would have gladly throttled him at that moment.

Now I had a *real* dilemma on my hands. Give in to Sam's blackmail or face Zworkin and the authorities back on the ground. It would not only be me who would be in trouble, but my entire crew. They did not deserve to suffer because of my bad decisions, but they would. We would all spend the rest of our lives shoveling cow manure in Siberia or running mining machines on the Moon.

I had been corrupted and I knew it. Oh, I had the best of motives, the loftiest of intentions. But how would they appear next to the fact that I had allowed my crew to watch disgusting pornographic films provided by a capitalist agent of the CIA? Corruption, pure and simple. I would be lucky to be sentenced to Siberia.

I gave in to Sam's demands. I told myself it was for the sake of my crew, but it was to save my own neck, and to save my dear family from disgrace. I had the technicians make three extra small diamonds and embedded them in the ice cream when Sam made his next visit.

That was the exact week, naturally, when the USSR and the Western powers were meeting in Geneva to decide on deployment of space weapons. Our own Red Shield system and the American Star Wars system were well into the testing phase. We had conducted a good many of the tests ourselves aboard Mir 5. Now the question was, does each side begin to deploy its own system or do we hammer out some method of working cooperatively?

Sam returned a few days later. I did not want to see him, but was afraid not to. He seemed happy and cheerful as usual, and carried no less than six new videos with him. I spoke to him very briefly, very coldly. He seemed not to be bothered at all. He laughed and joked. And passed me a note on a tiny scrap of paper as he handed me the new videos.

I read the note in the privacy of my cubicle, after he left. "Good stuff. Worth a small fortune. How many can you provide each week?"

I was accustomed to the weightlessness of zero gravity, but at that instant I felt as if I were falling into a deep, dark pit, falling and falling down into an utterly black well that had no bottom.

To make matters worse, after a few days of progress the conference at Geneva seemed to hit a snag for some unfathomable reason. The negotiations stopped dead and the diplomats began to snarl at each other in the old Cold War fashion. The world was shocked. We received orders to accelerate our tests of the Red Shield laser that had been installed in the laboratory module at the aft end of our station.

We watched the TV news broadcasts from every part of the world (without letting Zworkin or ground control know about it, of course). Everyone was frightened at the sudden intransigence in Geneva.

Zworkin summed up our fears. "The imperialists want an excuse to strike us with their remaining nuclear missiles before our Red Shield defense is deployed."

I had to admit that he was probably right. What scared me was the thought that *we* might strike at *them* before their Star Wars defense was deployed. Either way it meant the same thing: nuclear holocaust. Each side still had enough missiles to wipe out half the world.

Even thick-headed Korolev seemed worried. "Will we go to war?" he kept asking. "Will we go to war?" No one knew.

Needless to say, it was clear that if we did go to war Mir 5 would be a sitting duck for Yankee antisatellite weapons. As everyone knew, the war on the ground would begin with strikes against space stations and satellites.

To make matters even worse, in the midst of our laser test preparations Sam sent a radio message that he was on his way and would rendezvous with our station in three hours. He said he had "something special" for us.

The crisis in Geneva meant nothing to him, it seemed. He was coming for "business as usual." Zworkin had been right all along about him. Sam was a spy. I was certain of it now.

A vision formed in my mind. I would personally direct the test of the Red Shield laser. Its high-energy beam would happen to strike the incoming American spacecraft. Sam Gunn would be fried like a scrawny chicken in a hot oven. A regrettable accident. Yes. It would solve my problem.

Except—it would create such a furor on Earth that the conference in Geneva would break up altogether. It could be the spark that would lead to war, nuclear war.

Yet—Sam had no business flying a Yankee spacecraft so close to a Soviet station. Both the U.S. and Russia had clearly proclaimed that the regions around their stations were sovereign territory, not to be violated by the other side's craft. Sam's visits to Mir 5 were strictly illegal, secret, clandestine, except for his first "emergency" visit. If we fried him we would be within our legal rights.

On the other hand—could the entire crew remain silent about Sam's many visits? Would Zworkin stay silent or would he denounce me once we had returned to Mother Russia?

On the *other* hand—what difference would any of that make if we triggered nuclear war?

That is why I found myself sweating in the laser laboratory, a few hours after Sam's call. He knew that we were going to test the laser, he had to know. That was why he was cheerfully heading our way at this precise point in time.

The laboratory was chilly. The three technicians perating the giant laser wore bulky sweaters over their coveralls and gloves with the fingers cut so they could manipulate their sensitive equipment properly.

This section of the station was a complete module in itself; it could be detached and de-orbited, if necessary, and a new section put in its place. The huge laser filled the laboratory almost completely. If we had not been in zero gravity it would have been impossible for the technicians to climb into the nooks and crannies necessary to service all the hardware.

One wide optical-quality window gave me a view of the black depths of space. But no window could withstand the incredible intensity of the laser's high-power beam. The beam was instead directed through a polished copper pipe to the outside of the station's hull, which is why the laboratory was always so cold. It was impossible to keep the module decently warm; the heat leaked out through the laser beam channel. On the outer end of that channel was the aiming mirror (also highly polished copper) that directed the beam toward its target—hypothetical or actual.

One day we would have mirrors and a laser output window of pure diamond, once we had learned how to fabricate large sheets of the stuff in zero gravity. That day had not yet come. It seemed that ground control was more interested in growing gem-quality diamonds than large sheets.

I had calculated Sam's approach trajectory back at the control center and pecked the numbers into my hand computer. Now, as the technicians labored and grumbled over their big laser I fed those coordinates into the laser aiming system. As far as the technicians knew, they were firing their multimegawatt beam into empty space, as usual. Only I knew that when they fired the laser its beam would destroy the approaching Yankee spacecraft and kill Sam Gunn.

The moments ticked by as I sweated coldly, miserable with apprehension and—yes, I admit it freely—with guilt. I had set the target for the laser's aiming mirror. The big slab of polished copper hanging outside the station's hull was already tracking Sam's trajectory, turning ever so slightly each second. The relays directing its motion clicked inside the laboratory like the clicks of a quartz clock, like the tapping of a Chinese water torture.

Then I heard the sighing sound that happens when an airtight hatch between two modules of the station is opened. Turning, I saw the hatch swinging open, its heavy hinges groaning slightly. Zworkin pushed through and floated over the bulky master control console to my side.

"You show an unusual interest in this test," he said softly.

My insides blazed as if I had stuck my hand into the power outlet. "There is the crisis in Geneva," I replied. "Ground control wants this test to proceed flawlessly."

"Will it?"

I did not trust myself to say anything more. I merely nodded.

Zworkin watched the muttering technicians for a few endless moments, then asked, "Do you find it odd that the American is approaching us *exactly* at the time our test is scheduled?"

I nodded once again, keeping my eyes fixed on the empty point in space where I imagined the beam and Sam's spacecraft would meet.

"I received an interesting message from Moscow, less than an hour ago," Zworkin said. I dared not look into his face, but his voice sounded tense, brittle. "The rumor is that the Geneva conference has struck a reef made of pure diamond."

"What?" That spun me around. He was not gloating. In fact, he looked just as worried as I felt. No, not even worried. Frightened. The tone of voice that I had assumed was sarcasm was actually the tight, dry voice of fear.

"This is unconfirmed rumor, mind you," Zworkin said, "but what they are saying is that the Western intelligence service has learned we are manufacturing pure diamond crystals in zero gravity, diamond crystals that can be made large enough to be used as mirrors and windows for extremely high-power lasers. They are concerned that we have moved far ahead of them in this key area of technology."

Just at that instant Sam's cocky voice chirped over the station's intercom speakers. "Hey there, friends and neighbors, here's your Hollywood delivery service comin' atcha."

The laser mirror clicked again. And again. One of the technicians floated back to the console at my side and pressed the three big red rocker switches that turn on the electrical power, one after the other. The action made his body rise up to the low ceiling of the laboratory each time. He rose and descended slowly, up and down, like a bubble trapped in a sealed glass.

A low whine came from the massive power generators. Even though they were off in a separate module of the station I felt their vibration.

In my mind's eye I could see a thin yellow line that represented Sam's trajectory approaching us. And a heavier red line, the fierce beam of our laser, reaching out to meet it.

"Got something more than videos, this trip," Sam was chattering. "Managed to lay my hands on some really neat electronic toys, interactive games. You'll love 'em. Got the latest sports videos, too, and a bucketful of real-beef hamburgers. All you do is pop 'em in your microwave. Brought mustard and ketchup, too. Better'n that soy stuff you guys been eating . . ."

He was talking his usual blue streak. I was glad that the communications technicians knew to scrub his transmissions from the tapes that ground control monitored. Dealing with Zworkin was bad enough.

Through his inane gabbling I could hear the mirror relays clicking like the rifles of a firing squad being cocked, one by one. Sam approached us blithely unaware of what awaited him. I pictured his spacecraft being hit by the laser beam, exploding, Sam and his videos and hamburgers all transformed instantly into an expanding red-hot ball of bloody vapor.

I reached over and pounded the master switch on the console. Just like the technician I bounded toward the ceiling. The power generators wound down and went silent.

Zworkin stared up at me openmouthed as I cracked my head painfully and floated down toward him again.

I could not kill Sam. I could not murder him in cold blood, no matter what the consequences might be.

"What are you doing?" Zworkin demanded.

Putting out a hand to grasp the console and steady myself, I said, "We should not run this test while the Yankee spy is close enough to watch."

He eyed me shrewdly, then called to the two dumbfounded technicians. "Out! Both of you! Until your commander calls for you again."

Shrugging and exchanging confused looks, the two young men left the laboratory module. Zworkin pushed the hatch shut behind them, leaning against it as he gave me a long quizzical stare.

"Grigori Aleksandrovich," he said at last, "we must do something about this American. If ground control ever finds out about him—if *Moscow* ever finds out . . ."

"What was it you said about the diamond crystals?" I asked. "Do you think the imperialists know about our experiments here?"

"Of course they know! And this Yankee spy is at the heart of the matter."

"What should we do?"

Zworkin rubbed his chin but said nothing. I could not help thinking, absurdly, that his acne had almost totally disappeared.

So we allowed Sam aboard the station once again and I brought him immediately to my private cubicle.

"Kripes!" he chirped. "I've seen bigger coffins. Is this the best that the workers' paradise can do for you?"

"No propaganda now," I whispered sternly. "And no more blackmail. You will not return to this station again and you will not get any more diamonds from me."

"And no more ice cream?" He seemed entirely unconcerned with the seriousness of the situation.

"No more anything!" I said, straining to make it as strong as I could while still whispering. "Your visits here are finished. Over and done with."

Sam made a rueful grin and wormed his right hand into the hip pocket of his coveralls. "Read this," he said, handing me a slip of paper.

It had two numbers on it, both of them in six digits.

"The first is your private bank account number at the Bank of Zurich, in Switzerland."

"Russian citizens are not allowed to . . ."

"The second number," Sam went on, "is the amount of money deposited in your account, in Swiss francs."

"I told you, I am not—" I stopped and looked at the second number again. I was not certain of the exchange ratio between Swiss francs and rubles, but six digits are six digits.

Sam laughed softly. "Listen. My friends in New York have friends in Switzerland. That's how I set up the account for you. It's your half of the profit from those little stones you gave me."

"I don't believe it. You are attempting to bribe me."

His look became pitying. "Greg, old pal, three quarters of your Kremlin leaders have accounts in Switzerland. Don't you realize that the big conference in Geneva is stalled over—"

"Over your report to the CIA that we are manufacturing diamonds here in this station!" I hissed. "You are a spy, admit it!"

He spread his hands in the universal gesture of confession. "Okay, so I've passed some info over to the IDA."

"Don't you mean CIA?"

Sam blinked with surprise. "CIA? Why in hell would I want to talk to those spooks? I'm dealing with the IDA."

"Intelligence Defense Agency," I surmised.

With an annoyed shake of his head, "Naw—the International Diamond Association. The diamond cartel. You know, DeBeers and those guys."

I was too stunned with surprise to say anything.

"The cartel knew you were doing zero-gravity experiments up here, but they thought it was for diamond film and optical quality diamond to use on your high-power lasers. Once my friends in New York saw that you were also making gem-quality stones, they sent word hotfooting to Amsterdam."

"The international diamond cartel . . ."

"That's right, pal," said Sam. "They don't want to see diamonds manufactured in space kicking the bottom out of their market."

"But the crisis in Geneva," I mumbled.

Sam laughed. "The argument in Geneva is between the diamond cartel and your own government. It's got nothing to do with Star Wars or Red Shield. They've forgotten all about that. Now they're talking about *money*!"

I could not believe what he was saying. "Our leaders would never stoop—"

Sam silenced me with a guffaw. "Your leaders are haggling with the cartel like a gang of housewives at a warehouse sale. Your president is talking with the cartel's leaders right now over a private, two-way fiber-optic link."

"How do you know this?"

He reached into the big pocket on the thigh of his suit. "Special video recording. I brought it just for you." With a sly smile he added, "Can't trust those guys in Amsterdam, you know."

It was difficult to catch my breath. My head was swimming.

"Listen to me, Greg. Your leaders are going to join the diamond cartel; they're just haggling over the price."

"Impossible!"

"Hard to believe that your own leaders would help the evil cartel rig world prices for diamonds? But that's what's going on right now, so help me. And once they've settled on their terms, the conference in Geneva will get back to dealing with the easy questions, like nuclear war."

"You're lying. I can't believe that you are telling me the truth."

He shrugged good-naturedly. "Look at the video. Watch what happens in Geneva. Then, once things settle down, you and I can start doing business again."

I must have shaken my head without consciously realizing it.

"Don't want to leave all those profits to the cartel, do you? We can make a fair-sized piece of change—as long as we stay small enough so the cartel won't notice us. That's still a lot of money, pal."

"Never," I said. And I meant it. To do what he asked would mean working against my own nation, my own people, my own government. If the security police ever found out!

I personally ushered Sam back to the docking compartment and off the station. And never allowed him back on Mir 5 again, no matter how he pleaded and wheedled over the radio.

After several weeks he finally realized that I would not deal with him, that when Grigori Aleksandrovich Prokov says "never" that is exactly what I mean.

"Okay, friends," his radio voice said, the last time he tried to contact us. "Guess I'll just have to find some other way to make my first million. So long, Greg. Enjoy the workers' paradise, pal."

The old man's tone had grown distinctly wistful. He stopped, made a deep wheezing sigh, and ran a liver-spotted hand over his wrinkled pate.

Jade had forgotten the chill of the big lunar dome. Leaning slightly closer to Prokov she asked: "And that was the last you saw or heard of Sam Gunn?"

"Yes," said the Russian. "And good riddance, too."

"What happened after that?"

Prokov's aged face twisted unhappily. "What happened? Everything went exactly as he said it would. The conference in Geneva started up again, and East and West reached a new understanding. My crew achieved its mission goal; we spent two full years in Mir 5 and then went home. The Russian Federation became a partner in the international diamond cartel."

"And you went to Mars," Jade prompted.

Prokov's wrinkled face became bitter. "No. I was not picked to command the Mars expedition. Zworkin never denounced me, never admitted his own involvement with Sam, but his report was damning enough to knock me out of the Mars mission. The closest I got to Mars was a weather observation station in Antarctica!"

"Wasn't your president at that time the one who—"

"The one who retired to Switzerland after he stepped down from leading the nation? Yes. He is living there still like a bloated plutocrat."

"And you never dealt with Sam Gunn again?"

"Never! I told him never and that is exactly what I meant. Never."

"Just that brief contact with him was enough to wreck your career."

Prokov nodded stonily.

"Yet," Jade mused, "in a way it was *you* who got the Russian Federation into partnership with the diamond cartel. That must have been worth hundreds of millions each year to your government."

The old man's only reply was a bitter "Pah!"

"What happened to your Swiss bank account? The one Sam started for you?"

Prokov waved a hand in a gesture that swept the lunar dome and asked, "How do you think I can afford to live here?"

Jade felt herself frown with puzzlement. "I thought the Leonov Center was free . . ."

"Yes, of course it is. A retirement center for Heroes of the Russian Federation. Absolutely free! Unless you want some real beef in your Stroganoff. That costs extra. Or an electric blanket for your bed. Or chocolates—chocolates from Switzerland are the best of all, did you know that?"

"You mean that your Swiss bank account . . ."

"It is an annuity," said Prokov. "Not much money, but a nice little annuity to pay for some of the extra frills. The money sits there in the bank and every month the faithful Swiss gnomes send me the interest by telefax. Compared to the other Heroes living here I am a well-to-do man. I can even buy vodka for them now and then."

Jade suppressed a smile. "So Sam's bank deposit is helping you even after all these years."

Slowly the old man nodded. "Yes, he is helping me even after his death." His voice sank lower. "And I never thanked him. Never. Never spoke a kind word to him."

"He was a difficult man to deal with," said Jade. "A very difficult personality."

"A thief," Prokov replied. But his voice was so soft it sounded almost like a blessing. "A blackmailer. A scoundrel."

There were tears in his weary eyes. "I knew him for only a few months. He frightened me half to death and nearly caused nuclear war. He disrupted my crew and ruined my chance to lead the Mars expedition. He tricked me and used me shamefully . . ."

Jade made a sympathetic noise.

"Yet even after all these years the memory of him makes me smile. He made life exciting, vibrant. How I wish he were here. How I miss him!"

9

······

Decisions, Decisions

"Hey, that's not bad," said Jim Gradowsky as he turned off the tape recorder. He grinned across his desk at Jade. "You did a good job, kid."

She was sitting on the front inch and a half of her boss's couch. "It's only a voice tape," she said apologetically. "I couldn't get any video."

Gradowsky leaned back and put his slippered feet on the desktop. "That's okay. We'll do a simulation. There's enough footage on Sam Gunn for the computer graphics program to paint him with no sweat. The viewers'll never know the difference. And we can re-create what Prokov must've looked like from his current photo; I assume he'll have no objection to having his portrait done in 3-D."

"He might," Jade said in a small voice.

Shrugging, her boss answered, "Then we'll fake it. We'll have to fake the other people anyway, so what the hell. Public's accustomed to it. We put a disclaimer in small print at the end of the credits."

So that's how they do the historical documentaries, Jade said to herself, suddenly realizing how the networks showed such intimate details of people long dead.

"Okay, kid, you got the assignment," Gradowsky said grandly. "There must be dozens of people here in Selene and over at Lunagrad that knew Sam. Track 'em down and get 'em to talk to you."

She jumped to her feet eagerly. "I've already heard about a couple of mining engineers who're over at the base in Copernicus. And there's a hotel executive at the casino in Hell Crater, a woman who—"

"Yeah, yeah. Great. Go find 'em," said Gradowsky, suddenly impatient. "I'll put an expense allowance in your credit account."

"Thanks!" Jade felt tremendously excited. She was going to be a real reporter. She had won her spurs.

As she reached the door of Gradowsky's office, though, he called to her. "Don't let the expense account go to your head. And I want a copy of every bill routed to me, understand?"

"Yes. Of course."

The weeks rolled by. Jade found that the real trick of interviewing people was to get them started talking. Once they began to talk the only problem was how much tape her microrecorder carried. Of course, many of her intended subjects refused to talk at all. Almost all of them were suspicious of Jade, at first. She learned how to work around their suspicions, how to show them that she was not an ordinary network newshound, how to make them understand that she *liked* Sam Gunn and wanted this biography to be a monument to his memory. Still, half the people she tried to see refused to be interviewed at all.

Jade tried to plan her travels logically, efficiently, to make the best use of the network's expense money. But an interview in Copernicus led to a tip about a retired accountant living in Star City, all the way over on the Farside. The exotic woman who claimed that Sam had jilted her at the altar knew about a tour guide who lived by the Tranquility Base shrine, where the Apollo 11 lander sat carefully preserved under its meteor dome. And on, and on.

Jade traveled mostly by tour bus, trundling across the pockmarked lunar plains at a reduced fare packed in with visitors from Earth. For the first time she saw her home world as strangers see it: barren yet starkly beautiful, new and rugged and wild. When they talked of their own homes on Earth they mostly complained about the weather, or the taxes, or the crowds of people at the spaceport. Jade looked through the bus's big tinted windows at the lovely blue sphere hanging above the horizon and wondered if she would find Earth crowded and dirty and humdrum if she lived there.

Once she took a passenger rocket, for the jaunt from Selene to Aristarchus, crossing Mare Nubium and the wide Sea of Storms in less than half an hour. She felt her insides drop away for the few minutes the rocket soared in free-fall at the top of its ballistic trajectory. The retros fired and she felt weight returning before her stomach became unmanageable.

She piled up more voice tapes, more stories about Sam Gunn. Some were obviously fabrications, outright lies. Others seemed outrageous exaggerations of what might have originally been true events.

"You've got to get some corroboration for this stuff," Gradowsky told her time and again. "Even when your pigeons are talking about people who're now dead, their families could come out of nowhere and sue the ass off us."

Corroboration was rare. No two people seemed to remember Sam Gunn in exactly the same way. A single incident might be retold by six different people in six different ways. Jade had to settle for audio testaments, where her interviewee swore on tape that the information he or she had given was true, to the best of his or her recollection.

"Pretty shaky," Gradowsky muttered when she returned to his office. "The lawyers aren't going to like this."

Jade slumped in the battered old couch, feeling exhausted from her weeks of travel and tension.

"You don't mean that we can't use any of it, do you?"

"That's not my decision, kid," said Gradowsky from behind his desk. "We'll have to let the lawyers listen to what you've got."

She nodded glumly, too tired to argue. Besides, it would do no good to fight Gradowsky on this. His hands were tied. She began to get an inkling of how Sam Gunn had felt about being hemmed in by office procedures and red tape.

"So where do you go from here?" Gradowsky asked her.

Jade pulled herself up straighter in the chair, startled by the question. "You mean we're going on with the project?"

"Sure. Until the lawyers pull the plug on us. Why not? I think what you're getting is great stuff. I just worry about people suing us, that's all."

Jade's weariness seemed to wash away like waterpaint under a firehose.

"Well," she said, "several of the people I talked to said there's a man at space station Alpha who . . ."

"Alpha? That's in Earth orbit."

"Right."

"We don't have the budget to send you out there," Gradowsky said.

"We don't?"

"Hell, kiddo, you've just about used up the whole expense budget I gave you just traipsing around the different lunar settlements. Do you have any idea of what it costs to fly back Earthside?"

"I wouldn't be going all the way to Earth," Jade answered. "Just to the space station."

"Yeah, I know." Gradowsky seemed embarrassed with the recollection that Jade could not go to Earth even if she wanted to.

"I've covered just about everybody I could find here on the Moon," she said. "But there are plenty of people elsewhere: on Alpha, in the Lagrange habitats, even out in the Belt."

Gradowsky puffed his cheeks and blew out a heavy sigh. "The Asteroid Belt. Christ!"

Jade knew she had to do something, and quickly, or the Sam Gunn project was finished.

"When I first started this job," she said to her boss,

"you told me that a good reporter goes where the story is, regardless of how far or how difficult it might be."

He grinned sheepishly at her. "Yeah, I know. But I forgot to tell you the other half of it—*as long as the big brass okays the expenses.*"

Straightening her spine, Jade replied, "We'll have to talk to the big brass, then."

Gradowsky looked surprised for an instant. Then he ran both his hands over his ample belly and said, "Yeah. I guess maybe we will."

Several weeks later, one of the corporation's big brass came to Selene City for the annual "fear of God" meeting that every branch office of Solar News Network received from management.

His full name was Arak al Kashan, although he smilingly insisted on being called Raki. "Raki," he would say, almost self-deprecatingly, "not Rocky." Yet Jade overheard Gradowsky mumble to one of the technicians, "Count your fingers after you shake hands with him."

Raki was tall and tan and trim, dark of hair and eye, old enough to be a network vice president yet young enough to set women's hearts fluttering. The grapevine had it that he was descended from very ancient blood; his aristocratic lineage went all the way back to the earliest Persian emperors. He had the haughtiness to match the claim. Jade heard him with her own ears saying disdainfully, "The unlamented Pahlavi Shahs were nothing more than upstart peasants."

Jade thought he was the handsomest man she had ever seen. Raki dressed in hand-tailored suits of the latest fashion, darkly iridescent lapel-less jackets in shades of blue or charcoal that fit him like a second skin over pale pastel turtlenecks. Tight slacks that emphasized his long legs and bulging groin.

If Raki noticed Jade among the half-dozen employees at the Solar office, he gave no outward sign of it. His task, as vice president in charge of human resources, was to have a brief personal chat with each man and woman at the Selene City office, review their job performances, and assure them that headquarters, back in Orlando, had their best interests at heart—even though there were to be no salary increases this year.

"Be careful of him," Monica warned Jade when she saw the look in her young friend's eyes. "He's a lady-killer."

Jade smiled at Monica's antique vocabulary. With the Sam Gunn project stalled, Jade had been assigned to covering financial news. Her current project was a report on the growth in tourism at Selene. Next she would tackle the consortium that was trying to raise capital for building a new mass driver that would double Selene's export capacity. Hardly as thrilling as tracking down Sam Gunn's old lovers and adversaries.

"Jumbo Jim says that Raki could get headquarters to okay my Sam Gunn project," Jade told Monica.

"Honey, I'm warning you. All he'll want to do is get into your bed."

They were sitting in Monica's cubbyhole office, sipping synthetic coffee before starting the day's tasks. Through the window that took up one whole wall they could see the dimly lit editing room where two technicians were bent over their computers, using the graphics program to "re-create" the construction of the new mass driver, from the first ceremonial shovel of excavation to the ultimate finished machine hurling hundreds of tons of cargo into space per hour.

Monica's office was too small for a desk. There were only the two chairs and a computer console built into the back wall. Its keyboard rested on the floor until Monica needed it.

Jade appreciated Monica's warning. "Mother Monica," she called her older friend. But she had other ideas in mind.

Trying not to smile too broadly, she told Monica, "You know, Sam Gunn used to say that he wanted to get laid without getting screwed. Maybe that's what I've got to do."

Monica gave her a long, troubled look.

"I mean," Jade said, "I wouldn't mind having sex with him. It might even be fun. The question is, how do I make sure that he'll okay the project afterward?"

Shaking her head like the weary mother superior of a rowdy convent, Monica said, "My God, you kids have it easy nowadays. When I was your age we had to worry about herpes, and chlamydia—and AIDS. Sex was punishable by death in those days!"

Somewhat surprised, Jade said, "But you managed . . ."

With a huff, Monica replied, "Sure, we managed. But you had to get a guy's blood report first. There were even doctors making fortunes faking medical records!"

"That must have been tough," Jade said.

"Why do you think people got married back then? And then divorced?"

"But, Monica, he'll only be here for another three days. I've got to get him to okay the Sam Gunn biography by then!"

Monica's disapproving expression softened. "I know, honey. I understand. It's just that I hate to see you using yourself like this. Meaningless sex might seem like fun at first . . ."

"Sam always said that there's no such thing as meaningless sex."

"Sam's dead, child. And he left a trail of hurt people behind him. Women, mostly."

Jade had to admit that she was right. "There was one woman I interviewed. She works at Dante's Inferno, over in Hell Crater. She was Sam's fiancée. She claims he left her at the altar and went off to the Asteroid Belt."

"I'll bet. And what kind of work does she do at Dante's?" Monica asked, her eyes narrowing.

Ishtar's was acknowledged to be the finest restaurant not merely in Selene, but the finest in all the Moon. Carved out of the lunar rock at the end of a long corridor, Ishtar's interior was shaped like a dome, with video screens showing views of the heavens so cunningly devised that it actually looked as though the dome were up on the surface.

The restaurant was small, intimate. Each table was niched into its own semicircular banquette of high, plush lunar pseudo-leather, creating a semicircle of virtually complete privacy. Lovers could snuggle close, although at the prices Ishtar's charged the restaurant's clientele was mostly executives who had access to golden expense accounts. All the waiters were human; there were no robots at all, not even as busboys.

"I've never had champagne before," Jade said with a slight giggle.

Arak al Kashan leaned back in the plush banquette and steepled his long, manicured fingers in front of his chin, admiring her from across their damask-covered table.

"You should have it every evening," Raki said, smiling. "A creature as lovely as you should have oceans of champagne. You should bathe in champagne."

Jade lifted an eyebrow slightly. "I don't think there's that much champagne in Selene."

"Then you can come to France with me. We'll rent a chateau and bathe in champagne every night."

"Oh, I can't come to Earth," Jade said lightly.

"I could see to it that you get a much better position with the network. In France. Or in Florida. We could see each other every day if you came to Florida."

She had already drunk enough champagne to dull the pain of what she had to tell him. "I can never come to Earth, Raki. My bones are too brittle for it."

His mouth dropped open for an instant, but he immediately recovered his composure.

"Then I must come to Selene more often," he said gallantly.

Jade accepted the compliment with a smile and a totally unpremeditated batting of her eyelashes. In the center of the restaurant the head waiter supervised the creation of a spectacularly flaming dish that brought murmurs of approval from the watching diners.

He's a doll! Jade thought to herself. Raki is a handsome, elegant, charming living doll.

He was also an accomplished lover, as she found out later that night, in the suite that the network maintained for visiting executives. Jade felt herself swept away like a cork in a tidal wave under Raki's experienced hands and tongue. She felt as if she would suffocate; she felt as if her heart would burst in her chest. Electric thrills tingled every square centimeter of her skin.

Slowly, ever so slowly, she floated back to reality. As if awakening from a dream Jade gradually sensed the bed firmly beneath her, the darkness of the room eased only by the luminous digits of the clock on the night table, the animal heat of the man sleeping next to her naked body.

Jade could make out the form of Raki's body, coiled like a panther, his face half buried in his pillow.

She took a long, shuddering breath. Now you've done it, she told herself. It's over and done with. It was exciting, but it's finished now. Tomorrow he'll be leaving. Tomorrow he'll go back to Earth and you'll be alone again.

"What's the matter?" Raki's voice was whisper soft.

Startled that he was awake, she said, "What?"

"You were muttering. I thought you might be talking in your sleep."

Jade almost laughed. "Just talking to myself. Sorry if I woke you."

"It's all right," he said, turning over onto his back. "You'll be going home tomorrow."

"The day after—oh, yes, it's Tuesday morning now, isn't it? Yes, tomorrow."

"Do you live in Orlando?" Jade asked, her voice as flat and unemotional as she could make it.

He laughed softly. "You want to know if I'm married, don't you?"

"I already know that. I looked up your personnel file."

"You have access to the files?" He sounded surprised.

"No," she said. "But I'm a reporter."

"Ah."

Silence. Jade had watched enough old videos to know that this was the moment the lovers usually lit cigarettes. She wondered what it would taste like, whether she would feel the carcinogens attacking her lungs.

"You know that I am married and have two children," Raki said. "Statistically, it should be one point seven, but we found it difficult to produce only seven tenths of a child."

Jade did not laugh. "Is it a happy marriage?"

"Yes, I'm afraid it is."

"I'm glad," she lied.

"As a practicing Moslem," Raki said lightly, "I can take four wives, you know. The state of Florida would object, I'm sure, but I doubt that the government of Selene would mind."

"A wife in every port," Jade muttered. "That might get expensive."

"My wife is a practicing psychologist. She makes an excellent living. And you, of course, are employed as a reporter . . ."

"Don't joke about it!" Jade burst. "It isn't a joking matter."

"No, of course not. I'm sorry."

Silence again.

At length, Raki asked, "What is it you want?"

Jade tried to swallow down the lump in her throat.

Raki turned toward her. "I know I am devilishly handsome and utterly suave and urbane, practically irresistible. But you accepted my invitation to dinner knowing that it would lead here, and you accepted that because you want something from me. What is it?"

Jade blinked back tears.

"It's happened before, you know," Raki said. His voice was still gentle, almost sad. "Women seem so willing to offer their bodies in trade."

"You make it sound dirty."

"Oh, no! Not dirty. There's nothing dirty about making love. It's just . . . disappointing."

"Disappointing?"

He sighed like a heartbroken lover. "I had hoped that you liked me for myself, not for what I could do for you. But I knew better, all along. You want something: a raise in salary, a promotion . . . something."

Jade felt her spirits sinking out of sight.

"Well," Raki said, "you might as well tell me what it is."

Confused, Jade stammered, "There . . . there *was* something . . . I thought . . ." She did not know what to say.

Raki whispered, "You can tell me. I'm accustomed to being used."

"It isn't like that!" Jade burst. "Yes, all right, I admit that I wanted something from you—at first. But now, now that I know you . . ."

Raki smiled in the darkness and reached for her young trembling body. Jade flung herself into his arms and they made love until they both fell asleep exhausted.

"And then what happened?" Monica asked as they walked down the busy corridor from the cafeteria toward her office. It was nearly 0800 hours, the start of the business day. The women were dressed in their business clothes: Monica in comfortably loose black slacks and sweatshirt, Jade in a stylish auburn jumpsuit and glossy thigh-length boots.

"It was morning when we woke up," Jade answered with a small shrug. "I had to dash back to my place to change for work."

With an unhappy shake of her head Monica replied, "And Raki's in Jim's office bragging about how he screwed you all night long."

"No! He wouldn't . . ."

"Want to bet?"

Jade could not look Monica square in the face. "I've got to get to work," she said. "I'm interviewing that architect at ten sharp."

"Want to bet?" Monica repeated sternly.

"Yes!" Jade snapped, feeling anger surging within her. "I'll bet he's conducting ordinary business with Jim."

They had reached the door to Solar News's suite of cubbyhole offices. With a sweeping gesture, Monica ushered Jade through, then led the way past the trio of unoccupied desks to her own office. Gradowsky's office door was closed, Jade saw.

Monica plopped into her chair and picked the keyboard off the floor. Jade remained standing, her back to the window that looked into the editing room. No one was in there yet.

"Don't you ever tell Jumbo that I've bugged his office," Monica said, frowning slightly as she worked the keyboard.

"Bugged it! Why?"

"I might marry the bum one of these days, but that doesn't mean I altogether trust him." She pulled a pair of wire-thin headsets from the cabinet in the corner of the room and handed one of them to Jade.

Reluctantly Jade slipped the set over her hair. Monica plugged them both in, then held one earphone to her ear, her head cocked like a fat robin looking for a juicy worm.

". . . if I say so myself, I'm a very good teacher." Raki's voice. Unmistakable.

"Well, uh, you know she's just a kid. Got some good ideas, though." Gradowsky sounded uncomfortable, embarrassed.

"Really? I'll bet she's got better ones now." Raki laughed. Jade heard nothing from Jumbo Jim.

After a brief silence Raki asked, "You said she wants to do a biography?"

"Yeah. Of Sam Gunn. I think . . ."

"Sam Gunn! No, that would never wash."

"I dunno, Raki. She's already gotten a lot of really good stuff. Sam's good material. Sex, adventure, excitement."

Raki made a humming noise. Then, "You think so?"

"Yeah, I do."

"No, the executive board would never buy it. Half of them hate Sam's guts, even now, and the other half wouldn't give a damn."

"But if you recommended it," Gradowsky suggested.

"Listen, my friend, I didn't get this far in the network by sticking my neck out."

Jade sensed Jumbo Jim shaking his head. "Then what're you gonna tell her?"

"Me? Nothing?"

"You're not gonna see her again tonight?"

"Of course not. Why should I?"

Monica's face looked like a stone carving of vengeance. Jade felt her own cheeks flaming.

"I thought, well, after you had such a good time last night."

Raki laughed again. It sounded cruel. "The thrill is in the chase, James. Now that I've bagged her, what is there to getting her again? No, tonight I'll go to Hell Crater and enjoy myself with the professionals. I've had enough of little girls who must be taught everything."

Jade ripped the headset off so hard she thought her ears were coming off with it.

Monica looked as if she would cry. "I'm sorry, honey. But you had to know."

Jade went through her morning as if disembodied, watching this redheaded young woman from an enormous distance as she made her way down the gray tunnels of Selene, conducted a perfunctory interview with a dull, whining architect, then ate a solitary lunch in the darkest corner of the Pelican Bar, speaking to no one, not even a robot waiter. She punched up her order on the keyboard built into the wall of her booth.

There is no one you can trust, Jade told herself. Absolutely no one. Not even Monica. She's bugged her fiancé's office. Not one single human being in the whole solar system can be trusted. Not a damned one. I'm alone. I've always been alone and I always will be.

A robot brought her lunch tray. She ignored its cheerful programmed banter and it rolled away.

Jade could not eat more than a single mouthful. The food stuck in her throat. The cola tasted flat and sour.

She leaned her head against the back of the booth, eyes filling with tears, alone and lost in a world that had never cared whether she lived or died. It's not fair! she cried silently. It's just not fucking goddamned shitting fair.

Life is never fair. She remembered somebody told her that Sam Gunn had often said that. No, not quite. Sam had put it differently. "Life isn't fair, so the best thing you can do is load the dice in your own favor." That's what Sam had said.

Don't get mad, Jade told herself. Get even.

Grimly she slid out of the booth and headed for the ticket office of Lunar Transport.

"This is going to be kind of tough for me to talk about," Jade said.

"Don't give it a second thought, little one," said Yoni, Mistress of Ecstasy. "Monica filled my ears with the whole story while you were on your way here."

Here was the employee's lounge of Dante's Inferno, the biggest casino/hotel/house of pleasure in Hell Crater. It had been Sam Gunn's sardonic idea of humor to turn Hell into a complex of entertainment centers. The crater had been named after an eighteenth-century Jesuit astronomer, Maximilian Hell, who once directed the Vienna Observatory.

Jade had overspent her personal credit account to ride the passenger rocket from Selene, after telling Monica what she was going to do. Mother Monica apparently had gotten on the fiber-optic link with Yoni as soon as Jade hung up.

The lounge was small but quite plush. Yoni sat on a small fabric-covered couch; Jade on a softly cushioned easy chair.

Jade had interviewed the Mistress of Ecstasy weeks earlier. Yoni had been left at the altar by Sam Gunn more than twenty years ago. But although she had every reason to hate Sam, she said, "I guess I still have a soft spot in my heart for the little SOB."

Yoni claimed to be the child of a mystical pleasure cult from deep in the mysterious mountains of Nepal. Actually she had been born in the mining settlement at Aristarchus, of Chinese-American parents from San Francisco. She was tall for an oriental, Jade thought, and her bosom was so extraordinary, even though the rest of her figure was willowy slim, that Jade decided she must have been enhanced by implants. She wore a tight-fitting silk sheath of shining gold with a plunging neckline and skirt slashed to the hip.

She had worn a luxurious auburn wig when Jade had first interviewed her. Now she sat, relaxed, her hair cropped almost as short as a military cut. It was sprinkled with gray. Yoni was still beautiful, although to Jade she seemed awfully elderly for her chosen line of work. Cosmetic surgery had done its best, but there were still lines in her face, veins on the backs of her hands. Her dark almond eyes seemed very knowing, as if they had witnessed every possible kind of human frailty.

"Then you know," Jade choked out the words, "about Raki . . . and me."

Yoni smiled sadly and patted Jade's knee. "You're not the first woman to be roughed up by a man."

"Can you help me?"

Yoni's almond eyes became inscrutable. "In what way? I won't risk damaging this house's reputation just to help you get even with a jerk."

Jade blinked at her. "No, that isn't what I want at all."

"Then what?"

"I want him to approve my doing a biography of Sam Gunn."

It was Yoni's turn to look surprised. "Is that what you're after?"

"Yes."

Yoni leaned back in her couch and crossed her long legs. "Let me get this straight. You want me to make him change his mind about this video biography you want to do."

Jade nodded.

"Why should I help you?"

For a moment Jade had no answer. Then she heard herself say, "For Sam's sake."

"For Sam's sake!" Yoni tilted her head back and laughed heartily. "Why in the name of the seventy-seven devils of Tibet should I care an eyelash about Sam? He's dead and gone and that's that."

Jade said, "I thought you had a soft spot in your heart for him."

"In my heart, little one. Not my head."

"You don't feel any obligation toward Sam?"

"If he were here I'd kick him in the balls. And he'd know why."

"Even though he gave you the controlling interest in Dante's Inferno?"

After her interview with Yoni, Jade had accessed all the records she could find about Dante's. S. Gunn Enterprises, Unlimited, had originally built the place. Yoni had been a licensed prostitute in the European lunar settlement, New Europa, when Sam had briefly fallen in love with her. He had left her at the altar, true enough. He had also left her fifty-five percent of the shares of the newly opened Dante's Inferno. The rest he had sold off to help finance a venture to the Asteroid Belt.

Yoni gazed up at the smooth, faintly glowing ceiling panels, then across the lounge at the computer-graphics images mounted on the walls. They were all of tall, buxom women, blond, redheaded, gleaming black hair. They wore leather, or daintily feminine lace, or nothing but jewelry. They were all Yoni, Mistress of Ecstasy, in her various computer-simulated embodiments.

Finally she looked back at Jade. "You're right," she admitted. "I owe the little bastard."

"Then you'll help me?"

Without answering, Yoni got to her feet and started for the door. "Come on down to my office. I'll have to look up your john's file."

Yoni's office looked to Jade like a millionaire's living room. Bigger than any office she had ever seen; bigger than any apartment, for that matter. And there were doors leading to other rooms, as well. Oriental carpets on the floor. Video windows on every wall. The furniture alone must have cost millions to tote up from Earth: Chinese prayer tables of real wood, lacquered and glistening; long, low settees covered in striped fabrics; even a hologram fireplace that actually threw off heat.

Jade stood in the middle of the huge room, almost breathless with admiration, while Yoni went straight to a delicately small desk tucked into a corner and tapped on the keyboard cunningly built into its gleaming top. The silk painting of misty mountains above the desk turned into a small display screen.

"Most johns don't use their real names here," Yoni muttered, mostly to herself, "but we can usually trace their credit accounts, even when they've established a temporary one to cover their identity."

Jade drifted toward the desk, resisting the urge to touch the vases, the real flowers, the ivory figurines resting on an end table.

"You said he calls himself Rocky?"

"Raki." Jade spelled it.

"H'm. Here he is, full name and everything. He's not trying to hide from anybody."

"He's married . . ."

"Two wives," Yoni said as the data on the screen scrolled by. "One in Orlando and one in Istanbul. Plus a few girlfriends that he sees regularly, here and there."

Jade let herself drop into the little straight-backed chair beside the desk.

"He doesn't make any secret of it, so there's no way to use this information as leverage on him."

"Does he have . . . girlfriends . . . here on the Moon?"

Yoni gave her a sidelong look. "No, when he's here he comes to us. To me."

Jade felt her face redden.

Yoni smiled knowingly at her. "He's never seen me, little one. Not in the flesh. It's been years since I've done business with anyone flesh-to-flesh."

"Oh?"

"The VR nets," Yoni said, as if that explained everything. When she saw that Jade did not understand she went on, "Most of my customers come here for our simulations. They're quite lifelike, with the Virtual Reality systems. We just zip them up into a cocoon so the sensory net's in contact with every centimeter of their body, and then we play scenarios for them."

"They don't want sex with real women?" Jade felt stupid asking it.

"Some do, but what men want most is not sex so much as power. For most men, they feel powerful when they're screwing a woman. It makes them feel strong, especially when the woman is doing exactly what they desire. That's why the VR nets are so popular. A john can have any woman he wants, any number of women, for the asking."

"Really?"

Yoni gave her a knowing smile. "We have tapes of Cleopatra, Marilyn Monroe, Catherine the Great. One john wants Jacqueline Kennedy Onassis; nobody else, just her. Another has a fixation on Eleanor of Aquitaine. Thinks he's Richard the Lion Heart, I guess."

"And it's all pre-programmed simulations?"

"The basic scenario is pre-programmed. We always have a live operator in the loop to make sure everything's going right and to take care of any special needs that come up."

Jade completely missed Yoni's pun. But she caught the unspoken implication.

"You keep tapes of each session?"

"No!" Yoni snapped, almost vehemently. Then, more gently, "Do you realize the kinds of corporate and government people we have as clientele here? One hint, even the slightest rumor, that we tape their sessions and we would be out of business—or dead."

"Oh. I didn't realize . . ."

Yoni smiled mysteriously. "We don't have to blackmail our guests, or even threaten to. These V.R. sessions can be very powerful; they have a strong impact on the mind. Almost like a post-hypnotic suggestion, really."

"You can influence people?" Jade asked.

"Not directly. But—no one actually understands what long-term effects these V.R. sessions have on a person's mind. Especially a habitual user. I have commissioned a couple of psychologists to look into it, but so far their results have been too vague for any practical use."

"Could you—influence—Raki?"

With a shrug, Yoni said, "I don't know. He's been here often, that's true. But he's not an addict, like some I could name."

Jade hesitated, feeling embarrassed, then asked, "What kind of sex does he go in for?"

Glancing back at the computer screen, Yoni said, "I don't think you understand, little one. The man doesn't come here for sex. He gets his sexual needs fulfilled from flesh-and-blood creatures like yourself."

"Then what . . . ?"

"For power, little one. Not sexual power. *Corporate* power."

Jade's eyes went wide. She understood. And she knew what had to be done.

*   *   *

Arak al Kashan gazed through his office window at the Orlando skyline: tower after tower, marching well past the city limits, past the open acreage of Disney World, and on out to the horizon. There was power there, majesty and might in the modern sense. Beyond his line of sight, he knew, construction crews were hard at work turning swampland and citrus groves into more corporate temples of enduring concrete, stainless steel, and gleaming glass.

He leaned back in his plush leather chair and sighed deeply. The moment had come. His trip to the Moon had been relaxing, diverting. Now the moment of truth had arrived.

Getting to his feet, Raki squared his shoulders as he inspected his image in the full-length mirror on the door to his private lavatory. The jacket fits perfectly, he saw. Its camel's-hair tone brings out my tan. Good.

He snapped his fingers once and the mirror turned opaque. Then he stepped around the desk and started toward the door and the meeting of the board of directors of Solar News Network, Inc. This was going to be *the* meeting. The one where he took charge of the entire corporation, where he seized the reins of power from the doddering old hands of the CEO and won the board's approval as the new chief of Solar News.

The day had come at last.

But before he could take three steps across the precious Persian carpet, the door opened and a short, disheveled man rushed in.

"You're in trouble, pal. Deep shit, if you don't mind the expression."

"Who the hell are you?" Raki demanded.

"That's not important. You've got a real problem and I'm here to help you."

Raki took a step backward, then another, and felt his desk against the back of his legs. The little man seemed terribly agitated, perhaps insane. His wiry rust-red hair was cropped short, yet it still looked tangled and dirty. He wore coveralls of faded olive-green, stained here and there with what looked like grease or machine oil.

Raki groped with one hand toward the intercom on his desk, still facing the strange intruder.

"Never mind calling security," the man said. "I'm on your side, pal. I can help you."

"Help me? I don't need—"

"The hell you don't need help! They're waiting for you upstairs"—he cast his eyes toward the ceiling—"with knives sharpened and a vat of boiling oil. All for you."

"What do you mean?"

The man smiled, a lopsided sort of grin in his round, snub-nosed face.

"You think you're gonna waltz right in there and take control of the corporation, huh? You think the CEO's just gonna bend over and let you boot him in the butt?"

"What do you know about it?"

"Plenty, pal," said the little man. "I was never the guy for corporate politics. Had no time for boards of directors and all the crap that goes with a big bureaucracy. But lemme tell you, they're out to get you. They're gonna pin your balls to the conference table, Raki, old pal."

Raki felt his knees giving way. He sank to a half-sitting position on the edge of his desk.

His visitor strutted across the carpet, looked out the window. "Nice view. Not as good as the view from Titan, but what the hell, this is the best you can do in Florida, I guess."

"What did you mean?" Raki asked.

"About the view from Titan?"

"About the board of directors. They're waiting for me upstairs—"

"You bet your busy little ass they're waiting. With assorted cutlery and boiling oil, like I said."

"You're crazy!"

"Mad?" The little man screwed up his face and crossed his eyes. "Hannibal was mad. Caesar was mad. And surely Napoleon was the maddest of them all."

"Talk sense, dammit!"

The man chuckled tolerantly. "Look. You're going up to the board of directors to tell them that the corporation would be better off with you as CEO instead of the old fart that's running the network now. Right?"

"Right," said Raki.

"Well, what's your plan?"

"My plan?"

"Yeah. You need a plan to lay out on the table, a blue-print to show them what changes you're gonna make, how you're gonna do bigger and better things for dear ol' Solar News."

"I ... I ..." Raki suddenly realized he did not have a plan. Not an idea in his head. He could feel cold sweat breaking out all over his body.

"C'mon, c'mon," the little man demanded, "the board's waiting. What's your plan?"

"I don't have one!" Raki wailed.

His visitor shook his head. "Just as I thought. No plan."

"What can I do?" Raki was trembling now. He saw his dream of conquest crumbling. They'll fire me! I'll lose everything!"

"Not to worry, pal. That's why I'm here. To help you." The little man pulled a computer disk from his grubby coverall pocket. It was smaller than the palm of his hand, even though his hand was tiny.

He handed the disk to Raki. It felt warm and solid in his fingers.

"Show 'em that, pal. It'll knock 'em on their asses."

Before Raki could think of anything to say he was standing at the foot of the long, long conference table. The entire board of directors was staring at him from their massive chairs. The old CEO and his henchmen sat up near the head of the table, flanking the chairman of the board, a woman upon whom Raki had lavished every possible attention. She was smiling at him, faintly, but the rest of the board looked grim.

"Well," snapped the CEO, "what do you have there in your hand, young man?"

Raki took a deep breath. "I hold here in my hand," he heard his own voice saying, smoothly, without a tremor, "the salvation of Solar News."

A stir went around the conference table.

Holding up the tiny disk, Raki went on, "This is a

documented, dramatized biography of one of the solar system's most colorful personalities—the late Sam Gunn."

The board erupted into an uproar.

"Sam Gunn!"

"No!"

"It couldn't be!"

"How did you manage it?"

One of the truly elderly members of the board, frail and pasty-faced, waved his skeletal hands excitedly. "I have it on very good authority that BBC was planning to do a biography of Sam Gunn. You've beaten them to the punch, young man! Bravo."

The chairman turned a stern eye on her CEO. "How come you didn't do this yourself?" she demanded of the cowering executive. "Why did Raki have to do this all on his own?" And she gave Raki a wink full of promise.

The entire board of directors got to their feet and applauded. Walter Cronkite appeared, in a white linen double-breasted suit, to join the acclamation. The old CEO faded, ghostlike, until he disappeared altogether.

Raki smiled and made a little bow. When he turned, he saw that Yoni was waiting for him, reclining on a bank of satin pillows beside a tinkling fountain in a moonlit garden scented by warm blossoms.

His strange little visitor stepped out from behind an azalea bush, grinning. "Way to go, pal. Give her everything you've got."

Jade knew that her ploy had failed. Raki had returned to Orlando two weeks ago, and there was no word from him at all. Nothing.

She went through her assignments perfunctorily, interviewing a development tycoon who wanted to build retirement villages on the Moon, a visiting ecologist from Massachusetts who wanted a moratorium declared on all further lunar developments, a mining engineer who was trying to raise funds for an expedition to the south lunar pole to search for ice caves: "I *know* there's got to be water frozen down there someplace; I just know it."

All the help that Yoni had given her, all the support that Monica gave, had been for nothing. Jade saw herself trapped in a cell of lunar stone, blank and unyielding no matter which way she turned.

Gradowsky warned her. "You're sleepwalking, kid. Snap out of it and get me stories I can send to Orlando, not this high-school junk you've been turning in."

Another week went by, and Jade began to wonder if she really wanted to stay on as a reporter. Maybe she could go back to running a truck up on the surface. Or ship out to Mars: they needed construction workers there for the new base the scientists were building.

When Gradowsky called her into his office she knew he was going to fire her.

Jumbo Jim had a strange, uncomfortable expression on his face as he pushed aside a half-eaten hero sandwich and a mug of some foaming liquid while gesturing Jade to the chair in front of his desk.

Swallowing visibly, Gradowsky said, "Well, you did it."

Jade nodded glumly. Her last assignment had been a real dud: the corporate board of Selene City never gave out any news other than their official media release.

"The word just came in from Orlando. You leave for Alpha tomorrow."

It took Jade a moment to realize what Jumbo Jim was telling her. She felt her breath catch.

"Raki must have fought all the way up to the board of directors," Gradowsky was saying. "It must've been some battle."

Instead of elation, instead of excitement, Jade felt numb, smothered, encased in a block of ice. I've got to make it work, she told herself. I've got to get to every person who knew Sam and make them tell me everything. I owe it to Monica and Yoni. I owe it to Raki.

She looked past Gradowsky's fleshy, flabby face, still mouthing words she did not hear, and realized that Raki had put his career on the line. And so had she.

10

· — · · — · · — · · — · · — · · — · · — · · — · · — · · — · · — · · — · · — · ·

Space Station Alpha

THEY FACED EACH other suspiciously, floating weightlessly in emptiness.

The black man was tall, long-limbed, loose, gangling; on Earth he might have made a pro basketball player. His utilitarian coveralls were standard issue, frayed at the cuffs and so worn that whatever color they had been originally had long since faded into a dull gray. They were clean and pressed to a razor sharpness, though. The insignia patch on his left shoulder said ADMINISTRATION. A strictly non-regulation belt of royal-blue, studded with rough lumps of meteoric gold and clamped by a heavy gold buckle, cinched his pencil-thin waist and made him look even taller and leaner.

He eyed the reporter warily. She was young, and the slightly greenish cast to her pretty features told him that she had never been in zero gravity before. Her flame-red hair was shoulder-length, he judged, but she had followed the instructions given to groundlings and tied it up in a zero-gee snood. Terrific big emerald eyes, even if they did look kind of scared.

Her coveralls were spanking new white. She filled

106

them nicely enough, a trim, coltish figure that he almost admired. She looked like a forlorn little waif floating weightlessly, obviously fighting down the nausea that was surging through her.

Frederick Mohammed Malone was skeptical to the point of being hostile toward this female interloper. Jade could see the resentment smoldering in the black man's red-rimmed eyes. Malone's face was narrow, almost gaunt, with a trim little Vandyke jutting out from his chin. His forehead was high, receding; his hair cropped close to the skull. His skin was very black. She guessed Malone's age at somewhere in his early sixties, although she knew that living in zero gravity could make a person look much younger than his or her calendar age.

She tried to restart their stalled conversation. "I understand that you and Sam Gunn were, uh, friends."

"Why're you doing a story on Sam?" Malone asked, his voice low and loaded with distrust.

The two of them were in Malone's "office." Actually it was an observation blister in the central hub of space station Alpha. Oldest and still biggest of the Earth-orbiting commercial stations, Alpha was built on the old wheels-within-wheels scheme. The outermost rim, where most of the staff lived and worked, spun at a rate that gave it almost a full Earth gravity, out of bounds for Jade. Two thirds of the way toward the hub there was a wheel that spun at the Moon's one-sixth gee. That was where she was quartered for her visit. The hub itself, of course, was for all practical purposes at zero gee, weightless.

Malone's aerie consisted of one wall on which were located a semicircular sort of desk and communications center, a bank of display screens that were all blankly gray at the moment, and an airtight hatch that led to the spokes that radiated out to the various wheels. The rest of the chamber was a transparent glassteel bubble from which Malone could watch the station's loading dock—and the overwhelming majesty of the huge, curved, incredibly blue and white-flecked Earth as it slid past endlessly, massive, brilliant, ever changing, ever beautiful.

To Jade, though, it seemed as if they were hanging in empty space itself, unprotected by anything at all, and falling, falling, falling toward the ponderous world that filled her peripheral vision. The background rumble of the bearings that bore the massive station's rotation while the hub remained static sounded to her like the insistent bass growl of a giant grinding wheel that was pressing the breath out of her.

She swallowed bile, felt it burn in her throat, and tried to concentrate on the job at hand.

She said to Malone, "I've been assigned to do a biography of Mr. Gunn for the Solar News Network . . ."

Despite himself, Malone suddenly grinned. "First time I ever heard him called *Mr.* Gunn."

"Oh?" Jade's microchip recorder, imbedded in her belt buckle, was already on, of course. "What did the people here call him?"

That lean, angular black face took on an almost thoughtful look. "Oh . . . Sam, mostly. 'That tricky bastard,' a good many times." Malone actually laughed. "Plenty times I heard him called a womanizing sonofabitch."

"What did you call him?"

The suspicion came back into Malone's eyes. "He was my friend. I called him Sam."

Silence stretched between them, hanging as weightlessly as their bodies. Jade turned her head slightly and found herself staring at the vast bulk of Earth. Her adoptive mother was down there, somewhere, living her own life without a thought about the daughter she had run away from. And her real mother? Was she on Earth, too, forever separated from the baby she had born, the baby she had left abandoned, alone, friendless, and loveless?

Jade's mind screamed as if she were falling down an elevator shaft. Her stomach churned queasily. She could not tear her eyes away from the world drifting past, so far below them, so compellingly near. She felt herself being drawn toward it, dropping through the emptiness, spinning down the deep swirling vortex . . .

Malone's long-fingered hand squeezed her shoulder hard enough to hurt. She snapped her attention to his dark, unsmiling face as he grasped her other shoulder and held her firmly in his strong hands.

"You were drifting," he said, almost in a whisper.

"Was I . . . ?"

"It's all right," he said. "Gets everybody, at first. Don't be scared. You're perfectly safe."

His powerful hands steadied her. She fought down the panic surging inside.

"If you got to upchuck, go ahead and do it. Nothing to be ashamed of." His grin returned. "Only, use the bags they gave you, please."

He looked almost handsome when he smiled, she thought. After another moment he released her. She took a deep breath and dabbed at the beads of perspiration on her forehead. The retch bags that the technicians had attached to her belt were a symbol to her now. I won't need them, she insisted to herself. I'm not going to let this get to me. I'm not going to let *them* get to me.

"I . . . didn't think . . . didn't realize that zero gravity would effect me."

"Why not? It gets to everybody, one way or another."

"I'm from Selene," Jade said. "I've lived all my life under lunar gravity."

Malone gazed at her thoughtfully. "Still a big difference between one-sixth gee and none at all, I guess."

"Yes." It was still difficult to breathe. "I guess there is."

"Feel better?" he asked.

There was real concern in his eyes. "I think I'll be all right. Thanks."

"De nada," he said. "I didn't know you'd never been in weightlessness before."

His attitude had changed, she saw. The sullenness had thawed. He had insisted on conducting the interview in the station's zero-gravity area. He had allowed no alternative. But she was grateful that his shell of distrust seemed to have cracked.

It took several moments before she could say, "I'm not here to do a hatchet job on Mr. Gunn."

Malone made a small shrug. "Doesn't make much difference, one way or th'other. He's dead; nothing you can say will hurt him now."

"But we know so little about him. I suppose he's the most famous enigma in the solar system."

The black man made no response.

"The key question, I suppose . . . the thing our viewers will be most curious about, is why Sam Gunn exiled himself up here. Why did he turn his back on Earth?"

Malone snorted with disdain. "He didn't! Those motherfuckers turned their backs on him."

"What do you mean?"

"It's a long story," Malone said.

"That's all right. I've got as much time as it takes." Even as she said it Jade wished that Malone would volunteer to return back to the lunar-gee wheel, where the gravity was normal. But she dared not ask the man to leave his office. Once a subject starts talking, never interrupt! That was the cardinal rule of a successful interview. Jumbo Jim had drilled that into her. Besides, she was determined not to let weightlessness get the better of her.

"Would you believe," Malone was saying, "that it all started with a cold?"

"A cold?"

"Sam came down with a cold in the head. That's how the whole thing began."

"Tell me about it."

11

Isolation Area

SAM WAS A feisty little bastard—Malone reminisced—full of piss and vinegar. If there were ten different ways in the regulations to do a job, he'd find an eleventh, maybe a twelfth or a fourteenth, just because he couldn't abide being bound by the regs. A free spirit, I guess you'd call him.

He'd had his troubles with the brass in Houston *and* Washington. Why he ever became an astronaut in the first place is beyond me. Maybe he thought he'd be like a pioneer out on the frontier, on his own, way out in space. How he made it through training and into flight operations is something I'll never figure out. I just don't feature Sam sitting still long enough to get through kindergarten, let alone flight school and astronaut training.

Anyway, when I first met him he was finished as an astronaut. He had put in seven years, which he said was a biblical amount of time, and he wanted out. And the agency was glad to get rid of him, believe me. But he had this cold in the head and they wouldn't let him go back Earthside until it cleared up.

"Six billion people down there with colds, the flu, bad sinuses, and post-nasal drips and those assholes in Houston won't let me go back until this goddamned sniffle clears up."

Those were the first words Sam ever said to me. He had been assigned to my special isolation ward, where I had reigned alone for nearly four years. Alpha was under construction then. We were in the old Mac-Dac Shack, a glorified tin can that passed for a space station back in those primitive days. It didn't spin, it just hung there. Everything inside was weightless.

My isolation ward was a cramped compartment with four zero-gee sleep restraints Velcroed to the four walls together with lockers to stow personal gear. Nobody but me had ever been in it until that morning. Sam shuffled over to the bed next to mine, towing his travel bag like a kid with a sinking balloon.

"Just don't sneeze in my direction, Sniffles," I growled at him.

That stopped Sam for about half a second. He gave me that lopsided grin of his—his face sort of looked like a scuffed-up soccer ball, kind of round, scruffly. Little wart of a nose in the middle of it. Longest hair I ever saw on a man who works in space; hair length was one of the multitudinous points of contention between Sam and the agency. His eyes sparkled. Kind of an odd color, not quite blue, not really green. Sort of in-between.

"Malone, huh?" He read the nametag clipped over my sleep restraint.

"Frederick Mohammed Malone," I said.

"Jesus Christ, they put me in with an Arab!"

But he stuck out his hand. Sam was really a little guy; his hand was almost the size of a baby's. After a moment's hesitation I swallowed it in mine.

"Sam," he told me, knowing I could see his last name on the tag pinned to his coveralls.

"I'm not even a Muslin," I said. "My father was, though. First one in Arkansas."

"Good for him." Sam disengaged his Velcro shoes from the carpeting and floated over to one of the sleeping bags. His travel bag hung alongside. He ignored it and sniffed the air. "Goddamned hospitals all smell like somebody's dying. What're you in for? Hangnail or something?"

"Something," I said. "Acquired Immune Deficiency Syndrome."

His eyes went round. "AIDS?"

"It's not contagious. Not unless we make love."

"I'm straight."

"I'm not."

"Terrific. Just what I need, a gay black Arab with AIDS." But he was grinning at me.

I had seen plenty of guys back away from me once they knew I had AIDS. Some of them had a hangup about gays. Others were scared out of their wits that they'd catch AIDS from me, or from the medical personnel or equipment. I had more than one reason to know how a leper felt, back in those days.

Sam's grin faded into a puzzled frown. "How the hell did the medics put me in here if you've got AIDS? Won't you catch my cold? Isn't that dangerous for you?"

"I'm a guinea pig . . ."

"You don't look Italian."

"Look," I said, "if you're gonna stay in here, keep off the ethnic jokes, okay? And the puns."

He shrugged.

"The medics think they got my case arrested. New treatment that the gene therapy people have come up with."

"I get it. If you don't catch my cold, you're cured."

"They never use words like *cured*. But that's the general idea."

"So I'm a guinea pig, too."

"No, you are a part of the apparatus for this experiment. A source of infection. A bag of viruses. A host of bacteria. Germ city."

Sam hooked his feet into his sleep restraint's webbing and shot me a dark look. "And this is the guy who doesn't like ethnic jokes."

The Mac-Dac Shack had been one of the first space stations that the agency had put up. It wasn't fancy, but for years it had served as a sort of research laboratory, mainly for medical work. Naturally, with a lot of M.D.s in it, the Shack sort of turned into a floating hospital in orbit. With all the construction work going on in those days there was a steady stream of injured workmen and technicians.

Then some bright bureaucrat got the idea of using one module of the Shack as an isolation ward where the medics could do research on things like AIDS, Legionnaire's Disease, the New Delhi virus, and some of the paralytic afflictions that required either isolation or zero gravity. Or both. The construction crew infirmary was moved over to the yet-unfinished Alpha while the Shack was turned into a pure research facility with various isolation wards for guinea pigs like me.

Sam stayed in my ward for three–four days; I forget the exact time. He was like an energetic little bee, buzzing all over the place, hardly ever still for a minute. In zero gee, of course, he could literally climb the curved walls of the ward and hover up on the ceiling. He terrified the head nurse in short order by hanging near the ceiling or hiding inside one of the sleeping bags and then launching himself at her like a missile when she showed up with the morning's assortment of needles.

Never once did Sam show the slightest qualm at having his blood sampled alongside mine, although he watched the nurses taking the samples *very* closely. I've seen guys get violent from the fear that they'd get a needle contaminated by my blood and catch what I had. But Sam never even blinked. Me, I never liked needles. Couldn't abide them. Couldn't look when the nurse stuck me; couldn't even look when she stuck somebody else. Sam looked. He told me so.

By the end of the first day Sam noticed something. "All the nurses are women."

"All six of them," I affirmed.

"The doctors are all males?"

"Eight men, four women."

"That leaves two extra women for us."

"For you. I'm on the other side."

"How come all women nurses?" he wondered.

"I think it's because of me. They don't want to throw temptation in my path."

Sam started to frown at me but it turned into that lopsided grin. "They didn't think about *my* path."

He proceeded to cause absolute havoc among the nurses. With the single-minded determination of a sperm cell seeking blindly for an ovum, Sam pursued them all: the fat little redhead, the cadaverous ash-blonde, the really good-looking one, the kid who still had acne—all of them, even the head nurse, who threatened to inject him with enough estrogen to grow boobs on him if he didn't leave her and her crew alone.

Nothing deterred Sam. He would be gone for long hours from the ward, and when he'd come back he would be grinning from ear to ear. As politely as I could I'd ask him how he made out.

"It matters not if you win or lose," he would say. "It's how you play the game ... as long as you get laid."

When he finally left the isolation ward it seemed as if we had been friends for years. And it was damned quiet in there without him. I was alone again. I missed him. I realized how many years it had been since I'd had a friend.

I sank into a real depression of self-pity and despair. I had caught Sam's cold, sure enough. I was hacking and sneezing all day and night. One good thing about zero gravity is that you can't have a post-nasal drip. One bad thing is that all the fluids accumulate in your sinuses and give you a headache of monumental proportions. The head nurse seemed to take special pleasure in inflicting upon me the indignity of forcing tubes up my nose to drain the sinuses.

The medics were overjoyed. Their guinea pig was doing something interesting. Would I react to the cold like any normal person and get over it in a few days? Or would the infection spread through my body and worsen, turn into pneumonia or maybe kill me? I could see them writing their learned papers in their heads every time they examined me, which was four times a day.

I was really unfit company for anyone, including myself. I went on for months that way, just wallowing in my own misery. Other patients came and went: an African kid with a new strain of polio, an asthmatic who had developed a violent allergy to dust, a couple of burn victims from the Alpha construction crew who had to be suspended in zero gee. I stayed while they were treated in the other wards and sent home.

Then, without any warning at all, Sam showed up again.

"Hello, Omar, how's the tent-making business?" My middle name had become Omar, as far as he was concerned.

I gaped at him. He was wearing powder-blue coveralls and shoulder insignia of Global Technologies, Inc., which in those days was just starting to grow into the interplanetary conglomerate it has become.

"What the hell you doing back here?" My voice came out a full octave higher than normal, I was so surprised. And glad.

"I work here."

"Say what?"

He ambled over to me in the zero-gee strides we all learn to make: maintain just enough contact with the carpeted flooring to keep from floating off toward the ceiling. As Sam approached my bunk the head nurse pushed through the ward's swinging doors with a trayful of the morning's indignities for me.

"Global Technologies just won the contract for running this tin can. The medical staff still belongs to the government, but everybody else will be replaced by Global employees. I'm in charge of the whole place."

Behind him, the head nurse's eyes goggled, her mouth sagged open, and the tray slid from her hand. It just hung there, revolving slowly as she turned a full 180 and flew out of the ward without a word. Or maybe she was screaming so high that no human ear could hear it, like a bat.

"You're in charge of this place?" I was laughing at the drama that had been played out behind Sam's back. "No shit?"

Sam seemed happy that I seemed pleased. "I got a five-year contract."

We got to be *really* friends then. Not lovers. Sam was the most heterosexual man I have ever seen. One of the shrinks aboard the station told me Sam had a Casanova complex: he had to take a shot at any and every female creature he saw. I don't know how good his batting average was, but he surely kept busy—and grinning.

"The thrill is in the chase, Omar, not the capture," he said to me many times. Then he would always add, "As long as you get laid."

But Sam could be a true friend, caring, understanding, bringing out the best in a man. Or a woman, for that matter. I saw him help many of the station's female employees, nurses, technicians, scientists, completely aside from his amorous pursuits. He knew when to put his Casanova complex in the backseat. He was a surprisingly efficient administrator and a helluva good leader. Everybody liked him. Even the head nurse grew to grant him a grudging respect, although she certainly didn't want anybody to know it, especially Sam.

Of course, knowing Sam you might expect that he would have trouble with the chain of command. He had gotten himself out of the space agency, and it was hard to tell who was happier about it, him or the agency. You could hear sighs of relief from Houston and Washington all the way up to where we were, the agency was so glad to be rid of the pestering little squirt who never followed regulations.

It didn't take long for Sam to find out that Global Technologies, Inc., had its own bureaucracy, its own sets of regulations, and its own frustrations.

"You'd think a multibillion-dollar company would want to make all the profits it can," Sam grumbled to me, about six months after he had returned to the Shack. "Half the facilities on Alpha are empty, right? They overbuilt, right? So I show them how to turn Alpha into a tourist resort and they reject the goddamned idea. 'We are not in the tourism business,' they say. Goddamned assholes."

I found it hard to believe that Global Tech didn't understand what a bonanza they could reap from space tourism. It's not just twenty-twenty hindsight; Sam had me convinced then and there that tourism would be worth a fortune to Alpha. But Global just failed to see it, no matter how hard Sam tried to convince them. Maybe the harder he tried the less they liked the idea. Some outfits are like that. The old Not-Invented-Here syndrome. Or more likely, the old If-Sam's-For-It-I'm-Against-It syndrome.

Sam spent weeks muttering about faceless bureaucrats who sat on their brains, and how much money a zero-gravity honeymoon hotel could make. At least, that's what I thought he was doing.

The big crisis was mostly my fault. Looking back on it, if I could have figured out a different way to handle things, I would have. But you know how it is when your emotions are all churned up; you don't see any alternatives. Truthfully, I still don't see how I could have done anything else except what I did.

They told me I was cured.

Yeah, I know I said they never used words like that, but they changed their tune. After more than five years in the isolation ward of the station, the medics asked me to join them in the conference room. I expected another one of their dreary meetings; they made me attend them at least once a month, said it was important for me to "maintain a positive interaction with the research staff." So I dragged myself down to the conference room.

They were all grinning at me, around the table. Buckets of champagne stood at either end, with more bottles stashed where the slide projector usually hung.

I was cured. The genetic manipulations had finally worked. My body's immune system was back to normal. My case would be in the medical journals; future generations would bless my memory (but not my name, they would protect my anonymity). I could go back home, back to Earth.

Only, I didn't want to go.

"You don't want to go?" Sam's pudgy little face was screwing up into an incredulous expression that mixed in equal amounts of surprise, disapproval, and curiosity.

"Back to Earth? No, I don't want to go," I said. "I want to stay here. Or maybe go live on Alpha or one of the new stations they're building."

"But why?" Sam asked.

We were in his office, a tiny cubbyhole that had originally been a storage locker for fresh food. I mean, space in the Shack was *tight*. I thought I could still smell onions or something faintly pungent. Sam had walled the chamber with blue-colored spongy plastic, so naturally it came to be known as the Blue Grotto. There were no chairs in the Grotto, or course; chairs are useless in zero gee. We just hung in midair. You could nudge your back against the slightly rough wall surfacing and that would hold you in place well enough. There wasn't any room to drift around. Two people were all the chamber could hold comfortably. Sam's computer terminal was built into the wall; there was no furniture in the Grotto, no room for any.

"I got nothing to go back for," I answered, "and a lot of crap waiting for me that I'd just as soon avoid."

"But it's *Earth*," he said. "The world . . ."

So I told him about it. The whole story, end to end.

I had been a soldier, back in that nasty little bitch of a war in Mexico. Nothing glamorous, not even patriotism. I had joined the Army because it was the only way for a kid from my part of Little Rock to get a college education. They paid for my education and right afterward they pinned a lieutenant's gold bars on my shoulders and stuck me inside a heavy tank. Well, you know how well the tanks did in those Mexican hills. Nothing to shoot at but cactus, and we were great big noisy targets for those smart little missiles they brought in from Mongolia or wherever.

They knocked out my tank. I was the only one of the crew to survive. I wound up in an Army hospital in Texas where they tried to put my spine back together again. That's where I contracted AIDS, from one of the male nurses who wanted to prove to me that I hadn't lost my virility. He was a very sweet kid, very caring. But I never saw him again once they decided to ship me to the isolation ward up in orbit.

Now it was five years later. I was cured of AIDS, a sort of anonymous hero, but everything else was still the same. Earth would still be the same, except that every friend I had ever known was five years distance from me. My parents had killed themselves in an automobile wreck when I was in college. I had no sisters or brothers. I had no job prospects. Soldiers coming back five years after the war weren't greeted with parades and confetti, and all the computer stuff I had learned in college was obsolete by now. Not even the Army used that generation of software anymore.

And Earth was dirty, crowded, noisy, dangerous—it was also *heavy*, a full one gee. I tried a couple days in the one-gee wheel over at Alpha and knew that I could never live in Earth's full gravity again. Not voluntarily.

Sam listened to all this in complete silence, the longest I had ever known him to go without opening his mouth. He was totally serious, not even the hint of a smile. I could see that he understood.

"Down there I'll be just another nobody, an ex-soldier with no place to go. I can't handle the gravity, no matter what the physical therapists think they can do for me. I want to stay here, Sam. I want to make something of myself and I can do it here, not back there. The best I can be back there is another veteran on a disability pension. What kind of a job could I get? I can *be* somebody up here, I know I can."

He put his hand on my shoulder. Had to rise up off the floor a ways to do it, but he did it. "You're sure? You're absolutely certain that this is what you want?"

I nodded. "I can't go back, Sam. I just can't."

The faintest hint of a grin twitched at the corners of his mouth. "Okay, pal. How'd you like to go into the hotel business with me?"

You see, Sam had already been working for some time on his own ideas about space tourism. If Global Tech wouldn't go for a hotel facility over on Alpha, complete with zero-gee honeymoon suites, then Sam figured he could get somebody else interested in the idea. The people who like to badmouth Sam say that he hired me to cover his ass so he could spend his time working on his tourist hotel deal while he was still collecting a salary from Global. That isn't the way it happened at all; it was really the other way around.

Sam hired me as a consultant and paid me out of his own pocket. To this day I don't know where he got the money. I suspect it was from some of the financial people he was always talking to, but you never know, with Sam. He had an inexhaustible fund of rabbits up his sleeves.

Whenever I asked him about it he just grinned at me and told me not to ask questions.

I was never an employee of Global Technologies. And Sam worked full-time for them, eight hours a day, six days a week, and then some. They got their salary's worth out of him. More. But that didn't mean he couldn't spend nights, Sundays, and the odd holiday here and there wooing financiers and lawyers who might come up with the risk capital he needed for his hotel. Sure, sometimes he did his own thing during Global's regular office hours. But he worked plenty of overtime hours for Global, too. They got their money's worth out of Sam.

Of course, once I was no longer a patient whose bills were paid by the government Global sent word up from corporate headquarters that I was to be shipped back Earthside as soon as possible. Sam interpreted that to mean, when he was good and ready. Weeks stretched into months. Sam fought a valiant delaying action, matching every query of theirs with a detailed memorandum and references to obscure government health regulations. It would take Global's lawyers a month to figure out what the hell Sam was talking about and then frame an answering memo.

In the meantime Sam moved me from the old isolation ward into a private room—a coffin-sized cubbyhole—and insisted that I start paying for my rent and food. Since Sam was paying me a monthly consultant's stipend he was collecting my rent and food money out of the money he was giving me himself. It was all done with the Shack's computer system, so no cash changed hands. I had the feeling that there were some mighty weird subroutines running around inside that computer, all of them programmed by Sam.

While all this was going on the Shack was visited by a rather notorious U.S. senator, one of the most powerful men in the government. He was a wizened, shriveled old man who had been in the Senate almost half a century. I thought little of it; we were getting a constant trickle of VIPs in those days. The bigwigs usually went to Alpha, so much so that we began calling it the Big Wheels' Wheel. Most of them avoided the Shack. I guess they were scared of getting contaminated from our isolation ward patients. But a few of the VIPs made their way to the Shack now and then. Sam took personal charge of the senator and his entourage and showed him more attention and courtesy than I had ever seen him lavish on a visitor before. Or since, for that matter. Sam, kowtowing to an authority figure? It astounded me at the time, but I laughed it off and forgot all about it soon enough.

Then, some six months after the senator's visit, when it looked as if Sam had run out of time and excuses to keep me in the Shack and I would have to pack my meager bag and head down the gravity well to spend the rest of my miserable days in some overcrowded ghetto city, Sam came prancing weightlessly into my microminiaturized living quarters, waving a flimsy sheet of paper.

"What's that?" I knew it was a straight line but he wasn't going to tell me unless I asked.

"A new law." He was smirking, canary feathers all over his chin.

"First time I ever seen you happy about some new regulation."

"Not a regulation," he corrected me. "A *law*. A federal law, duly passed by the U.S. Congress and just today signed by the president."

I wanted to play it cool but he had me too curious. "So what's it say? Why's it so important?"

"It says"—Sam made a flourish that sent him drifting slowly toward the ceiling as he read—" 'No person residing aboard a space facility owned by the United States or a corporation or other legal entity licensed by the United States may be compelled to leave said facility without due process of law.' "

My reply was something profound, like "Huh?"

His scrungy little face beaming, Sam said, "It means that Global can't force you back Earthside! As long as you can pay the rent, Omar, they can't evict you."

"You joking?" I couldn't believe it.

"No joke. I helped write this masterpiece, kiddo," he told me. "Remember when old Senator Winnebago was up here, last year?"

The senator was from Wisconsin but his name was

not Winnebago. He had been a powerful enemy of the space program until his doctors told him that degenerative arthritis was going to make him a pain-racked cripple unless he could live in a low-gee environment. His visit to the Shack proved what his doctors had told him: in zero gee the pains that hobbled him disappeared and he felt twenty years younger. All of a sudden he became a big space freak. That's how Sam was able to convince him to sponsor the "pay your own way" law, which provided that neither the government nor a private company operating a space facility could force a resident out as long as he or she was able to pay the going rate for accommodations.

"Hell, they've got laws to protect tenants from eviction in New York and every other city," Sam said. "Why not here?"

I was damned glad of it. Overjoyed, in fact. It meant that I could stay, that I wouldn't be forced to go back Earthside and drag my ass around at my full weight. What I didn't realize at the time, of course, was that Sam would eventually have to use the law for himself. Obviously, *he* had seen ahead far enough to know that he would need such protection sooner or later. Did he get the law written for his own selfish purposes? Sure he did. But it served *my* purpose, too, and Sam knew that when he was bending the senator's tin ear. That was good enough for me. Still is.

For the better part of another year I served as Sam's leg man—a job I found interesting and amusingly ironic. I shuttled back and forth from the Shack to Alpha, generally to meet big-shot business persons visiting the Big Wheel. When Sam was officially on duty for Global, which was most of the time, he'd send me over to Alpha to meet the visitors, settle them down, and talk about the money that a tourist facility would make. I would just try to keep them happy until Sam could shake loose and come over to meet them himself. Then he would weave a golden web of words, describing how fantastic an orbital tourist facility would be, bobbing weightlessly around the room in his enthusiasm, pulling numbers out of the air to show how indecently huge would be the profit that investors would make.

"And the biggest investors will get their own suites,

all for themselves," Sam promised, "complete with every luxury—every service that the well-trained staff can provide." He would wink hard enough to dislocate an eyelid at that point, to make certain the prospective investor knew what he meant.

I met some pretty interesting people that way: Texas millionaires, Wall Street financiers, Hollywood sharks, a couple of bull-necked types I thought might be Mafia but turned out to be in the book and magazine distribution business, even a few very nice middle-aged ladies who were looking for "good causes" in which to invest. Sam did not spare them his "every service that the staff can provide" line, together with the wink. They giggled and blushed.

"It's gonna happen!" Sam kept saying. Each time we met a prospective backer his enthusiasm rose to a new pitch. No matter how many times a prospect eventually turned sour, no matter how often we were disappointed, Sam never lost his faith in the idea or the inevitability of its fruition.

"It's gonna happen, Omar. We're going to create the first tourist hotel in orbit. And you're going to have a share of it, pal. Mark my words."

When we finally got a tentative approval from a consortium of Greek and Italian shipping magnates Sam nearly rocked the old Shack out of orbit. He whooped and hollered and zoomed around the place like a crazy billiard ball. He threw a monumental party for everybody in the Shack, doctors, nurses, patients, technicians, administrative staff, security guards, visitors, even the one consultant who lived there—me. Where he got the caviar and fresh brie and other stuff I still don't know. But it was a party none of us will ever forget. The Shack damned near exploded with merriment. It started Saturday at five P.M., the close of the official work week. It ended, officially, Monday at 8 A.M. There are those who believe, though, that it's still going on over there at the Shack.

Several couples sort of disappeared during the party. The Shack wasn't so big that people could get lost in it, but they just seemed to vanish. Most of them showed up by Monday morning, looking tired and sheepish. Three of the couples eventually got married. One pair of them was stopped by a technician when they tried to go out an airlock while stark naked.

Sam himself engaged in a bit of EVA with one of the nurses, a tiny little elf of fragile beauty and uncommon bravery. She snuggled into a pressure suit with Sam and the two of them made several orbits around the Shack, outside, propelled by nothing more than their own frenetic pulsations and Newton's Third Law of Motion.

Two days after the party the Beryllium Blonde showed up.

Her real name was Jennifer Marlow, and she was as splendidly beautiful as a woman can be. A figure right out of a high-school boy's wettest dreams. A perfect face, with eyes of china blue and thickly glorious hair like a crown of shining gold. She staggered every male who saw her, she stunned even me, and she sent Sam into a complete tailspin.

She was Global Technology's ace troubleshooter. Her official title was administrative assistant (special projects) to the president. The word we got from Earthside was that she had a mind like a steel trap, and a vagina to match.

The official excuse for her visit was to discuss Sam's letter of resignation with him.

"You stay right beside me," Sam insisted as we drifted down the Shack's central corridor, toward the old conference room. "I won't be able to control myself if I'm in there alone with her."

His face was as white as the Moon's. He looked like a man in shock.

"Will you be able to control yourself *with* me in there?" I wondered.

"If I can't, rap me on the head. Knock me out. Give me a Vulcan nerve pinch. Anything! Just don't let me go zonkers over her."

I smiled.

"I'm not kidding, Omar!" Sam insisted. "Why do you think they sent her up here instead of some flunky? They know I'm susceptible. God knows how many scalps she's got nailed to her teepee."

I grabbed his shoulder and dug my Velcroed slippers into the floor carpeting. We skidded to a stop.

"Look," I said. "Maybe you want to avoid meeting with her altogether. I can represent you. I'm not ... uh, susceptible."

His eyes went so wide I could see white all around the pupils. "Are you nuts? Miss a chance to be in the same room with her? I want to be protected, Omar, but not that much!"

What could I do with him? He was torn in half. He knew the Beryllium Blonde was here to talk him out of resigning, but he couldn't resist the opportunity of letting her try her wiles on him any more than Odysseus could resist listening to the Sirens.

Like a couple of schoolboys dragging ourselves down to the principal's office we made our way slowly along the corridor and pushed through the door to the conference room. She was already standing at the head of the table, wearing a Chinese-red jumpsuit that fit her like skin. I gulped down a lump in my throat at the sight of her. I mean, she was *something*. She smiled a dazzling smile and Sam gave a weak little moan and rose right up off the floor.

He would have launched himself at her like a missile if I hadn't grabbed his belt and yanked him down to the table level. Being in zero gee, there was no need for chairs around the table. But I sure wished I had one then; I would have tied Sam into it. As it was, I hovered right next to him and kept the full length of the polished imitation wood table between us and the Blonde.

"I think you know why I'm here," she said. Her voice was music.

Sam nodded dumbly, his jaw hanging open. I thought I saw a bit of saliva foaming at the corner of his mouth.

"Why do you want to leave us, Sam? Don't you *like* us anymore?"

It took three tries before he could make his voice work. "It's ... not that. I ... I ... I want to go into ... uh, into business ... for myself."

"But your employment contract has almost two full years more to run."

"I can't wait two years," he said in a tiny voice. "This opportunity won't keep ..."

"Sam, you're a very valued employee of Global Technologies, Incorporated. We want you to stay with us. *I* want you to stay with us."

"I . . . can't."

"But you signed a contract with us, Sam. You gave us your word."

I stuck in my dime's worth. "The contract doesn't prohibit Sam from quitting. He can leave whenever he wants to." At least, that's what the lawyers Sam had hired had told us.

"But he'll lose all his pension benefits and health care provisions."

"He knows that."

She turned those heartbreakingly blue eyes on Sam again. "It will be a big disappointment to us if you leave, Sam. It will be a *personal* disappointment to me."

To his credit, Sam found the strength within himself to hold his ground. "I'm awfully sorry . . . but I've worked very hard to create this opportunity and I can't let it slip past me now."

She nodded once, as if she understood. Then she asked, "This opportunity you're speaking about: does it have anything to do with the prospect of opening a tourist hotel on space station Alpha?"

"That's right! But not just a hotel, a complete tourist facility. Sports complex, entertainment center, zero-gravity honeymoon suites . . ." He stopped abruptly and his face turned red. Sam blushed! He actually blushed.

Miss Beryllium smiled her dazzling smile at him. "But, Sam dear, that idea is the proprietary intellectual property of Global Technologies, Incorporated. Global owns the idea, not you."

For a moment the little conference room was absolutely silent. I could hear nothing except the faint background hiss of the air circulation fans. Sam seemed to have stopped breathing.

Then he squawked, *"What?"*

With a sad little shake of her gorgeous head, the Blonde replied, "Sam, you developed that idea while an employee of Global Technologies. We own it."

"But you turned it down!"

"That makes no difference, Sam. Read your employment contract. It's ours."

"But I made all the contacts. I raised the funding. I worked everything out—on my own time, goddammit! *On my own time!*"

She shook her golden locks again. "No, Sam. You did it while you were a Global employee. It is not your possession. It belongs to us."

Sam leapt out of my grasp and bounded to the ceiling. This time he was ready to make war, not love. "You can't do this to me!"

The Blonde looked completely unruffled by his display. She stood there patiently, a slightly disappointed little pout on her face, while I calmed Sam down and got him back to the table.

"Sam, dear, I know how you must feel," she cooed. "I don't want us to be enemies. We'd be happy to have you take part in the tourist hotel program as a Global employee. There could even be a raise in it for you."

"It's mine, dammit!" Sam screeched. "You can't steal it from me! It's mine!"

She shrugged deliciously. "I suppose our lawyers will have to settle it with your lawyers. In the meantime I'm afraid there's nothing for us to do but to accept your resignation. With reluctance, of course. With my own personal and very sad reluctance."

That much I saw and heard with my own eyes and ears. I had to drag Sam out of the conference room and take him back to his own quarters. She had him whipsawed, telling him that he couldn't claim possession of his own idea and at the same time practically begging him to stay on with Global and run the tourist project for them.

What happened next depends on who you ask. There are as many different versions of the story as there are people who tell it. As near as I can piece it all together, though, it went this way:

The Beryllium Blonde was hoping that Sam's financial partners would go along with Global Technologies once they realized that Global had muscled Sam out of the hotel deal. But she probably wasn't as sure of everything as she tried to make Sam think. After all, those backers had made their deal with the little guy; maybe they didn't want to do business with a big multinational corporation. Worse still, she didn't know exactly what kind of a deal Sam had cut with his backers. If Sam had legally binding contracts naming him as their partner they just might scrap the whole project when they learned that Global had cut Sam out. Especially if it looked like a court battle was shaping up.

So she showed up at Sam's door that night. He told me that she was still wearing the same skintight jumpsuit, with nothing underneath it except her own luscious body. She brought a bottle of incredibly rare and expensive cognac with her. "To show there's no hard feelings."

The Blonde's game was to keep Sam with Global and get him to go through with the tourist hotel deal. Apparently, once Global's management got word that Sam had actually closed a deal for creating a tourist facility on Alpha, their greedy little brains told them they might as well take the tourist business for themselves. Alpha was still badly underutilized; a tourist facility suddenly made sense to those jerkoffs.

So instead of shuttling back to Phoenix, as we had thought she would, the Blonde knocked on Sam's door that night. The next morning I saw him floating along the Shack's central corridor. He looked kind of dazed.

"She's staying here for a few more days," Sam mumbled. It was like he was talking to himself instead of to me.

But there was that happy little grin on his face.

Everybody in the Shack started to make bets on how long Sam could hold out. The best odds had him capitulating in three nights. Jokes about Delilah and haircuts became uproariously funny to everybody—except me. My future was tied up with Sam's. If the tourist project collapsed it wouldn't be long before I got shipped back to Earth, I knew.

After three days there were dark circles under Sam's eyes. He looked weary. Dazed. The grin was gone.

After a week had gone by I found Sam snoring in the Blue Grotto. As gently as I could I woke him.

"You getting any food into you?" I asked.

He blinked, gummy-eyed. "Chicken soup. I been taking chicken soup. Had some yesterday . . . I think it was yesterday . . ."

By the tenth day more money had changed hands among the bettors than on Wall Street. Sam looked like a case of battle fatigue. His cheeks were hollow, his eyes haunted.

"She's a devil, Omar," he whispered hoarsely. "A devil."

"Then get rid of her, man!" I urged. "Send her packing!"

He smiled wanly, like a man who knew he was addicted. "And quit show business?" he said weakly.

Two weeks to the day after she arrived, the Blonde packed up and left. Her eyes were blazing with anger. I saw her off at the docking port. She looked just as perfectly radiant as the day she had first arrived at the Shack. But what she was radiating now was rage. *Hell hath no fury* . . . I thought. But I was happy to see her go.

Sam slept for two days straight. When he managed to get up and around again he was only a shell of his old self. He had lost ten pounds. His eyes were sunken into his skull. His hands trembled. His chin was stubbled. He looked as if he had been through hell and back. But his crooked little grin had returned.

"What happened?" I asked him.

"She gave up."

"You mean she's going to let you go?"

He gave a deep, soulful, utterly weary sigh. "I guess she finally figured out that she couldn't change my mind and she couldn't kill me—at least not with the method she was using." His grin stretched a little wider.

"We all thought she was wrapping you around her little finger," I said.

"So did she."

"You outsmarted her!"

"I outlasted her," Sam said, his voice low and truly sorrowful. "You know, at one point there, she almost had me convinced that she had fallen in love with me."

"In love with you?"

He shook his head slowly, like a man who had

crawled across miles of burning desert toward an oasis that turned out to be a mirage.

"You had me worried, man."

"Why?" His eyes were really bleary.

"Well . . . she's a powerful hunk of woman. Like you said, they sent her up here because you're susceptible."

"Yeah. But once she tried to steal my idea from me I stopped being so susceptible. I kept telling myself, 'She's not a gorgeous hot-blooded sexpot of a woman. She's a company stooge, an android they sent here to nail you, a bureaucrat with boobs. Great boobs.'"

"And it worked."

"By a millimeter. Less. She damned near beat me. She damned near did. She should never have mentioned marriage. That woke me up."

What had happened, while Sam was fighting the Battle of the Bunk, was that when Sam's partners-to-be realized that Global was interested in the tourist facility, they became absolutely convinced that they had a gold mine on their hands. They backed Sam to the hilt. *Their* lawyers challenged Global's lawyers, and once the paper-shufflers down in Phoenix saw that, they understood that Miss Beryllium's mission to the Shack was doomed. The Blonde left in a huff when Phoenix ordered her to return. I guess she was enjoying her work. Or maybe she thought she had Sam weakening.

"Now lemme get another week's worth of sleep, will you?" Sam asked me. "And, oh yeah, find me about a ton and a half of vitamin E."

So Sam became the manager and part owner of the human race's first extraterrestrial tourist facility. I was his partner and, the way things worked out, a major shareholder in the project. Global got some rent money out of it. Actually, so many people enjoyed their vacations and honeymoons aboard the Big Wheel that a market eventually opened up for low-gravity retirement homes. Sam beat Global on that, too. But that's another story.

Malone was hanging weightlessly near the curving transparent dome of his chamber, staring out at the distant Moon and cold unblinking stars.

Jade had almost forgotten her fear of weightlessness. The black man's story seemed finished. She blinked and turned her attention to here and now. Drifting slightly closer to him, she turned off the recorder with an audible click, then thought better of it and turned it on again.

"So that's how this hotel came into being," she said.

Malone nodded, turning in midair to face her. "Yep. Sam got it started and then lost interest in it. He had other things on his mind, bigger fish to fry. He went into the advertising business, you know."

"Oh, yes, everybody knows about that," she replied. "But what happened to the woman, the Beryllium Blonde? And why didn't Sam ever return to Earth again?"

"Two parts of the same answer," Malone said tiredly. "Miss Beryllium thought she was playing Sam for a fish, using his Casanova complex to literally screw him out of his hotel deal. Once she realized that *he* was playing *her*, fighting a delaying action until his partners got their lawyers into action, she got damned mad. Powerfully mad. By the time it finally became clear back at Phoenix that Sam was going to beat them, she took her revenge."

"What do you mean?"

"Sam wasn't the only one who could riffle through old safety regulations and use them for his own benefit. She found a few early NASA regs, then got some bureaucrats in Washington—from the Office of Safety and Health, I think—to rewrite them so that anybody who'd been living in zero gee for a year or more had to undertake six months worth of retraining and exercise before he could return to Earth."

"Six months? That's ridiculous!"

"Is it?" Malone smiled with humor. "That regulation is still on the books, lady. Nobody pays attention to it anymore, but it's still there."

"She did that to spite Sam?"

"And she made sure Global put all its weight behind enforcing it. Made people think twice before signing an employment contract to work up here. Stuck Sam, but good. He wasn't going to spend no six months retraining! He just never bothered going back to Earth again."

"Did he want to go back?"

"Sure he did. He wasn't like me. He *liked* it back there. There were billions of women on Earth! Sam wanted to return but he just could never take six months out of his life to do it."

"That must have hurt him terribly."

"Yeah, I guess. Hard to tell with Sam. He didn't like to bleed where other people could watch."

"And you never went back to Earth."

"No," Malone said. "Thanks to Sam I stayed up here. He made me manager of the hotel, and once Sam bought the rest of this Big Wheel from Global, I became manager of the whole Alpha station."

"And you've never had the slightest yearning to see Earth again?"

Malone gazed at her solemnly for long moments before answering. "Sure I get the itch. But when I do I go down to the one-gee section of the Wheel here. I sit in a wheelchair and try to get around with these crippled legs of mine. The itch goes away then."

"But they have prosthetic legs that you can't tell from the real thing," she said. "Lots of paraplegics ..."

"Maybe *you* can't tell them from the real thing, but I guarantee you that any paraplegic who uses those legs can tell." Malone shook his head stubbornly. "Naw, once you've spent some time up here in zero gee you realize that you don't need legs to get around. You can live a good and useful life here instead of being a cripple down there."

"I see," Jade said softly.

"Yeah. Sure you do."

"Sure I do," Jade said softly. "I can never go to Earth, either."

"Never?" Malone sounded skeptical.

"Bone disease. I was born with it."

An uncomfortable silence rose between them. She turned off the recorder in her belt buckle, for good this time.

Finally Malone softened. "Hey, I'm sorry. I shouldn't be nasty with you. It's just that ... thinking about Sam again. He was a great guy, you know. And now he's dead and everybody thinks he was just a troublemaking bastard."

"I don't," she said. "A womanizing sonofabitch, like you said. A male chauvinist of the first order. But after listening to you tell it, even at that he doesn't seem so awful."

The black man smiled at her. "Look at the time! No wonder I'm hungry! Can I take you down to the dining room for some supper?"

"The dining room in the lunar-gravity section?"

"Yes, of course."

"Won't you be uncomfortable there? Isn't there a galley in the microgravity section?"

"Sure, but won't you be uncomfortable there?"

She laughed. "I think I can handle it."

"Really?"

"I can try. And maybe you can tell me how Sam got himself into the retirement home business."

"All right. I'll do that."

As she turned she caught sight of the immense beauty of Earth sliding past the observation dome; the Indian Ocean a breathtaking swirl of deep blues and greens, the subcontinent of India decked with purest white clouds. The people who lived there, she thought. All those people. And the two, in particular, who were hiding away from her.

"But . . ." she looked at Malone, then asked in a whisper, "do you ever miss being home, being on Earth? Don't you feel isolated here, away from . . ."

His booming laughter shocked her. "Isolated? Up here?" Malone pitched himself forward into a weightless somersault, then pirouetted in midair. He pointed toward the ponderous bulk of the planet and said, "*They're* the ones who're isolated. Up here, I'm free!"

Then he offered his arm to her and they floated together toward the gleaming metal hatch, their feet a good eight inches above the chamber's floor.

Still, Jade glanced back over her shoulder at the gleaming expanse of cloud-decked blue. She thought of the two women who lived among the billions down there, the two women who would never see her, whom she could never see. There are many kinds of isolation, Jade thought. Many kinds.

12

■━•━■━•━■━•━■━•━■━•━■━•━■━•━■━•━■━•━■

Lagrange Habitat
Jefferson

THE DINING ROOM in Alpha's zero-gravity section was actually a self-service galley. Malone helped Jade to fill her tray with prepackaged courses, then they fit their slippered feet into loop restraints on the spindly legs of a table, Jade using the highest level of the plastic loops, long-legged Malone the lowest.

Their dinner together was relaxed and pleasant. Malone recommended for dessert what he called "the Skylab bomb": a paper-thin shell of vanilla ice cream filled with strawberries.

"You can only make it this thin in zero gee," he pointed out.

As they finished their squeezebulbs of coffee, Malone said, "Y'know, there's a guy over in the new habitat at L5, the one they've named Jefferson. You'd do well to talk to him."

Jade turned on her belt recorder to get the man's name and location.

"Yeah. Spence Johansen," Malone continued. "He

knew Sam when they were both astronauts with the old
NASA. Then they went into business together."

"What kind of business?" Jade asked.

Malone grinned at her. "Junk collecting."

"It's just a small increment on the fare," Jade said to
Raki's image on the phone screen. She was leaning against
the side wall of the cubicle she had rented aboard Alpha,
her bags packed, ready to head back to Selene by way of
habitat Jefferson.

Raki had a strange smile on his darkly handsome face.
"You got the story from this man Malone?" he asked.

"Yes. It's really good, Raki. Very personal stuff. Great
human interest. And Malone told me about this Spencer
Johansen who's living at Jefferson. I can get there on the
transfer ship that's leaving in half an hour."

He shook his head. "What would you do if I said no?"

She grinned at his image. "I'd go there anyway; the
difference in fare is so small I'd pay it myself."

He puffed out a sigh. "Do you realize how far out on
a limb I am with you? The CEO *hates* Sam Gunn. If Sam
were alive today the old man would want to have him
murdered."

Jade said nothing. She merely hung there weightlessly, her back plastered to the wall to prevent her from
drifting out of range of the phone's camera eye.

"All right," Raki said finally, with a little shrug of acquiescence. "I think it's crazy. I think maybe *I'm* crazy. But
go ahead, get everything you can."

"Thanks!" Jade said. "You won't regret it, Raki."

"I already regret it."

"Call me Spence," he said, dropping his lanky, sweaty
frame onto the bench beside her.

In spite of herself, Jade felt her heart skip a couple of
beats. She was breathless, but not merely from the exertion
of a hard game of low-gee tennis.

Spencer Johansen was tall and lean, with the flat midsection and sharp reflexes that come only from constant exercise. His eyes were sky-blue, his face handsome in a
rugged, clean-cut, honest way. When he smiled, as he was

doing now, he looked almost boyish despite his silver-gray hair. He was older than Raki, she knew. Yet he seemed more open; innocent, almost.

The smile was *deadly*. Jade had to remind herself that this man was the subject of an interview, not an object of desire. She was here to get a story out of him, and he was refusing to talk.

Jefferson was the newest of the Lagrange habitats being built at the L4 and L5 libration points along the Moon's orbit. A vast tube of asteroidal steel, twenty kilometers long and five wide, its interior was landscaped to look like a pleasant Virginia countryside, with rolling wooded hills and picturesque little villages dotting the greenery here and there. Best of all, from Jade's point of view, was that Jefferson rotated on its long axis only fast enough to give an almost lunar feeling of weight inside. The entire habitat, with its population of seventy-five thousand, was pleasantly low gee.

"Why Sam?" Johansen asked, still smiling. But those clear blue eyes were wary, guarded.

They were both still puffing from their punishing game. Out on the huge low-gee court, safely behind a shatterproof transparent wall, the next two players were warming up with long, slow low-gravity lobs and incredible leaps to hit the ball five meters above the sponge metal surface of the court.

"Solar Network wants to do his biography," Jade replied, surreptitiously pressing the microswitch that activated the recorder built into her belt buckle.

"Solar, huh?" Spencer Johansen huffed.

"Well . . . it's really me," Jade confessed. "I've become fascinated by the man. *I* want to get Solar to do a special on him. I need all the help I can get. I need your story."

Johansen looked down at her. Sitting beside him she looked small, almost childlike, in a loose-fitting sleeveless gym top and shorts of pastel yellow.

"You're not the first woman to be fascinated by ol' Sam," he muttered. His own tennis outfit was nothing more than an ancient T-shirt and faded denim cutoffs.

"Couldn't you tell me *something* about him? Just some personal reminiscences?"

"We made a deal, you and me."

She sighed heavily. "I know. And I lost."

His smile returned. "Yeah, but you played a helluva game. Never played tennis before?"

"Never," she swore. "There's no room for tennis courts in Selene."

He seemed to look at her from a new perspective. The smile widened. "Come on, hit the showers and put on your drinking clothes."

"You'll give me the interview? Even though I lost the game?"

"You're too pretty to say no to. Besides, you played a damned good game. A couple days up here and you'll be beating me."

13

•━•━•━•━•━•━•━•━•━•━•━•━•━•━•

Vacuum Cleaner

BACK IN THE old NASA days Sam Gunn and I were buddies—said Johansen to Jade over a pair of L5 "libration libations."

They had height limitations for astronauts back then, even for the old shuttle. I just barely made it under the top limit. Little Sam just barely made it past the low end. Everybody used to call us Mutt and Jeff. In fact, Sam himself called me Mutt most of the time.

I never figured out exactly why it was, but I *liked* the little so-and-so. Maybe it's because he was always the underdog, the little guy in trouble with the big boys. Although I've got to admit that most of the time Sam started the trouble himself. I'm no angel; I've raised as much hell as the next guy, I guess. But Sam—he was unique. A real loose cannon. He *never* did things by the book. I think Sam regarded the regulations as a challenge, something to be avoided at all costs. He'd drive everybody nuts. But he'd get the job done, no matter how many mission controllers turned blue.

He quit the agency, of course. Too many rules. I've got to confess that flying for the agency in those days was a lot like working for a bus line. If those desk jockeys in Washington could've used robots instead of human astronauts they would've jumped at the chance. All they wanted was for us to follow orders and fill out their damned paperwork.

Sam was itching to be his own boss. "There's m-o-n-e-y to be made out there," he'd spell out for me. "Billions and billions," he'd say in his Carl Sagan voice.

He got involved in this and that while I stayed in the agency and tried to make the best of it despite the bureaucrats. Maybe you heard about the tourist deal he got involved in. Later on he actually started a tourist hotel at Alpha. But at this point Alpha hadn't even been started yet; the only facilities in orbit were a couple of Russian jobs and the American station Freedom. Sam had served on Freedom, part of the very first crew. Ended the mission in a big mess.

Well, meantime, all I really wanted was to be able to fly. That's what I love. And back in those days, if you wanted to fly you either worked for the agency or you tried to get a job overseas. I just couldn't see myself sitting behind a desk or working for the French or the Japs.

Then one fine day Sam calls me up.

"Pack your bags and open a Swiss bank account," he says.

Even over the phone—we didn't have videophones back then—I could hear how excited he was. I didn't do any packing, but I agreed to meet him for a drink. The Cape was just starting to boom again, what with commercial launches (unmanned, in those days) and the shuttles ferrying people to space stations and all that. I had no intentions of moving; I had plenty of flight time staring me in the face even if it was nothing more than bus driving.

Sam was usually the center of attention wherever he went. You know, wisecracking with the waitresses, buying drinks for everybody, buzzing all over the bar like a bee with a rocket where his stinger ought to be. But that afternoon he was just sitting quietly in a corner booth, nursing a flat beer.

Soon as I slid into the booth Sam starts in, *bam*, with no preliminaries. "How'd you like to be a junk collector?"

"Huh?"

Jabbing a thumb toward the ceiling he says, "You know how many pieces of junk are floating around in low orbit? Thousands! Millions!"

He's talking in a kind of a low voice, like he doesn't want anybody to hear him.

I said back to him, "Tell me about it. On my last mission the damned canopy window got starred by a stray piece of crap. If it'd been any bigger ..."

There truly were thousands of pieces of debris floating in orbit around the Earth back then. All kinds of junk: discarded equipment, flakes of paint, pieces of rocket motors, chunks of crap of all kinds. Legend had it that there was still an old Hasselblad camera that Mike Collins had fumbled away during the Gemini 10 mission floating around out there. And a thermal glove from somebody else.

In fact, if you started counting the really tiny stuff, too small to track by radar, there might actually have been millions of bits of debris in orbit. A cloud of debris, a layer of man-made pollution, right in the area where we were putting space stations in permanent orbits.

Sam hunched across the table, making a shushing gesture with both his hands. "That's just it! Somebody's gonna make a fuckin' fortune cleaning up that orbiting junk, getting rid of it, making those low orbits safe to fly in."

I gave him a sidelong look. Sam was trying to keep his expression serious, but a grin was worming its way out. His face always reminded me of a leprechaun: round, freckled, wiry red hair, the disposition of an imp who never grew up.

"To say nothing," he damn near whispered, "of what they'll pay to remove defunct commsats from geosynchronous orbit."

He didn't really say "geosynchronous orbit," he called it "GEO" like we all do. "LEO" is low Earth orbit. GEO is 22,300 miles up, over the equator. That's where all the communications satellites were. We damned near got into a shooting war with half a dozen equatorial nations in

South America and Africa over GEO rights—but that's a
different story.

"Who's going to pay you to collect junk?" I asked.
Damned if my voice didn't come out as low as his.

Sam looked very pleased with himself. "Our dear old
Uncle Sam, at first. Then the fat-cat corporations."

Turns out that Sam had a friend who worked in the
Department of Commerce, of all places, up in Washington.
I got the impression that the friend was not a female,
which surprised me. Seemed that the friend was a Commerce Department bureaucrat, of all things. I just couldn't
picture Sam being chummy with a desk jockey. It seemed
strange, not like him at all.

Anyway, Commerce had just signed off on an agreement with the space agency to provide funding for removing junk from orbit. Like all government programs, there
was to be a series of experimental missions before anything else happened. What the government calls a "feasibility study." At least two competing contractors would be
funded for the feasibility study.

The winner of the competition, Sam told me, would
get an exclusive contract to remove debris and other junk
from LEO on an ongoing basis.

"They've gotta do something to protect the space station," Sam said.

"Freedom?"

He bobbed his head up and down. "Sooner or later
she's gonna get hit by something big enough to cause real
damage."

"The station's already been dinged here and there.
Little stuff, but some of it causes damage. They've got
guys going EVA almost every day for inspection and re-
pair."

"And the corporations who own the commsats are going to be watching this competition very closely," Sam
went on, grinning from ear to ear.

I knew that GEO was getting so crowded that the International Telecommunications Authority had put a moratorium on launching new commsats. The communications
companies were only being allowed to replace old satel-

lites that had gone dead. They were howling about how their industry was being stifled.

"Worse than that," Sam added. "The best slots along the GEO are already so damned crowded that the commsat signals are interfering with one another. Indonesia's getting porno movies from the Polynesian satellite!"

That made me laugh out loud. Must have played holy hob with Indonesia's family planning program.

"How much do you think Turner or Toshiba would pay to have dead commsats removed from orbit so new ones can be spotted in the best locations?" Sam asked.

"Zillions," I said.

"At least!"

I thought it over for all of ten seconds. "Why me?" I asked Sam. I mean, we had been buddies but not all that close.

"You wanna fly, don'tcha? Handling an OMV, going after stray pieces of junk, that's going to call for *real* flying!"

An OMV was an orbital maneuvering vehicle: sort of a little sports car built to zip around from the space station to other satellites; never comes back to Earth. Compared to driving the space shuttle, flying an OMV would be like racing at Le Mans.

I managed to keep a grip on my enthusiasm, though. Sam wasn't acting out of altruism, I figured. Not without some other reason to go along with it. I just sat there sipping at my beer and saying nothing.

He couldn't keep quiet for long. "Besides," he finally burst out, "I need somebody with a good reputation to front the organization. If those goons in Washington see my name on top of our proposal they'll send it to the Marianas Trench and deep-six it."

That made sense. Washington was full of bureaucrats who'd love to see Sam mashed into corn fritters. Except, apparently, for his one friend at Commerce.

"Will you let me be president of the company?" I asked.

He nodded. The corners of his mouth tightened, but he nodded.

I let my enthusiasm show a little. I grinned and stuck

my hand out over the table. Sam grinned back and we shook hands between the beer bottles.

But I had a problem. I would have to quit the agency. I couldn't be a government employee—even on long-term leave—and work for a private company. Washington's ethics rules were very specific about that. Oh, yeah, Sam formed a private company to tackle the job. Very private: he owned it all. He called it VCI. That stood for Vacuum Cleaners, Inc. Cute.

I solved my problem with a single night's sleepless tussling. The next morning I resigned from the agency. Hell, if Sam's plan worked I'd be getting more flying time than a dozen shuttle jockeys. And I'd be doing some real flying, not just driving a big bus.

If things didn't work out with Sam I could always re-up with the agency. They'd take me back, I felt sure, although all my seniority and pension would be gone. What the hell. It was only money. Most of my salary went to my first three wives anyway.

Jade nearly dropped the tall frosty glass from which she had been sipping.

"Your first three wives?" she gulped.

Johansen inched back in the fabric-covered slingchair. He looked frustrated, embarrassed. "Uh, I've been married six times," he said in a low, fumbling voice.

"Six?"

He seemed to be mentally counting. Then he nodded. "Yeah, six. Funny thing, Sam always had the reputation for chasing . . . women. But somehow I always wound up getting married."

Jade's heart fluttered with disappointment. Yet a tiny voice deep within her noted that seven is a lucky number. She felt shocked, confused.

It took an effort of will to pull her eyes away from Johansen and gaze out at the scenery. The patio on which they sat hung out over the curving landscape of the gigantic habitat. Jade saw gentle grassy hills with a lazy stream meandering among them, in the distance a little village that looked like a scene for a Christmas card except there was no snow. Farther still there were farms, kilometers off, like a checkerboard of different shades of green. Her eyes followed the curve of this vast structure, up and up, woods and fields and more villages overhead, all the way around until her gaze settled on Johansen's relaxed, smiling face once again.

"It's quite a sight, isn't it?" he said. "A complete self-sufficient ecology, man-made, inside a twenty-kilometer cylinder."

"Quite a sight," she murmured.

Putting the glass down on the little cocktail table between them, Jade forced herself to return to the subject at hand. "You were talking about leaving the agency to go to work for Sam."

Oh, yeah—Johansen replied, deftly ordering a new round of drinks with a hand signal to their robot waiter.

Sam had two problems to wrestle with: how to raise the money to make VCI more than a bundle of paper, and how to get the government to award us one of the two contracts for the experimental phase of the junk removal program.

Sam raised the money, just barely. He got most of it from a banker in Salt Lake City who had a daughter that needed marrying. And did *that* cause trouble later on! Let me tell you.

But I don't want to get ahead of myself.

We rented a dinky office on the second floor of a shopping mall, over a women's swimwear shop. Sam spent more time downstairs than he did in the office. At least, when the stores were open. Nights he worked with me writing our proposal. He seemed to work better after the sun went down. Me, I worked night and day. Writing a proposal was not easy for me.

Sam went out and hired a wagonload of big-time consultants from academia and industry, guys with fancy degrees and lists of publications longer than a gorilla's arm.

"Gee, Sam, how can we afford all these fancy pedigrees?" I asked him.

He just grinned. "All we need 'em for is to put their names on our letterhead and their resumés in our proposal. That doesn't cost a damned thing. They only get

paid when we ask them to consult with us, and we don't
have to ask 'em a thing once we win the contract."

That sounded a little shady to me, but Sam insisted
our proposal needed some class and I had to agree with
him there. Our only real employees were two bright kids
who were still students at Texas A&M, and four local technicians who were part-time until we got the government
contract. We leased or borrowed every piece of office
equipment. Most of the software our Texas kids invented
for us or pirated from elsewhere. We really needed that
impressive list of consultants.

Those two youngsters from Texas had come up with a
great idea for removing debris from orbit. At least, it
looked like a great idea to me. On paper. I knew enough
engineering to get by, but these kids were really sharp.

"How'd you find them?" I asked Sam.

"They wrote a paper about their idea," he said. "Published it in an aerospace journal. Their professor put his
name on it, just like they all do, but I found those two kids
who did the real work and put 'em on the payroll."

I was impressed. I had never realized that Sam kept
up with the technical journals.

Well, we finished writing the proposal and faxed it up
to Washington just under the deadline. You know how the
government works: you could have the greatest invention
since canned soup but they won't look at it if it isn't in
their hands by "close of business" on the day they specify.
Thank God for the fax machines. We just barely made it.

Then we waited. For weeks. Months.

I got nervous as hell. Sam was as cool as liquid hydrogen. "Relax, Mutt," he told me a thousand times during
those months. "It's in the bag." And he would smile a
crooked little smile.

So there I sat, behind a rented desk in a dinky office,
while the days ticked by and our money ran out. I was
president of a company that was so close to bankruptcy I
was starting to think about moonlighting as a spare pilot
for Federal Express.

Then we got the letter from Washington. Very official,
with a big seal on it and everything.

We were invited to send a representative to a meeting

in Washington to defend our proposal against a panel of government experts. The letter said that there were four proposals being considered. The four companies were Rockledge International, Lockwood Industries, Texas Aerospace, and VCI—us.

"Holy Christmas!" I said when I read the letter. "We're never going to get a contract. Look at who the competition is: three of the biggest aerospace corporations in the world!"

Sam made like a Buddha. He folded his hands over his little belly and smiled enigmatically.

"Don't worry about it, Mutt," he said for the thousand-and-first time. "It's in the bag. If there's any real problem, I've got four magic words that will take care of everything."

"What did you say?"

"Four magic words," Sam repeated.

I did not share his confidence. In fact, I thought he had gone a little nutty under the pressure.

I was nervous as a kid on his first solo as I flew to Washington on the appointed day. I had spent every day and night since we'd received that letter cramming every bit of technical and financial data into my thick skull. We had even flown over to College Station for a week, where our two bright Texas A&M youngsters stuffed all their info into me directly.

I was surprised to see that one of Sam's two young geniuses was female. Sort of round and chubby, but she had huge, dark, soulful Mediterranean eyes that followed Sam wherever he moved like twin radar dishes locked onto a target. I figured that maybe Sam had met her *before* he had read their paper in that journal.

Anyway, there I was, stepping into an office in some big government building in Washington, my head bursting with facts and figures. As offices go, it wasn't much bigger or better furnished than our own little place in Florida. Government-issue desk, table, and chairs. Metal bookcases on one side. Faded pastel walls, hard to tell what color they were supposed to be originally. Everything looked kind of shabby.

I was the last one to arrive. Representatives of our

three competitors were already sitting side by side on one end of the long table that took up most of the room. They sure looked well off, knowledgeable, slick and powerful. I felt like an intruder, an outsider, well beyond my depth.

But Sam had given me those four magic words of his to use in an emergency, and I whispered them to myself as I took the last chair, at the foot of the table.

Sitting at the head of the table was a guy from the agency I had met once, when he had visited the Cape for the official ceremonies when we opened space station Freedom. That had been years ago, and I hadn't seen him anywhere around the working parts of the agency since then. On his right-hand side sat three more government types: old suits, gray hair or none at all, kind of pasty faces from being behind desks all their lives.

The three industry reps were dressed in much better suits: not flashy, but obviously expensive. Two of them were so young their hair was still all dark. The third, from Rockledge International, was more my own age. His hair was kind of salt-and-pepper; looked like he spent plenty on haircuts, too. And tanning parlors. He was the only one who smiled at me as I sat down and introduced myself. I didn't know it right at that moment, but it was the kind of smile a shark gives.

"We're glad you could make it, Mr. Johansen," said the guy at the head of the table. The others sort of snickered.

"My flight was delayed in Atlanta," I mumbled. In those days, when you flew out of Florida, even if you died and were sent to hell you had to go by way of Atlanta.

He introduced himself as Edgar Zane. Thin hair, thin lips, thin nose, and thin wire-frames on his bifocals. But his face looked round and bloated, too big for his features. Made him look like a cartoon character, almost. From what I could see of his belly behind the table, that was bloated, too.

Zane introduced everybody else around the table. The government types were from the Department of Transportation, the Environmental Protection Agency, and the Department of Commerce.

Commerce? Was this bald, sallow-faced, cranky-looking old scarecrow Sam's pigeon in the Commerce Department? He sure didn't give me any reason to think so. He squinted at me like an undertaker taking measurements.

"Before we begin," said the Rockledge guy, Pierre D'Argent, "I'd like to ask Mr. Johansen for a clarification."

Zane peered at him through the top half of his bifocals. "You're here to answer questions, Mr. D'Argent, not ask them."

He beamed a smile toward the head of the table. "Yes, I understand that. But I believe we all have the right to know exactly who we are dealing with here."

He turned his handsome face to me. "VCI is a new firm in this field. I think we'd all like to know a bit more about your company's financial backing and management structure."

I knew right away what he wanted. He wanted me to tell them all that Sam Gunn was the man behind VCI.

I gave him the standard spiel that Sam had drummed into me, like a POW reciting name, rank, and serial number. VCI is a privately held company. I am the president and chief executive officer. While our staff is small and elite, we have an extensive list of consultants who can provide world-class technical, management, and financial expertise on every aspect of our program. VCI's principal financial backer is the First Federal Bank of Utah. Our accounting firm is Robb and Steele, of Merritt Island, Florida.

D'Argent smiled at me with all his teeth. "And what role does Mr. Gunn play in VCI?"

"Who?" My voice squeaked a little.

"Sam Gunn," D'Argent said.

I looked up the table. Zane was scowling at me through his wire-frame glasses. He knew Sam, that was for sure.

Never lie to the government, Sam had instructed me, when there's a good chance that they'll catch you at it.

"Mr. Gunn is the founder of VCI," I said.

"His name doesn't appear in your proposal," Zane practically snarled.

"Yes it does, sir," I corrected him. "On page four hundred and sixty-three." That was back in the boilerplate section where we were required to put in a history of the company. Ordinarily nobody read the boilerplate, but now I knew that Zane and his three harpies would go over it with electron microscopes. How Sam managed to produce forty-seven pages of history about a company that wasn't even forty-seven weeks old was beyond me.

Zane gave D'Argent a glance, then asked me, "Is Sam Gunn going to be actively involved in the project—if you should be fortunate enough to win one of the contracts?"

"We have no intention to actively involve him in the day-to-day work," I said. It was pretty close to the truth.

Zane looked as if he didn't believe a word of it. I figured we had been shot down before we even got off the runway. D'Argent gave me another one of his shark smiles, looking pleased with himself.

But the bald scarecrow from Commerce cleared his throat and rasped, "Are we here to discuss the competing proposals or to conduct a witch hunt? Sounds to me like a cult of personality."

Zane huffed through his pinched nose and started the official proceedings.

The one thing we had going for us was our technical approach. I quickly saw that all three of our giant corporate competitors had submitted pretty much the same proposal: the old nerf-ball idea. You know, launch a balloon and blow it up to full size once it's in orbit. The balloon's surface is sort of semisticky. As it runs into debris in space it bounces them into orbits that spin down into the atmosphere, where the junk burns up. The idea had been around for decades. It was simple and would probably work—except for sizable chunks of debris, like discarded pieces of rocket stages or hand tools that got away.

It also required a lot of launches, because the nerf ball itself got slowed down enough after a few orbits to come spiraling back into the atmosphere. The nerfs could be launched with small unmanned boosters pretty cheaply, or ride piggyback on bigger boosters. They could even be tucked into spare corners of shuttle payload bays and injected into orbit by the shuttle crews.

Our proposal was different. See, the junk hanging

around up there picked up an electrical charge after a couple of orbits. From electrons in the solar wind, if I remember correctly. Sam's idea was to set up a big electromagnetic bumper on the front end of space station Freedom and deflect the debris with it, neatly clearing out the orbit that the station was flying through. Kind of like the cowcatcher on the front of an old locomotive, only instead of being made of steel our bumper was an invisible magnetic field that stretched hundreds of meters into space out in front of the station.

"The equipment we need is small enough to fit into a shuttle's student experiment canister," I explained. "The bumper itself is nothing more than an extended magnetic field, generated by a superconducting coil that would be mounted on the forward-facing side of the space station."

"The costs . . ." Zane started to mutter.

"The program will cost less than a continuing series of nerf-ball launches," I said before he could turn to the relevant pages in our proposal. "And the elegant thing is that since this program's primary aim is to keep Freedom's orbit clear of debris, we will be doing exactly that."

"And nothing else," D'Argent sniped.

I smiled at him for a change. "Once Freedom's orbit has been cleared we could always detach the equipment, mount it in an orbital maneuvering vehicle, and clean out other orbits. The equipment is very portable, yet durable and long-lasting."

We went into some really heavy-duty arguing, right through lunch (a plate of soggy sandwiches and cans of soda brought in to us by a delivery boy who had dirt under every one of his fingernails) and all through the long afternoon.

"I've got to admit," Zane finally said as it started to get dark outside, "that VCI's technical proposal is extremely interesting."

"But can a newly hatched company be expected to carry through?" D'Argent asked. "I mean, after all, they have no track record, no real financial strength. Do you really trust Sam Gunn, of all people, to get the job done?"

I held on to my temper. Partly because Sam had drilled it into me that they'd drop our proposal if they thought I was as flaky as he was. But mostly because I heard Sam's four magic words.

"Small business set-aside."

They were spoken by the cadaver from Commerce. Everything stopped. The room fell so quiet I could hear the going-home traffic from out on the streets below even through the double-paned sealed windows of the office.

"This program has a small business set-aside provision," the Commerce scarecrow said, his voice crackling as if it were coming over a radio link from Mars. "VCI is the only small business firm to submit a proposal. Therefore, if their proposal is technically sound—which we all agree that it is—and financially in line, we have no choice but to award them one of the two contracts."

D'Argent's handsome chin dropped to his expensive rep tie. Zane glared at his crony from Commerce. The others muttered and mumbled to themselves. But there was no way around it. Decades earlier the Congress had set up a system so that little companies could compete against the big guys. Sam had found that old government provision and used it.

Later, when I told Sam how things had gone, he whooped and danced on my desktop. Nothing made him happier than using the government's own red tape to his advantage.

"Wait a minute," Jade said, putting down the tall cool glass she had been holding for so long that its contents had melted down to ice water.

Johansen, who had hardly touched his own drink, eyed her quizzically.

"Was that old man Sam's contact in the Commerce Department, after all? Had he tipped Sam off about the small business set-aside?"

I thought the same thing—Johansen answered—but the guy slipped out of the meeting room like a ghost disappearing into thin air. And when I asked Sam about it, back in Florida, he just got quiet and evasive. There was something going on, but I couldn't figure out what it was. Not until a lot later.

Anyway, about six weeks afterward we got the official notification that we had won one of the two contracts for what the government called "The Orbital Debris Removal Test and Evaluation Program, Phase I." The other contract went to Rockledge.

"We're in!" Sam yelped. "We did it!"

We partied all that weekend. Sam invited everybody from the swimwear shop downstairs, for starters, and pretty soon it seemed like the whole shopping mall was jammed into our little office. Sometime during the weekend our two geniuses from Texas A&M showed up and joined the fun.

The hangover was monumental, but the party was worth it. Then the work began.

I saw trouble right away. The kids from Texas were really brilliant about superconductors and magnetic bumpers, but they were emotionally about on the level of junior high school.

The girl—uh, woman—her name was Melinda Cardenas. It was obvious that she had the hots for Sam. She followed him with those big brown eyes of hers wherever Sam went. She was kind of cute although pretty badly overweight. Could have been a real beauty, I guess, if she could stay away from sweets and junk food. But that's just about all she ate. And every time I looked at her, she was eating.

Her boyfriend—Larry Karsh—ate as much junk food as she did, but never put on an ounce. Some people have metabolisms like that. He never exercised. He just sat all day long at the desktop computer he had brought with him, designing our magnetic bumper and munching on sweet rolls and greaseburgers from the fast-food joint a few doors down the mall from our office. He could lose weight just by breathing, while Melinda gained a pound and a half every time she inhaled.

It took me a while to figure out that Larry was plying Melinda with food so she'd stay too fat for anybody else to be interested in her. They were rooming together, but "like brother and sister," according to Melinda. One look at Larry's pasty, unhappy face, sprinkled with acne, told me that the brother-and-sister thing was making him miserable.

"You gotta get her away from me," Sam told me, a little desperation in his voice, one evening down in the bar where we had originally formed VCI.

"Melinda?"

"Who else?"

"I thought you liked her," I said.

"She's just a kid." Sam would not meet my eyes. He concentrated instead on making wet rings on the tabletop with his beer bottle.

"Pretty well-developed kid."

"You gotta get her off me, Mutt." He was almost pleading. "If you don't, Larry's going to pack up and leave."

I finally got the picture. Sam had used his charm to get Melinda to join VCI because he had known that Larry would come wherever she went. But now Larry was getting resentful. If he broke up our design team VCI would be in deep yogurt.

"Just how much charm did you use on her?" I asked.

Sam raised his hands over his head. "I never touched her, so help me. Hell, I never even took her out to dinner without Larry coming with us."

"Did he have acne back in Texas?"

"Yeah. I think they're both virgins." Sam said it as if it were a crime.

I can see now, with twenty-twenty hindsight, that what I should have done was buddy up to Larry, give him a few pointers about personal grooming and manners. The kid was brilliant, sure, but his idea of evening wear was an unwashed T-shirt and a pair of cutoffs. And he was so damned shy that he hid behind his computer just about all the time. He never went anywhere and he never did anything except massage his computer. And eat junk food. He had that dead-fish complexion of a guy in solitary confinement. He was about as much fun as staring at a blank wall.

To tell the truth, I just couldn't see myself buddying up to the kid. So, instead, I made the mistake of trying to get Melinda interested in me, rather than Sam. I invited her out to dinner. That's all it took. I didn't even hold her hand, but the next morning there was a love poem on my desk, signed with a flowery M. And Larry didn't show up in the office.

"Where is he?" Sam snapped the minute he entered the office—around ten-thirty. He headed straight for his desk, which I called "Mount Blanc," because of the mountain of paperwork heaped on top of it. Sam paid practically no attention to any incoming paper. The mountain just grew bigger. How he ever found anything in that pile I never knew, but whenever I couldn't find some form or some piece of important correspondence, Sam would rummage through the mountain and pull out the right piece of paper in half a minute.

Neither Melinda nor I answered Sam's question. I didn't know where the kid was. Melinda was watching me shyly from behind her computer. Then I realized that Larry's desk was bare. He had taken his computer.

"Where the hell is he?" Sam screeched.

It took me about ten seconds to figure out what had happened. Ten seconds, plus reading Melinda's poem. It was pretty awful. Can you imagine a poem that rhymes *dinner, winner,* and *thinner*?

"Where the hell is Larry?" Sam asked her directly.

She shrugged from behind her computer screen. "He's very immature," she said, batting her eyelashes at me. Good Lord, I realized that she was wearing makeup. Lots of it.

"Of all the gin joints in all the towns in all the world," Sam growled, scurrying from behind his desk and heading for the door. "Come on, Mutt! I've got to meet Bonnie Jo at the airport and you've got to find that kid before he runs back to Texas!"

"Bonnie Jo?" I called after him. I flicked my phone console to automatic answer and then dashed out after him. Melinda sat where she had been since eight that morning; her only exercise was reaching for a bag of nacho chips.

Bonnie Jo Murtchison was the daughter of our financial backer, the banker who wanted his daughter married.

"She's coming in on the eleven o'clock plane," Sam said over his shoulder as we rattled down the stairs and ran out to his leased Jaguar convertible. I never saw it with the top up, yet somehow it was always under shelter when Florida decided to have a cloudburst. Sam was uncanny that way.

"You'll never make it to the airport by eleven," I said, vaulting over the Jag's door.

Sam gave me a sour look as he slid behind the wheel. "And when's the last time *any* goddamned commercial airliner arrived on schedule?"

He had a point there.

The apartment that Larry and Melinda shared was on the way to the airport. Sam's intention was to drop me off, assuming Larry was still there, and hustle on to the airport.

We spotted him on the driveway of the old frame three-story house, packing all his belongings into their battered old Volvo station wagon. As far as I could see, Larry's belongings consisted of one duffel bag of clothes and seventeen cartons of computer hardware and documentation books.

He was just getting into the car when we pulled up and blocked the driveway, just like the highway patrol.

"Where're you going?" Sam yelped as he bounded out of the Jag. I followed behind, my boots crunching on the driveway's gravel.

The three of us looked like a set of Russian dolls, the kind that fit one inside of the other. Sam stood about shoulder-high to Larry, who stood little more than shoulder-high to me.

"Back to Texas," he said, his voice kind of cracking. "You want Melinda, she's all yours."

"I don't want her!" Sam said. "I want her to stop pestering me, for cryin' out loud."

Larry put down the cardboard carton he was carrying on the tailgate of the Volvo and drew himself up to his full height.

"She's not interested in you anymore, Mr. Gunn. She's gone batty over this guy." He jutted his lower lip at me.

For a ridiculous instant I felt like a gunslinger in a western, about to be challenged by a callow youth.

"Listen, son," I said as reasonably as I could, "I was just trying to get her mind off Sam."

He kind of sagged, as if he'd been holding himself together for so long that his strength had given out. I thought he might drop to the ground and start crying.

But he didn't. "Sam, you—what's the difference? She doesn't like me anymore. I guess she never really liked me in the first place."

I looked at Sam and he looked at me. Then he got a sort of strange, benign smile on his face, an almost saintly kind of expression I had never seen on Sam before.

He went over to Larry and slid an arm around the kid's skinny shoulders, as much to prop him up as anything else. "Larry," he asked in a quiet, kindly sort of voice, "have you ever heard of a fella named Cyrano de Bergerac?"

"Who?"

"Cyrano?" Jade looked sharply into Johansen's sparkling blue eyes.

"You know the play?" he asked.

"I played Roxane in our high-school drama class," she said.

"Oh." Johansen looked slightly uncomfortable. "I think I saw it on video once. Had a lot of sword fighting in it."

She sighed and nodded. "Yes, a lot of sword fighting. And Cyrano coached Christian so that he could win Roxane's heart—even though Cyrano loved her himself."

Johansen nodded back at her. "Yep. That's just what Sam did. Or at least, that's what he got me to do."

It was sheer desperation—Johansen continued. Without Larry we'd never be able to build our hardware on the schedule we had promised in our proposal. Or maybe not at all.

"Don't worry about a thing," Sam told the kid, right there in the driveway. "Mutt and I know everything there is to know about women. With us helping you, she'll fall into your arms in no time flat."

The kid's face reddened. "I get kind of tongue-tied when I t-try to t-talk sw-sw-sweet to her."

Sam stared at the kid. A stuttering lover? It didn't look good.

Then I got the idea of the century. "Why don't you talk to her through your computers?"

Larry got really excited about that. Computers were something he understood and trusted. As long as he didn't have to actually speak to her face-to-face he could say anything we gave him.

"Okay," Sam said, glancing at his wristwatch. "Mutt, you take our lovesick friend here to the library and borrow as many poetry books as they'll let you take out. I gotta get to the airport and meet Bonnie Jo."

Melinda looked surprised when we came back into the office; those big brown eyes of hers flashed wide. But then she stuck her nose into her computer screen and began pecking at the keyboard as fast as her chubby little fingers would go.

It was getting near to noon. I went to my desk and ran off the phone's answering machine. There was only one call, from Sam. Bonnie Jo's plane from Salt Lake City was running late. Delays and congestion in Dallas.

So what else is new? I sat Larry down at his desk and helped him unfold his computer and set it up again. Melinda glanced at us from time to time, but whenever she saw me looking she quickly snapped her eyes back to her own screen.

Larry hadn't said a word to her. While he checked out his machine I thumbed madly through one of the poetry books. God almighty, I hadn't even looked at that stuff since they made me read it in high-school English classes. I ran across one that I vaguely remembered.

Without speaking, I showed the page to Larry, then left the book on his desk and went over to my own, next to the window. As nonchalantly as I could I booted up my own machine, waiting to see if the kid actually worked up the nerve to send the poem to Melinda, sitting four and a half feet away from him.

Sure enough, the words began to scroll across the screen: "Come live with me and be my Love . . ."

I don't know what Melinda was working on, but I guess when she saw the message light blink on her machine she automatically set the screen to receive it.

Her eyes went *really* wide. Her mouth dropped open as she read the lines of poetry scrolling onto her screen. To make sure she didn't think they were coming from me, I picked up the telephone and tapped the first button on my automatic dialer. Some guy's bored voice told me that the day's high would be eighty-two, with an seventy-five percent chance of showers in the afternoon.

Melinda looked at me kind of puzzled. I ignored her and looked out my window, where I could watch her reflection without her knowing it. I saw a suspicion on her face slowly dawn into certainty. She turned and looked at Larry, who promptly turned flame-red.

A good beginning, I thought.

Then Sam burst into the office, towing Bonnie Jo Murtchison.

When it came to women Sam was truly democratic. Tall or short, plump or anorexic, Sam made no distinctions based on race, creed, color, or previous condition of servitude. But he did seem to hit on blondes preferentially.

Bonnie Jo Murtchison was blond, the kind of golden blond with almost reddish highlights that is one of the triumphs of modern cosmetic chemistry. Her hair was frizzed, shoulder-length, but pushed back off her face enough to show two enormous bangle earrings. She had a slight figure, almost boyish. Good legs, long and strong and nicely tanned. A good tennis player, I thought. That was the first thing that popped into my mind when I saw her.

She was wearing a neat little miniskirted sleeveless frock of butter-yellow, the kind that costs a week's pay. More jewelry on her wrists and fingers, necklaces dangling down her slim bosom. She clattered and jangled as she came into the office, towering over Sam by a good five–six inches.

The perfect spoiled princess, I thought at once. Rich father, beautiful mother, and no brothers or sisters. What a pain in the butt she's going to be.

I was right, but for all the wrong reasons.

The first thing that really jolted me about Bonnie Jo was her voice. I expected the kind of shrill yapping that you hear from the cuties around the condo swimming pool; you know, the ones who won't go into the water because it'd mess up the hairdo they just spent all morning on.

Bonnie Jo's voice was low and ladylike. Not quite husky, and certainly not soft. Controlled. Strong. She didn't hurt your ears when she talked.

Sam introduced her to Larry, who mumbled and avoided her eyes, and to Melinda, who looked her over like a professional prizefighter assessing a new opponent. Then he brought her across the room to my desk.

"This is our president, Spence Johansen," Sam said. "I call him Mutt."

She reached across the desk to take my hand in a firm grip. Her eyes were gray-green, a color that haunted me so much I looked it up in a book on precious stones at the local library. The color of Brazilian tourmaline: deep, mysterious, powerful grayish-green.

"And what would you like me to call you, Mr. Johansen?" she asked in that marvelous voice.

She just sort of naturally drew a smile out of me. "Spence will be fine," I said.

"Good. I'm Bonnie Jo."

I think I fell in love with her right then and there.

"That was pretty quick," Jade sniffed.

Johansen shrugged. "It happens that way, sometimes."

"Really?"

"Haven't you ever fallen in love at first sight?"

She tried to conjure up Raki's image in her mind. The drinks she had been swilling made her head spin slightly.

"Yes, I guess I have, at that," she said at last. That smile of his made her head swim even more.

Johansen looked out across the grassy hills that stretched below them to the edge of the toylike village. Sunlight filtering through the big solar windows slanted long shadows down there.

"It's going to be sunset pretty soon," he said. "I know

a fine little restaurant down in Gunnstown, if you're ready for dinner."

"Gunnstown?" she asked.

"That's the name of the village down there." He pointed with an outstretched arm.

"Should I change?"

Grinning, "I like you the way you are."

"My clothes," she said.

He cocked his head slightly. "It's a very nice little continental restaurant. Tablecloths and candles, that sort of thing."

She said. "Meet me at my hotel room in an hour."

When he called for her, precisely one hour later, Johansen was wearing a comfortable pair of soft blue slacks and a slate-gray velour pullover, the closest thing to formal attire on the space habitat. Jade had shopped furiously in Gunnstown's two and only boutiques until she found a miniskirted sleeveless frock of butter-yellow.

Once they were sitting across a tiny table, with a softly glowing candle between them, she saw that Johansen was staring at her intently.

Almost uncomfortable, Jade tried to return to the subject of Sam Gunn.

But Johansen said, "Your eyes are beautiful, you know? The prettiest I've ever seen."

Silently Jade retorted, Prettier than Bonnie Jo's? But she dared not say it aloud. Instead, she said: "Just before you suggested dinner, you were telling me about Bonnie Jo." Jade struggled to keep her voice even. "About falling in love with her."

It wasn't a tough thing to do—Johansen replied. I had expected a spoiled rich kid. Her father, the banker, had insisted on having one of his own people join the VCI team as treasurer. Apparently his daughter insisted just as stubbornly that she take the job. So there she was, at the desk we shoehorned into our one little office, two feet away from mine.

She had degrees in economics and finance from BYU, plus an MBA from Wharton. She really knew her business. And she was strictly no-nonsense. Sam wined and dined her, of course, but it didn't go any further than that, far as I could tell. I knew Sam had no real intention of getting married to anybody. I didn't think she did, either. Or if she did, she was willing to wait until VCI started making big bucks.

We were all living practically hand-to-mouth, with every cent we got from the government and from Bonnie Jo's father's bank poured into building the hardware for removing debris from orbit. Bonnie Jo was never hurting for spending money, of course, but she never lorded it over us. The weeks rolled by and we sort of became a real team: you know, working together every day, almost living together, you come to know and respect each other. Or you explode.

Bonnie Jo even started helping Melinda in her personal life. Gave her hints about her clothes. Even went on a diet with her; not that Bonnie Jo needed it, but Melinda actually started to slim down a little. They started going to exercise classes down the way in the shopping mall.

I was giving myself a cram course in romantic poetry and passing it all on to Larry. On Valentine's Day he wanted to give Melinda a big heart-shaped box of chocolates. I suggested flowers, instead. I figured she wouldn't eat flowers, although I wasn't altogether certain.

"And write a note on the card they put in with the flowers," I insisted.

He gulped. "Sh-should I s-s-s-sign my n-n-name?"

"Damned right."

Larry turned pale. But I marched him to the florist section of the supermarket and we picked out a dozen posies for her. I towed him to the counter where they had a little box full of blank cards. I handed him my government-issue ballpoint pen, guaranteed to write underwater or in zero gravity.

He looked at me, panic-stricken. "Wh-what'll I say?"

I thought for a second. " 'To the woman who has captured my heart,' " I told him.

He scribbled on the little card. His handwriting was awful.

"Sign it."

He stared at me.

"Better yet," I said. "Just put your initial. Just an 'L.' "

He did that. We snuck the bouquet into the office while Melinda and Bonnie Jo were out at their exercise class. Larry laid the flowers on her desk with a trembling hand.

Well, the last time I had watched a scene like what followed was in an old video called *Love Is a Many Splendored Thing*. Melinda sort of went into shock when she saw the flowers on her desk, but only for a moment. She read the card, then spun around toward Larry—who looked white as a sheet, scared—and launched herself at him. Knocked him right off his desk chair.

Sam gave them the rest of the day off. It was Friday, so they had the whole weekend to themselves.

A few minutes after the lovers left the office, Sam frowned at his computer screen.

"I gotta check out the superconducting coils down at the Cape," he said. "Those suckers in Massachusetts finally delivered them. Arrived this morning."

Two weeks late. Not good, but within the tolerable limits we had set in our schedule. The manufacturer in Massachusetts had called a couple months earlier and said that delivery would be three months late, due to a big order they had to rush for Rockledge International.

Sam had screamed so loud and long into the phone that I thought every fiber-optic cable between Florida and Massachusetts would have melted. The connection actually broke down three times before he finished convincing our manufacturing subcontractor that: (a) their contract with us had heavy penalty clauses for late delivery; (b) since this order from Rockledge had come in *after* our order we clearly had priority; and (c) this was obviously an attempt by Rockledge to sabotage us.

"Tell your goddamned lawyers to stock up on No Doz," Sam yelled into the phone. "I'm going to sue you sneaking, thieving bastards sixteen ways from Sunday! You'll go down the tubes, buddy. Bankrupt. Broke. Dead in the water. Kaput! You just watch!"

He slammed the phone down hard enough to make the papers on my desk bounce.

"But, Sam," I pleaded, "if you tie them up or shut

them down *we'll* go out of business with them. We need
that superconducting coil. And the backup."

A sly grin eased across his face. "Don'tcha think I
know that? I'm just putting the fear of lawyers into them.
Now," he reached for the phone again, "to put the fear of
God almighty into them."

I didn't eavesdrop on purpose, but our desks were
jammed so close together that I couldn't help hearing him
ask for Albert Clement. At the Department of Commerce.

Sam's tone changed enormously. He was stiffly formal
with Clement, almost respectful, explaining the situation
and his suspicion that Rockledge was trying to club us to
death with their money. I wondered if this guy Clement
was the same Commerce Department undertaker who had
been at the evaluation hearing in D.C.

Well, it all got straightened out. The next day I got a
very apologetic phone call from the director of contracts at
the Massachusetts firm, some guy with an Armenian name.
Terrible misunderstanding. Of course they wouldn't let this
enormous order from Rockledge get in the way of deliver-
ing what they had promised to us. On schedule, absolutely.
Maybe a week or so late, nothing more than that. Guaranteed. On his mother's grave.

I said nice things back to him, like "Uh-huh. That's
fine. I'm glad to hear it." Sam was watching me, grinning
from ear to ear.

The guy's voice dropped a note lower, as if he was
afraid he'd be overheard. "It's so much pleasanter dealing
with you than that Mr. Gunn," he said. "He's so excitable!"

"Well, I'm the president of the firm," I said back to
him, while Sam held both hands over his mouth to stifle
his guffaws. "Whenever a problem arises, feel free to call
me."

He thanked me three dozen times.

I no sooner had put the phone down than it rang
again. Pierre D'Argent, calling from Rockledge headquarters in Pennsylvania.

In a smarmy, oily voice he professed shock and surprise that *anyone* would think that Rockledge was trying to
sabotage a smaller competitor. I motioned for Sam to pick
up his phone and listen in.

"We would never stoop to anything like that," he assured me. "There's no need for anyone to get hysterical."

"Well," I said, "it seemed strange to us that Rockledge placed such a large order with the outfit that's making our teeny little coils, and then tried to muscle them into shunting our work aside."

"We never did that," D'Argent replied, like a saint accused of rifling the poor box. "It's all a misunderstanding."

Sam said sweetly into his phone, "We've subpoenaed their records, Oh silver-tongued devil."

"What? Who is that? Gunn, is that you?"

"See you in Leavenworth, Pee-air."

D'Argent hung up so hard I thought a gun had gone off in my ear. Sam fell off his chair laughing and rolled on the floor, holding his middle and kicking his feet in the air. We had not subpoenaed anybody for anything, but it cost Rockledge a week's worth of extremely expensive legal staff work to find that out.

Anyway, that had happened months earlier, and now the superconducting coils had finally arrived at the Cape and Sam had to buzz over there to inspect them. Leaving Bonnie Jo and me alone in the office. Friday afternoon. The weekend looming.

I did my level best to avoid her. She was staying at the Marriott hotel in Titusville, so I steered clear of the whole town. Kept to myself in my little rattrap of a one-room apartment. Worked on my laptop all day Saturday, ate a microwaved dinner, watched TV. Then worked some more. Did not phone her, although I thought about it now and then. Maybe once every other minute.

Sunday it rained hard. I started to feel like a convict in prison. By noontime I had convinced myself that there was work to do in the office; anything to get out of my room. It was pouring so thick I got soaked running from my parking space to the covered stairs that led up to our office. First thing I did there was phone Sam's hotel down at the Cape. Checked out. Then I phoned his apartment. Not there.

I slid into my desk chair, squishing wet. Okay. He's back from the Cape. He's with Bonnie Jo. Good. I guess.

But I guessed wrong, because Bonnie Jo came into

the office, brighter than sunshine in a bright yellow slicker and plastic rain hat.

"Oh," she said. "I didn't know you'd be here."

"Where's Sam?" I asked her.

She peeled off the hat and slicker. "I thought he'd be here. Probably he stayed at the Cape for the weekend."

"Yeah. He's got a lot of old buddies at the Cape."

"And girlfriends?"

"Uh, no. Not really." I was never much good at shading the truth.

Bonnie Jo sat at her desk and picked up the phone. "Highway patrol," she said to the dialing assistance computer program.

She saw my eyebrows hike up.

"On a stormy day like this, maybe he drove off the road."

The highway patrol had no accidents to report between where we were and the Cape. I puffed out a little sigh of relief. Bonnie Jo put the phone down with a bit of a dark frown on her pretty face.

"You worry about Sam that much?" I asked her.

"My job is to protect my daddy's investment," she said. "And my own."

Well, one thing led to another and before I knew it we were having dinner together in the Japanese restaurant down at the end of the mall. I had to teach Bonnie Jo how to use chopsticks. She caught on real fast. Quick learner.

"Are you two engaged, or what?" I heard myself ask her.

She smiled, kind of sad, almost. "It depends on who you ask. My father considers us engaged, although Sam has never actually popped the question to me."

"And what do you think?"

Her eyes went distant. "Sam is going to be a very rich man someday. He has the energy and drive and willingness to swim against the tide that will make him a multimillionaire, eventually. If somebody doesn't strangle him first."

"So that makes him a good marriage prospect."

Her unhappy little smile came back. "Sam will make a terrible husband. He's a womanizer who doesn't give a thought to anybody but himself. He's lots of fun to be with, but he'd be hell to be married to."

"Then why . . . ?"

"I already told you. To protect my daddy's invest-ment."

"You'd *marry* him? For that?"

"Why not? He'll have his flings, I'll have mine. As long as I can present my daddy with a grandson, everyone will be satisfied."

"But . . . love. What about love?"

Her smile turned bitter. "You mean like Melinda and Larry? That's for the peasants. In my family marriage is a business proposition."

I dropped the chunk of sushi in my chopsticks right into my lap.

Bonnie Jo leaned across the little table. "You're really a very romantic guy, aren't you, Spence? Have I shocked you?"

"Uh, no, not . . . well, I guess I never met a woman with your outlook on life."

"Never dated an MBA before?" Her eyes sparkled with amusement now. She was teasing me.

"Can't say that I have."

She leaned closer. "Sam's out at the Cape chasing cocktail waitresses and barmaids. Maybe I ought to go to a bar and see what I can pick up."

"Maybe you ought to go home before you pick up something that'll increase your father's health insurance premiums," I said, suddenly feeling sore at her.

She gave me a long look. "Maybe I should, at that."

And that was our dinner together. I never touched her. I never told Sam about it. But the next morning when he showed up at the office looking like every blue Monday morning in the history of the world—bleary-eyed, pasty-faced, muttering about vitamin E—I knew I couldn't hang around there with Bonnie Jo so close.

Melinda and Larry arrived hand in hand. I swear his stuttering had cleared up almost entirely in just that one weekend. Bonnie Jo came in around ten, took a silent look at Sam, and went to her desk as cool as liquid nitrogen.

Sam was inhaling coffee and orange juice in roughly equal quantities.

"Sam," I said, my voice so loud that it startled me, "since I'm president of this outfit, I've just made an executive decision."

He looked over toward me with bloodshot eyes.

"I'm going over to the Cape," I announced.

"I was just there," he croaked.

"I mean to stay. Hardware's starting to arrive. We need somebody to direct the assembly technicians, somebody there on the scene all the time, not just once a week. Somebody with the power to make decisions."

"The techs know what they're doing better than you do, Mutt," argued Sam. "If they run into any problems they've got phones, modems, faxes—they can even use the agency's video link if they have to."

"It'll be better if I'm on the scene," I insisted, trying not to look at Bonnie Jo. "We can settle questions before they become problems."

Sam shook his head stubbornly. "We haven't budgeted for you to be living in a hotel at the Cape. You know how tight everything is."

"The budget can be stretched," Bonnie Jo said. "I think Spence is right. His being on the Cape could save us a lot of problems."

Sam's head swiveled from her to me and back to her again. He looked puzzled, not suspicious. Finally he shrugged good-naturedly and said, "Okay, as long as it won't bust the bank."

So I moved to the Cape. During the weeks I was there supervising the assembly and checkout of our equipment I actually did save a couple of minor glitches from growing into real headaches. Larry drove over once a week to check the hardware against his design; then he'd drive back to Melinda again that evening. I knew I could justify the expenses legitimately, if it came to that. Most important, though, was that I had put some miles between myself and Bonnie Jo. And she must have realized how attracted I was to her, because she convinced Sam I should get away.

A couple of my old agency buddies snuck me some

time on the OMV simulator, so I spent my evenings and spare weekends brushing up on my flying. Our official program didn't call for any use of orbital maneuvering vehicles. What we had proposed was to set up our magnetic bumper on the forward end of space station Freedom and see how well it deflected junk out of the station's orbital path. Called for some EVA work, but we wouldn't need to fly OMVs.

But Sam had warned me to be prepared for flying an OMV, back when we first started writing the proposal.

"Whattaya think we oughtta do," he had asked me, "if we scoop up something valuable?"

"Valuable?" I had asked.

"Like that glove Ed White lost. Or the famous Hasselblad camera from back in the Gemini days."

I stared at him. "Sam, those things reentered and burned up years ago."

"Yeah, yeah, I know." He flapped an annoyed hand in the air. "But suppose—just suppose, now—that we scoop up something like that."

We had been sitting in our favorite booth in our favorite bar. Sam liked Corona in those days; slices of lime were littered across his side of the table, with little plastic spears stuck in their sides. They looked like tiny green harpooned whales. Me, I liked beer with more flavor to it: Bass ale was my favorite.

Anyway, I thought his question was silly.

"In the first place," I said, "the magnetic field won't scoop up objects, it'll deflect them away from the path of the station. Most of them will be bounced into orbits that'll spiral into the atmosphere. They'll reenter and burn up."

"But suppose we got to something really *valuable*," Sam insisted. "Like a spacer section from the Brazilian booster. Or a piece of that European upper stage that blew up. Analysts would pay good money to get their hands on junk like that."

"Analysts?"

"In Washington," Sam said. "Or Paris, for that matter. Hell, even our buddy D'Argent would like to be able to present his Rockledge lab boys with chunks of the competition's hardware."

I had never thought of that.

"Then there's the museums," Sam went on, kind of dreamy, the way he always gets when he's thinking big. "How much would the Smithsonian pay for the *Eagle*?"

"The Apollo 11 lunar module?"

"It's lower section is still up there, sitting on the Sea of Tranquility."

"But that's the Moon, Sam. A quarter-million miles away from where we'll be!"

He gave me his sly grin. "Brush up on your flying, Mutt. There are interesting times ahead. Ve-r-r-y interesting."

I could see taking an OMV from the space station and flitting out to retrieve some hunk of debris that looked important or maybe valuable. So I spent as many of my hours at the Cape as possible in the OMV simulator. It helped to keep me busy; helped me to not think about Bonnie Jo.

At first I thought it was an accident when I bumped into Pierre D'Argent in the Shuttle Lounge. It was late in the afternoon, too soon for the after-work crowd. The lounge was cool and so dark that you could break your neck tripping over cocktail tables before your eyes adjusted from the summer glare outside.

I actually did bump into D'Argent. He was sitting with his back to the aisle between tables, wearing an expensive dark suit that blended into the shadows so well I just didn't see him.

I started to apologize, then my eyes finally adjusted to the dimness and I saw who he was.

"Mr. Johansen!" He professed surprise and asked me to join him.

So I sat at his little table. With my back to the wall. Just the two of us, although there were a few regulars up at the bar watching a baseball game from Japan.

I ordered a Bass. D'Argent already had a tall frosted glass of something in front of him, decorated with enough fruit slices to start a plantation. And a little paper umbrella.

"Your friend Gunn sent our legal department into quite a spin," he said, smiling with his teeth.

"Sam's a very emotional guy," I said as the waitress

brought my ale. She was a cute little thing, in a low-cut black outfit with a teeny-tiny skirt.

"Yes, he is indeed." D'Argent let out a sigh. "I'm afraid Mr. Gunn has no clear idea of where his own best interests lie."

I took a sip of ale instead of trying to answer.

"Now you, Mr. Johansen," he went on, "you look like someone who understands where your best interests lie."

All I could think of to say was "Really?"

"Really." D'Argent leaned back in his chair, looking like a cool million on the hoof: elegant from his slicked-back salt-and-pepper hair to the tips of his Gucci suede loafers.

"I must confess that I thought your technical proposal was little short of daring. Much better than the job my own technical people did. They were far too conservative. Far too."

Was he pumping me for information? I mumbled something noncommittal and let him go on talking.

"In fact," he said, smiling at me over his fruit salad, "I think your technical approach is brilliant. Breathtaking."

The smile was very slick. He was insurance-salesman handsome. Trim gray mustache neatly clipped; expensive silk suit, dark gray. I couldn't tell the color of his eyes, the lighting in the lounge was too dim, but I expect they were gray, too.

I shrugged off his compliment. But he persisted. "A magnetic deflector system actually mounted on the space station. Very daring. Very original."

"It was Sam's idea," I said, trying to needle him.

It didn't faze him a bit. "It was actually the idea of Professor Luke Steckler, of Texas A&M. Our people saw his paper in the technical literature, but they didn't have the guts to use the idea. You did."

"Sam did."

He hiked his eyebrows a bit. They were gray, of course. "You're much too modest, Spence. You don't mind if I call you Spence, do you?"

I did mind. I suddenly felt like I was in the grip of a very slick used-car salesman. But I shook my head and hid behind my mug of ale.

D'Argent said, "Spence, I know that my technical people at Rockledge would love to have you join their team. They need some daring, someone willing to take chances."

I guess my eyebrows went up, too.

Leaning forward over the tiny table, D'Argent added in a whisper, "And we'll pay you twice what Gunn is paying."

I blinked. Twice.

The lounge was slowly filling up with "happy hour" customers: mostly engineers from the base and sales people trying to sell them stuff. They all talked low, almost in whispers. At least, until they got a couple of drinks into them. Then the noise volume went up and some of the wilder ones even would laugh now and then. But while I was sitting there trying to digest D'Argent's offer without spitting beer in his face, I could still hear the soft-rock music coming through the ceiling speakers, something old and sad by the Carpenters.

"I would like you to talk with a few of my technical people, Spence. Would you be willing to do that?"

Twice my VCI salary. And that was just for openers. It was obvious he'd be willing to go higher. Maybe a lot higher. I'd been living on Happy Hour hors d'oeuvres and junk food. I was four months behind on the rent for my seedy dump of an apartment—which was sitting empty, because of Bonnie Jo.

But I shook my head. "I'm happy with VCI." *Happy* wasn't exactly the right word, but I couldn't leave Sam in the lurch. On the other hand, this might be the best way to make a break with Bonnie Jo.

Turning slightly in his chair, D'Argent sort of nodded toward a trio of guys in suits sitting a few tables away from us.

"I've taken the liberty of asking a few of my technical people to come here to meet you. Would you be willing to talk with them, Spence? Just for a few minutes."

Son of a bitch! It was no accident that we bumped into each other. It was a planned ambush.

"I think, with your help, we can adapt the magnetic bumper concept easily enough," he was saying, silky-smooth. "We'd even pay you a sizable bonus for joining Rockledge: say, a year's salary."

They wanted to steal Sam's idea and squeeze him out of the picture. And they thought I'd help them do it. For money.

I got to my feet. "Mr. D'Argent, Rockledge doesn't have enough money in its whole damned corporate treasury to buy me away from VCI."

D'Argent shrugged, very European-like, and made a disappointed sigh. "Very well, although your future would be much more secure with Rockledge than with a con man such as Mr. Gunn."

Through gritted teeth I said, "I'll take my chances with Sam." And I stalked out of the lounge, leaving him sitting there.

"That was a pretty noble thing to do," Jade said.

They were more than halfway through their dinners. She had ordered trout from the habitat's aquaculture tanks. Johansen was eating braised rabbit. Jade had to remind herself that rabbit was bred for meat here in the space habitat, just as it was on Selene. But she had never eaten rabbit at home and she could not bring herself to order it here.

"Nothing noble about it," he said easily. "It made me feel kind of slimy just to be sitting at the same table with D'Argent. Working with the ... gentleman, well, I just couldn't do it."

"Even though you were trying to get away from Bonnie Jo."

He shook his head slightly, as if disappointed with himself. "That was the really tough part. I wanted to get away from her and I wanted to be with her, both at the same time."

"So what did you do?"

He grinned. "I got away. I went up to space station Freedom."

Sam had served aboard Freedom when he'd been in the agency—Johansen explained. He was definitely persona non grata there, as far as the bureaucrats in Washing-

ton and the Cape were concerned, even though all the
working stiffs—the astronauts and mission specialists—
they all asked me how he was and when he would be coming up. Especially a couple of the women astronauts.

Living aboard Freedom was sort of like living in a bad
hotel, without gravity. The quarters were cramped, there
was precious little privacy, the hot water was only luke-
warm, and the food was as bland as only a government
agency can make it. I spent ten–twelve hours a day inside
a space suit, strapped into an MMU—a manned maneuvering unit—assembling our equipment on a special boom
outside the station.

The agency insisted that the magnetic field could not
be turned on until every experiment being run inside the
lab module was completed. Despite all our calculations
and simulations (including a week's worth of dry run on
the station mock-up in Huntsville) the agency brass was
worried that our magnetic field might screw up some delicate experiment the scientists were doing. It occurred to
me that they didn't seem worried about screwing up the
station's own instrumentation or life-support systems. That
would just have threatened the lives of astronauts and mission specialists, not important people like university scientists on their campuses.

Anyway, after eleven days of living in that zero-gee
tin can I got the go-ahead from mission control to turn on
the magnetic field. Maybe the fact that one of the big solar
panels got dinged with a stray chunk of junk hurried their
decision. The panel damage cut the station's electrical
power by a couple of kilowatts.

Rockledge had already launched two of their nerf
balls, one on a shuttle mission and the other from one of
their own little commercial boosters. They were put into
orbits opposite in direction to the flow of all the junk floating around, sort of like setting them to swim upstream.

Right away they started having troubles. The first nerf
ball expanded only partway. Instead of knocking debris out
of orbit it became a piece of junk itself, useless and beyond anybody's control. The second one performed okay,
although the instrumentation aboard it showed that it was
getting sliced up by some of the bigger pieces of junk.

Rather than being nudged out of orbit when they hit the sticky balloon, they just rammed right through it and came out the other end. Maybe they got slowed enough to start spiraling in toward reentry. But it wouldn't take more than a couple of weeks before the nerf ball was ripped to shreds—and became still yet another piece of orbiting junk.

"They're part of the problem," I said to Sam over the station's videophone link, "instead of being part of the solution."

Sam's round face grinned like a jack-o'-lantern. "So that's why D'Argent's looking like a stockbroker on Black Tuesday."

"He's got a lot to be worried about," I said.

Sam cackled happily. Then, lowering his voice, he said, "A friend of mine at the tracking center says the old original Vanguard satellite is going to reenter in a couple weeks."

"The one they launched in '58?"

"Yep. It's only a couple of pounds. They called it the grapefruit back then."

I looked over my shoulder at Freedom's crew members working at their stations. I was in the command module, standing in front of the videophone screen with my stockinged feet anchored in floor loops to keep me from floating around the place weightlessly. The crew—two men and a woman—were paying attention to their jobs, not to me. But still . . .

"Sam," I said in a near whisper, "you want me to try to retrieve it?"

"Do you have any idea of what the Smithsonian will pay for it?" he whispered back. "Or the *Japanese*?"

I felt like a fighter pilot being asked to take on a risky mission. "Shoot me the orbital data. I'll see what I can do."

It took a lot of good-natured wheedling and sweet-talking before Freedom's commander allowed me to use one of the station's OMVs. There was a provision for it in our contract, of course, but the station commander had the right to make the decision as to whether VCI might actually use one of the little flitters. She was a strong-willed professional astronaut; I'd known her for years and we'd even dated now and then. She made me promise her the Moon, just about. But at last she agreed.

The orbital maneuvering vehicles were sort of in-between the MMUs that you could strap onto your back and the orbital transfer vehicles that were big enough for a couple of guys to go all the way to GEO. The OMVs were stripped-down little platforms with an unpressurized cockpit, a pair of extensible arms with grippers on their ends, and a rocket motor hanging out the rear end.

I snatched the old Vanguard grapefruit without much trouble, saving it from a fiery death after it had spent more than half a century in space. It was just about the size and shape of a grapefruit, with a metal skin that had been blackened by years of exposure to high-energy radiation. Its solar cells had gone dead decades ago.

Anyway, Sam was so jubilant that he arranged to come up to Freedom in person to take the satellite back to Earth. Under his instructions I had not brought the grapefruit inside the station; instead I stored it in one of the racks built into the station's exterior framework. Sam was bringing up a special sealed vacuum container to bring the satellite back to the ground without letting it get contaminated by air.

Sam was coming up on one of the regular shuttle resupply flights. Since there wasn't any room for more personnel aboard the station he would only stay long enough to take the Vanguard satellite and bring it back to Earth with him.

That was the plan, anyway.

Well, the news that a private company had recaptured the old satellite hit the media like a Washington scandal. Sam was suddenly hot news, proclaiming the right of salvage in space while all sorts of lawyers from government agencies and university campuses argued that the satellite by rights belongs to the government. The idea of *selling* it to the Smithsonian or some other museum seemed to outrage them.

I saw Sam on the evening TV news the night before he came up to the station. Instead of playing the little guy being picked on by the big bullies, Sam went on the attack.

"That grapefruit's been floating around up there as dead as a doornail since before I was born," he said to the blonde who was interviewing him. "My people located it, my people went out and grabbed it. Not the government. Not some college professor who never even heard of the Vanguard 1958b until last week. My people. VCI. Part of S. Gunn Enterprises, Unlimited."

The interviewer objected, "But you used government facilities . . ."

"We are *leasing* government facilities, lady. We pay for their use."

"But that satellite was paid for by the American taxpayer."

"It was nothing but useless junk. It went unclaimed for decades. The law of salvage says whoever gets it, owns it."

"But the law of salvage is from maritime law. No one has extended the law of salvage into space."

"They have now!" Sam grinned wickedly into the camera.

It didn't help, of course, when some Japanese billionaire offered thirty million yen for the satellite.

Next thing you know, the shuttle resupply flight has no less than five guests aboard. They had to bump an astronomer who was coming up to start a series of observations and a medical doctor who was scheduled to replace the medic who'd been serving aboard the station for ninety days.

Five guests: Sam, Ed Zane from the space agency, Albert Clement from the Department of Commerce, Pierre D'Argent of Rock-by-damn-ledge.

And Bonnie Jo Murtchison.

Sam was coming up to claim the satellite, of course. Zane and Clement were there at the request of the White House to investigate this matter of space salvage before Sam could peddle the satellite to anyone—especially the Japs. I wasn't quite sure what the hell D'Argent was doing there, but I knew he'd be up to no good. And Bonnie Jo?

"I'm here to protect my investment." She smiled when I asked her why she'd come.

"How did you get them to allow you . . . ?"

We were alone in the shuttle's mid-deck compartment, where she and Sam and the other visitors would be sleeping until the shuttle undocked from the station and returned to Earth—with the satellite, although who would have ownership of the little grapefruit remained to be seen.

Bonnie Jo was wearing a light blue agency-issue flight suit that hugged her curves so well it looked like it was tailor-made for her She showed no signs of space adaptation syndrome, no hint that she was ill at ease in zero gee. Looked to me as if she enjoyed being weightless.

"How did I talk them into letting me come up here with Sam? Simple. I am now VCI's legal counsel."

She sure was beautiful. She had cropped her hair real short, almost a crew cut. Still, she looked terrific. I heard myself ask her, as if from a great distance away, "You're a lawyer, too?"

"I have a law degree from the University of Utah. Didn't I tell you?" The whole situation seemed to amuse her.

When a government employee gets an order from the White House, even if it's from some third assistant to a janitor, he jumps as high as is necessary. In the case of Zane and Clement, they had been told to settle this matter about the Vanguard satellite, and they had jumped right up to space station Freedom. Clement looked mildly upset at being in zero gravity. I think what bothered him more than anything else was that he had to wear coveralls instead of his usual chalky gray three-piece suit. Darned if he didn't find a gray flight suit, though.

Zane was really sick. The minute the shuttle went into weightlessness, Sam gleefully told me, Zane had started upchucking. The station doctor took him in tow and stuck a wad of antinausea slow-release medication pads on his neck. Still, it would take a day or more before he was well enough to convene the hearing he'd been sent to conduct.

Although the visitors were supposed to stay aboard the shuttle, Sam showed up in the command module and even wheedled permission to wriggle into a space suit and go EVA to inspect our hardware. It was working just the way we had designed it, deflecting the bits of junk and debris that floated close enough to the station to feel the influence of our magnetic bumper.

"I must confess that I didn't think it would work so well."

I turned from my console in the command module and saw Pierre D'Argent standing behind me. "Standing" is the wrong word, almost, because you don't really stand straight in zero gee; your body bends into a sort of question-mark kind of semicrouch, as if you were floating in very salty water. Unless you consciously force them down, your arms tend to drift up to chest height and hang there.

It made me uneasy to have D'Argent hanging (literally) around me. My console instruments showed that the bumper system was working within its nominal limits. I could patch the station's radar display onto my screen to see what was coming toward us, if anything. Otherwise there were only graphs to display and gauges to read. Our equipment was mounted outside and I didn't have a window. The magnetic field itself was invisible, of course.

"The debris actually gains an electrical charge while it orbits the Earth," he murmured, stroking his gray mustache as he spoke.

I said nothing.

"I wouldn't have thought the charge would be strong enough to be useful," he went on, almost as if he were talking to himself. "But then your magnetic field is very powerful, isn't it, so you can work with relatively low charge values."

I nodded.

"We're going to have to retrieve our nerf balls," he said with a sad little sigh. "The corporation will have to pay the expense of sending a team up to physically retrieve them and bring them back to Earth for study. We won't be launching any more of them until we find out where we went wrong with these."

"The basic idea is wrong," I said. "You should have gone magnetic in the first place."

"Yes," D'Argent agreed. "Yes, I see that now."

When I told Sam about our little conversation he got agitated.

"That sneaky sonofabitch is gonna try to steal it out from under us!"

"He can't do that," I said.

"And rain makes applesauce."

It all came to a head two days later, when Zane finally got well enough to convene his meeting.

It took place in the shuttle's mid-deck compartment, the six of us crammed in among the zippered sleeping bags and rows of equipment trays. Bonnie Jo anchored herself next to the only window, the little round one set into the hatch. D'Argent managed to get beside her, which made me kind of sore. I plastered my back against the airlock hatch at the rear of the compartment; that gave me enough traction to keep from floating around.

Sam, being Sam, hovered up by the ceiling, one arm wrapped casually on a rung of the ladder that led up to the cockpit. Zane and Clement strapped themselves against the rows of equipment trays that made up the front wall of the compartment.

Zane still looked unwell, even more bloated in the face than usual and queasy green. His coveralls showed off his pearlike shape. Clement seemed no different than he'd been in Washington; it was as if his surroundings made no impact on him at all. Even in a flight suit he was a thin, gray old man and nothing more.

Yet he avoided looking at Sam. And I noticed that Sam avoided looking at him. Like two conspirators who didn't want the rest of us to know that they were working secretly together.

"This is a preliminary hearing," Zane began, his voice a little shaky. "It's purpose is to make recommendations, not decisions. I will report the results of this meeting directly to the vice president, in his capacity as chairman of the Space Council."

Vice President Benford had been a scientist before going into politics. I doubted that he would look on Sam's free-enterprise salvage job with enthusiasm.

"Before we begin . . ." There was D'Argent with his finger raised in the air again.

"What's he doing here, anyway?" Sam snapped. "What's Rockledge got to do with this hearing?"

Zane had to turn his head and look up to face Sam. The effort made him pale slightly. I saw a bunch of faint rings against the skin of his neck, back behind his ear, where medication patches had been. Looked like he'd been embraced by a vampire octopus.

"Rockledge is one of the two contractors currently engaged in the orbital debris removal feasibility program," Zane said carefully, as if he was trying hard not to throw up.

Sam frowned down at Zane, then at D'Argent.

Bonnie Jo said, "VCI has no objection to Rockledge's representation at this hearing."

"We don't?" Sam snapped.

She smiled up at him. "No, we don't."

Sam muttered something that I couldn't really hear, but I could imagine what he was saying to himself.

D'Argent resumed, "I realize that this hearing has been called to examine the question of space salvage. I merely want to point out that there is a larger question involved here, also."

"A larger question?" Zane dutifully gave his straight line.

"Yes. The question of who should operate the debris removal system once the feasibility program is completed."

"Who should operate . . ." Sam turned burning red.

"After all," D'Argent went on smoothly, "the debris removal system should be used for the benefit of its sponsor—the government of the United States. It should *not* be used as a front for shady fly-by-night schemes to enrich private individuals."

Sam gave a strangled cry and launched himself at D'Argent like a guided missile. I unhooked my feet from the floor loops just in time to get a shoulder into Sam's ribs and bounce him away from D'Argent. Otherwise I think he would have torn the guy limb from limb right then and there.

Bonnie Jo yelled, "Sam, don't!" Clement seemed to faint. My shoulder felt as if something had broken in there.

And Zane threw up over all of us.

That broke up the meeting pretty effectively.

It took Bonnie Jo and me several hours to calm Sam down. He was absolutely livid. We carried him kicking and screaming out of the shuttle and into the station's wardroom, by the galley. The station physician, the guy who had to stay aboard longer than the usual ninety days because of Sam and the others commandeering the shuttle seats, came in and threatened to give him a shot of horse tranquilizer.

What really sobered Sam up was Bonnie Jo. "You damned idiot! You're just proving to those government men that you shouldn't be allowed to operate anything more sophisticated than a baby's rattle!"

He blinked at her. I had backed him up against the wall of the wardroom and was holding him by his shoulders to stop him from thrashing around. The station's doctor was sort of hovering off to one side with a huge hypodermic syringe in his hand and an expectant smile on his face. Bonnie Jo was standing squarely in front of Sam, her eyes snapping like pistols.

"I screwed up, huh?" Sam said sheepishly.

"You certainly showed Zane and Clement how mature you are," said Bonnie Jo.

"But that sonofabitch is trying to steal the whole operation right out from under us!"

"And you're helping him."

I waved the medic away. He seemed disappointed that he wouldn't have to stick a needle in Sam's anatomy. We drifted over to the table. There was only one of them in the cramped little wardroom, rising like a flat-topped toadstool from a single slim pedestal. It was chest-high; nobody used chairs in zero gee, you stuck your feet in the floor loops and let your arms drift to their natural level.

Sam hung on to the table, letting his feet dangle a few inches off the floor. He looked miserable and contrite.

Before I could say anything, the skipper poked her brunette head into the wardroom.

"Can I see you a minute, Spence?" she asked. From the look on her face I guessed it was business, and urgent.

I pushed over to her. She motioned me through the

hatch and we both headed for the command module, like a pair of swimmers coasting side by side.

"Got a problem," she said. "Mission control just got the word from the tracking center that Rockledge's damned nerf ball is on a collision course with us."

I got that sudden lurch in the gut that comes when your engine quits or you hear a hiss in your space suit.

"How the hell could it be on a collision course?" I didn't want to believe it.

She pulled herself through the hatch and swam up to her command station. Pointing to the trio of display screens mounted below the station's only observation window, she said, "Here's the data, see for yourself."

I still couldn't believe it, even though the numbers made it abundantly clear that in less than one hour the shredded remains of one of the nerf balls was going to come barreling into the station at a closing velocity of more than ten miles per second.

"It could tear a solar panel off," the commander said tightly. "It could even puncture these modules if it hits dead center."

"How the hell . . ."

"It banged into the spent final stage of the Ariane 4 that was launched last week. Got enough energy from the collision to push it up into an orbit that will intersect with ours in"—she glanced at the digital clock on her panel—"fifty-three minutes."

"The magnetic field won't deflect it," I said. "It hasn't been in space long enough to build up a static electrical charge on its skin."

"Then we'll have to abandon the station. Good thing the shuttle's still docked to us."

She moved her hand toward the communications keyboard. I grabbed it away.

"Give me five minutes. Maybe there's something we can do."

I called Sam to the command module. Bonnie Jo was right behind him. Swiftly I outlined the problem. He called Larry, back in Florida, who immediately agreed that the magnetic bumper would have no effect on the nerf ball. He didn't look terribly upset; to him this was a the-

oretical problem. I could see Melinda standing behind
him, smiling into the screen like a chubby Mona Lisa.

"There's no way we could deflect it?" Sam asked, a
little desperation in his voice.

"Not unless you could charge it up," Larry said.

"Charge it?"

"Spray it with an electron beam," he said. "That'd
give it enough of a surface charge for the magnetic field to
deflect it."

Sam cut the connection. Forty-two minutes and
counting.

"We have several electron beam guns aboard," the
skipper said. "In the lab module."

"But they're not powerful enough to charge the
damned nerf ball until it gets so close it'll hit us anyway,"
Sam muttered.

"We could go out on one of the OMVs," I heard myself suggest.

"Yeah!" Sam brightened. "Go out and push it out of
the way."

I had to shake my head. "No, Sam. That won't work.
The nerf ball is coming toward us, it's in an opposite orbit. The OMV doesn't have enough delta-vee to go out
there, turn around and match orbit with it, and then
nudge it into a lower orbit."

"You'd have to ram the OMV into it," the commander
said. "Like a kamikaze."

"No thanks," Sam said. "I'm brave but I'm not suici-
dal." He started gnawing his fingernails.

I said, "But we could go out on an OMV and give it
a good squirt with an electron gun as we passed it. Charge
it up enough for the magnetic bumper to do the job."

"You think so?"

"Forty minutes left," Bonnie Jo said. Not a quaver in
her voice. Not a half tone higher than usual. Not a hint of
fear.

The commander shook her head. "The OMVs aren't
pressurized. You don't have enough time for pre-breathe."

See, to run one of the OMVs you had to be suited up.
Since the suits were pressurized only to a third of the normal air pressure that the station used, you had to pre-

breathe oxygen for about an hour before sealing yourself inside the suit. Otherwise nitrogen bubbles would collect in your blood and you'd get the bends, just like a deep-sea diver.

"Fuck the pre-breathe," Sam snapped. "We're gonna save this goddamned station from Rockledge's runaway nerf ball."

"I can't let you do that, Sam," the skipper said. Her hand went out to the comm keyboard again.

Sam leveled a stubby finger at her. "You let us give it a shot or I'll tell everybody back at the Cape what *really* happened when we were supposed to be testing the lunar rover simulator."

Her face flushed dark red.

"Listen," Sam said jovially. "You get everybody into the shuttle and pull away from the station. Mutt and I will go out in the OMV. If we can deflect the nerf ball and save the station you'll be a hero. If not, the station gets shredded and you can give the bill to Rockledge International."

I hadn't thought of that. Who would be responsible for the destruction of this twenty-billion-dollar government installation? Who carried damage insurance on the space station?

"And the two of you will die of the bends," she said. "No, I won't allow it. I'm in charge here and . . ."

"Stick us in an airlock when we get back," Sam cajoled. "Run up the pressure. That's what they do for deep-sea divers, isn't it? You've got a medic aboard, use the jerk for something more than ramming needles into people's asses!"

"I can't, Sam!"

He looked at her coyly. "I've got videotapes from the lunar simulator, you know."

Thirty-five minutes.

The skipper gave in, of course. Sam's way was the only hope she had of saving the station. Besides, whatever they had done in the lunar simulator was something she definitely did not want broadcast. So ten minutes later Sam and I are buttoning ourselves into space suits while the skipper and one of her crew are floating an electron gun down the connecting tunnel to the airlock where the

OMVs are docked. Everybody else was already jamming themselves into the shuttle mid-deck and cockpit. It must have looked like a fraternity party in there, except that I'll bet everybody was scared into constipation.

Everybody except Bonnie Jo. She seemed to have ice water in her veins. Cool and calm under fire.

I shook my head to get rid of my thoughts about her as I pulled on the space-suit helmet. Sam was already buttoned up. My ears popped when I switched on the suit's oxygen system, but otherwise there were no bad effects.

The orbital maneuvering vehicle had a closed cockpit, but it wasn't pressurized. I lugged the electron gun and its power pack inside. "Lugged" isn't the right word, exactly. The apparatus was weightless, just like everything else. But it was bulky and awkward to handle.

Sam did the piloting. I set up the electron gun and ran through its checks. Every indicator light was green, although the best voltage I could crank out of it was a bit below max. That worried me. We'd need all the juice we could get when we whizzed past the nerf ball.

We launched off the station with a little lurch and headed toward our fleeting rendezvous with the runaway. Through my visor I saw the station dwindle behind us, two football fields long, looking sort of like a square double-ended paddle, the kind they use on kayaks, with a cluster of little cylinders huddled in its middle. Those were the habitat and lab modules. They looked small and fragile and terribly, terribly vulnerable.

For the first time in my life I paid no attention to the big beautiful curving mass of the Earth glowing huge and gorgeous below us. I had no time for sightseeing, even when the sights were the most spectacular that any human being had ever seen.

The shuttle was pulling away in the opposite direction, getting the hell out of the line of fire. Suddenly we were all alone out there, just Sam and me inside this contraption of struts and spherical tanks that we called an OMV.

"Just like a World War I airplane movie," Sam said to me over the suit radio. "I'll make a pass as close to the nerf ball as I can get. You spray it with the gun."

I nodded inside my helmet.

"Five minutes," Sam said, tapping a gloved finger on the radar display. In the false-color image of the screen the nerf ball looked like a tumbling mass of long thin filaments, barely hanging together. Something in my brain clicked; I remembered an old antimissile system called Homing Overlay that looked kind of like an umbrella that had lost its fabric. When it hit a missile nose cone it shattered the thing with the pure kinetic energy of the impact. That's what the tatters of the aluminized plastic nerf ball would do to the thin skin of the space station, if we let it hit. I could picture those great big solar panels exploding, throwing off jagged pieces that would slice up the lab and habitat modules like shards of glass going through paper walls.

"Three minutes."

I swung the cockpit hatch open and pushed the business end of the electron gun outside with my boots.

"How long will the power pack run?" I asked. "The longer we fire this thing the more chance we'll have of actually charging up the ball."

Sam must have shrugged inside his suit. "Might as well start now, Mutt. Build up a cloud that the sucker has to fly through. Won't do us a bit of good to have power still remaining once we've passed the goddamned spitball."

That made sense. I clicked the right switches and turned the power dial up to max. In the vacuum I couldn't hear whether it was humming or not, although I thought I felt a kind of vibration through my boots. All the dials said it was working, but that was scant comfort.

"One minute," Sam said. I knew he was flying our OMV as close to the nerf ball as humanly possible. Sam was as good as they came at piloting. Better than me; not by much, but better. He'd get us close enough to kiss that little sucker, I knew.

We were passing over an ocean, which one I don't know to this day. Big, wide deep blue below us, far as the eye could see, bright and glowing with long parades of teeny white clouds marching across it.

I saw something dark hurtling toward us, like a black

octopus waving all its arms, like a silent banshee coming to grab us.

"There it . . . was," Sam said.

The damned thing thrashed past us like a hypersonic bat out of hell. I looked down at the electron gun's gauges. Everything read zero. We had used up all the energy in the power pack.

"Well, either it works or it doesn't," Sam said. All of a sudden he sounded tired.

I nodded inside my helmet. I felt it, too: exhausted, totally drained. Just like the electron gun, we had given it everything we had. Now we had nothing left. We had done everything we could do. Now it was up to the laws of physics.

"We'll be back at the station in an hour," Sam said. "We'll know then."

We knew before then. Our helmet earphones erupted a few minutes later with cheers and yells, even some whistles. By the time we had completed our orbit and saw the station again, the shuttle was already redocked. Freedom looked very pretty hanging up there against the black sky. Gleaming in the sunlight. Unscathed.

So all we had to worry about was the bends.

"Was it very painful?" Jade asked.

Johansen gave her a small shrug. "Kind of like passing kidney stones for sixteen or seventeen hours. From every pore of your body."

She shuddered.

"We came out of it okay," he said. "But I wouldn't want to go through it again."

"You saved the station. You became heroes."

We saved the station—Johansen agreed—but we didn't become heroes. The government didn't want to acknowledge that there had been any danger to Freedom, and Rockledge sure as hell didn't want the public to know that their nerf ball had almost wrecked the station.

Everybody involved had to sign a secrecy agreement. That was Ed Zane's idea. To give the guy credit, though, it was also his idea to force Rockledge to pay a cool million bucks for the cost of saving the station from their runaway nerf ball. Rockledge ponied up without even asking their lawyers and Zane saw to it that the money was split among the people who had been endangered—which included himself, of course.

Each of us walked away with about fifty thousand dollars, although it wasn't tax-free. The government called it a hazardous duty bonus. It was a bribe, to keep us from leaking the story to the media.

Everybody agreed to keep quiet except Sam, of course.

The medics took us out of the airlock, once we stopped screaming from the pain, and hustled us down to a government hospital on Guam. Landed the blessed shuttle right there on the island, on the three-mile-long strip they had built as an emergency landing field for the shuttle. They had to fly a 747 over to Guam to carry the orbiter back to Edwards Space Base. I think they got Rockledge to pay for that, too.

Anyway, they put Sam and me in a semiprivate room. For observation and tests, they said. I figured they wouldn't let either one of us out until Sam signed the secrecy agreement.

"Fifty thousand bucks, Sam," I needled him from my bed. "I could pay a lot of my bills with that."

He turned toward me, frowning. "There's more than money involved here, Mutt. A lot more."

I shrugged and took a nap. I wouldn't sign their secrecy agreement unless Sam did, of course. So there was nothing for me to do but wait.

Zane visited us. Sam yelled at him about kidnapping and civil rights. Zane scuttled out of the room. A couple of other government types visited us. Sam yelled even louder, especially when he heard that one of them was from the Justice Department in Washington.

I was starting to get worried. Maybe Sam was carrying things too far. They could keep us on ice forever in a place like Guam. They wouldn't let us call anybody; we were being held incommunicado. I wondered what Bonnie Jo was doing, whether she was worried about us. About me.

And just like that, she showed up. Like sunshine breaking through the clouds she breezed into our hospital room the third day we were there, dressed in a terrific pair of sand-colored slacks and a bright orange blouse. And a briefcase.

She waltzed up between the beds and gave us each a peck on the cheek.

"Sorry I couldn't get here sooner," she said. "The agency wouldn't answer any questions about you until my Uncle Ralph issued a writ."

"Your Uncle Ralph?" Sam and I asked in unison.

"Justice Burdette," she said, sounding a little surprised that we didn't recognize the name. "The Supreme Court. In Washington."

"Oh," said Sam. "*That* Uncle Ralph."

Bonnie Jo pulled up a chair between our beds, angling it to face Sam more than me. She placed her slim briefcase neatly on the tiled floor at her feet.

"Sam, I want you to sign the secrecy agreement," she said.

"Nope."

"Don't be stubborn, Sam. You know it wouldn't be in the best interests of VCI to leak this story to the media."

"Why not? We saved the friggin' space station, didn't we?"

"Sam—you have proved the feasibility of the magnetic bumper concept. In a few months the agency will give out a contract to run the facility. If you don't sign the secrecy agreement they won't give the contract to VCI. That's all there is to it."

"That's illegal!" Sam shot upright in his bed. "You know that! We'll sue the bastards! Call the news networks! Call . . ."

She reached out and put a finger on his lips, silencing him and making me feel rotten.

"Sam, the more fuss you make the less likely it is that the government will award you the contract. They can sit there with their annual budgets and wait until you go broke paying lawyers. Then where will you be?"

He grumbled under his breath.

Bonnie Jo took her finger away. "Besides, that's not

really what you want, is it? You want to operate the debris removal system, don't you? You want to sell the Vanguard satellite to the Smithsonian, don't you?"

He kind of nodded, like a kid being led to the right answer by a kindly teacher.

"And after that?"

"Remove defunct commsats from GEO. Retrieve the Eagle from Tranquility Base and sell it to the highest bidder."

Bonnie Jo gave him a pleased smile. "All right, then," she said, picking up the briefcase. She placed it on her lap, opened it, and pulled out a sheaf of papers. "You have some signing to do."

"What about me?" I asked, kind of sore that she had ignored me.

Bonnie Jo peeled the top sheet from the pile and held it up in the air by one corner. "This one's for Sam. It's the secrecy agreement. There's one for you, too, Spence. All the others have to be signed by the president of VCI."

"Over my dead body," Sam growled.

"Don't tempt me," Bonnie Jo answered sweetly. "Read them first. All of them. Engage brain before putting mouth in gear."

Sam glared at her. I tried not to laugh and wound up sputtering. Sam looked at me and then he grinned, too, kind of self-consciously.

"Okay, okay," he said. "I'll read."

He put the secrecy agreement on the bed to one side of him and started going through the others. As he finished each document, he handed it to me so I could read it, too.

The first was a sole-source contract from the agency to run the debris removal system for space station Freedom for five years. Not much of a profit margin, but government contracts never give a high percentage of profit. What they do is give you a steady income to keep your overhead paid. On the money from this contract Larry and Melinda could get married and take a honeymoon in Tasmania, if they wanted to.

The second document made my eyes go wide. I could actually feel them dilating, like camera lenses. It was a contract from Rockledge International for VCI to remove six of their defunct commsats from geosynchronous orbit. I paged through to the money numbers. More zeroes than I had seen since the last time I had read about the national debt!

When I looked up, Bonnie Jo was grinning smugly at me. "That's D'Argent's peace offering. You don't blab about the nerf ball incident and you can have the job of removing their dead commsats."

"What about retrieving the nerf balls before they reenter the atmosphere?" I asked. "I'd think that Rockledge would want to get their hands on them, see why they failed."

"Yeah," Sam said. "I want a separate contract from Rockledge to retrieve their nerf balls and . . ."

"Keep reading," Bonnie Jo said. "It's in the pile there."

She had done it all. VCI would be the exclusive contractor for garbage removal not only for the government, but for Rockledge as well. With that kind of a lead, we'd be so far ahead of any possible competitors that nobody would even bother to try to get into the business against us.

I signed all the contracts. With a great show of reluctance, Sam signed the secrecy agreement. Then I signed mine.

"You're marvelous," I said to Bonnie Jo, handing her back all the documents. "To do all this . . ."

"I'm just protecting my daddy's investment," she said coolly. There was no smile on her face. She was totally serious. "And my own."

I couldn't look into those gray-green eyes of hers. I turned away.

Somebody knocked at the door. Just a soft little tap, kind of weak, timid.

"Now what?" Sam snapped. "Come on in," he yelled, exasperated. "Might as well bring the Mormon Tabernacle Choir with you."

The door opened about halfway and Albert Clement slipped in, thin and gray as ever, back in his usual charcoal three-piece undertaker's suit.

"I'm sorry if I'm intruding," he said softly, apologetically.

Sam's frown melted. "You're not intruding."

Clement sort of hovered near the door, as if he didn't
dare come any farther into the room.

"I wanted to make certain that you were all right," he
said.

"You came all this way?" Sam asked. His voice had
gone tiny, almost hollow.

Clement made a little shrug. "I had a few weeks annual leave coming to me."

"So you came out to Guam."

"I wanted to . . . that was a very courageous thing you
did, son. I'm proud of you."

I thought I saw tears in the corners of Sam's eyes.
"Thanks, Dad. I—" He swallowed hard. "I'm glad you
came to see me."

"Dad?" Jade was startled. "That withered old man
was Sam's father?"

"He sure was," Johansen replied. "He and Sam's
mother had divorced when Sam was just a baby, from what
Sam told me later on. Sam was raised by his stepfather;
took his name. Didn't even know who his real father was
until just before he started up VCI."

Jade felt her own heart constricting in her chest. Who
is my father? My mother? Where are they? Why did they
abandon me?

"Hey, are you okay?" Johansen had a hand on her
shoulder.

"What? Oh, yes. I'm fine . . . just . . . fine."

"You looked like you were a million miles away," he
said.

"I'm all right. Sorry."

He leaned back away from her, but his eyes still
looked worried.

"So it was his father who fed him the inside information from the Department of Commerce," Jade said, trying
to recover her composure.

"Right. That's how Sam learned that the program had
a small business set-aside," Johansen explained. "Which

was public knowledge. Clement didn't do anything wrong."

"But he certainly didn't want anyone to know about their relationship, either, did he?"

Johansen nodded. "I guess not. You know, I never saw Sam so—I guess *subdued* is the right word. He and Clement spent a solid week together. Once the hospital people let us get up and walk around, they even went deep-sea fishing together."

"I'll have to check him out," Jade said, mostly to herself.

"Clement died a few years later. He retired from the Commerce Department and applied for residency in the first of the L4 habitats, the old Island One. Thought the low gravity would help his heart condition, but he died in his sleep before the habitat was finished building. Sam gave him a nice funeral. Quiet and tasteful. Not what you'd expect from Sam at all."

"And his mother? Is she still alive?"

Johansen shook his head. "He would never talk about his mother. Not a word. Maybe he discussed her with Clement, but I just don't know."

Jade sat back in her chair, silent for a long moment while the candlelight flickered across her face. She had not seen her adopted mother, not even spoken with her by videophone, in more than ten years. The link between them was completely broken.

"So that's how Sam made his first fortune. With Vacuum Cleaners, Incorporated," she said at last.

"VCI," Johansen corrected. "Yeah, he made a fortune all right. Then he squandered it all on that bridge ship deal a couple years later. By then he was completely out of VCI, though. I stayed on as president until Rockledge eventually bought us out."

"Rockledge?"

"Right. The big corporations always win in the end. Oh, I got a nice hunk of change out of it. Very nice. Set me up for life. Allowed me to buy a slice of this habitat and become a major shareholder."

"Did Sam ever marry Bonnie Jo?"

Johansen grimaced.

* * *

That got decided while we were still on Guam—Johansen replied.

Bonnie Jo hung around, just like Clement did. Sam seemed to spend more time with his father than with her, so I would end up walking the hospital grounds with her, taking her out to dinner, that kind of stuff.

Finally, one night over dinner, she told me she and Clement would be leaving the next day.

I said something profound, like "Oh."

"When will you and Sam be allowed to leave the hospital?" she asked. We were in the best restaurant in the capital city, Agana. It was sort of a dump; the big tourist boom hadn't started yet in Guam. That didn't happen until a few years later, when Sam opened up the orbital hotel and built the launch complex there.

Anyway, I shrugged for an answer. I hadn't even bothered to ask the medics about when we'd be let go. The week had been very restful, after all the pressures we had been through. And as long as Bonnie Jo was there I really didn't care when they sent us packing.

"Well," she said, "Albert and I go out on the morning flight tomorrow." There was a kind of strange expression on her face, as if she were searching for something and not finding it.

"I guess you'll marry Sam once we get back to the States," I said.

She moved her eyes away from mine and didn't answer. I felt as low as one of those worms that lives on the bottom of the ocean.

"Well . . . congratulations," I said.

In a voice so low I could barely hear her, Bonnie Jo said, "I don't want to marry Sam."

I felt my jaw muscles tighten. "But you still want to protect your father's investment, don't you? And your own."

Her eyes locked onto mine. "I could do that by marrying the president of VCI, couldn't I?"

I know how it feels to have your space suit ripped open. All the air whooshed out of me.

"Spence, you big handsome lunk, *you're* my investment," she said. "Didn't you know that?"

"Me?"

"Yes, you."

I nearly knocked the table over kissing her. I never felt so happy in all my life.

"Which number wife was she?" Jade was surprised at the acid in her voice.

Johansen pushed his chair slightly back from the restaurant table. "Number four," he said, somewhat reluctantly.

"And it didn't work out?"

"Wasn't her fault," he said. "Not really. I spent more time in orbit than at home. She met this kid who was an assistant vice president at her father's bank. They had a lot more in common ..."

Johansen's voice trailed off. The candle between them was guttering low. The table was littered with the crumbs of dessert, emptied coffee cups. The restaurant was deserted except for one other couple and the stumpy little robot waiters standing impassively by each table.

Jade had one more question to ask. "I know that nobody ever retrieved the Apollo 11 lunar module. What happened to Sam's plan?"

Johansen made a tight grin. "The little guy was nobody's fool. Once the World Court decided that the right of salvage was pretty much the same in space as it was at sea, we went to the Moon and laid claim to all the hardware the Apollo astronauts had left behind, at all six landing sites."

"But it's all still there," Jade said. "I've been to Tranquility Base. And Gamma and all the others ..."

"That's right." Johansen's smile broadened, genuinely pleased. "Sam's original thought was to auction the stuff off to the highest bidder. The Japanese were hot for it. So was the Smithsonian, of course. And some group of high-tech investors from Texas."

"So who bought them?"

"Nobody," Johansen said. "Because Sam got the bright idea of offering it for free to Selene. I think it was still called Moonbase then. Anyway, the people there loved him for it. Thanks to Sam, Selene legally owns all the Apollo hardware resting on the Moon. Those landing sites are big tourist attractions for them."

"That was generous."

"Sure was. And, of course, Sam could get just about anything he wanted from Selene for years afterward."

"I see," said Jade.

Johansen signaled for the bill. The robot trundled over, digits lighting up on the screen set into its torso. Johansen tapped out his okay on the robot's keyboard and let the photocell take an impression of his thumbprint. Jade turned off her recorder.

Johansen moved gracefully around the little table and held her chair while she stood up, feeling strangely unhappy that this interview was at an end.

As they strolled slowly down the footpath that led to the hotel where she was staying, Johansen suggested, "How'd you like to go hang gliding tomorrow morning? In this low gravity there's no danger at all."

Jade was surprised at how much she wanted to say yes.

"I can't," she heard herself say. "I'm leaving tomorrow morning."

"Oh," said Johansen, sounding disappointed.

They walked along the footpath in the man-made twilight toward the little cluster of low buildings that was Gunnstown, where her hotel was situated. Johansen pointed out the lights of other towns overhead. In the darkness they could not see that the habitat's interior curved up and over them.

"They're like stars," Jade said, gazing up at the lights.

"Some people even see constellations in them," he told her. "See, there's a cat—over there. And the mouse, down farther . . ."

She leaned closer to him as he pointed out the man-made constellations.

"Do you think you'll ever marry again?" she asked in a whisper.

"Not until I'm certain it will last," he answered immediately. "I've had enough hit-and-runs in my life. I want somebody I can settle down with and live happily ever after."

Happily ever after, Jade said to herself. Does anyone ever do that? She pulled away from Johansen slightly, thinking of Raki and what she owed him, what she owed herself.

I'm leaving tomorrow. Good. I'll leave and go out and interview more of Sam's friends and enemies. I'll leave and never see this man again. It's better that way. Six wives! Who can trust a man who's had six wives?

She felt almost glad that she was leaving habitat Jefferson in the morning.

Almost glad.

14

Selene City

"BUT NONE OF them will see me!" Jade repeated for the twelfth time. "Not one of them!"

Jumbo Jim Gradowsky leveled a stern finger at her. "You mean you haven't gotten to any of them, that's what you're really saying."

"I've tried, I've really tried."

Gradowsky leaned both his heavy forearms on his desktop, nearly flattening a chocolate bar that lay there half unwrapped. Jade, sitting tensely on the cubbyhole office's shabby couch, unconsciously leaned back away from his ponderous form.

"They're all on Earth, aren't they?" he asked, his voice slightly softer.

Nodding, Jade defended herself. "But I've been hounding them, Jim. I could interview them by videophone, but not one of them will even answer my calls! The best I've gotten is a return call from one of their lawyers telling me to stop annoying them."

"Orlando claims that some private detective agency ran a check on you."

"To see if I'm really a Solar News reporter?"

199

Gradowsky knitted his brows slightly. "More than that, looks like. They wanted a complete dossier on you: age, date and place of birth, previous employment, the whole nine yards."

"Who was the agency working for?"

"One of the people you're trying to interview."

"Which one?"

"The Margaux woman; the recluse who lives in Maine."

"Why would she . . . ?"

"Who the hell knows? That's why you've got to get to these people, Jade. What you've got about Sam Gunn is piffling compared to what they're trying to hide. I can feel it in my bones. There's something big they're hiding down there!"

"But I can't go to Earth, Jim. You know that. Raki knows it, too."

Gradowsky fixed her with an unhappy frown. "How many times have I told you, kid? A reporter has to go to where the story is. You've got to camp on their doorsteps. You've got to *force* them to see you."

"On Earth?"

He shrugged so hard that his wrinkled short-sleeved shirt almost pulled free of his pants.

"On Earth," Jade repeated.

"Raki's under pressure to get this show finished, one way or the other. What you've got so far is fine, but if you could get an interview with one of the survivors of that asteroid jaunt—just one of them—both of you would look like angels to the board of directors."

"I'd have to wear an exoskeleton," Jade said. "Get a powered wheelchair. A heart booster pump."

Gradowsky's fleshy face broke into a grin. "That's the stuff! They couldn't turn you down if you showed up like that! They'd have to talk to you. Hell, you might drop dead right on their doorsteps!"

"Yes," Jade muttered. "I might."

"So? What's keeping you?"

"There's one survivor living off-Earth," she said.

"Yeah, you told me. On a bridge ship. That's too far away, kid. It'd cost a fortune to send you there, all the way out to Mars. And we can't wait for the ship to loop back here."

"The ship goes past Mars and on to the Belt."

"I know."

"The sculptress lives on an asteroid out there. The woman who worked with Sam when he got into the advertising business."

Gradowsky shook his head. "We can't let you spend two years tootling around on a bridge ship."

"I could hire a high-boost shuttle. They run back and forth to the bridge ships all the time."

With an exaggerated show of patience, Gradowsky said, "Jade, honey, there are six survivors of Sam's first expedition to the asteroids. Five of them live on Earth. Any other reporter would be there now, chasing them down."

"I can't go to Earth!"

"Then you're off the assignment," Gradowsky said flatly. "I can't help it, but those are the orders from Orlando. Either you get the job done or they'll give the assignment to another reporter."

"Is that what Raki said?"

"It's out of his hands, kid. There's a dozen staff reporters down there salivating for the chance to get in on this. You've opened a big can of worms, Jade. Now they're all hot to grab the story away from you."

Jade felt cold anger clutching at her heart. "So either I go to Earth or I'm off the Sam Gunn bio?"

"That's the choice you have, yeah." Gradowsky tried to look tough, but instead he simply looked upset.

Without another word Jade got up from the chair and made her way from Gradowsky's office to Monica's. There was nowhere else for her to run. She had no office of her own; in Solar News's tight-fisted policy, a reporter's "office" was his or her pocket computer.

Before Jade could say anything Monica handed her keyboard to her. "There was a call for you. From Earth. Maine, USA."

"Jean Margaux lives in Maine," Jade said, suddenly breathless with expectation. She sat in Monica's spare chair and tapped the proper keys on the board.

A man's long, hound-sad face appeared on the wall

screen. He was sitting behind a huge desk of polished wood, bookcases neatly lined with leather volumes at his back. He wore a suit jacket of somber black and an actual necktie, striped crimson and deep blue.

"This message is for Ms. Jane Avril Inconnu. Would you kindly hold your right thumb up to the screen so that the scanner can check it? Otherwise this message will terminate now."

With a glance at Monica, Jade put her right thumb up and leaned forward until it almost touched the screen. The image of the gravely unsmiling man froze for a few seconds. Then:

"Thank you, Ms. Inconnu. I have the unpleasant task of informing you that Ms. Jean Margaux was killed yesterday in an automobile accident. As her attorney, I have been empowered by the four other partners in the *Argo* expedition who live on Earth to inform you that any further attempts to call, interview, photograph, or contact them in any way, by any employee of the Solar News Network, Inc., will be regarded as a breach of privacy and will result in an appropriate suit against said Solar News Network, Inc. Thank you."

The screen went blank.

Jade felt just as blank, empty, as if her insides had just been pulled out of her, as if she had suddenly stepped out of an airlock naked into the numbing vacuum of deep space.

Monica broke the spell. "Well, I'll be a daughter of a bitch! How do you like that?"

Fifteen minutes later Jade was back in Gradowsky's office and Raki's handsome face shone on the display screen built into the office wall.

"Yes, we've been notified, too," Raki was saying. He looked annoyed, tight-lipped. Lawyers and threats to sue were taken very seriously in Orlando.

"What the hell are they trying to hide?" Gradowsky asked, his newsman's nose twitching.

"Whatever it is, we'd better stay clear of the four remaining survivors for the time being. I've got the legal staff checking into this, but you know how long it takes them to come up with a recommendation."

"That's 'cause you pay them by the hour," Gradowsky said.

Raki was not amused. "They always give us the most conservative advice. They'll tell us to avoid the risk of a lawsuit, stay away from the remaining four."

Jade was listening with only part of her mind. An inner voice was puzzling over the fact that Jean Margaux had detectives investigate her background, and then she was killed in an auto accident. Was it an accident? Or murder? She remembered hearing somewhere that many people on Earth commit suicide by crashing their cars and making it look like an accident. That way they left their heirs the double indemnity money from their insurance.

But Jean Margaux was a very wealthy woman. Jade knew that from her own research into the survivors of Sam Gunn's expedition out to the asteroids. And childless. As far as Jade could learn, she had no heirs.

I'll have to check out the terms of her will, she told herself. Did one of the other four murder her? Not for money, maybe, but because they were afraid she would eventually talk to me?

"That finishes it," Raki was saying, his lips turned down into an unaccustomed frown. "The Sam Gunn bio stops right here and now."

"There's a fifth survivor of the expedition," Jade heard herself say. "And he isn't part of this threatened lawsuit."

Gradowsky immediately replied, "Yeah, but he's all the way to hell out by Mars on a bridge ship."

"They're hiding something," Jade snapped. "Something so important to them that Jean Margaux died to keep it secret."

It took a couple of seconds for Raki to answer from Earth, "It was an accident, Jade."

"Was it? Are we sure of that?"

Neither man replied.

Jade hunched forward in her chair. "The only other survivor of that expedition is on the bridge ship *Golden Gate*. The sculptress who made Sam's statue is living out in the Belt. And the professor who was with Sam when he died is outfitting a deep-space mission at Titan. I could get to all three of them!"

"And not get back for two years," Gradowsky grumbled.

"Okay, so what?" Jade felt eagerness trembling through her. "Raki, you can put the Sam Gunn bio on hold, can't you? Let those lawyers think we've dropped the project. Meantime I'll get out to the *Golden Gate* and see what they're trying to hide. And then go on to the other two. I can do it! I know I can!"

Gradowsky was staring at her. Raki had a faraway look in his eyes.

"We'd have to pay your salary for two years while you're doing nothing," Raki said.

"I'm getting minimum," Jade shot back. "You won't be losing much. Or just pay my travel costs while I'm going back and forth; put me on salary only for the time I'm actually working."

"H'mm."

"We could slip her aboard a high-boost shuttle," Gradowsky said. "Trade her fare for advertising time. Get her out to the *Golden Gate* in a few weeks, maybe for free. Or at a reduced fare, at least."

Raki rubbed his cleanly shaven chin. Jade felt her heart stop while he pondered.

Finally he said, "Very well. Travel expenses only unless you're actually working. Jim, see what you can do about getting her to that bridge ship quickly. And not a word about this to anybody!"

"We won't let their lawyers know what we're doing," Gradowsky said, grinning. "Don't worry."

"I'm not worried about their damned lawyers," Raki answered. "I don't want the CEO to know what I've just agreed to!"

15

●━●━●━●━●━●━●━●━●━●━●━●━●━●━●━●━●

Bridge Ship *Golden Gate*

YES, I WAS one of the investors in that mad expedition,"
said Rick Darling. "It was probably the most foolish thing
I've ever done, in a long life of foolishness."

Jade could not quite fathom the expression on Darling's face. He was immensely fat, the kind of obesity that
can only be achieved in a low-gravity environment. He
looked like a layered mountain, rolls upon rolls of fat bulging beneath his flamingo-pink robe.

In the shadowy half-light of his private quarters, his
face looked like a gibbous moon, bloated cheeks and tiers
of chins. He was smiling, but his eyes were so deeply set
in folds of fat that Jade could not tell if his smile was
pleased or pained.

"Sam Gunn." Darling sighed heavily and took a sip
from the gem-encrusted goblet engulfed in his fat,
bejeweled hand. "I thought I'd never hear his name
spoken in polite society again. The little bastard."

Jade felt ill at ease, despite the fact that Darling's
quarters were at a comfortable lunar gravity. But of all
the people she had interviewed over the months of her
travels, of all the people that Sam Gunn had worked with,

lived with, loved and hated with, Rick Darling gave her a strong sense of disquiet.

His private quarters were little short of sybaritic, from the pile of sumptuous pillows on which Darling reclined like an overweight maharajah to the splendid tapestries lining the walls and the richly carved genuine wood low tables scattered across the room. The tables were the only furniture she could see. Like her host, Jade sat on a mound of pillows, softly yielding yet comfortably supportive. The scenes embroidered on the pillows were wildly erotic. The tapestries flaunted every form of perversion she had ever heard of and several that were totally new to her.

Darling himself wore more rings and bracelets and heavy necklaces of gold and glittering jewels than she had ever seen on one person, male or female. She felt distinctly shabby in her jade-green slacks and vest, adorned by nothing more than a faux pearl necklace and matching earrings.

The very air of this latter-day Arabian Nights chamber was sickly sweet with perfume. Or was it more than perfume? It would be simple enough for this smiling pile of flesh to put a narcotic in the air-circulation system. Or an aphrodisiac.

The thought alarmed her.

Sitting up straight, a current of apprehension tingling through her body, she asked in as businesslike a voice as she could summon up: "You didn't like Sam Gunn?"

"*No one* liked him, dear lady," replied Rick Darling. His voice was a clear sweet tenor, almost angelic. "Sam was not a likable person, believe me."

"Yet you knowingly invested in his venture. Nobody forced you to go out and spend two years of your life in that spacecraft with him."

Darling's smile revealed that he even had diamonds set into his teeth. For the first time she noticed the earrings half hidden beneath his glistening tightly curled hair. The man looked like a jewelry display case.

"No *one* forced me to go, true enough." He sighed again, like a mountain heaving. "But there were circumstances, my dear. Circumstances often force us to do things we really would rather not do."

"Really?"

"Certainly." Darling reached for the splendid gold pitcher on the low table at his side. He raised the pitcher and his eyebrows.

"No thanks, I'm fine," said Jade. And I intend to stay that way, she added silently. She had taken one sip of what Darling had claimed to be the finest wine produced off-Earth. She had no intention of taking more.

"Circumstances," Darling went on as he filled his own cup, "dictate our actions. For example, you yourself are not comfortable here. You are not comfortable with me, are you?"

Jade blinked several times before admitting, "No, I guess I'm not."

Darling nodded, sending ripples through his many chins. "You fought and battled to get to me. You argued and bribed your way past the ship's security people. You literally camped at my door until I finally agreed to see you. Now that you are here, you frown with disapproval at my decor, my life-style, myself. Yet you remain, because of circumstances."

She forced a smile. "I thought *I* was interviewing *you*."

He smiled back, glittering diamonds at her. "I live the way I live. I am rich enough to afford whatever it takes to make me happy. And, to a considerable extent, whoever."

"You got rich because of Sam Gunn."

"Yes, that's true. Damn him."

"Why?" She leaned forward, eager for the answer. "I've tried to interview all of the other surviving members of that expedition and none of them would even speak to me. What happened? What did Sam do?"

Darling heaved another titanic sigh. "I have his tapes, you know."

"What?"

"I suppose you could call them the ship's log. After all, he *was* the captain of the vessel."

"You have Sam's log of the mission?"

"Yes."

"In his own voice?"

"Yes."

She could not hide her eagerness. "Can . . . can I hear them? Copy them?"

He hesitated a long moment, whether from true indecision or merely to dangle her on the hook of her own impatience, Jade could not tell.

Finally Darling said slowly, "You can listen to them, but not copy them. You must agree to the conditions I insist on before I will allow you to hear the tapes."

She tensed. "What conditions?"

He raised a thick, blunt, ringed finger. "Before that, you must also agree to grant me one request after you have heard the tapes."

"One request."

"You must agree beforehand. Now."

"Without knowing what the request is?"

He nodded solemnly.

She glanced around at the scenes on the tapestries. *Mother of mercy, suppose he wants me to do something like that?*

"What are the conditions?"

"You will listen to the tapes here in this room. You will strip yourself naked and give all your clothing and your shoulder bag to me before I present you with the tapes."

Jade felt a surge of bile rising in her throat.

"I assure you," Darling quickly added, "that the nudity is entirely a security precaution. I do not want the tapes copied. I must make certain that you do not have a copying device on you.,"

She stared hard at him, her thoughts swirling.

"I will leave the room," Darling said. "A robot will take your clothing and bag to me."

"Uh-huh."

"I will insist, however, on making certain that you are entirely—unequipped—by making a visual inspection of you via a video intercom."

Dieu, she thought, *he's a voyeur.* And immediately she regretted the three kilos she had gained over the past month. In low gravity the body puffs up anyway; I'll look pretty bad. Or maybe he likes flab. He's got plenty of his own.

"Do you agree?" Darling asked, just a hint of anxiousness in his high, rich voice.

"To the conditions, yes," she heard herself say, almost surprised. "But I can't agree to grant you whatever request you want afterward. After all . . ."

"I promise you that it will not involve pain or humiliation," Darling said.

Her heart froze inside her. *Sacre coeur,* what does he have in mind?

"Wh-what is it?" she asked timidly.

Darling folded his heavy hands over his immense belly. His arms were barely long enough to make it.

"You have worked very hard to get this far. Now you can listen to Sam Gunn's tapes, if you wish to. I will grant your request. If you will grant mine. That is all I intend to tell you."

The log of the mission that made Sam Gunn a billionaire. In his own voice. It had been an epic, pioneering flight, the first true expedition out beyond the orbit of Mars, the first commercial voyage out to the rich bonanza of the Asteroid Belt.

Rick Darling had never returned to Earth after his voyage with Sam Gunn. He lived in isolated splendor aboard the *Golden Gate.* Isolated, but not alone. *Golden Gate* was one of the huge "bridge" spacecraft that plied a long parabolic orbit that looped from the Earth / Moon system out to the Asteroid Belt and back again. Darling was rich enough to set himself up in magnificent style in a private villa aboard the ten-kilometer-long spacecraft. Yet, even in the midst of never less than four thousand human souls, Darling saw almost no one. He preferred to be served by robots.

There were five "bridge" ships sailing the years-long orbit out to the Belt. Way stations on the road to the asteroids. Bridges between the worlds. Their very existence was based on ideas that Sam Gunn had pioneered. Not that anybody gave him credit for it. Or a share of their profits.

But that was a different matter. Jade looked at Darling's fleshy face, tried to peer into those fat-hidden eyes.

"Well?" he demanded.

She took a deep breath. "All right, I'll grant your request, whatever it is," she said, thinking that if it got too nasty she would knee him in the balls and run the hell out of there.

Even though the room was far from cold, she shivered as the robot took the last item of her clothing, flowered bikini panties, into its velvet-padded steel claw of a hand. She felt defenseless, exposed, vulnerable.

"The earrings, please," said the robot with Rick Darling's voice.

The bastard is watching me. She unscrewed the tiny faux pearls and handed them to the patient robot. One of those earrings was an emergency screamer that would bring the *Golden Gate*'s security team crashing in if she activated it. She was truly on her own now.

She stood totally naked before the robot, knowing that Darling was inspecting her through its eyes.

"Turn around please."

She pirouetted slowly, hoping that he would not insist on an internal examination. She heard a brief buzzing sound, barely enough to register on her consciousness.

"Thank you," Darling's voice said from the speaker in the robot's head. "The X-ray scan is finished."

Planting her fists on her hips, she snapped, "X rays? What's next, neutrinos?"

No reply. Instead the robot reached into a slot in its torso and handed her six spools of tape, each of them roughly the size of a walnut. She took them eagerly into her hands.

"There is a laser tape player built into the table set against the far wall, beneath the video screen," Darling's voice instructed. "Unfortunately, Sam chose to make an audio log only. There is no video. I assume that you know what he looked like. If you would like, I can project still pictures of Sam and the various others who made the voyage onto the screen. I also have some video footage of our ship, the *Argo*. And blueprints, if you want."

Forgetting her nudity, she answered, "Yes, all the visual images you have. I'd like to see them."

"I will project them in sync with Sam's tapes, as closely as I can." Darling's voice sounded pleased, almost amused.

She hurried across the room and sat cross-legged before the low table. What looked at first like inlays and carvings were actually the controls for a laser player. The legs of the table held its speakers. Spreading the six tiny spools on the tabletop, she saw that they were clearly numbered.

As she inserted the first one into the slot the screen above her lit up with a view of the *Argo*. She smiled at the name. Sam certainly didn't lack for hubris. What was the Yiddish word for it? Chutzpah.

The ship was shaped like a fat tubular wheel, with slender spokes running down to a large hub. She recognized the design instantly: living quarters in the "tire" section, which was spun to give a feeling of gravity; the hub was low gravity, practically zero gee at its very center.

Sam's voice startled her.

"Log of the *Argo* expedition to the Asteroid Belt. Date: thirty-one March."

Knowing Sam from interviewing his friends and enemies, she had expected a sharp, insistent, irritating voice from him. Instead, he spoke in a calm baritone, a little on the reedy side perhaps, but a much softer and more relaxed voice than she had anticipated.

"It feels kinda funny being captain of this ship, commander of this expedition, CEO of this operation. I've always been under other people's thumbs, pretty nearly always, at least. I wonder how I'm going to like being the guy in charge?"

16

● ▬ ● ▬ ● ▬ ● ▬ ● ▬ ● ▬ ● ▬ ● ▬ ● ▬ ● ▬ ● ▬ ● ▬ ●

Two Years
Before the Mast

THEY'RE ALREADY MAKING wisecracks about this voyage—
Sam's voice continued. Since we break Earth orbit tomorrow we're officially launching the expedition on April first.
Some of the media jerkoffs are already calling us The Ship
of Fools.

I had nothing to do with selecting the launch date. The
goddamned International Astronautical Council picked the
date, with their usual infinite wisdom. Had to wait two
weeks here in orbit because their tracking facilities were
completely tied up on the second Mars expedition. Six scientists and three astronauts going to spend ninety days on
the Martian surface—some big-time expedition!

Anyway, the two-week delay gave those nervous nel-
lies down in the banks a chance to send up their so-called
experts for *another* check of all the ship's systems. Everything's fine, all systems go, they couldn't find anything
wrong. Even though we'll be out for at least two years,
they had to admit that the ship and the crew I picked are
fully up to the mission.

Wish I could say the same about my partners.

I had to form a limited partnership to get this venture going. Seven limited partners. Very limited. Three men and four women who were willing to put up ten million bucks apiece for the privilege of being the first human beings to ride out to the Asteroid Belt. Without their backing the banks wouldn't have even looked at my deal. I needed their seed money, but now I'm gonna have to put up with them for two years or more.

What the hell! I'm the captain. If any of them gives me a hard time I'll make the sucker walk the plank.

Jade stopped the tape.

"I don't have my notes with me," she said to the empty room. "I want to refresh my memory of who those partners were—besides you."

Darling did not answer, but the picture on the screen above her changed to show a group of eight people, four women and four men, all dressed in snappy flight suits. Sam was front and center, the shortest of the men and shorter than two of the women. His round, freckled face gave him the look of an aging leprechaun. Wiry red hair cropped close. Sly grin. The beginnings of wrinkles in the corners of his eyes.

"Which one is you?" Jade called out.

A long moment, then a circle appeared around the face of the man standing farthest to the left.

"My God, you were beautiful!" she blurted.

Rick Darling, at that age, was little less than an Adonis. Handsome face, tanned, full-lipped, framed by dark wavy hair. Broad shoulders, muscular build that showed even through the flight suit. Not a single piece of jewelry on him.

"Yes, I was, wasn't I?" Darling's voice, even through the speakers, sounded unutterably sad.

She leaned forward and touched the tape player's control button once again.

The computer can fill in the date—Sam's voice said. He sounded edgy, almost out of breath.

Well, we're off, on schedule. High-energy boost. We'll

pass the Mars expedition in a couple of weeks. Too bad we won't get close enough to wave to 'em. Good friend of mine from back in my astronaut days is commanding the flight. She'll be the first woman to set foot on Mars; the fifth human being. Hope that makes her happier than I ever could.

Everything's okay here, all systems in the green. My partners are having a ball. Literally, some of them. I introduced two of the women to zero-gee fun and games last night. They liked it so much that I almost had to call for help. Almost.

Women are blabbermouths! Now the two that I *didn't* take down to the hub are sore at me. And one of the men, that Darling character, is starting to make hints.

I hired one of the crewmen to help keep the passengers amused. Erik Klein. He's a blond, tanned, beachboy type. Not too bright, but muscular enough to keep the women happy. The other two—my *real* crew—I've got to keep separated from the partners. These seven dwarf-brained numbskulls think they're here for fun and games. I thought they'd entertain each other, pretty much. With Erik and me helping out a little, now and then.

Two years of this. Two years of *this*?

I had to give them a lecture. Imagine it! Me, laying down the rules to somebody else.

But they're going to wreck this mission before we get halfway to where we're going. Hell, they could even wreck the damned ship and kill us all.

Trouble is, they think they're here to be entertained. I guess that's the impression they got, somehow, from the way I described the trip to them, way back when.

Seven partners. Seven movers and shakers from the media, high society, the arts and sciences. Hell, even the astronomer is acting like a freshmen away from home for the first time in his life.

And they're bothering the crew. I don't mind if they screw themselves into catatonia, among themselves. But the crew's gotta run this ship. They've got to be in top physical and mental condition when we start prospecting among the asteroids.

It all seemed so simple, back on Earth. Get seven prominent scatterbrains to put up the seed money for an expedition to the asteroids. Use their credentials to impress the banks enough to put up the real backing. Go out to the asteroids, find a nice chunk of nickel-iron, smelt and refine it on the way back to Earth, then sell it for enough to give everybody a nice profit.

It's the sweetest deal I've ever put together, especially since the seven dwarfs will be getting their shares from the *net* profit we make, while I'll be drawing my own off the top, from the gross.

But, Lord, are those seven airheads a shipload of trouble! I may have to shove one of them out an airlock, just to impress the others that I mean business.

Imagine it! *Me* trying to enforce discipline on *them*.

I hate this job.

Listen, this log is going to have to be confidential. I'm going to give the computer a security code word so nobody can break into it and hear what I've got to say.

Let's see ... computer, this is a command. Code this log under, uh, umm—code word "supercalifragelisticexpialidotious."

[Computer]: Code word accepted.

Okay, good. I hadn't intended to get so paranoid, but I'm stuck here for the next twenty-three months with nobody I can trust. I've got to talk to *somebody* or I'll go nuts. So I'll talk to you, computer.

[Computer]: I contain artificial intelligence programs that can provide limited responses to your inputs.

When I want you to answer me, I'll tell you! Otherwise, keep your voice synthesizer quiet. Understood?

[Computer]: Understood.

Part of the reason for locking up this log is that I'm going to start naming names and I don't want anybody else to know what those names are. Christ knows I've done enough screwing around in my time, but I've always believed a gentleman doesn't kiss and tell. Well, maybe I'm not a gentleman and I certainly ain't talking about just kissing, but I've never gone around embarrassing anybody I was lucky enough to bed with.

But I can't talk things out without naming names. It just won't work. Am I making any sense?

[Pause.]

Hey, computer, am I making any sense?

[Computer]: Your statements are internally consistent.

Great. How do I call up your psychotherapy program?

[Computer]: Ask for Guidance Counselor.

Jeez, just like in high school. Okay, gimme the Guidance Counselor.

[Computer, same voice]: How may I help you?

Just listen and then tell me what I should do after I finish, okay?

[Computer]: If that's what you really want.

Oh, brother!

[Computer]: Is that part of your problem, your brother? I have your biographical dossier in my files, but there is no mention of a brother.

No, no, no! I haven't started yet!

[Computer]: I see.

I'm starting now. Got it?

[Computer]: Go on.

Let's see ... I think it was Nelson Algren who said there are three rules for a happy life. One, never play cards with any man named "Doc." Two, never eat at any place called "Mom's." and three, never, never go to bed with a woman whose troubles are worse than your own.

[Computer]: Um-h'mm.

I went to bed with Sheena Chang last night. Big mistake.

[Computer]: Sheena Chang, video actress. Proclaimed one of the ten most beautiful women in the world by 21st-Century Fox/ United Artists/ MGM/ Fujitsu Corporation. Latest starring role: Tondaleo, the sultry Eurasian prostitute with a heart of gold, in *Invasion of the Barbarians from Outer Space*. Age: twenty-seven. Height ...

Yeah, yeah, yeah. That's her. Sultry Eurasian, all right. I was really surprised when her agent told me she had agreed to come on this voyage. I had only called her on a lark; thought it'd be fun to be on a slow boat to China with her.

[Computer]: To China? Navigational data shows we are heading . . .

Just a figure of speech, dammit! Stop interrupting!

Anyway, I never thought she'd give up two years in the middle of her career to come sailing out to the Asteroid Belt with me. But she did. Last night I found out why.

She was all hot breath and sizzle until I got her clothes off her and put her in my bed. We had made it before, in the threesome with Marj Dupray down in the zero-gee section. Sheena had been a wild woman then; Marj wasn't so bad herself, for a skinny fashion designer. They were both tanked up on champagne and whatnot. After all, that was our first night out.

[Computer]: I see.

Well, anyway, last night Sheena and I have a private little supper in my quarters. She's wearing a low-cut dress so slinky she must have sprayed it on. One thing leads to another and finally we're both in the buff and on the bed.

I say to her, "I was really knocked out when you agreed to come on this trip."

That's all it took. The floodgates opened.

[Computer]: Floodgates?

She started crying! At first I thought she had drunk too much wine with dinner, but then I remembered that she had downed a tub of champagne that first night without batting an eye. She just blubbered away and babbled for hours, right there in the bed. Naked. One of the ten most beautiful women in the world.

[Computer]: Why was she crying?

That's what I asked her. And she told me. And told me. And told me! Her career is going down the tubes; her last three videos lost money; her implants are slumping; her husband is suing her for divorce; her boyfriend's left her for a younger starlet; her agent's making bad deals for her; her cat died . . . Jeez, she just went on and on about how her life was ruined and she was going to kill herself.

[Computer]: Perhaps she should speak to me. I may be able to help her.

Yeah, maybe. Anyway, it turns out that her publicity

agent convinced her that taking this voyage would be just
the thing to give her career a boost. When she comes back
she'll be the first actress to have flown to the Asteroid
Belt. They'll make a docudrama out of it. They'll get Mi-
chael J. Fox IV, to play my role. Ta-da, ta-dum, ta-dee—so
off she goes on the good ship *Argo*.

[Computer]: Ta-da, ta-dum, ta-dee?

Ignore it. Two days out, Sheena starts thinking that
maybe she made a mistake. Two weeks out she's certain of
it. Her publicity guy and her agent have connived behind
her back to get her out of the way so that the new starlet
her boyfriend's shacked up with can take her place. Her
career is ruined. Her body's falling apart and she can't sue
the plastic surgeons because the publicity would ruin her
even more. She'll be out of the limelight for two whole
years. By the time she gets back everybody'll have forgotten who the hell she is, and she'll be an old woman by
then anyway, past thirty.

[Computer]: According to her dossier she will be only
twenty-nine when this mission ends.

So she lied about her age! Anyway, Sheena doesn't
want to make love, she wants to kill herself. It took me all
goddamned night to calm her down, cheer her up, and
convince her that when we get back from the asteroids
she'll be rich enough to *buy* 21st-Century, et al.

[Computer]: According to the prospectus filed with
the Securities and Exchange Commission . . .

I know, I know! So I exaggerated a little. She needed
cheering up.

By the time I got her to stop talking about killing herself, it was damned near morning. I had to get dressed and
go to the bridge for the first-shift systems review. She
wriggled back into that slinky dress of hers, still sniffling
a little. Then she dropped the bombshell.

[Computer]: Should I activate the damage-control
program?

No, stupid. But gimme the logistics program.

[Computer]: Logistics.

Sheena Chang is not to receive any drugs, medications, or pharmaceuticals of any kind. Understand? In fact,
all requests for medication, stimulants, or relaxers from

any of the partners is to be reported to me immediately. Understood?

[Computer]: Understood.

Okay. Get the Guidance Counselor back.

[Computer]: Guidance Counselor.

The bombshell Sheena handed me was metaphorical. You understand what metaphorical means?

[Computer]: I have a thorough command of twenty languages, including English.

Wonderful. She told me that one of the partners is an agent for Rockledge International, the multinational megacorporation, the soulless bloodsucking vampires of the corporate world, the gutless sneaking bastards who'd steal your *cojones* and sell them to the highest bidder if you gave them the chance. I've tangled with them before; they're always trying to grab everything for themselves, the two-bit sonsofbitches.

[Computer]: You disapprove of them.

Only as much as I disapprove of cannibalism, genocide, and selling your mother to a Cairo brothel.

[Computer]: I see.

So there's Sheena sniffling and squeezing her boobs into her dress, and she tells me I've been so nice and kind and patient that she's going to warn me that one of the partners is secretly working for Rockledge.

"Which one?" I asked her.

"I don't know," she says.

"Then how do you know that one of them is on Rockledge's payroll?"

She finally gets her bosom adjusted—believe me, it took all my powers of concentration not to go over to her and give her a hand.

Anyway, she says: "A couple of nights ago, it was kind of late and we were in the lounge having a nightcap or two . . ."

"We? Who?"

She shrugged. I was still in the buff and immediately came to attention. Sheena paid no attention and I thought she'd probably seen bigger. But not better.

I asked her again, "Who was in the lounge with you?"

"Oh, golly, we had been drinking for a while. And

Rick had handed out some really weird candy; he's got a whole trunkful of shit, you know ..."

"I know." I was starting to get exasperated with her birdbrain act. "So Darling was there. Who else?"

"Oh, Marjorie, and Dr. Hubble. Grace Harcourt, she was sitting with me. I don't remember if Bo Williams was there or not. And I'm sure Jean Margaux wasn't. She wouldn't be, the snob."

"So who said what? What'd you hear?"

"It was just a snatch of conversation, a man's voice, I'm pretty sure. Somebody said something about money piling up at a bank in Liechtenstein ..."

"Liechtenstein?"

"That's right. He's getting a monthly stipend from Rockledge International and it's gathering compound interest all the time we're away on this trip!"

She looked pleased that she remembered that much. But that was all she could remember. Or so she said. Somebody was on Rockledge's payroll, in secret. And it was probably a man.

[Computer]: Why does that bother you so?

Why? Why? Because Rockledge'll try to steal the profits of this mission out from under me, that's why! It's just like those sleazy bastards—let the little guy do all the work and then they come in and snatch the money. Rape and pillage, that's the way they work.

[Computer]: I assume those are metaphors again.

Listen, you stupid hunk of germanium, I want you to get me a Dun & Bradstreet on each one of my partners. One of them's a ...

[Computer]: You will have to call up the financial program.

Okay! Gimme the financial program!

[Computer]: Financial.

I want a complete rundown on each one of my partners.

[Computer]: Displaying.

No, no, no! Not the data already in your memory! That's months old, for chrissakes. I want the up-to-the-minute stuff. And check the banks in Liechtenstein.

[Computer]: That will take several hours. Transmission time to Earth is currently . . .

Just do it! Fast as you can. Do it.

Jeez, I feel like a kid in a confessional booth. It's been three months since my last entry in this log. A pretty quiet three months.

Things have gone along okay, really smoother than I expected. One of the plasma thrusters crapped out last week, but Will Bassinio and I went EVA and replaced it with a spare. Will's my electronics specialist; a real whiz at chips and circuits and stuff like that. Lonz—Alonzo Ali, my first mate—monitored us from the command center while Erik did what he does best: charmed the passengers.

Erik's a good kid. Not a deep thinker, but he smiles pretty and the passengers seem to like him, especially the female passengers. On the official manifest he's my logistics specialist. Not much of a technician, but he does his job okay.

I think of them as passengers now, rather than partners. In this phase of the flight we're running sorta like a cruise liner. There won't be any real work to do until we get past the orbit of Mars and start actively prospecting for an asteroid to mine. In the meantime it's six meals a day and all the entertainment I can dream up for my magnificent seven.

They're not as much trouble right now as I thought they'd be. Darling's happy as a mugger in an old lady's home. He's always in the galley or the dining salon, stuffing himself on all the gourmet food I stored aboard. He's gaining weight fast; his clothes look like they're gonna start popping seams any minute.

Sheena has calmed down a lot. Maybe what I told her about being a celebrity when she comes back to Earth has helped. But I think it's Lowell Hubble who's made the real difference. He's the oldest man on board, lean, gray-haired fatherly type. Neat little mustache that's still almost dark. Dresses in rumpled slacks and baggy cardigan sweaters. Even smokes a pipe. Sheena's taken up with him and they both seem delighted about it. He's even teaching her astronomy.

Is Hubble the Rockledge agent? I've been wondering about that. He's an astronomer, for chrissake. They don't make much money. There's no Dun & Bradstreet report on him, although he comes from a pretty wealthy family. But was the ten million he ponied up his own money, or Rockledge's?

I asked Grace Harcourt to snoop around for me and see what she could find out.

"Me? Spy for you?" She laughed out loud.

I had invited her up to the command center, what would be called the bridge on a ship at sea, I guess. I like Grace. She's tough and feisty; has to be, to make it as an entertainment industry gossip columnist. There's a lot of competition in that business. And a lot of lawsuits.

I had met her years ago, when I was a NASA astronaut-in-training and she was still a local TV news reporter in Houston. We had gotten along really well right from the start, but my so-called career took me to Florida and she aimed for Hollywood. And hit it big.

Grace is tiny, a good two inches shorter than me. But she's smart, sharp. Not bad-looking, either. A little more on her hips than there ought to be, but otherwise she's got a nicely curved figure that looks good in frilly blouses and pleated skirts. She also has a pleasant, heart-shaped face that knows how to smile.

But now she was laughing. "I'm a gossip columnist, Sam," she said, "not a secret agent."

"Snooping is snooping," I told her. "Just keep your pretty eyes and ears open for me, will you?"

She gave me a funny look. "How do you know I'm not working for Rockledge?"

That made me grin. "You're a gossip columnist, right? You never kept a secret in your life."

She laughed and admitted I was right. I've got no worries about Grace. She tapes her column every day and we transmit it to Earth. She bases her stuff on the same reports from her spies and finks that she'd be getting if she were at home in Beverly Hills. She also throws in a couple tidbits about our voyage now and then and shows her viewers some of the ship. No other daily column has ever been taped from deep space before.

Then I had the run-in with Marjorie Dupray. She had been my zero-gee companion, along with Sheena, that first night. A very successful fashion designer, Marj had started out as a model and she's kept that lean, long-legged model's figure. But she's got a mean look to her, if you ask me. Maybe it's that buzz cut of hers, with her hair dyed like a neon flamingo. Or the biker's leathers she likes to wear. She doesn't give off much of a female aura.

Why would a fashion designer agree to come on this voyage? And put up ten mil, to boot? I decided to question her, subtly, so she wouldn't know I was suspicious.

I invited her up to the command center one evening when I had the watch alone. She seemed moderately bored as I showed her the navigational computer and the Christmas tree lights of the life-support systems monitor board. But she perked up a bit when we got to the comm console.

"How long does it take a message to get back to Earth now?" he asked.

"Nearly half an hour," I said. "And longer every day. We are going where no man has gone before, you know."

"And no woman."

I made a little bow to acknowledge her feminist point of view, which surprised me. Then I asked: "Are you getting any work done? Is our voyage into deep space inspiring you to create new clothing designs?"

She shook her head. It was a finely sculptured head, with a haughty nose and strong chin, high cheekbones that threw shifting shadows across her face. Marj is damned near a foot taller than me. I have nothing against tall women; in fact, I consider them a challenge. But that butch haircut of hers bothered me. And now the color was burnt orange.

But I was after information, not challenges.

"Don't you have contracts to fulfill? I thought this voyage was going to be a working session for you. How can you afford to take two years off?"

She gave me a pitying look. "I don't have to push it, Sam. When I get back from this trip I'll be the first and only designer to have been in deep space. I'll be able to throw rags together and the fashion industry will gobble them up and call them works of inspired genius."

"Oh." Maybe she was telling the truth. The fashion industry has always seemed kind of weird to me. "I thought maybe you were independently wealthy. Or you had another source of income."

"I have a few investments here and there," she said with a slight smile.

"Like in Liechtenstein?" I blurted.

Her sculptured face turned cold as ice. "Is that what this is all about, Sam? You think I'm spying on you?"

I gave her my innocent-little-boy look. "What makes you think . . ."

"Sheena told me how upset you got. How you think one of us is working for Rockledge Industries."

"Well, yeah, I am upset about that. Wouldn't you be?"

"Me? Upset about something Sheena thinks she might have heard while she was guzzling booze and frying what little brains she's got on Rick's junk?" Marj smirked at me.

"Whoever made that slip about Liechtenstein must've also been high," I said.

"Well, it wasn't me."

"I'm glad to hear it," I said. But either my expression or my tone told her I didn't altogether believe her profession of innocence.

Marj patted my cheek with one long, slender-fingered hand. "Sam, dear, there are times when I would gladly kick you in the balls."

If there's one thing I hate, it's condescension. "You'd hurt your delicate little foot, tall lady. I wear a lead jockstrap."

She laughed out loud. "I'll bet you do, at that."

I assured her that I did.

Anyway, that was almost a month ago. Since then nobody's said or done anything suspicious, and the cruise is going along without a hitch.

Which worries me. Maybe Grace really is the Rockledge agent. Maybe she's kept lots of secrets, especially about herself. How would I know? Or Marg. Or any one of them.

Jeez, I'm getting paranoid!

Anyway, we pass the point of no return in another six days. The ship is under a constant acceleration from the plasma thrusters. It's a very low acceleration; in the hub of the ship you still feel like you're in zero gee, that's how low the acceleration is. But although those little thrusters don't give you much push, they're very fuel efficient and can run for years at a time (when they don't crap out) and keep building up more and more velocity for you.

As an emergency backup, we're also carrying three pods of chemical rockets with enough delta vee among 'em to change our course, swing past Mars, and head back to the Earth / Moon system. So we can cut this ride short and go back home if there's any major trouble—up to the point of no return. Then, if we have a problem, no matter what the hell it may be, we've still got to coast all the way out to the Asteroid Belt and swing back to Earth on a trajectory that'll take us at least eleven months.

So, six days from now we become hostages to Newton's laws of motion and momentum. The point of no return. I hate to admit it, but I'm nervous about it.

Those mother-humping, slime-sucking, illegitimate sons of snakes from Rockledge! Now I know what they're up to, and why they've got an agent on board!

We passed the point of no return two days ago.

Today the main food freezers crapped out. All three of 'em, at the same time. Bang! Gone. Sabotage, pure and simple. Nineteen months more to go, and all our food is thawing out!

I wish I was an Arab, or even a Spaniard. Those people know how to curse!

It makes perfect sense. We die of starvation. That's all. Those bastards from Rockledge murder us—all except their own agent, who waits until we're all dead, then sends a distress call back to Earth where Rockledge has a high-energy booster all set and ready to zoom out to rescue their man. Or woman.

Or maybe they let the poor sucker die, too. Dead spies tell no tales. And you don't have to pay them.

Oh, hell, I know that doesn't make any sense! I'm starting to babble, I'm so pissed off.

All three food freezers shut down. We don't know exactly when because there was no indication on the Christmas tree of the main control console. All the goddamned lights stayed clean green while our food supply started to thaw out.

It was Erik who noticed the problem. Bright-smiling, genial, slow-witted Erik.

I was showing off the command center to Jean Margaux, our high-society lady from Boston's North Shore. (She pronounces it Nawth Show-ah.) She's the one who got jealous the first night about my zero-gee antics with Sheena and Marj. What the hell, if I'm naming names I might as well name all of them.

Jean is the tall, stately type. Handsome face; good bones. Really beautiful chestnut-colored hair, and I think it's her natural shade. Not much bosom, but nice long legs and a cute backside. She likes to wear long, slim skirts with slits in them that show off those legs when she moves.

Cool and aloof, looks down her nose at you. It's not as if she gives the impression that her shit don't stink; she gives the impression that she doesn't ever shit. But touch her in the right place and she dissolves like a pat of butter in a rocket exhaust. She turns into a real tigress. All it takes is a touch, so help me—and then afterward she's the Ice Queen again. Weird.

So I'm showing her the Christmas tree, with all its red and green lights, only there wasn't a single red one showing. The ship was humming along in perfect condition, if you could believe the monitor systems. Alonzo Ali was on duty at the command console; Lonz is not only my first mate, he's a Phi Beta Kappa astronautical engineer and navigator from the International Space University.

So Erik comes into the command center with a puzzled frown on his normally open, wide-eyed face.

"There are no windows," Jean was saying. Coming from her, it sounded more like a compliant than a comment.

"Nope," I said. "With the ship swinging through a complete revolution every two minutes, you'd get kind of dizzy looking out a window."

"But we have windows in the lounge," she said. "And in our suites."

"Those are video screens," I corrected as gently as I

could. "They show views from the cameras at the ship's hub, where they don't rotate."

"Oh," she said, as if I'd stuck a dead skunk in front of her.

Erik was kind of hanging around behind her, in my line of vision, not interrupting but sort of jiggling around nervously, like a kid who has to pee.

"Excuse me," I said to Jean. Her high-society airs sort of made me act like a butler in a bad video.

I stepped past her to ask Erik, "Is something wrong?"

"I think so," he said, furrowing his brow even deeper.

"What is it?" I asked softly.

"I'm not really sure," said Erik.

Jean was watching us intently. I restrained my urge to grab Erik by the throat and pull his tongue out of his head.

"What seems to be the trouble?" I asked, as diffidently as possible. No roughneck, I.

"Funny smell."

"Ah. A strange odor. And where might this odd scent be coming from?"

"The food freezers."

All this polite badinage had lulled me into a sense of unreality.

"The food freezers? Plural?"

"Yah."

"The food freezers," I repeated, smiling and turning toward the blue-blooded Ms. Margaux. Then it hit me. *"The food freezers!"*

I lunged past Erik to the command console. The goddamned Christmas tree was as green as Clancy's Bar on St. Patrick's Day.

"No malfunctions indicated," Lonz said in that deep rich basso of his. He's from Kenya, and anytime he gets tired of space he can take up a career in the opera.

My heart rate went back to normal, almost, but I decided to go down to the freezers and check them out anyway. Jean asked if she could accompany me. There was a strange light in her eyes, something that told me she anticipated a lesson in arctic survival.

I nodded and headed for the hatch.

"Isn't Erik coming, too?" Jean asked.

Oh-ho, I thought. She wants the cram course in arctic survival.

"Yeah, right. Come on, Erik. Show me where you smelled this funny odor."

The logistics section is almost exactly on the opposite side of the wheel from the command center. We could have gone down one of the connecting tubes and through the hub, but I decided with Jean along it'd be better if we just walked around the wheel and stayed at a full one gee.

It's always a little strange, walking along inside the wheel. Your feet and your inner ear tell you that you're strutting along on a flat surface, while your eyes see that the floor is curving up in front of you, right out of sight. Anyway, we walked down the central corridor, past the lounge, the galley and dining salon, the passengers' living quarters, and the gym before we got to the logistics section. The workshops and maintenance facilities are all on the other half of the wheel. Our factory and processing smelter are down near the hub, of course, in microgravity.

Erik opens the big door to the first of the walk-in food freezers. It smells like a camel caravan had died in there several days ago. The second one smelled worse. By the time we got to the third one I guess our noses were suffering from sensory overload: it only smelled as bad as rancid milk poured over horse manure.

Jean kept her oh-so-proper attitude, but her face looked like she had stopped breathing. Erik was giving me a sort of hang-dog grin, like he expected me to blame him for the catastrophe.

I kept my cool. I did not puke or even gag. I just raised my clenched fists over my head and uttered a heart-felt "Son of a *BITCH!*"

Jean couldn't control her ladylike instincts any further; she yanked a facial tissue from a pocket in her blouse, pressed it to her face, and fled back toward her quarters.

I left Erik there and zipped back to the lounge to call the passengers together to ask for volunteers to help with the cleanup.

It's a very nice lounge, if I say so myself. Plush chairs,

deep carpeting, big video screens that can serve as windows to the splendors of the universe outside. At the moment they were showing a tape of some tropical beach: gentle waves lapping in, palm trees swaying against a clean blue sky, no people in sight. Must have been a clip from some travel agency's come-on. There hasn't been a beach that clean and empty of tourists since the first commercial flights of the hypersonic airliners.

"Wait just a moment, Sam," said Lowell Hubble, our pipe-smoking astronomer. No tobacco, of course, that stuff had been outlawed way back in '08 or '09. Whatever he had in the blackened, long-stemmed pipe he always held clamped in his teeth was smokeless and sweet-smelling. I think it was a bubble-gum derivative.

"Are you telling us," he said from around the pipe, "that our food supply is ruined?"

"Most of the frozen food, yes," I admitted. "Looks that way. I need some help checking out the situation."

"We'll starve!" Rick Darling yelped.

"You'll starve last," quipped Grace Harcourt. Good old Grace: she could be tough or tender, and she knew when to be which.

Darling stuck out his lower lip at her. The others were staring at me apprehensively. They had been sitting in the recliner chairs scattered about the room; now they were hunching forward tensely on the front two inches of each chair. I was standing in front of the bar, trying to look cool and competent.

"Nobody's going to starve," I told them. "It's only the frozen food that's affected and I think we can save a good deal of it, if we move quickly enough."

"Isn't all the food frozen?" asked Bo Williams, our Pulitzer Prize author, the man who had already signed a megabuck contract to write the book about this voyage. Bo looked more like a professional wrestler than an author: shaved bullet head, no neck, heavy shoulders and torso, bulging out.

"Most of it. But we have a backup supply of packaged food. And the reprocessors, of course."

"Canned food." Darling shuddered.

"Some of it's canned. Most of it's been preserved by

irradiation. Food's been stored for half a century and more that way."

"Radiation?" Sheena Chang's big eyes went wider than usual. She was wearing violet contacts to go with the color of her outfit, a Fredericks of Hollywood version of a flight suit, real tight, with lots of zippers.

"It's all right," Hubble said, leaning over from his chair to pat her head reassuringly. "Nothing to worry about."

"What was that about reprocessors?" Grace asked.

This was not a subject I wanted to discuss in any detail. "We can recycle the food, to a certain extent."

"Recycle?" For once I was not happy that Grace was a newshound.

"It's been done on space stations and long-duration missions." I tried to pass the whole thing off. "The Mars expedition has a recycling system."

"The food we eat will be recycled?" Damn Grace and her goddamned tenacity!

"Right," I snapped. "Now, I need . . ."

Rick Darling was catching on. "You mean our *garbage* will be recycled into fresh food?"

"Not just our garbage, sweetheart," Grace told him.

Jean Margaux, she who gave the impression she did not do that sort of thing, stared at me as if I had insulted her entire family tree.

Marjorie Dupray said grimly, "I'll starve first."

Marj wouldn't have far to go before she starved. She was all skin and bones already. As usual, she was wearing the crummiest clothes of the group: a shapeless sweater of dingy gray and baggy oversize slacks decorated with fake machine-oil stains. But I knew that underneath that camouflage was a body as sleek and responsive as a racing yacht.

"Nobody needs to starve," I said, getting irritated with the bunch of them. Maybe this was The Ship of Fools, after all.

"Sure," Darling groused. "We can spend the next year and a half eating recycled . . ."

"Don't say it!" Jean snapped. "I can't bear even to think of it."

"Let's see how much of the frozen food we can rescue," I urged. "Who's gonna help us clean up the freezers?"

Not a hand was raised. None of my partners would volunteer to help.

"That's the crew's responsibility, not ours," said the always-gracious Jean Margaux.

The others agreed.

It was grisly work.

We had to go in there and see what was spoiled beyond recovery, what could be saved if we cooked it immediately, and what was still reasonably okay. At the same time I wanted to figure out how all three freezers could fail without any warning lights showing up on the command console.

Erik and I did the dirty work with the food. Will checked out the freezers' electrical systems. He wore an oxygen mask with a little supply bottle on the belt of his flight suit. Sensitive kid.

"Where I grew up in South Philadelphia used to smell like this," he grumbled through the clear plastic mask as he entered the first of the freezers. "I never thought I'd get a whiff of home out here in space."

"Don't get homesick on me," I told him. "Just find out what went wrong."

About half of the food had turned to green slime, really putrid. The stench didn't seem to affect Erik at all, he just cleaned away with the same obtuse smile on his chiseled features as ever.

"Doesn't the smell bother you?" I asked him.

"What smell?"

"For chrissakes, you're the one who reported it in the first place!"

"Oh, that. Yah, it is rather annoying, isn't it?"

I just shook my head and Erik went back to work in blond, blue-eyed innocence.

So we shoveled several tons of spoiled food into the reprocessor, which chugged and burped and buzzed for hours on end, turning out neat little bricks of stuff, some colored reddish-gray, others colored greenish-gray. They were supposed to be synthetic meat and synthetic vegetables. I nibbled on one each, then wished we had brought a cargo bay filled with Worcester sauce, ketchup, soy sauce, and Texas three-alarm salsa.

Will Bassinio just showed me what went wrong with the freezers.

He looked really worn out when he reported to me this morning in the command center. Eyes red from lack of sleep, a black ring around his nose and mouth from the oxygen mask he'd been wearing for nearly twelve hours straight. He didn't smell so good, either. The rotting food had impregnated his coveralls.

"You been at it all night?" I asked him.

He nodded wearily. "Whoever did the job on the freezers was pretty fuckin' smart."

Will pulled three tiny chips from the chest pocket of his smelly, stained coveralls. They were so small I couldn't make out what they were.

"Timers," he explained before I could ask. "Somebody spliced 'em into the control unit of each freezer. Really neat job; took me all fuckin' night to find 'em. Interrupted the current flow and shut the freezers down, while at the same time sending an okay reading to the monitors up here on the bridge. Pretty fuckin' ingenious."

"Can you fix the freezers before all the food thaws out?" I asked.

Will gave me a sad shake of his head. "Whoever did this job knew what he was doing. I'd have to rebuild the whole control unit in each freezer. Take two–three weeks, maybe more."

"We don't have spares?"

"We were supposed to. They're listed in the logistics computer but the bin where they ought to be stored is dead-empty."

I felt my blood seething. Sabotage.

"Were they put into the control units before we launched or during the flight?" I asked.

Will gave me a shrug. "Can't tell."

"There aren't any locks on the freezer doors," I muttered.

"Never saw anybody goin' in there," he muttered

back. "Except that Darling guy, once. He said he was looking for a key lime pie."

Darling. The art critic. The guy who'd been stuffing
himself ever since we had left Earth orbit.

The file I had on Darling claimed that he had inher-
ited a modest fortune from his mother, a real estate broker
in Florida. It would've been a larger fortune if his father
hadn't kept frittering money away on half-baked schemes
like opening a fundamentalist Christian theme park in Bei-
rut. The old man died, eventually: gunned down by a
crazed ecologist on the Ross Ice Shelf where he was trying
to build a hotel and penguin-hunting lodge.

Darling claimed his ten million investment in the
Argo expedition came from his inheritance. Said it was all
the money he had in the world.

I called a lady in Anaheim that I knew, Kay Taranto.
She specialized in tracking down deadbeats for the Disney
financial empire. I asked her to find out if any money from
Rockledge had suddenly appeared in Darling's chubby
hands. Told her to check Liechtenstein. Kay was as persist-
ent and dogged as a heat-seeking missile. If there was anything to find out about Darling, she was the one to do it.

Meanwhile, I told Will to go through the entire ship
millimeter by millimeter to see if there were any other
nasty little surprises planted here or there.

"Don't sleep, don't eat, don't even waste time breathing," I told him. "From now on you're my bug inspector.
Look everywhere."

He gave me a sly grin. "Even under the beds?"

"And in them, if you have to," I said. "For every bug
you find I'll give you a bonus—say, a week's salary?"

"How about a month's?"

I nodded an okay. It'd be worth it, easy.

I don't know whose idea it was to have a continuous
banquet until all the food that was about to spoil was eaten
up. Probably Darling's. Kind of thing his perverted brain
would think up.

For the past three days and nights the seven of them
have been stuffing themselves like ancient Romans during
Saturnalia. Ship of bulemics. They must know that every-

thing they upchuck is going into the reprocessor, but it looks like they just don't care. Not right now.

Of course, they're drinking all the wine on board, too. My only joy is that they're going to be so sick when they get to the end of the food that they'll just lay in their sacks for a *long* time and let me get on with the real job of this mission.

I'm staying up here at the command center for the duration of their orgy. I've got some old synthesized Dixieland playing on the intercom so I can't hear their laughing and shouting from down in the dining room. Or their puking. I've ordered the crew to stay out of the passengers' area.

"Let 'em bust their guts," I told my men. "We've got work to do."

When you read that there's millions of asteroids out in the Belt you get the mental picture of a kind of forest of chunks of rock and metal, you know, clustered so thick that you can't sail a ship through without getting dinged.

No such luck.

Sure, there's millions of asteroids in the Belt. Some as big as mountains; a few of 'em are a couple of hundred kilometers wide. But most of 'em are the size of pebbles, even grains of sand. And they've got a tremendously wide volume of space to wander around in, out there between the orbits of Mars and Jupiter. You could put all the planets and moons of the solar system in that region and it'd still be almost entirely empty space.

The first thing I'm looking for is a nice little nickel-iron asteroid, maybe a couple hundred meters across. Nothing spectacular; a piece as small as a Little League baseball field will do fine. She'll contain more high-grade iron ore than the whole Earth's steel industry uses in ten years. Maybe fifty to seventy-five tons of platinum, an impurity that'd set a man up for life. To say nothing of the gold and silver that's sprinkled around in her.

Such an asteroid is worth billions of dollars. Maybe hundreds of billions.

Then there's the carbonaceous-type rocky asteroids. They contain something more valuable than gold, a lot more valuable. They contain water.

There's a new frontier being built in cislunar space, the region between low Earth orbit and the Moon's surface. We've got zero-gee factories in orbit and mining operations on the Moon. We've got big condominium habitats being built in the L4 and L5 libration points. Nearly fifty thousand people live and work in space now.

They get most of their raw materials from the Moon. Lunar ores give our frontier workers aluminum and titanium, even some iron, although it's low-grade stuff and expensive as hell to mine and smelt. There's plenty of silicon on the Moon; they've got a thriving electronics industry growing there.

But the people on the space frontier have got to import their heavy metals from Earth. And their water. They buy high-grade steels from outfits like Rockledge International, and pay enormous prices for lifting the tonnage up from Earth. Same thing for water, except the corporate bastards charge even more for that than they do for steel or even platinum.

Which is why Rockledge and the other corporate giants don't want to see me succeed on this venture. If I come coasting back to the Earth / Moon system with several thousand tons of high-grade steel and enough water to start building swimming pools in Moonbase—and undercutting the corporations' Earth-based prices—I'll have broken the stranglehold those fat-cat bastards have on the space settlements.

They don't like that. Which is why they're out to stop me. I've got to be on the lookout for their next attempt. They can't launch anything to intercept us or attack us outright; the IAC would know that they'd done it and there'd be criminal charges filed against them.

No, Rockledge and any partners-in-crime they may have are working from within. They've got an agent on board my ship and they've got a plan for wrecking this expedition. This sabotage of the food freezers is just their first shot. Will hasn't found any more time bombs yet, but that doesn't mean the ship's clean. Not by a long shot. They could hide a ton of surprises aboard the *Argo*; I just hope Will digs 'em up before they go off.

I know it sounds paranoid, but even paranoids have enemies.

Kay Taranto finally answered me today. We're so far beyond the orbit of Mars by now that messages take nearly an hour to travel from Earth, even at the speed of light. So two-way conversations are out of the question.

I took her call in my personal quarters, just off the command center. The transmission was scrambled, of course, and it took a little coaxing of the computer before I got a clear picture on my screen. Kay had never been a great beauty: she's got a lean, scruffy, lantern-jawed look to her. The only time I've ever seen her smile was when she nailed a victim who was trying to escape Disney's clutches. Now her face in my screen was unsmiling, dead serious.

"No joy, Sam," she said. "Far as I can tell, Darling is virginally pure, money-wise. No large sums deposited in any of his accounts. No deposits at all in the past four years. He's been living off the income from several nice chunks of blue-chip stocks. No accounts in Liechtenstein that I could find. No Rockledge stock in his portfolio, either. He just about cleaned out his piggy bank to raise the ten mil for your wacky venture. And that's all there is to it."

Then she let a faint glimmer of a smile break her iron-hard facade. "That'll be seventy-five thou, pal. And dinner's on you when you get back."

Thanks a friggin' lot, I said silently to her image on the screen. *Por nada.*

Okay, so we found a carbonaceous chondrite first.

From everything the astrogeologists had told me, metallic asteroids are much more plentiful than the carbonaceous stones. But it's just happened that our sensors picked up a carbonaceous rock, *bang!* right off the bat. I fired two automated probes at it as soon as we got close enough. This morning Lonz initiated the course change we need to match orbit with the rock and rendezvous with it. We'll catch up to it in ten days.

The passengers—partners—have finally recovered

from their food orgy. For a week or so they were pretty hung over, and pretty shame-faced. It's a pity I didn't think to make a video of their antics. I could blackmail them for the rest of their lives if I had it all on tape.

Anyway, I called a meeting in the lounge. They all looked pretty dreary, worn out, like they were recuperating from some tropical disease. All except Darling, who seemed pink and healthy. And a lot heavier than he was before. He's ditched his normal clothing and he's now wearing some kind of robe that looks like he stitched it together himself. It took me a couple of minutes of staring at it before I recognized what it was: two tablecloths from the dining lounge, with some designs hand-painted on them.

Shades of the Emperor Nero! Was he wearing eye makeup, too?

"We've located a carbonaceous asteroid," I announced, turning away from Darling. "We'll make rendezvous with it in ten days."

Hubble's ears perked up. "I'd like to see the data, if I may." His voice was still hoarse from all the Roman feather-throating he'd gone through. You'd think that his being an older man, a scientist and all that, he would've set a better example for the other bubbleheads. But no, he'd been just as wild as the rest of them.

I noticed, though, that Sheena was no longer sitting next to him. His father image had apparently gone down the toilet along with everything else.

"Sure," I said to him. "Come on up to the command center afterward. Right now, though, I thought it'd be a good idea if we came up with a proper name for the rock."

"You can't claim it, can you?" Grace asked.

Bo Williams shook his bald head. "No one can claim any natural object in space. That's international law."

"You can use it, though," Hubble said. "There's no law against mining or otherwise utilizing an astronomical body, even if you can't claim ownership."

"First come, first served," said Rick Darling. With a smirk.

"You're all well versed on interplanetary law," I said, making myself smile at them. "But I still think we ought to give this rock a name. It's going to make us rich, the least we can do is name it."

"What will we get from it?" Sheena asked.

"Water," responded five or six voices simultaneously, including mine.

"Is that all?"

"Tons of water," I said. "Water sells for about one million U.S. dollars per ton at Lagrange One. Considering the size of this asteroid and its possible water content, we ought to clear a hundred million, easy."

"That would pay back our investment!" Marj Dupray piped.

"With a profit," added Jean Margaux, the first time I had seen her say something spontaneous.

"There'll be other valuables on a carbonaceous chondrite, as well," Hubble said, taking out his pipe for the first time. "Carbon, of course. A fair amount of nitrogen, I would suppose ... It could be quite profitable."

Not bothering to explain to them the difference between gross income and net profit, I said, "So let's pick a name for the rock and register it with the IAC."

They fell silent.

"I was sort of thinking we might name it Gunn One," I suggested modestly.

They booed and hooted. Each and every one of them.

"Aphrodite," said Sheena, once the razzing had quieted down.

Everybody turned to stare at her. Aphrodite?

She blinked those gorgeous eyes of hers; they were emerald-green this morning. "I remember some painting by some old Italian of the birth of Venus, coming out of the sea. You know, like she's the gift of the sea."

"But what's that got to do with ..."

"And that's Venus. There's already a planet named Venus."

"I know," Sheena said. "That's why I thought we could use her Greek name, Aphrodite."

I had never realized she knew anything at all about anything at all. But she knew abut the goddess of love's different names. I went behind the bar to the computer terminal and checked on the names already registered for asteroids. There was a Juno and a Hera, a Helena and even a Cleopatra. But no Aphrodite.

"Aphrodite looks good," I said.

"I still fail to see what it has to do with a lump of rock floating around in space," Jean complained.

But we voted her down and sent a message to the IAC headquarters in Geneva: a new asteroid has been discovered and its name is Aphrodite.

A hundred and twenty-seven tons of water. Boy, do I feel good about that! A hundred and twenty-seven million bucks safely stowed in our inflatable tanks!

We've been working hard for a solid month, chewing up Aphrodite and baking the volatiles out of her rocks. The grinding equipment worked fine; so did the ovens. No sabotage there, thank God.

There isn't much of old Aphrodite left. Sheena got kind of upset when she realized we were tearing up the rock and grinding it and baking the pieces. We left a small chunk so the name's still valid, although we've perturbed its orbit so much that Hubble claims she'll fall in toward the Sun and cross the orbit of Mars and maybe even Earth's orbit.

Thirty-one thousand seven hundred and fifty gallons of water, according to the volume of tankage we've filled. That masses out to one hundred and twenty-seven tons. Plus an almost equal amount of ammonia and methane. We've got an even dozen of our inflatable storage tanks hanging outside the ship's hub. I've already made a contract with Moonbase Corporation to buy the whole kit and kaboodle at ten percent below Rockledge's price. They'll process the ammonia and methane for the nitrogen and carbon, then mix the leftover hydrogen with oxygen from lunar ores to make still more water.

We're gonna drown Rockledge!

My partners have been happy and pretty well behaved this past month. The news media back home have been interviewing them almost constantly; they're all becoming famous. This isn't The Ship of Fools anymore. The media's describing us now as "the grandest entrepreneurial venture in history."

I love the publicity, because the more attention the media pays us the harder it'll be for Rockledge or one of those other big corporate monsters to attack us.

And Lonz has found a *bee-yoo-tiful* nickel-iron asteroid hanging out there just two weeks from where we are. Laser measurements show she's a little over a hundred meters by thirty by twenty or so. Enough high-grade iron ore in her to give us a corner on the steel market for all the Lagrange construction jobs!

We're gonna be rich!

I need the guidance counselor.
[Computer]: How may I help you?
I've got a problem.
[Computer]: Yes?
About a woman. Two women, really.
[Computer]: Go on.
It's Grace Harcourt and Sheena Chang. They're snarling and spitting at each other like a pair of cats.
[Computer]: Why do you think they're behaving that way?
It's over me, stupid! Why else?
[Computer]: Tell me what happened.
We're cruising toward this nickel-iron asteroid, going to make rendezvous in a few days. So I call the partners together in the lounge again to decide on a name for the rock.

And Sheena pipes up, "I don't think it's right for us to be destroying these asteroids."

That surprised me. But coming from her, I tried to explain things gently.

"Look, Sheena," I said. "The whole reason we're out here, the reason you and everybody else joined this expedition, is to get the natural resources that these asteroids contain and bring them back home, where people need them."

"You smashed up Aphrodite until there's practically nothing left of her, and now she's going to crash into Mars or the Earth or maybe even fall into the Sun and burn to death!"

"Sheena, it's just a hunk of rock."

"It's part of nature. It's part of the natural environment. We shouldn't be tampering with the environment. That's wrong."

"Oh, good Christ!" said Grace with a huff like a disgusted steam engine. She was sitting on one side of Sheena; Hubble was sitting on the other, sucking on his smokeless pipe.

"There's nothing alive on these asteroids," Hubble told her, back to his patient fatherly voice once more. "It doesn't hurt anyone to mine them."

"I still think it's wrong," Sheena insisted. I saw tears in her eyes.

"How long are we going to put up with this drivel?" Grace snarled.

Sheena went almost rigid in her chair, like somebody had wired it with a couple thousand volts.

Grace said, "I've spent most of my working days listening to airheaded actors and actresses attach themselves to 'causes.' Sheena, what the hell's the matter with your brain? We're talking about a dead chunk of rock. There's millions of them out here. Get real!"

Sheena just sat there for a minute or so, looking shocked. Jean Margaux was sitting right behind Grace; she had a funny kind of eager grin on her face, like she was waiting to see the gladiators rip each other's guts open. And Rick Darling was right beside Jean, with a cynical smirk on his bloated puss.

[Computer]: His cat was smirking?

Puss! Face! It's slang, you dumb pile of germanium.

[Computer]: You are expressing your suppressed hostilities; good.

I've never suppressed a goddamned hostility in my whole goddamned life!

[Computer]: Go on.

Where was I—oh, yeah. I was just as surprised at Grace's outburst as any of the others. Marj and Bo Williams were sitting in the back of the lounge. Bo started to say something but Sheena got there first.

"Listen, Miss High-and-Mighty Columnist," she said to Grace, "I had to kiss your backside when I was in the acting business, but now I'm going to be independently wealthy, thanks to Sam, and you can go scribble yourself!"

"You plasticized bitch," Grace shot back, "I'll bet my backside is the only one in southern California you haven't kissed."

"Jealous?"

"Of you? Take away the implants and what've you got?"

"A dumpy broad with cellulite on her hips, like you."

"At least I've got a brain in my head!"

"So does a rat!"

They were nose to nose now, yelling, starting to get out of their chairs.

I jumped between them. "Hey, hey! Calm down, both of you!"

"Get this airhead out of here, Sam," Grace said. "There's nothing going on above her neck anyway."

Sheena's eyes were blazing fury. "She's jealous, jealous, jealous! Look at her, she's turning green all over!"

Hubble got up and coaxed Sheena back toward her quarters. I held Grace by the shoulders until they left. She was trembling with rage.

"This meeting's over," I told the others. "We'll pick a name for the asteroid later."

I walked Grace forward, toward the command center, away from the other passengers' quarters where Sheena and Hubble had gone.

I kept some good cognac in my quarters. Hardly ever touched it myself, but it looked good in its cut-crystal decanter and I thought it might help calm Grace down. Me, I prefer beer.

"What the hell happened in there?" I asked Grace.

She sat in the couch, still quivering so much there were almost whitecaps on her cognac. I pulled up the powered recliner chair to face her, with the coffee table between us. My quarters aren't luxurious, but there's a little more space to them than the passengers' suites. Rank hath its privileges, after all.

Grace knocked back half her cognac, then said, "I can't take any more of her, Sam. She's driving me nuts."

"Sheena?"

"Who else? The way she flaunts herself. Makes eyes at all the men."

"I thought she had settled onto Hubble."

"She's after you, Sam. Can't you see that?"

"Me? I haven't laid a glove on her since the first month out."

"And she resents it."

"That's crazy."

Grace put her snifter down on the coffee table. It was plastic, of course, but painted to look like ebony.

"Sam, she's looking for a father figure. That's you."

"That's Hubble," I corrected her.

Grace shook her head. "It was Hubble until the food orgy. Then she saw that Lowell was just as human and silly as the rest of us. But, you, *mon capitaine,* were aloof and noble and doing your duty on the bridge while the rest of us were stuffing ourselves—in more ways than one, I might add."

"I don't want to hear about it," I said.

"You've got to listen to me, Sam! You asked me to find out who the Rockledge agent is . . ."

"Sheena?"

"No, of course not. But if she's sore at you, if she feels you've rejected her, she could become a very willing tool for whoever among us is working for Rockledge."

That stopped me. "Sheena, helping Rockledge. Hmp. With an enemy like that, who needs friends?"

"This isn't funny, Sam."

But it made me laugh anyway.

Suddenly Grace got up from the couch, came around the coffee table, and plopped herself in my lap.

"You big dummy," she said. "I'm trying to protect you. Can't you see that?"

Then she said the words that strike terror into the heart of any man.

"Sam—I think I've fallen in love with you."

Well, what could I do? I mean with her sitting in my lap and all? One thing led to another and we wound up in bed. Grace is very tender, very sweet, underneath that facade of the tough Hollywood columnist that she wears most of the time.

But now she wants to hang around my neck. And this ship isn't big enough for me to hide! Besides, if she's right about Sheena I ought to be working on her, getting on her good side, so to speak.

[Computer]: In bed, you mean?

That's her best side, pal.

[Computer]: Is that necessary? It will complicate the interpersonal relationships . . .

Everything's already so goddamned complicated that I feel like I'm a pretzel trapped in a spaghetti factory. What should I do?

[Computer]: What do you want to do?

I want to get them both off my back!

[Computer]: And what would be the best way to do that, do you think?

That's what I'm asking you!

[Computer]: How do you feel about this situation?

Oh, Christ! I know this program. Whenever you're stuck you ask me how I feel. Get lost! Turn off!

[Computer]: Are you certain you want to do this?

End the program, dammit! When I want to jerk off I'll do it in the bathroom.

Well, those sneaking, slithering, slimy bastards at Rockledge have struck again.

This morning we got an order from the International Astronautical Council—bless 'em—that forbids us from mining any more asteroids until further notice.

A moratorium on asteroid mining! Only temporary, they say. But "temporary" to those lard-bottomed bureaucrats could mean years! I could be old and senile before they lift the moratorium.

Those fat-headed drones claim that we've perturbed the orbit of Aphrodite so much that there's a chance it might strike the Earth. There's not much left of Aphrodite, but she's still big enough to cause damage wherever she lands. The media are already talking about the "killer asteroid" and running stories about how an asteroid hit wiped out the dinosaurs sixty-five million years ago.

Absolute bullshit!

What's happened is that Rockledge and the other big

boys are putting pressure on the IAC to stop me—uh, us, that is. Now that they know we can undercut their price for water, they're using Aphrodite as an excuse. If the asteroid's orbit poses a threat, the IAC can send a team out with enough rocket thrusters to nudge it away from the Earth, for chrissakes. I'll pay the friggin' cost of the mission, if I have to. Take it off as a business expense; lower my goddamned taxes.

But what the IAC's done is put a moratorium on all operations that might change an asteroid's natural orbit. Hell, we're the only operation out here in the Belt. They're trying to stop us.

Well, fuck them!

I ordered Lonz to ignore the message. I'm not even going to acknowledge receiving it. We're going ahead and mining that big chunk of nickel-iron, and then we'll head back home with enough high-grade metal to make all the off-Earth settlements drool. They'll want to do business with us, and there's nothing the friggin' IAC can do to stop them from buying what I'm selling.

Then we'll let the lawyers fight it out. I'll have all the space settlements on my side, and the media will love a story that pits us little guys against the big bad corporate monsters.

Moratorium, my ass!

Yesterday we named the asteroid Pittsburgh. I called the partners together again and told them, not asked them, what the name would be. I was born in Pittsburgh, and back in its heyday it was a big steel-making town. So will this asteroid be. Our sensors show she's practically solid metal.

This morning I sent my claim in to the IAC. I haven't acknowledged their moratorium order, and I haven't told the partners about it. Filing a claim for the asteroid doesn't violate their moratorium, of course, but it'll sure make them suspicious. What the hell! There's nothing they can do about it. It'd take them a year to get a ship out here to try to stop us.

You're not allowed to claim possession of an astronomical body, but once you've informed the IAC that you've established a working facility someplace you've got the right to use the natural resources there without anybody else coming in to compete with you. The facility can be scientific, industrial, or a permanent habitat. It could even be commercial, like a tourist hotel.

That's how the various settlements on the Moon were established; no nation owns them, but once a group lays claim to a territory, the IAC prevents any other group from muscling in on the same territory.

With a chunk of metal like Pittsburgh the IAC ought to give S. Gunn Enterprises, Unlimited, exclusive rights to mine its resources—moratorium or no fucking moratorium. The asteroid's too small to allow another company to start whittling away at it. At least, that's the legal position that the IAC agreed to before the *Argo* left Earth orbit. Now we'll have to see if they stick to it.

In the meantime, there's work to do.

Pittsburgh's a beauty! We're hovering about five hundred meters from her. At this distance she's huge, immense, like a black pitted mountain hanging over our heads. I've spent most of the day taking the partners out for EVAs. To say they were impressed would be the understatement of the decade.

Imagine an enormous lump of coal-black metal, its surface roughened and pitted, its ridges and crater rims gleaming where the Sun strikes them. It's so big it dwarfs you when you go outside, makes you feel like it's going to crush you, almost.

I brought the partners out in twos. Each time a pair of them floated free of the airlock and looked up through their bubble helmets I heard the same sound out of them: a gasp—surprise, awe, fear, grandeur, all that and more.

Hubble asked for permission to chip some samples for himself, to study in the little lab he's set up in his quarters. Bo Williams started reciting poetry, right there in his space suit. Even Jean Margaux, the Ice Queen, was audibly impressed.

Everybody except Darling came out to look.

"There's our fortune," I told each one of them over the suit-to-suit comm link. "Considering the mass of this beauty and the prices on today's metals market, you're looking at ten billion dollars, on the hoof. At least."

That made them happy. Which was a good thing, because we're getting down to the last of the preserved food. In a day or two we're going to have to start eating the recycled stuff.

The IAC is still sending their moratorium to us, every hour on the hour. I've instructed the crew to ignore it and not to tell the partners about it. I've ordered them not to acknowledge any incoming messages from anybody. Then I sent out a message to my own office in Florida that we were experiencing some kind of communications difficulty, and all the incoming transmissions were so garbled we couldn't make them out.

Lonz gave me a funny look when I sent that out. A guilty look.

"Nobody's gonna hold you responsible," I told him. "Don't worry about it."

"Right, boss," he said. But he still looked uneasy. And he's never called me boss before.

I spent most of the night watching the video tapes of Darling's movements during the time I was taking the other partners outside to see Pittsburgh close-up.

It bothered me that he refused to go EVA like the rest of them. So I activated the ship's internal monitoring system, the cameras that are set unobtrusively into the overhead panels of every section of the ship. I suppose I could have been watching everything that everybody does since the moment we left Earth orbit. Maybe that would've told me who the Rockledge fink is. Certainly it would have been as good as watching porno flicks.

But there are seven of them and only one of me. I'd have to spend seven times the hours I actually have in the hopes of catching somebody performing an act of sabotage—or doing something in bed I haven't done myself, and better.

Anyway, I discovered Darling's secret. Trouble is, it's got nothing to do with Rockledge or possible sabotage. The sneaky lard-ass has been hoarding food! While the rest of the partners were up in the command center or suiting up at the main airlock, he was tiptoeing down to the food lockers and hauling armfuls of goodies back to his own suite. He's got packaged food stored in his bureau drawers, canned food stuffed under his bed, whole cases of food hidden in his closets.

God knows how long he's been stealing the stuff. His personal wine cooler is filled with frozen food, which the bastard must have been stealing since before the freezers went on the fritz.

Did he know the freezers were going to commit hara-kiri?

The work on Pittsburgh is going slower than I had planned. The metal's so good that it's tougher than we had expected. So it takes longer for the laser torches to cut through it. Once we've got a slice carved off, the smelting and refining equipment works fine. We're building up a nice payload of high-quality steel for the Lagrange habitats and the steel-hungry factories in Earth orbit.

To say nothing of the lovely ingots of twenty-four-karat gold and pure silver that we're cooking out of the ore. And the sheets of platinum!

The *Argo* is starting to look like a little toy doughnut sitting alongside a cluster of shiny steel grapes. See, in zero gravity, when we melt down a slab of ore it forms itself into a very neat sphere of molten metal. Like a teeny little sun, glowing outside the ship. After we remove the impurities (the gold and silver platinum, that is) we inject gas into the sphere to hollow it out while it's solidifying. A hollow sphere is easier for our customers to work with than a solid ball of steel. The gas comes right from the asteroid itself, of course; a by-product of our mining operation.

All this is done remotely, without any people outside. Lonz and Will control the operation from the command center. They only go EVA if something goes wrong, some piece of equipment breaks down. Even then, the little maintenance robots can take care of the routine repairs. They've only had to go EVA twice in all the weeks we've been working on Pittsburgh.

We'll have to leave the asteroid soon if we want to get

back to Earth on a reasonable schedule. The partners are
grumbling about the recycled food—Darling's bitching the
loudest, the lying thief. He's feasting on the real food he's
cached in his suite while the rest of us are nibbling on
shit-burgers. All the other partners are marveling that he's
gaining weight while the rest of us are slimming down.

Finally I couldn't stand it anymore. This evening
when I came into the dining lounge there was fat-ass Darling in his homemade togs, holding a green briquette or
recycled crap in one hand with his chubby pinkie up in
the air.

"I will *never* come out on a fly-by-night operation like
this again," he was saying.

Jean Margaux sniffed at the red briquette she had in
front of her. They were odorless, but her face looked as if
she were getting a whiff of a pigsty on a blazing afternoon
in August. Marj Dupray and Bo Williams were off at a table by themselves, whispering to each other with their
heads nearly touching over their table.

"I'm sorry you don't like the food," I said to Darling.
I could feel the tightness in my face.

"It's inedible," he complained.

"Then you'll just have to go back to your suite and
gorge yourself on the food you've got hidden there," I said.

His fleshy face turned absolute white.

Jean looked amused. "Don't tell me you've got a
candy bar hidden under your bed," she said to Darling.

"I resent your implication," the fat bastard said to me.

"Resent it all you like," I shot back. "After you've
taken us to your suite and opened up your wine cooler."

He heaved himself to his dainty little feet. "I won't
stay here and be insulted."

Jean looked kind of curious now. Bo and Marj had
stopped their tête-à-tête and were staring at us.

With as much dignity as a small dirigible, Darling
headed for the hatch.

I called after him, "Come on, Rick, invite us to your
suite. Share the food you've hoarded, you puffed-up
sonofabitch."

He spun around to face me, making the fringes of his
toga flap and swirl. "You retract that statement or, so help

me, when we get back to Earth I'll sue you for every penny you've got!"

"Sure, I'll retract it. After you've invited us to your suite."

"That's an invasion of my privacy!" he said.

Jean drew herself up to her full height. "Richard, dear, are you actually hiding food from us?"

Bo Williams got off his chair, too. "Yeah—what's the story, Rick? How come you're getting fatter while we're all getting thinner?"

Darling's eyes swung from one of them to the other. Even Marjorie was on her feet now, scowling at him.

"Can't you see what he's doing?" Darling spluttered and pointed a fat finger at me. "He's trying to make a scapegoat out of me! He's trying to get you all to hate me and forget that *he's* the one who's gotten us into this mess!"

"There's an easy way to prove you're innocent," Williams said. "Invite us in to your suite."

Bo can look menacing in his sleep, with that burly build of his and the shaved scalp. He's really a gentle guy, a frustrated poet who makes his living writing documentaries. But he looks like a Turkish assassin.

"I don't have to prove anything," Darling answered, edging back toward the hatch. "A man's innocent until proven guilty. That's the law."

What little patience I have snapped right then and there. "I'm the law aboard this vessel," I said. "And I order you to open up your suite for inspection. Now."

He hemmed and hawed. He blubbered and spluttered. But with Bo and me pushing him, he backed all the way down the corridor to his suite. Sure enough, there was enough food cached away in there to cater a party.

Which is exactly what we had. I called Grace, Sheena, and Lowell Hubble. Even invited the crew while I went up to the command center and kept an eye on the automated equipment. They ate and drank everything Darling had squirreled away. He just sat on his own bed and cried until there was nothing left but crumbs and empty bottles.

Served him right. But I couldn't help feeling sort of

sorry for the poor jerk when they all left him in his own suite, surrounded by the mess.

I kind of hate to leave Pittsburgh. This asteroid has made me filthy rich. We can't stay long enough to mine everything she's got to give us; even if we did the *Argo* would be toting so much mass that our thrusters would never be able to get us back to Earth.

No, we'll leave Pittsburgh with our smelting equipment and a beacon on her, to verify our claim. If the IAC works the way they should, nobody else will be able to touch her. In a few years the lawyers ought to have wrangled out this moratorium business, and I'll be able to send out a fleet of ships to finish carving her up and carting the refined metals back Earthward.

I'll be a billionaire!

Marooned.

Those bastards at Rockledge have shown their hand at last. They're going to kill me and my partners and steal my claim to Pittsburgh and the metals we've mined. As well as the water and volatiles we got from Aphrodite.

I'm beyond anger. A kind of a cold freeze has gripped me. I can't even work up the satisfaction of screaming and swearing. They've marooned us on the asteroid; me and all my partners. We'll die on Pittsburgh. I'm talking into the recording system built into my space suit. Maybe someday after we're all dead somebody will find us and listen to this tape. If you do, take our bodies—and this tape— straight to the IAC's law-enforcement people. Murder, piracy, grand larceny, conspiracy, kidnapping—and it all goes right to the top of Rockledge. And God knows who else.

I don't even feel scared. I'm just kind of numb. Dumbstruck. Like being paralyzed.

Erik is the one. Smiling, blond, slow-witted Erik is the mastermind that Rockledge planted on the *Argo*. It's like one of those damned mystery novels where the murderer turns out to be the stupid butler. Who would have suspected Erik? Not me, that's for sure.

Lonz, Will, and I had put in a long, tough day finishing up our operations on Pittsburgh. All the mining and smelting equipment we had put onto the asteroid was finally shut down. That cluster of steel grapes bulked very nicely on one side of the ship. The sheets of platinum and the ingots of gold and silver were all neatly tucked into our cargo bays. Our identification beacon was on the asteroid, beeping satisfactorily.

I scrolled through the checklist on the main console's screen one final time. We had done everything we had to do. The partners were all asleep—at least they were all in their beds. Or somebody's beds.

"Okay," I said to Lonz. "That's it. Let's see the nav program and set up the trajectory for home."

"Um, there's been a change in the mission plan, Sam," Erik said.

I turned around from the console to look at him. I hadn't even realized he'd entered the control center. His usual station was down by the galley, next to the lounge. He stood in the middle of the floor, smiling that slow, genial smile of his, like always.

"Whattaya mean?" I asked.

"We can't start the homeward trip just yet," he said.

"Why not?"

His smile didn't change one iota as he explained, "We've got to put you and your partners off the ship first."

"Put me and . . . ?"

"You're staying here, Sam," Erik told me. "You're not coming back." And he pulled a slim little automatic pistol from his belt. It looked big enough to me, probably because he pointed it straight at my eyes.

"What the hell are you talking about?" But the sinking sensation in the pit of my stomach told me that I knew the answer to my own question.

I spun around toward Lonz and Will. They both looked unhappy, but neither one of them made a move to help me.

"You guys, too?" All of a sudden I felt like Julius Caesar.

"You wouldn't believe how much money we'll be getting," Will muttered.

"For chrissakes, didn't I treat you guys fair and square?" I yelped.

"You didn't make us partners, Sam," said Lonz.

"Holy shit. Why didn't you *tell* me you were un-happy? I could've . . ."

"Never mind," Erik said, suddenly forceful, in charge. "Sam, you'll have to stay in your quarters until we get ev-erything arranged. Don't try anything. I don't want to make this messy."

Three against one would have made a mess all right, and the mess would be me. So I huffed and puffed and slinked to my quarters like a good, obedient prisoner. My mind was spinning, looking for an out, but I didn't know what they planned to do. That made it tough to figure out my next move. I heard them attach some kind of a lock to the outside of the door as soon as I closed it after me. And then all my lights went off; not even the emergency lamps lit. They had cut off all electrical power to my quarters. No lights, no computer access, no communications with any-body, nothing but darkness.

And waiting.

After a few hours they bundled us all into space suits and—one by one—had each of us jet from the *Argo's* main airlock to the surface of Pittsburgh, where we had left the mining and smelting equipment. I was the last one to be pushed out.

"We've set up an inflated dome for the eight of you," Erik said, with that maddening slow grin of his, "and stocked with enough food to last a few months."

"Thanks a bunch!" I snapped.

"We could have killed you all outright," he said. "I thought I was going to have to after I made that slip about Liechtenstein in the lounge one of the first nights out."

I felt like a complete idiot. It never occurred to me that one of the guys I hired might be the Rockwell plant.

The sonofabitch knew what he was doing; I have to hand him that. If he had tried anything violent all eight of us would have fought for our lives. As far as I could tell the only weapon they had was Erik's one pistol. He might have killed several of us, but we might have swarmed him under. Lonz and Will, too. Eight against three. We might have carried it off.

But Erik worked it like an expert. He isolated us into

individuals and, instead of killing us outright, merely forced us to go from the ship to the asteroid. Merely. It was a slow way of killing us. Food and shelter notwithstanding, nobody will return to Pittsburgh in less than a couple of years. Nobody can, even if Erik would leave us a radio and we screamed our lungs out for help.

"This is piracy," I said as the three of them nudged me toward the airlock. "To say nothing of murder."

"It's business, Sam," Erik said. "Nothing personal."

I turned to Lonz. "Do you think he's going to let you live?" Then to Will. "Or you? Neither one of you is going to make it back to Earth."

Lonz looked grim. "They're giving us enough money to set us up for life. There's no reason for us to talk, and no reason for Erik to worry about us."

I huffed at him from inside my helmet. "Dead men tell no tales, pals." Then I snapped the visor shut and stepped into the airlock.

"I'm sorry, Sam," I heard Will's voice say, muffled by my helmet.

"Sorry don't get the job done," I answered in my bravest John Wayne imitation.

Then the hatch closed and the pumps started sucking the air out of the lock.

The outer hatch slid open. There was Pittsburgh, hanging big and black and ugly against the even blacker background of space. Through the heavy tinting of my visor I could only see a few of the brighter stars. They looked awfully cold, awfully far away.

"Get going, Sam," Erik's voice sounded genially in my earphones, "or we'll have to open your suit with a laser torch."

Like walking the goddamned plank. I jetted over to the asteroid. Sure enough, there was an inflated dome next to the equipment we had left. And seven space-suited figures standing outside it. Even in the bulky suits they looked scared shitless, huddled together, clinging to one another.

I planted my feet on the asteroid and turned back toward the *Argo*, spinning lazily against the backdrop of stars.

Raising one clenched fist over my head I yelled into my suit radio's microphone, "I'll see you—all of you—hanging from the highest yardarm in the British fleet!"

It was the only damned thing I could think of. About five minutes later a blazing flare of light bellowed from the *Argo*'s rocket nozzles and the ship—*my* ship—suddenly leapt away and dwindled in the dark sky until I couldn't see it anymore.

To say that my partners are upset is putting it so mildly that it's like saying that Custer's Seventh Cavalry was not terribly friendly with the Sioux Nation.

They're terrified. They're weeping. They're cursing and swearing and calling down the wrath of the gods. Who (as usual) remain totally aloof and unconcerned about our plight. It took me nearly half an hour to get them to stop babbling, and by that time I finally got it through my thick skull that they're mad at *me*!

"This is all your fault!" Rick Darling screamed at me. "I *begged* them to let me stay on the ship. I promised them I'd never inform on them. I even told them that I was *glad* they wanted to get rid of you! But they wouldn't listen! Now I'm going to die and it's all your fault!"

Funny thing is, each and every one of them is yelling some variation of the same story. Each one of them begged Erik to let them stay aboard, promised to go along with killing me—and all the others—providing they were allowed to get home safely.

Erik didn't take any of them up on their offers. Not even Sheena, who had a helluva lot to offer. The sonofabitch must be made of very strong stuff. Either that or he's gay, which I doubt, because Darling would've probably bent over backward for him if that's what he wanted.

They're being so goddamned rotten that they've almost made me forget who our real enemy is. I let them babble and gabble and just clumped across the rough, pitted surface of Pittsburgh and went inside the dome Erik had so thoughtfully left for us. I ought to mention that the asteroid's too small to have any noticeable gravity. We're all outfitted with small magnets on our boots, which work very nicely on a body made predominantly of iron. But even though walking is as easy as stepping across a newly painted floor that's still slightly tacky, my body's feeling all the old sensations of nearly zero gravity.

I'm smiling to myself. As soon as my partners calm down enough to take stock of their situation, they're going to get good and sick. I'm certain that Erik hasn't included space-sickness medications in the pile of supplies he's left us.

Good! Serves the whining little pricks right.

Sure enough, they've all been sick as dogs for the past two days. I felt kind of queasy myself for the first few hours, but I got over it quickly enough.

I've spent the time checking out just how much Erik left us, in his less-than-infinite kindness. It's not much. Eight crates of food briquettes; about enough to last six months. No medical supplies, not even aspirin. The dome's got air and water recyclers, off-loaded from *Argo*'s spares. But no backup equipment and no spare parts. If anything goes wrong with the machinery, we die pretty quickly.

So our prospects are (1) we starve to death in six months; (2) we die from lack of water or air if either of the recyclers craps out on us; or (3) we start murdering each other because there's nothing else for us to do but get on each other's nerves.

At least inside the dome we can get out of the space suits. There's no furniture in here; nothing to sit on but the crates of food briquettes, eight inflatable sleeping rolls, and a zero-gee bathroom facility. The toilet seems to work okay, although there's only the one of them. The women bitch about that constantly. Me, I worry about how much radiation we're absorbing; the metallized plastic of this dome doesn't stop cosmic ray primaries, and if there's a solar flare we'll probably get cooked inside of an hour or two.

There's also the possibility that a smaller asteroid might puncture our dome. That would be absolutely poetic: killed by an asteroid striking another asteroid.

Reality is setting in.

My seven keen-minded partners are mostly recovering from their zero-gee puking and starting to realize that we are well and truly marooned on this chunk of nickel-iron. With only six months worth of food.

They've even stopped hollering at me. They're getting morose, just sitting around this cramped little dome like a bunch of prisoners waiting for dawn and the firing squad.

"Would've been kinder of Erik to kill us outright and get it over with," said Bo Williams.

The others are sad-faced as basset hounds with toothaches. Trying to sleep on a three-centimeter-thick inflatable bag laid over a rough floor of solid nickel-iron does nothing to improve anybody's disposition.

"If that's the way you feel about it," Lowell Hubble said to Bo, from behind his inevitable pipe, "why don't you just commit suicide and save us the self-pity? That would leave an extra ration of food to the survivors."

Williams's shoulder muscles bunched underneath his grimy shirt. "And why don't you try sucking on something else other than that damned pacifier?"

"Why don't you both shut up?" Marj snapped.

"I think this entire line of conversation is disgraceful," said Jean. "If we can't behave like polite adults we should leave the dome until we've learned how to act properly."

We all stared at her. I started to laugh. In her own prissy way, Jean was right. We need some discipline. Something to keep our minds off our predicament.

"Maybe we ought to draw lots," Grace suggested with mock cheerfulness. "Short straw goes outside without a suit. Maybe we could stretch the food long enough . . ."

"And even add to our food supply," Williams said, eyeing Darling grimly. "Like the Donner party."

Sheena's eyes went like saucers. "Eat . . . ? Oh, I could never do that!"

"People do strange things when they're starving," Hubble said. He looked over at our overfed Mr. Darling, too.

If Rick understood what was going through their minds, he didn't show it. "If only there was some hope of rescue," he mewled. "Some slightest shred of hope."

It hit me right then.

"Rescue, my ass!" I said. And before Jean could even frown at me, I added. "We're gonna save ourselves, by damn!"

They laughed at Columbus. They laughed at Edison and the Wright brothers and Marconi.

None of my beloved partners laughed at me when I said we'd save ourselves. They just kind of gaped for a moment, and then ignored me, as if I had farted or done something else stupid or vulgar.

But what the hell, there isn't anything else we can do. And we need some discipline, some goal, some objective to keep our brains busy and our minds off starvation and death. Instead of breaking down into an octet of would-be murderers and cannibals, I dangled the prospect of salvation in front of their unbelieving eyes.

"We can do it!" I insisted. "We can save ourselves. We can turn this little wordlet of ours into a lifeboat."

"And pigs can fly," Bo Williams growled.

"They can if they build wings for themselves," I shot back.

Darling started, "How on earth do you propose ..."

"We're not on Earth, O corpulent critic of the arts. Erik thinks he's got us marooned here on Pittsburgh. But we're gonna ride this rock back to the Earth / Moon system."

Jean Margaux: "That's impossible!"

Marj Dupray: "It beats sitting around and watching the food supplies dwindle."

Grace Harcourt: "Can you really do it, Sam?"

Sheena Chang: "What do you think, Lowell?"

Hubble, our resident astronomer, took the pipe out of his mouth and squinted at me as if he had never seen me before. His mustache was getting ragged and grayer than usual. He needed a shave. All of us men looked pretty shaggy, except for Darling, whose cheeks were still as smooth as a baby's backside. Is he permanently depilated, or doesn't he have enough testosterone in him to raise a beard?

Hubble said, "To move this asteroid out of its present

orbit we'd need a propulsion system and navigational equipment."

"We've got 'em," I said. "Or at least, we can make 'em."

I know the mining and smelting facilities inside out. We had left the equipment here on Pittsburgh. My idea had been, why drag them all the way back home when you'll want them at the asteroid on the next trip out? The equipment's nuclear-powered, of course: you'd need solar-cell panels as big as cities to generate enough electricity at this distance from the Sun.

When Sheena found out we had two (count 'em, two) nukes on Pittsburgh, she gasped with alarm. "But nuclear power is bad, Sam. It's got radiation."

"Don't worry about it, kiddo," I told her. "They're shielded real well." I didn't bother to inform her that her gorgeous body was getting more radiation from cosmic primaries than all the nuclear power plants on Earth gave off.

My idea is to use the mining lasers to slice off chunks of the asteroid, then use the smelting facility to vaporize the metal instead of just melting it down. If we can direct the vapor properly it'll push us like a rocket exhaust. I figure we can scoop out a pit in the asteroid's surface and use it as a rough-and-ready rocket nozzle. Or maybe one of the existing craters that've put the *pit* in ol' Pittsburgh will do.

We won't need pinpoint navigation. All I need is to get us moving at a good clip toward the Earth / Moon system. Once we cross the orbit of Mars the automated meteor-watch radars'll pick us up. Hell, Pittsburgh's big enough to scare the bejesus out of the IAC. An asteroid this big, heading for the Earth / Moon system? They'll at least send a robot probe to check us out; maybe a manned spacecraft with enough extra propulsion aboard to nudge us away from the inhabited region. Either way, there'll be a radio aboard and we can yell for help.

Damn! Hubble's done some calculations on his wrist computer and given me the bad news. Oh, my scheme will work all right, but it'll take seventy or eighty years before Pittsburgh gets past the orbit of Mars.

"She's just too massive," Hubble said. "If we want to

accelerate this asteroid that quickly we need a lot more energy than we can get by burning off mass at the rate the smelting facility can produce."

Gloom. All seven of them became even more morose than ever. I felt down, too. For a while. Then Sheena saved the day.

Not that we can tell day from night on Pittsburgh. The only way we can keep track of time is by the clocks built into our wrist computers. Even though the asteroid's slowly tumbling as it swings through space, inside the dome we get no sensation of daylight or nighttime. The sky's always dark, even when the Sun is visible outside. Our mood matched our environment: cold, dark, dreary.

Sheena came up to me while I was trying to decide whether I'd make dinner out of a green briquette or a red one. They both looked kind of brown to me, but that may have been just the lighting inside the dome, which was pretty low and murky.

"Sam," she said. "Can I ask you a favor?"

We were all so glum and melancholy that I had forgotten how beautiful Sheena was. Whether it was natural or surgically enhanced, even in the shabby unwashed blouse and slacks she'd been wearing for days on end, she looked incredibly lovely. I forgot about food, temporarily.

"A favor?" I said. "Sure. What is it?"

"Well ..." she hesitated, as if she had to put her thoughts together. "Since we won't be using the mining equipment and all that other stuff, can't we toss those ugly old nuclear generators out? I mean, they can't be doing us any good sitting out there making radiation ..."

I jumped to my feet so hard that my magnetic soles couldn't hold me and I went skyrocketing straight up to the top of the dome.

"*Yahoo!*" I yelled. My seven partners gaped up at me. To say they were startled would be a very large understatement.

I turned in midair and glided down onto Lowell Hubble's shoulders. "The nukes!" I yelled, tapping out a jazz rhythm on his head. "Instead of using them to generate electricity we can *explode* the mothers!"

It took a while for me to calm down enough to explain it to them. There was enough energy in the nuclear piles of our two generators to blast out a sizable portion of Pittsburgh—enough to propel us back toward the inner solar system.

"Like atomic bombs?" Bo Williams actually shuddered. "You've got to be crazy, Sam."

But Hubble was pecking away at his wrist computer. I could tell he was almost as excited as I was: he had even dropped his pipe.

"You can't set off nuclear explosions here," Grace said, looking kind of scared. "You'll get us all killed."

I gave her a grin and a shrug. "Might as well go down fighting. You want to wait until we put long pig on the menu?"

She didn't answer.

But Jean did. "Interplanetary law forbids using nuclear explosives in space unless specifically permitted by the IAC and under the supervision of their inspectors."

"So sue me," I told her. "Better yet, *call* the friggin' IAC and have them come out here and arrest me!"

Hubble had a different kind of objection. "Sam, I don't know if you can get those power piles to explode. They have all sorts of safeguards built into them. They're designed to fail-safe, you know."

"Then we'll have to pull 'em out of the generators and disengage all their safety systems."

"But the radiation!"

"That's what robots are for," I said grandly.

I should've known that those friggin' simpleminded robots we have for working the mining and smelting equipment couldn't handle the task of disassembling the nuclear reactors. Three of our five stupid tin cans can't even move across the goddamned surface of Pittsburgh; it's too rough for their delicate goddamned wheels. They're stranded where they sit. The two that can move aren't strong enough to pry the power piles out of the generators. Sure, everything here is in microgee, but those piles are imbedded inside deep shielding, and friction makes it tough to slide them out.

I won't bore you with all the details. I had to ask for

volunteers. I knew I'd have to go out there myself, but I'd need more than my two hands to get the job done.

I didn't expect any of my brave little partners to volunteer. They never had before, and what I was asking them to do now was really risky, maybe fatal.

To my surprise, Lowell Hubble raised his hand. "I'm too old to start a family," he said quietly, glancing at Sheena sideways.

We were standing in a little circle inside the dome. I had outlined what needed to be done and what the dangers were. I had also told them very firmly that I would accept only male volunteers.

"Nonsense!" Jean snapped. "That's male chauvinist twaddle."

As soon as Hubble put his hand up, Jean raised hers. "I'm too old to *want* to start a family," she said firmly.

The others glanced around at one another uneasily. Slowly, very slowly, each of them raised their hands. Even Sheena, although her hand was trembling. I felt kind of proud of them.

We did it by lottery. Almost. I wouldn't let Hubble out of the dome. I needed him for all the calculations we had to do, and maybe later for navigation, if all goes well. Bo Williams hated that, I could tell, but he didn't complain. He could see that there's no use risking the one guy who can handle the scientific end of this madness. It's not just the radiation. What'll we do if Hubble trips out there and one end of the power pile mashes his head?

Chauvinist or not, I just took Bo and Darling out with me. Darling looked so scared I thought he was going to crap in his space suit, but he didn't dare complain a peep. We got the first pile out from behind its shielding okay, and then skeedaddled back inside the dome and let the robots finish the work. The dosimeters built into our suits screeches a little and flashed their yellow warning lights. Once we got back into the dome they went back to green, though.

A good day's work. Maybe we'll make it after all.

According to Hubble's calculation, if we can make just one of the power piles explode it'll provide enough impetus to push Pittsburgh out of its orbit and send it zooming toward the inner solar system.

"You're sure?" I asked him.

He nodded like a college professor, the pipe back between his teeth. "If you can get it to explode."

"It'll explode, don't worry. Even if I have to beat it with a baseball bat."

He gave me a slightly amused look. "And where are you going to find a baseball bat?"

"Never mind that," I said. "Will we be safe? I don't really want to kill us if I can avoid it."

"Oh, safe enough, if you place the pile on the far end of Pittsburgh and set it off there. I've worked out the precise location for you."

"We won't get a fatal dose of radiation or anything?"

"No, the mass of the asteroid will protect us from radiation. Since there's no air outside the dome there will be no aerodynamic shock wave. No heat pulse or fallout, either, if the pile is properly sited in a crater."

"Then we'll be okay."

"We should be. The only thing to worry about is the seismic shock. The explosion will send quite a jolt through the body of the asteroid, of course."

"I was wondering about that? How many gees?"

He frowned slightly. "That's right, you astronauts think in terms of gee forces."

"Don't you?"

"No. I was more concerned with Pittsburgh's modulus of elasticity."

"Its what?"

He gave me a faraway look. "The explosion will send a shock wave through the solid body of the asteroid."

"You already said that."

"Yes. The question is, will that shock wave break up the asteroid?"

"Break it up? Break up Pittsburgh?"

"Yes."

"Well, will it? Will it?"

"I don't think so. But I simply don't have enough data to be certain."

"Thanks," I said.

So our choice is to sit on this rock until we starve to death or maybe blow it to smithereens with a jury-rigged atomic bomb.

I'm going with the bomb. And keeping my fingers crossed.

Okay, we're all in our pressure suits, inside the dome, lying flat inside our pitiful little inflated sleeping bags. When I press the button on the remote control unit in my hand the feeble-minded robot out there on the other end of Pittsburgh will pull the control rods out of the power pile and it'll go critical in a matter of seconds.

Here we go.

Soon's I work up the nerve.

Good news and bad news.

The pile exploded all right, and jolted Pittsburgh out of its orbit. The asteroid didn't break up. None of us got killed. No significant radiation here in the dome, either.

That's the good news.

There's plenty of bad. First off, the explosion slammed us pretty damned hard. Like being kicked in the ribs by a big bruiser in army boots. We all slid and tumbled in our air bags and went sailing splat into the wall of the dome. Damned near tore it open before we untangled ourselves. Arms, legs, yelling, bitching. Good thing we were in the space suits; they cushioned some of the shock. The sleeping bags just added to the confusion.

Even so, Bo Williams snapped a shin bone when he slammed into a food crate. The rest of us are banged up, bruised, but Bo is crippled and in a lot of pain. Jean, of all people, pulled the leg straight and set the bone as well as anybody could without X-ray equipment.

"The last time I had to do anything like this was on a walking tour of Antarctica," she calmly told us.

We tore the offending food crate apart to make a splint for Bo's leg. A walking tour of Antarctica?

But the really bad news came from Lowell Hubble. He took a few observations of the stars, made a couple of calculations on his wrist computer, and told me—privately, very quietly—that the blast didn't do enough.

"Whaddaya mean, not enough?" I wanted to yell, but I whispered, just like he did. The rest of the gang was clustered around Bo, who was manfully trying to bear his pain without flinching. The undivided attention of the four women helped.

"The explosion just didn't have enough energy in it to push our orbit toward the Earth," Hubble whispered. Drawing circles in the air with the stem of his pipe, he explained, "We're moving inward, toward the Sun, all right. We'll cross the orbit of Mars, eventually. But we won't get much closer to Earth than that."

"Eventually? How soon's that?"

He stuck the pipe back in his mouth. "Three and a half years."

I let out a weak little whistle. "That won't do us a helluva lot of good, will it?"

"None at all," he said, scratching at his scruffy chin.

I felt itchy, too. In another week or two my beard will be long enough to be silky. Right now it just irritates the hell out of me.

"We've got the other nuke," I said.

"We're going to need it."

"I hate to have to go through the whole damned exercise again—pulling the pile out of its shielding, dismantling the control systems. We're down to one usable robot."

"I'll volunteer, Sam."

I turned and there was Rick Darling standing two meters away, a kind of little-boy look of mixed fear and anticipation on his fuzzless face.

"You'll volunteer?" My voice squeaked with surprise.

"To work with you on the nuclear pile," he said. "You tell me what to do and I'll do it."

"You're sure you want to?"

His lower lip was trembling. "Sam, I've been completely wrong about you. You are the bravest and strongest man I've ever met. I realize now that everything you've done has been for our own good. I'm willing to follow you wherever you choose to lead."

I was too shocked to do much more than mumble,

"Okay. Good." Darling smiled happily at me and went back to his food crate.

Saints in heaven! I think Rick Darling is in love with me.

Well, we both took enough radiation out there to make our suit dosimeters screech. They went all the way into the red. Lethal dose, unless we get medical attention pretty damned quick. Fat chance.

We got the pile out of the generator, ripped out most of the safety rods, and put it where Hubble told us it has to be in order to push us closer to Earth. It took hours. The goddamned tin shitcan of a robot broke down on us halfway through the job and Darling and I had to manhandle the load by ourselves.

We didn't do much talking out there, just a lot of grunting and swearing. Don't let anybody tell you that working in microgravity is easy. Sure, things have no weight, but they still have mass and inertia. You try traipsing across the surface of an asteroid with the core of a nuclear reactor practically on your back, see how much fun you get out of it.

Anyway, we're back in the dome. Hubble's gone outside to check the position of the pile and to rig a line so we can yank out the last of the control rods manually. Marj and Grace are out there helping him. Sheena and Jean are here in the dome, hovering over Bo Williams. He's got a fever and he doesn't look too damned good.

While we were taking off our space suits Darling said to me, "You don't have to be afraid of me, Sam. I know you don't like me."

"I never saw anything to like," the words popped out of my mouth before I knew it, "until today."

"I just want your respect," he said.

"You've got it."

"Would—would you stop calling me names, then? Please? They really hurt."

There were tears in his eyes. "I'm sorry . . . Rick. I did it without thinking."

He said, "I know you're hetero. I'm not trying to seduce you, Sam. I just want to be your friend."

I felt about an inch tall. "Yeah. That's fine. You've earned it."

He put out his fleshly hand. I took it in mine. We didn't really shake; we just grasped each other's hand for a long moment until I was too embarrassed to look at him any longer. I had to pull away.

It's boom time again.

We're all back in our suits, lying on the floor, wedged against the food cartons that are now up against the dome wall. Hubble's calculated which way the blast will push us, and I've tried to arrange us so we won't go sliding and slamming the way we did last time.

It took hours to get Bo Williams into his space suit, with his leg in Jean's makeshift cast. He's hot as a microwaved burger, face red, half unconscious and muttering deliriously. Doesn't look good.

I've got the control box in my hand again. If this blast doesn't do the job we're finished. Probably finished anyway. I've picked up enough radiation to light a small city. No symptoms yet, but that'll come, sure enough.

Okay. Time to press the button. Wonder if this rock'll stand up to another blast?

What a ride!

The seismic shock lifted us all off our backs and bounced us around a bit, but no real damage. Bo Williams must've been unconscious when the bomb went off, or else the belt knocked him out.

A few new bruises, that's all. Otherwise we're okay. Hubble went outside and took some sightings. We're definitely going to cross Mars's orbit, but it's still going to take a couple–three months. Then it's just a matter of time before the IAC notices us.

If we don't starve first.

Tape's running low.

Bo Williams died today, probably from infection that we didn't have the medicine to deal with. We sealed him inside his space suit. Erik's legally a murderer now. I guess Lonz and Will are, too. Or accessories, at least.

Been fourteen days since we lit off the second nuke. Hubble says we'll cross Mars's orbit in ten weeks. Definitely. He thinks.

Dome's starting to smell bad. I think the air recycler's breaking down. Food's holding out okay; nobody has much of an appetite.

The air recycler's definitely on the fritz. All of us are dopey, sluggish. And irritable! Even sweet-tempered me is—am?—snapping at the others.

There's nothing to do. Terminal boredom. We just lay around and try to avoid each other. Munch on a crapburger now and then.

And wait.

Tape's almost gone. I won't say anything else until it's the end.

The air in here's as bad as Los Angeles before they went to electric cars. Grace is coughing all the time. My eyes burn and I feel as slow and stupid as a brain-damaged cow on downers.

Most of the others sleep almost all the time. Like babies. They only get up to eat and use the toilet. And snarl at each other.

Hubble's looking grim. We're nowhere near the orbit of Mars yet and he knows as well as I do that the air's giving out.

Darling popped the question. Said it was his dying wish. I gave him a backhand smack across the chops and told him to get lost. He burst into tears and skittered away. Should've been kinder to him, I guess. We *are* dying. Not much further to go.

The Lord helps those who help themselves!

I am sitting in a private cubicle aboard the bridge ship *Bosporus*. A friggin' luxury yacht, compared even to the good old *Argo*.

You know the IAC intends to place five bridge ships in constant transit between Earth and Mars. Like trains running on a regular schedule. They'll be loaded up in the

Earth / Moon region and then ply their way out to Mars
with all the supplies and personnel that the scientists need
for their ongoing exploration of the Red Planet.

And the bridge ships will make it safer and a lot
cheaper for settlers to move out past the Earth / Moon system. I had thought that they'd help a lot with the eventual
spread of the frontier into the Asteroid Belt and even beyond.

Well, anyway, *Bosporus* is the first of the bridge ships,
and she's on her shakedown cruise. The IAC diverted her
to come out and take a look at Pittsburgh.

Why? Because the old automated surveillance satellites still orbiting the Earth detected our two nuclear
blasts, that's why! Three cheers for bureaucracy!

Way back in the middle of the last century, when
there was something called a Cold War simmering between the U.S. of A. and what used to be the Soviet
Union, both sides were worried sick about the other guy
testing nuclear weapons. So they each put satellites into
orbit to spot nuke tests anywhere on Earth—or even in
space.

Well, the Cold War ended and the Neo–Cold War
started up and then *it* ended, but the surveillance satellites
kept being replaced and even upgraded. The bureaucracy
just kept rolling along, building new and better satellites
and putting them on station regular as clockwork. Oh, they
gave a lot of excuses for doing it: making sure that small
nations didn't develop nuclear weapons, using the satellites to make astronomical observations, that kind of garbage. I think the satellites are now tied into the IAC's
overall surveillance net: you know, the sensors that look
for meteoroids that might hit the Earth or endanger habitats in the Earth / Moon region.

Whatever—our two nuclear blasts rang alarm bells all
over the IAC's sensor net. Then they saw good old Pittsburgh all of a sudden trucking toward the inner solar system. The *Argo* was on its preplanned trajectory, cruising
back toward lunar orbit with its cargo of metals, water, and
volatiles. Erik, bless him, had already reported a fatal accident that had killed the eight of us.

Somebody pretty high up in the IAC decided to send

the *Bosporus* out for a look at Pittsburgh. We got saved. It wasn't just in the nick of time; we could have probably lasted another few days, maybe a week.

But good enough for government work.

You never saw such a commotion. I'm not only rich, I'm a friggin' hero!

The media swarmed all over us. They didn't wait for the *Bosporus* to make its way back to the Earth/Moon area. They bombarded us electronically; interviews, book contracts, video deals. And right behind them came the lawyers: IAC red-tape types wanting to know how dare I set off unauthorized nuclear explosions in space. Litigation sharpies trying to get their slice of the profits that both Rockledge and S. Gunn Enterprises, Unlimited, are now claiming. Criminal prosecutors, too, once they learned about Bo Williams's death and heard me screaming about piracy.

See, Erik and the Rockledge guys who hired him had already reported to the IAC that an accident had killed me and all my partners. They already had a high-acceleration ship zipping out to Pittsburgh so they could get rid of our bodies and claim the asteroid for Rockledge's use. Only, Pittsburgh wasn't where they thought it would be anymore, and, except for Bo, we were very much alive and screaming bloody murder.

Sheena's a star again. She's already shooting footage for a docudrama about the flight. Grace is negotiating a book contract. Marj has seventeen design salons from around the world begging for her talents.

Hubble—well, he's an academic, really. He'll go back to his university and try to live down the notoriety. Rick Darling. I just don't know what he's going to do. He's independently wealthy now; or he will be, once we sort out the legalities and split the profits. He hasn't made another pass at me. In fact, he's been staying as far away from me as he can.

Which suits me okay. I took Jean to dinner in the *Bosporus*'s one and only wardroom last night, fed her a bottle of their best wine, and relocated that vulnerable spot of hers. We spent the night making the stars dance.

They're treating us for radiation disease, of course. When the *Bosporus*'s medical officer found out how much radiation I had absorbed he put on a long face and tried to break it to me gently that I would never be able to father any children. I grinned at that, which I guess puzzled him. Until he asked me to strip and he saw the neat lead-lined jockstrap I wear.

This is just to put a finish on these tapes. I'm going to lock them away with orders that they're not to be touched by anybody until ten years after my death.

Erik was sentenced to life imprisonment, which means he'll be frozen in a vat of liquid nitrogen and kept like a corpsicle until social scientists prove they can rehabilitate murderers. Maybe they'll thaw him out in a century or two. I hope not. I would've preferred it if they'd stuck him on an asteroid and sent him sailing out beyond the orbit of Mars. See how he'd like it.

I feel bad about Lonz and Will. They were both sentenced to twenty years at the penal colony on Farside. I had to testify at the trial, and even though I put all the blame on Erik, I had to admit that Will and Lonz went along with him in the whole nasty deal.

Okay. That's it. Funny sitting here listening to my own voice for hours on end. There's a lot more I could put into these tapes, more details and stuff, but what the hell, enough's enough.

They'll be sore as hell at me if any of this leaks out. Every one of my erstwhile partners is telling his or her version of the story. Selling, I should say, not just telling. Sheena's got a video series going, "Queen of the Asteroids." She's fun to watch, but the stories are *yecchh*.

Oh, yeah. One thing that I shouldn't forget. The IAC scientists propositioned each of the women partners. I guess "propositioned" isn't the right word.

Once we were landed at the Moonbase medical facility for further antiradiation therapy and the inevitable psychological counseling, a group of scientists asked each of the women if they would consider having a baby. In the interests of science. To see what effect the radiation exposure would have. Maybe they'd be sterile. Maybe they'd have two-headed triplets.

It would all be clinically clean and scientifically pure. Artificial insemination and all that. Two with sperm from the males who were also on the asteroid, two with donor sperms from strangers. Maybe they even wanted to throw in a placebo, I don't know.

Each of the women turned them down flat. I think. Jean is staying at Moonbase for the time being, which is not like her at all. Marj set herself up in Bermuda, where she's franchising various Dupray space-inspired fashion lines to the highest bidders. Good old Grace gave me a kiss good-bye and hightailed it to California as soon as the medics would let her go. Her book's going to be a best-seller, I guess, even though what I've managed to see of it looks more like fiction to me than fact. But what the hell!

They've all gone their separate ways. Rick Darling's bought himself a villa in the big new bridge ship *Golden Gate*.

Me, I'm heading back for Pittsburgh. The asteroid's swung around the Sun and she's heading back toward the Belt. She's still got billions and billions of dollars worth of valuable metals, and I intend to get them, now that the courts have given me clear title.

But this time I'm going alone, except for some really top-notch robots.

It'll be lonely, out there all by myself.

Thank God!

17

■·•·■·•·■·•·■·•·■·•·■·•·■·•·■·•·■·•·■

Bridge Ship *Golden Gate*

JADE SAT IN deep silence for a long while before she noticed that the robot had returned, bearing her clothing in its spindly metal arms.

She dressed absently, her thoughts literally millions of kilometers away. The robot gathered up the scattered spools of tape and left her alone in the big luxurious room.

It can't be, she told herself over and over. It just can't be. If it's true it means . . .

"Now you've heard Sam's tapes."

Turning from her pale reflection in the blank screen above the tape player, she asked Darling, "How did you get them?"

He shrugged, a seismic movement of flesh beneath his robes. He had changed into a pure white costume decorated with gold and silver star bursts.

"I stole them," Darling said. "How else?"

"From Sam?"

Laboriously, Darling lowered himself onto the same pile of pillows he had been sitting on when she had first entered his chamber. He took a deep breath, like an exhausted athlete, as he sank into the cushions.

"Oh, no, not from Sam. He was far too clever to allow anyone to steal them from him. But once Sam's will was probated, we discovered that he had left the tapes to Grace Harcourt. Ever since she won the Pulitzer for her exposé of Rockledge's industrial hanky-panky, she's been living . . ."

"On Pitcairn Island, I know. I tried to interview her but she wouldn't see me." Jade sat on the other set of cushions, facing Darling, her mind seething in growing turmoil.

"Yes, of course. I had the tapes purloined from the plane that was taking them out to her."

"Why?"

Darling's fleshy face set almost into hardness. "You heard what he said about me. Do you think I want Grace—or anyone else in the world—to hear all that?"

"You fell in love with Sam?"

The hardness melted immediately. "I thought I did. It must have been the radiation. Or the excitement. He certainly did nothing to deserve love. Mine, or anyone else's."

"No one else has heard the tapes?"

"No one."

There were more questions Jade knew she would have to ask. But she dreaded them, put them off, while the enormity of what she had just learned from the tapes boiled over her like a tidal wave, smothering her, drowning her. She fought to maintain her composure, her life. She did not want Darling to see what was tearing away at her innards.

Darling seemed to sense her apprehension the way a snake senses the terror it instills in a small bird. He thinks it's because of him, Jade realized. He doesn't know, doesn't realize.

"Sheena married Lowell Hubble, after her Queen of the Asteroids series went into syndication," Darling ticked off on his beringed fingers, his eyes watching her intently. "Marjorie finally retired on Bermuda. Jean Margaux died recently in a traffic accident in Maine, not far from her summer home, I understand. There was some talk about foul play, even suicide."

Jade's heart nearly stopped.

"I checked that out," she said through gritted teeth. "No foul play. Suicide is possible, of course, but all that can be said for certain is that she lost control of her car and went over a cliff into the sea."

"Strange that she'd be driving her own car, though, don't you think? I would imagine a woman such as Jean would have a chauffeur on hand at all times. A young handsome chauffeur, undoubtedly." He smiled wickedly.

Jade barely managed to say, "Maybe."

"That leaves just me." Darling heaved a titanic sigh. "Living alone here in the midst of all this splendor."

Get him talking about himself, Jade thought desperately. Get away from Jean Margaux's death.

"Why alone?" she asked, trying to sound inquisitive. "You're wealthy. Your columns about art are world-famous. You could be surrounded by friends, associates, admirers."

He made a laugh that sounded forced and self-deprecating. "It would take quite a few of them to surround me, wouldn't it?"

"I didn't mean ..."

"Dear lady, I live the way I live because I choose to. I know my limitations. My columns are frauds; how can *anyone* write valid art criticism without going to see the artwork in its actual setting? I write about holograms that are sent to me. People read my pieces for the personal nasties I throw in about the artists and dealers and other critics. I'm a worse gossip columnist than Grace Harcourt ever was, on her most vicious day."

"I see."

"Do you? Do you know what that radiation did to me? I can never father children! That's not bad enough. It also unbalanced my entire endocrine system so completely that I've blown up to this monstrous size you see!" He spread his arms and the robe billowed out like a silken cloud.

"I didn't know that," Jade said softly.

"Sam accused me of gluttony and called me terrible names," Darling said, his voice shaking, "but the truth is I was a slim and handsome man when I started out on that voyage of his. You saw the pictures! Did I look anything like *this*?"

"No," she admitted. "You certainly didn't."

"Thanks to that unkind bastard Sam I've become a balloon, a blimp, a mountain of fat—and it's all his fault! I've got to hide myself from the rest of the human race, because of that little unloving snot of a man!"

Tears were rolling down Darling's cheeks. "I loved him. I truly did. And he treated me worse than dirt. He turned me into *this*."

"He may be my father," Jade blurted.

Darling coughed and sputtered, cleared his throat, wiped at his eyes. "What did you say?"

Shocked at her own admission, Jade sat there in stunned silence. She had not intended to tell Darling what she had learned, what she now feared was true. She had intended to remain silent, to keep her secret to herself and share it with no one.

Instead, her voice trembling, Jade said, "Sam and Jean Margaux had a fling aboard the *Bosporus*. Jean stayed on the Moon for nearly a year. I was born at Moonbase. An orphan."

"But that doesn't mean . . ."

"How could someone be orphaned at birth in a place like Moonbase?" Jade demanded, painful urgency in her question. "It was a small town in those days, only a few hundred people, and most of them were retirees. The medical staff didn't allow pregnancies to come to term there; as soon as they found that a woman was pregnant they shipped her back to her home on Earth."

"But you were born there," Darling whispered, the truth slowly dawning on him.

"You'd have to have a lot of money to get away with it," said Jade. "Money to keep the medics quiet. Money to erase the computer records. Money to pay off the woman who . . . who adopted the abandoned baby."

"Jean Margaux . . . ?" Darling seemed stunned.

Jade nodded bitterly. "Twenty years later, when she heard there was a reporter looking into the time she'd spent at Moonbase, when she found out who the reporter was, where she'd been born, how old she was—she told her chauffeur to take the day off, and then drove her car off a cliff."

"My God."

"I'm really an orphan now," said Jade. "Sam died off at the end of the solar system, and I killed my own mother."

Suddenly she was crying uncontrollably. Her world dissolved and she was bawling like a baby. She found herself in Darling's arms, wrapped and held and protected by this strange man who was no longer a stranger.

"It's all right," Darling was crooning to her, rocking her gently back and forth. "It's all right. Cry all you want to. We'll both cry. For all the love that we never had. For all the love that we've lost."

She had no idea how long they cried together. Finally, though, she disengaged herself gently from his arms. Darling pointed to a door in the opulent room and suggested she freshen up. She saw that tears had runneled streaks down the makeup on his face.

By the time she returned to the main room a small meal sat steaming on the low table in front of her host and Darling's makeup had been newly applied. Although she felt anything but hungry, Jade sat on the cushions set up opposite Darling. He poured her a cup of tea.

"Are you all right now?" he asked softly.

Jade nodded. I'll never be all right, she knew. I made my own mother kill herself. She killed herself rather than face her own daughter. Killed herself rather than admit she had a daughter—me.

"There's the matter of your promise," Darling said as he uncovered a bowl of diced meat chunks. She saw that the bowl next to it was filled with bubbling melted cheese.

"Yes. My promise." She almost laughed. Nothing he could do to her could bother her now.

"I had intended," he said, spearing a square of meat deftly on a little skewer, "to demand that you never reveal anything you heard on Sam's tapes."

She looked up at him. "That was going to be it?"

"Yes." He smiled at her. "What did you think?"

Glancing at the erotic scenes on the tapestries, she smiled back. "Something more physical."

"Dear me, no! Not at all!"

"I can understand why you're sensitive about Sam's tapes."

"Yes. Of course you can."

"But I'm a reporter . . ."

"You don't have to convince me. You can have the tapes."

For a moment she was not sure she had heard him correctly. "I can have them?"

Darling nodded, and a tide of ripples ran across his cheeks and chins to disappear beneath the open collar of his robe.

"It's strange," he said wistfully. "You nurse your own pain until there's virtually nothing left in your life but the pain."

"That's a terrible way to live," she said. But a pang of loss and sadness and guilt pulsed through her.

"When I realized how much you've suffered, it made me see how I've been flagellating myself, blaming Sam for what's become of me."

"I've got my work," Jade said, as much to herself as Darling. "I've got a life."

"And I don't. I've become a hermit. I've withdrawn from the human race."

"It's not too late to come back."

"Like this?" He looked down at himself, layer upon layer of bulging fat.

"Endocrine imbalances can be corrected," Jade said tenderly.

"Yes, I know," he confessed. "It's nothing but an excuse to keep myself hidden away from the rest of the world."

She smiled at him. "You'd need some discipline. Or a thick hide."

"You still owe me a promise. You said you'd do whatever I asked."

She felt no fear now. "I remember. What do you want?"

Darling took in a deep breath. His eyes studied her face, as if searching for the courage to make his request.

"Will you be my friend?" he asked at last. "You're going to be on the *Bosporus* for months. Will you come and visit me and . . . and help me to come out and meet other people?"

"I . . ." She had other commitments, a career, a longing for love and fulfillment, a gnawing guilt that burned sullenly within her like a hot coal. But in that instant of time she realized that love takes many forms, and that saving a man's life bears an obligation for a lifetime.

She saw an automobile tumbling off a cliff into the angry sea below. She saw Sam Gunn's round, slightly lopsided face grinning at her. She saw Raki's darkly handsome scowl and Spence Johansen's heart-fluttering smile and the tearful last memory of her adoptive mother as she left the Moonbase hospital forever. She saw Rick Darling staring at her with his entire life in his eyes.

"I'd be happy to be your friend," she said. "I need a friend, too."

The two of them—enormous overweight man and tiny elfin woman—leaned across the low table and embraced each other in newfound charity.

18

Asteroid Ceres

JADE CELEBRATED, IF that is the correct word, her twenty-first birthday alone.

Rick Darling had thrown an immense party for her the day before she left the *Golden Gate* at the farthermost point in its orbit and took the bulbous shuttle craft to the surface of Ceres. Nearly half the population of the huge bridge ship had poured into Darling's posh villa, eating, laughing, drinking, narcotizing themselves into either frenzied gaiety or withdrawn moroseness.

Through it all, Darling had remained close to Jade's side, his new figure almost trim compared to his former obesity. At first Jade thought he stayed near her because he was afraid of the crowd. Slowly, as the party proceeded and Darling played the genial, witty, gracious host, Jade began to realize that *he* wanted to protect *her*.

Jade tried to relax at the party and have a good time, but she was still haunted by the thoughts of her newly discovered and newly lost mother. Despite the happy oblivious crowd swirling around her, she still saw the automobile plunging over the rocky cliff and into the unforgiving sea.

Now, more than a week later, it was her birthday. Twenty-one years old. An entire lifetime ahead of her. An entire lifetime already behind her.

She stood at the window of her room in the Hotel Ceres and gazed out at the empty sky. There were no moons to be seen, no Earth hanging huge and tantalizingly close. Here in the Asteroid Belt, beyond the orbit of Mars, even giant Jupiter was merely another star in the sky, brighter than the rest but still little more than a distant pinpoint of light against the engulfing dark.

Slightly wider than a thousand kilometers, Ceres was the largest of the asteroids. Still, its gravity was negligible, a quarter of the Moon's, barely enough to give a sense of up and down. The hotel manager who had personally shown Jade to her room had smilingly demonstrated that you could drop a fragile crystal vase from your hand, then go fill a glass of water and drink it, and still have time to retrieve the vase before it hit the carpeted floor.

Twenty-one years old, Jade mused to herself as she stared out at the dark sky. Time to make something of yourself. Time to leave the past behind; there's nothing you can do to change it. Only the future can be shaped, altered. Everything else is over and done with.

She lost track of how long she stood at the window, sensing the cold of the airless eternity on the other side of the glassteel. Perhaps time passes differently here, with no worlds or moons in the sky. Nothing but stars endlessly spinning through the sky. Never any real daylight, always darkness—or twilight, at best. This little world is like the ancient Greek idea of the afterlife: gray twilight, emptiness, a shadow existence.

It took a real effort of will for Jade to pull herself from the window. You've got a job to do, she told herself sternly. You've got a life to lead. Then she added, Once you've figured out what you want to do with it.

The message light on the phone was on. She walked past the bed, carefully. Ceres's gravity was almost nonexistent; everyone in the hotel wore Velcro slippers and walked across the carpeting in a hesitant low-gee shuffle.

Jade smiled when she saw Jim Gradowsky's beefy face fill the phone screen. He was munching on something, as usual.

"Just a note to tell you that Raki got promoted to vice president in charge of special projects. Thanks mostly to the Sam Gunn tapes you beamed us, and the interview with Rick Darling. You're on full salary, kid. Plus expenses. Raki is *very* happy with you. Looks like he'll be getting a seat on the board of directors next."

But Raki himself did not call, Jade said to herself. Then she thought, Perhaps it's best that way.

"Oh, yeah," Gradowsky went on. "Monica says hello and happy birthday. From me, too. You're doin' great work, Jade. We're proud of you."

The screen blanked but the message light stayed on. Jade touched it again.

Spencer Johansen smiled at her. Jade's breath caught in her throat.

"Hey there, Jade. I'm sending this message to your office, 'cause I haven't a clue as to where in the solar system you might be. How about giving a fella a call now and then? I mean, I'd like to see you, talk to you. Maybe I could even come out to wherever you are and visit. You know, this old habitat feels kinda lonesome without you. Send me a message, will you? I'd like to see you again."

Jade plopped down on the edge of the bed, surprised that her knees suddenly felt so weak. Would Spence come all the way out here just to see me? No, it wouldn't be fair to ask him. I'll be leaving as soon as my interview comes through, anyway. And then out to Titan. It could be another two years before I see him again.

And why would he want to leave Jefferson and come out to see me? Jade asked herself. Is he a romantic fool or—suddenly she remembered Raki's cruel words: "The thrill is in the chase. Now that I've bagged her, what is there to getting her again?"

She shook her head. No, Spence isn't like that. He's not. I know he's not. But what if he is? an inner voice demanded. What if he is? Good thing there's several million miles between you.

Still, that did not mean she could not send him the message he asked for. Jade leaned forward and touched the phone's keyboard. She was stunned to find that two hours had elapsed before she ran out of things to say to Spence Johansen.

19

- - • - - • - • - • - - • - • - - • - - • - • - - • - • - - • - • - - • - - • - - • - - •

Space University

REGAL WAS THE only possible word for her.

Jade stared in unabashed awe. Elverda Apacheta was lean, long-legged, stately, splendid, dignified, intelligent— regal. The word kept bobbing to the surface of Jade's mind.

Not that the sculptress was magnificently clad: she wore only a frayed jumpsuit of faded gray. It was her bearing, her demeanor, and above all her face that proclaimed her nobility. It was an aristocratic face, the face of an Incan queen, copper-red, a study in sculptured planes of cheek and brow and strong Andean nose. Her almond-shaped deeply dark eyes missed nothing. They seemed to penetrate to the soul even while they sparkled with what appeared to be a delight in the world. The sculptress's thick black hair was speckled with gray, as much the result of exposure to cosmic radiation as age, thought Jade. It was tied back and neatly bound in a silver mesh. Her only other adornment was a heavy silver bracelet that probably concealed a communicator.

"Yes, I knew Sam well," she replied to Jade's lame opening question, in a throaty low voice. She spoke English, in deference to Jade, but there was the unmistakable memory of the high Andes in her accent. "Very well indeed."

Jade was wearing coral-colored parasilk coveralls with the stylized sunburst of the Solar Network logo emblazoned above her left breast pocket and the miniature recorder on her belt. She was surprised at her worshipful reaction to Elverda Apacheta. The woman was renowned as not only the first space sculptress, but the best. Yet Jade had interviewed other personalities who were very famous, or powerful, or notorious, or talented. None of them had been this breathtaking. Did this Incan queen affect everyone this way? Had she affected Sam Gunn this way?

The two women were sitting in the faculty lounge of the minuscule Ceres branch of the Interplanetary Space University. Little more than an extended suite of rooms in the same shielded dome as the hotel, the university was mainly a communications center where Cerean workers and their children could attend classes through interactive computer programs.

The lounge itself was a small, windowless, quiet room tastefully decorated with carpeting of warm earth colors that covered not only the floor but the walls, as well. The ideal place for recording an interview. Must have cost a moderate-sized fortune to bring this stuff all the way out here, Jade thought.

The sculptress reclined regally on a high-backed armchair of soft nubby pseudo-wool, looking every inch a monarch who could dispense justice or mercy with the slightest arch of an eyebrow. Jade felt drab sitting on the sofa at her right, despite the fact that her coveralls were crisply new while Apacheta's were worn almost to holes.

"I appreciate your agreeing to let me interview you," Jade said.

Elverda Apacheta made a small nod of acknowledgment.

"Many other of Sam's . . . associates, well, they either tried to avoid me or they refused to talk at all."

"Why should I refuse? I have nothing to hide."

No, you didn't have an illicit pregnancy, Jade thought. You didn't abandon your infant daughter.

Forcing herself to focus on the task at hand, Jade said, "There are rumors that you and Sam were"—she hesitated half a heartbeat—"well, lovers."

The sculptress smiled sadly. "I loved Sam madly. For a while I thought perhaps he loved me, too. But now, after all these years"—strangely, the smile grew more tender—"I am not so sure."

We were all much younger then—said Elverda Apacheta—and our passions were much closer to the surface. I could become enraged at the slightest excuse, the smallest problem could infuriate me.

You must remember, of course, that I had packed off to the asteroid where I had been living alone for almost three years. Even my supply shipments came in unmanned spacecraft. So it was a big surprise when a transfer ship showed up and settled into a rendezvous orbit a few hundred meters off my asteroid.

I thought of it as *my* asteroid. Nobody could own it, according to international law. But there were no restrictions against carving on it. Aten 2004 EA was the name the astronomers had given it, which meant that it was the one hundred thirty-first asteroid discovered in the year 2004 among the Aten group. The astronomers are very efficient in their naming, of course, but not romantic at all.

I called my asteroid Quipu-Camayoc, which means "The Rememberer." And I was determined to carve the history of my people upon it. The idea was not merely romantic, it was absolutely poetic. After all, we have lived in the mountains since before time was reckoned. Even the name of my people, my very own name—Apacheta—means a group of magical stones. Now my people were leaving their ancient mountain villages, scattering down to the cities, losing their tribal identities in the new world of factory jobs and electronic pleasures. Someone had to mark their story in a way that could be remembered forever.

When I first heard of the asteroid, back at the university at La Paz, I knew it was my destiny. The very name the astronomers had given it signified my own name: Aten 2004 EA—Elverda Apacheta. It was a sign. I am not superstitious, of course, and ordinarily I do not believe in signs and omens. But I knew I was destined to carve the history of my people on Aten 2004 EA and turn it into the memory of a vanishing race.

Quipu-Camayoc was a large stone streaked with metals, a mountain floating in space, nearly one full kilometer long. It was not in the Belt, of course; in those days no one had gone as far as the Belt. Its orbit was slightly closer to the Sun than Earth's orbit, so nearly once a year it came near enough to Earth for a reasonably easy flight to reach it in something like a week; that is when I usually got my supplies. This was many years ago, of course, before the first bridge ships were even started. The frontier had not expanded much beyond the Earth / Moon system; the first human expedition to Mars had barely gotten under way.

As I said, I was surprised when a transfer ship came into view instead of the usual unmanned spacecraft. I was even more surprised when someone jetted over to my quarters without even asking permission to come aboard.

I lived in my workshop, a small pod that contained all my sculpting equipment and the life-support systems, as well as my personal gear—clothing, sleeping hammock, things like that.

"Who is approaching?" I called on the communicator. In its screen I centered a magnified picture of the approaching stranger. I could see nothing, of course, except a white space suit topped with a bubble helmet. The figure was enwrapped by the jet unit, somewhat like a man sitting in a chair that had no legs.

"Sam Gunn is my name. I've got your supplies aboard my ship."

Suddenly I realized I was naked. Living alone, I seldom bothered with clothing. My first reaction was anger.

"Then send the supplies across and go on your way. I have no time for visitors."

He laughed. That surprised me. He said, "This isn't just a social call, lady. I'm supposed to hand you a legal document. It's got to be done in person. You know how lawyers are."

"No, I don't know. And I don't want to." But I hur-

riedly pushed over to my clothes locker and rummaged in
it for a decent set of coveralls.

I realize now that what I should have done was to
lock the access hatch and not allow him to enter. That
would have delayed the legal action against me. But it
would only have delayed it, not prevented it altogether.
Perhaps allowing Sam to enter my quarters, to enter my
life, was the best course after all.

By the time I heard the pumps cycling in the airlock
I was pulling a pair of old blue denim coveralls over my
shoulders. The inner hatch cracked open as I zipped
them up to the collar.

Sam coasted through the hatch, his helmet already removed and floating inside the airlock. He was small, not
much more than 160 centimeters, although to his last
breath he claimed to be 165. Which is nonsense. I myself
was a good six centimeters taller than he.

It would be difficult to capture his face in a sculpture.
His features were too mobile for stone or even clay to do
him justice. There was something slightly irregular about
Sam's face: one side did not quite match the other. It made
him look just the tiniest bit off-center, askew. It fitted his
personality very well.

His eyes could be blue or gray or even green, de-
pending on the lighting. His mouth was extremely mobile:
he had a thousand different smiles, and he was almost always talking, never silent. Short-cropped light brown hair,
with a tinge of red in it. A round face, a touch unbalanced
toward the left. A slightly crooked snub nose; it looked as
if it had been broken, perhaps more than once. A sprin-
kling of freckles. I thought of the *Norte Americano* character from literature, Huckleberry Finn, grown into boyish
manhood.

He hung there, framed in the open hatch, his booted
feet dangling several centimeters from the grillwork of the
floor. He was staring at me.

Suddenly I felt enormously embarrassed. My quarters
were a shambles. Nothing but a cramped compartment
filled with junk. Equipment and computer consoles scattered everywhere, connecting wires looping in the
microgravity like jungle vines. My hammock was a twisted

disaster area, the entire little cabin was filled with the flotsam of a hermit who had not seen another human being in three years. I was bone-thin, I knew. Like a skeleton. I could not even begin to remember where I had left my last lipstick. And my hair must have looked wild, floating uncombed.

"God, you're *beautiful*!" said Sam in an awed whisper. "A goddess made of copper."

Immediately I distrusted him.

"You have a legal paper for me?" I asked as coldly as I could. I had no idea of what it was; perhaps something from the university in La Paz about the new grant I had applied for.

"Uh, yeah . . ." Sam seemed to be half dazed, unfocused. "I, uh, didn't bring it with me. It's back aboard my ship."

"You told me you had it with you."

"No," he said, recovering slightly. "I said I was supposed to hand it to you personally. It's back on the ship."

I glared at him. How dare he invade my privacy like this? Interrupt my work? My art?

He did not wilt. In fact, Sam brightened. "Why don't you come over and have a meal with me? With us, I mean. Me and my crew."

I absolutely refused. Yet somehow, several hours later, I was on my way to his transfer ship, riding on the rear saddle of a two-person jet scooter. I had bathed and dressed while Sam had returned to his ship for the scooter. I had even found a bright golden yellow scarf to tie around the waist of my best green coveralls, and a matching scarf to tie down my hair. Inside my space suit I could smell the perfume I had doused myself with. It is surprising how you can find things you thought you had lost, when the motivation is right.

What was my motivation? Not to accept some legal document, certainly. Sam's sudden presence made it painfully clear to me that I had been terribly alone for such a long time. I had not minded the loneliness at all—not until he punctuated it as he did. My first reaction had been anger, of course. But how could I remain angry with a man who was so obviously taken with my so-called beauty?

My asteroid was in shadow as we sailed toward his ship, so we could not see the figures I had already carved upon it. It bulked over us, blotting out the Sun, like some huge black pitted mountain, looming dark and somehow menacing. Sam kept up a steady chatter on the suit-to-suit radio. He was asking me questions about what I was doing and how my work was going, but somehow he did all the talking.

His ship was called *Adam Smith,* a name that meant nothing to me. It looked like an ordinary transfer vehicle, squat and ungainly, with spidery legs sticking out and bulbous glassy projections that housed the command and living modules. But as we approached it I saw that Sam's ship was large. Very large. I had never seen one so big.

"The only one like it in the solar system, so far," he acknowledged cheerfully. "I'm having three more built. Gonna corner the cargo business."

He rattled on, casually informing me that he was the major owner of the orbital tourist facility, the Earth View Hotel.

"Every room has a view of Earth. It's gorgeous."

"Yes, I imagine it is."

"Great place for a honeymoon," Sam proclaimed. "Or even just a weekend. You haven't lived until you've made love in zero gee."

I went silent and remained so the rest of the short journey to his ship. I had no intention of responding to sexual overtures, no matter how subtle. Or blatant.

Dinner was rather pleasant. Five of us crowded into the narrow wardroom that doubled as the mess. Cooking in zero gravity is no great trick, but presenting the food in a way that is appetizing to the eye without running the risk of its floating off the plate at the first touch of a fork— that calls for art. Sam managed the trick by using plates with clear plastic covers that hinged back neatly. Veal piccata with spaghetti, no less. The wine, of course, was served in squeezebulbs.

There were three crew persons on *Adam Smith.* The only woman, the communications engineer, was married to the propulsion engineer. She was a heavyset blonde of about thirty who had allowed herself to gain much too much weight. Michelangelo would have loved her, with her thick torso and powerful limbs, but by present standards she was no great beauty. But then her husband, equally fair-haired, was also of ponderous dimensions.

It is a proven fact that people who spend a great deal of time in low gravity either allow themselves to become tremendously fat, or thin down to little more than skin and bones, as I had. The physiologists have scientific terms for this: I am an *agravitic ectomorph*, so I am told. The two oversize engineers were *agravitic endomorphs*. Sam, of course, was neither. He was Sam—irrepressibly unique.

I found myself instinctively disliking both of the bloated engineers until I thought of the globulous little Venus figures that prehistoric peoples had carved out of hand-sized round rocks. Then they did not seem so bad.

The third crewman was the payload specialist, a lanky dark taciturn biologist. Young and rather handsome, in a smoldering sullen way. Although he was slim, he had some meat on his bones. I found that this was his first space mission, and he was determined to make it his last.

"What is your cargo?" I asked.

Before the biologist could reply, Sam answered, "Worms."

I nearly dropped my fork. Suddenly the spaghetti I had laboriously wound around it seemed to be squirming, alive.

"Worms?" I echoed.

Nodding brightly, Sam said, "You know the Moralist Sect that's building an O'Neill habitat?"

I shook my head, realizing I had been badly out of touch with the rest of the human race for three years.

"Religious group," Sam explained. "They decided Earth is too sinful for them, so they're building their own paradise, a self-contained, self-sufficient artificial world in a Sun-circling orbit, just like your asteroid."

"And they want worms?" I asked.

"For the soil," said the biologist.

Before I could ask another question Sam said, "They're bringing in megatons of soil from the Moon, mostly for radiation shielding. Don't want to be conceiving two-headed Moralists, y'know. So they figured that as long as they've got so much dirt they might as well use it for farming, too."

"But lunar soil is sterile," the biologist said.

"Right. It's got plenty of nutrients in it, all those chemicals that crops need. But no earthworms, no beetles, none of the bugs and slugs and other slimy little things that make the soil *alive*."

"And they need that?"

"Yep. Sure do, if they're gonna farm that lunar soil. Otherwise they've gotta go to hydroponics, and that's against their religion."

I turned from Sam to the biologist. He nodded to confirm what Sam had said. The two engineers were ignoring our conversation, busily shoveling food into their mouths.

"Not many cargo haulers capable of taking ten tons of worms and their friends halfway around the Earth's orbit," Sam said proudly. "I got the contract from the Moralists with hardly any competition at all. Damned profitable, too, as long as the worms stay healthy."

"They are," the biologist assured him.

"This is the first of six flights for them," said Sam, returning his attention to his veal and pasta. "All worms."

I felt myself smiling. "Do you always make deliveries in person?"

"Oh, no." Twirling the spaghetti on his fork beneath the plastic cover of his dish. "I just figured that since this is the first flight, I ought to come along and see it through. I'm a qualified astronaut, you know."

"I didn't know."

"Yeah. Besides, it lets me get away from the hotel and the office. My buddy Omar can run the hotel while I'm gone. Hell, he runs it while I'm there!"

"Then what do you do?"

He grinned at me. "I look for new business opportunities. I seek out new worlds, new civilizations. I boldly go where no man has gone before."

The biologist muttered from behind a forkful of veal, "He chases women." From his dead-serious face I could not tell if he was making a joke or not.

"And you deliver ten tons of worms," I said.

"Right. And the mail."

"Ah. My letter."

Sam smiled broadly. "It's in my cabin, up by the bridge."

I refused to smile back at him. If he thought he was going to get me into his cabin, and his zero-gee hammock, he was terribly mistaken. So I told myself. I had only taken a couple of sips of the wine; after three years of living like a hermit, I was careful not to make a fool of myself. I wanted to be invulnerable, untouchable.

Actually, Sam was an almost perfect gentleman. After dinner we coasted from the wardroom along a low-ceilinged corridor that opened into the command module. I had to bend over slightly to get through the corridor, but Sam sailed along blithely, talking every millimeter of the way about worms, Moralists and their artificial heaven, habitats expanding throughout the inner solar system, and how he was going to make billions from hauling specialized cargoes.

His cabin was nothing more than a tiny booth with a sleeping hammock fastened to one wall, actually just an alcove built into the command module. Through the windows of the bridge I could see my asteroid, hovering out there with the Sun starting to rise above it. Sam ducked into his cubbyhole without making any suggestive remarks at all, and came out a moment later with a heavy, stiff, expensive-looking white envelope.

It bore my name and several smudged stamps that I presume had been affixed to it by various post offices on its way to me. In the corner was the name and address of a legal firm: Skinner, Flaymen, Killum and Score, of Des Moines, Iowa, USA, Earth.

Wondering why they couldn't have sent their message electronically, like everyone else, I struggled to open the envelope.

"Let me," Sam said, taking one corner of it in two fingers and deftly slitting it with the minuscule blade of the tiniest pocketknife I had ever seen.

I pulled out a single sheet of heavy white parchment, so stiff that its edges could slice flesh.

It was a letter for me. It began, "Please be advised . . ."

For several minutes I puzzled over the legal wordings while Sam went over to the control console and busied himself checking out the instruments. Slowly the letter's meaning became clear to me. My breath gagged in my throat. A searing, blazing knot of pain sprang up in my chest.

"What's wrong?" Sam was at my side in a shot. "Cripes, you look like you're gonna explode! You're red as a fire engine."

I was so furious I could hardly see. I handed the letter to Sam and managed to choke out, "Does this mean what I think it means?"

He scanned the letter quickly, then read it more slowly, his eyes going wider with each word of it.

"Jesus Christ on a crutch!" he shouted. "They're throwing you off the asteroid!"

I could not believe what the letter said. We both read it half a dozen times more. The words did not change their meaning. I wanted to scream. I wanted to kill. The vision came to my mind of lawyers stripped naked and staked out over a slow fire, screaming for mercy while I laughed and burned their letter in the fire that was roasting their flesh. I looked around the command module wildly, looking for something to throw, something to break, anything to release the terrible, terrible fury that was building inside me.

"Those sons of bitches!" Sam raged. "Those slimy dogooder bastards!"

The lawyers represented the Moralist Sect of The One True God, Inc. The letter was to inform me that the Moralists had notified the International Astronautical Council that they intended to capture asteroid Aten 2004 EA and use it as structural material for the habitat they were building.

"They can't do that!" Sam bellowed, bouncing around the bridge like a weightless Ping-Pong ball. "You were there first. They can't throw you out like a landlord evicting a tenant!"

"The white man has taken the Indian's lands whenever he chose to," I said, seething.

He mistook my deathly quiet tone for acquiescence. "Not anymore! Not today. This is one white man who's on the side of the redskins."

He was so upset, so outraged, so vociferous that I felt my own fury cooling, calming. It was as if Sam were doing all my screaming for me.

"This letter," I hissed, "says I have no choice."

"Hell no, you won't go," Sam snapped. "I've got lawyers, too, lady. Nobody's going to push you around."

"Why should you want to involve yourself?"

He shot me an unfathomable glance. "I'm involved. I'm involved. You think I can sit back and watch those Moralist bastards steal your rock? I *hate* it when some big outfit tries to muscle us little guys."

It occurred to me that at least part of Sam's motivation might have been to worm his way into my affection. And my pants. He would act the brave protector of the weak, and I would act the grateful weakling who would reward him with my somewhat emaciated body. From the few words that the taciturn biologist had said at dinner, and from my observation of Sam's own behavior, it seemed to me that he had a Casanova complex; he wanted every woman he saw.

And yet—his outrage seemed genuine enough. And yet—the instant he saw me he said I was beautiful, even though clearly I was not.

"Don't you worry," Sam said, his round little face grim and determined. "I'm on your side and we'll figure out some way to stick this letter up those lawyers' large intestines."

"But the Moralist Sect is very powerful."

"So what? You've got me, kiddo. All those poor praying sonsofbitches have on their side is God."

I was still angry and confused as Sam and I climbed back into our space suits and he returned me to my pod on my—no, *the* asteroid. I felt a burning fury blazing within me, bitter rage at the idea of stealing my asteroid away from me. They were going to break it up and use it as raw material for their habitat!

Normally I would have been screaming and throwing things, but I sat quietly on the two-person scooter as we left the airlock of Sam's ship. He was babbling away with a mixture of bravado, jokes, obscene descriptions of lawyers in general and Moralists in particular. He made me laugh. Despite my fears and my fury, Sam made me laugh and realize that there was nothing I could do about the Moralists and their lawyers at the moment, so why should I tie myself into knots over them? Besides, I had a more immediate problem to deal with.

Sam. Was he going to attempt to seduce me once we were back at my quarters? And if he did, what would my reaction be? I was shocked at my uncertainty. Three years is a long time, but to even think of allowing this man . . .

"You got a lawyer?" His voice came through the earphones of my helmet.

"No. I suppose the university will represent me. Legally, I'm their employee."

"Maybe, but you . . ." His voice choked off. I heard him take in his breath, like a man who has just seen something that overpowered him.

"Is that *it*?" Sam asked in an awed voice.

The Sun was shining obliquely on "The Rememberer," so that the figures I had carved were shown in high relief.

"It's not finished," I said. "It's hardly even begun."

Sam swerved the little scooter so that we moved slowly along the length of the carvings. I saw all the problems, the places that had to be fixed, improved. The feathered serpent needed more work. The Mama Kilya, the Moon Mother, was especially rough. But I had to place her there because the vein of silver in the asteroid came up to the surface only at that point and I needed to use the silver as the tears of the Moon.

Even while I picked out the weak places in my figures I could hear Sam's breathing over the suit radio. I feared he would hyperventilate. For nearly half an hour we cruised slowly back and forth across the face of the asteroid, then spiraled around to the other side.

The one enormous advantage of space sculpture, of course, is the absence of gravity. There is no need for a base, a stand, a vertical line. Sculpture can be truly three-dimensional in space, as it was meant to be. I had intended to carve the entire surface of the asteroid.

"It's fantastic," Sam said at last, his voice strangely muted. "It's the most beautiful thing I've ever seen. I'll be hung by the *conjones* before I'll let those double-talking bastards steal this away from you!"

At that moment I began to love Sam Gunn.

True to his word, Sam got his own lawyers to represent me. A few days after *Adam Smith* disappeared from my view, on its way to the Moralists' construction site, I was contacted by the firm of Whalen and Krill, of Port Canaveral, Florida, USA, Earth.

The woman who appeared on my comm screen was a junior partner in the firm. I was not important enough for either of the two senior men. Still, that was better than my university had done: their legal counsel had told me bleakly that I had no recourse at all and I should abandon my asteroid forthwith.

"We've gotten the IAC arbitration board to agree to take up the dispute," said Ms. Mindy Rourke, Esq. She seemed very young to me to be a lawyer. I was especially fascinated by her long hair falling luxuriantly past her shoulders. She could only wear it like that on Earth. In a low-gee environment it would have spread out like a chestnut-colored explosion.

"I'll have my day in court, then."

"You won't have to be physically present," Ms. Rourke said. Then she added, with a doubtful little frown, "But I'm afraid the board usually bases its decisions on the maximum good for the maximum number of people. The Moralists will house ten thousand people in their habitat. All you've got is you."

What she meant was that Art counted for nothing as compared to the utilitarian purpose of grinding up my asteroid, smelting it, and using its metals as structural materials for an artificial world to house ten thousand religious zealots who want to leave Earth forever.

Sam stayed in touch with me electronically, and hardly a day passed that he did not call and spend an hour or more chatting with me. Our talk was never romantic, but each call made me love him more. He spoke endlessly about his childhood in Nebraska, or was it Baltimore? Sometimes his childhood tales were based in the rainy hillsides of the Pacific Northwest. Either he moved around ceaselessly as a child or he was amalgamating tales from many other people and adopting them as his own. I never tried to find out. If Sam thought of the stories as his own childhood, what did it matter?

Gradually, as the weeks slipped into months, I found myself speaking about my own younger years. The half-deserted mountain village where I had been born. The struggle to get my father to allow me to go to the university instead of marrying, "as a decent girl should." The professor who broke my heart. The pain that sent me fleeing to this asteroid and the life of a hermit.

Sam cheered me up. He made me smile, even laugh. He provided me with a blow-by-blow description of his own activities as an entrepreneur. Not content with owning and operating the Earth View Hotel *and* running a freight-hauling business that ranged from low Earth orbit to the Moon and out as far as the new habitats being built in Sun-circling orbits, Sam was also getting involved in building tourist facilities at Moonbase, as well.

"And then there's this advertising scheme that these two guys have come up with. It's kinda crazy, but it might work."

The "scheme" was to paint enormous advertisement pictures in the ionosphere, some fifty miles or so above the Earth's surface, using electron guns to make the gases up at that altitude glow like the aurora borealis. The men that Sam was speaking with claimed that they could make actual pictures that could be seen across whole continents.

"When the conditions are right," Sam added. "Like, it's gotta be either at dusk or at dawn, when the sky looks dark from the ground but there's still sunlight up at the right altitude."

"Not many people are up at dawn," I said.

It took almost a full minute between my statement and his answer, I was so distant from his base in Earth orbit.

"Yeah," he responded at last. "So it's gotta be around dusk." Sam grinned lopsidedly. "Can you imagine the reaction from the environmentalists if we start painting advertisements across the sky?"

"They'll fade away within a few minutes, won't they?"

The seconds stretched, and then he answered, "Yeah, sure. But can you picture the look on their faces? They'll *hate* it! Might be worth doing just to give 'em ulcers!"

All during those long weeks and months I could hardly work up the energy to continue my carving. What good would it be? The whole asteroid was going to be taken away from me, ground into powder, destroyed forever. I knew what the International Astronautical Council's arbitrators would say: Moralists, ten thousand; Art, one.

For days on end I would stand at my console, idly fingering the keyboard, sketching in the next set of figures that the lasers would etch into the stone. In the display screen the figures would look weak, misshapen, distorted. Sometimes they glared at me accusingly, as if *I* were the one killing them.

Time and again I ended up sketching Sam's funny, freckled, dear face.

I found reasons to pull on my space suit and go outside. Check the lasers. Adjust the power settings. Recalibrate the feedback sensors. Anything but actual work. I ran my gloved fingers across the faces of the *hauqui*, the guardian spirits I had carved into this metallic stone. It was a bitter joke. The *hauqui* needed someone to guard them from evil.

Instead of working, I cried. All my anger and hate was leaching away in the acid of frustration and waiting, waiting, endless months of waiting for the inevitable doom.

And then Sam showed up again, just as unexpectedly as the first time.

My asteroid, with me attached to it, had moved far along on its yearly orbit. I could see Earth only through the low-power telescope that I had brought with me, back in those first days when I had fooled myself into believing I would spend my free time in space studying the stars. Even in the telescope the world of my birth was nothing more than a blurry fat crescent, shining royal-blue.

My first inkling that Sam was approaching was a message I found typed on my comm screen. I had been outside, uselessly fingering my carvings. When I came in and took off my helmet I saw on the screen:

HAVE NO FEAR, SAM IS HERE. WILL
RENDEZVOUS IN ONE HOUR.

My eyes flicked to the digital clock reading. He would be here in a matter of minutes! At least this time I was wearing clothes, but still I looked a mess.

By the time his transport was hovering in a matching orbit and the pumps in my airlock were chugging, I was decently dressed in a set of beige coveralls he had not seen before, my hair was combed and neatly netted, and I had applied a bit of makeup to my face. My expression in the mirror had surprised me: smiling, nearly simpering, almost as giddy as a schoolgirl. Even my heart was skipping along merrily.

Sam came in, his helmet already off. I propelled myself over to him and kissed him warmly on the lips. He reacted in a typical Sam Gunn way. He gave a whoop and made three weightless cartwheels, literally heels over head, with me gripped tightly in his arms.

For all his exuberance and energy, Sam was a gentle, thoughtful lover. Hours later, as we floated side by side in my darkened quarters, the sweat glistening on our bare skins, he murmured: "I never thought I could feel so . . . so . . ."

Trying to supply the missing word, I suggested, "So much in love?"

He made a little nod. In our weightlessness, the action made him drift slightly away from me. I caught him in my arms, though, and pulled us back together.

"I love you, Sam," I whispered, as though it were a secret. "I love you."

He gave a long sigh. I thought it was contentment, happiness even.

"Listen," he said, "you've got to come over to the ship. Those two nut cases who want to paint the ionosphere are on their way to the Moralists' habitat."

"What does that have to do with . . ."

"You gotta meet them," he insisted. Untangling from me, he began to round up his clothes, floating like weightless ghosts in the shadows. "You know what those Moralist hypocrites are going to call their habitat once it's finished? Eden! How's that for chutzpah?"

He had to explain the Yiddish word to me. Eden. The Moralists wanted to create their own paradise in space. Well, maybe they would, although I doubted that it would be paradise for anyone who deviated in the slightest from their stern views of right and wrong.

We showered, which in zero gee is an intricate, intimate procedure. Sam washed me thoroughly, lovingly, using the washcloth to tenderly push the soapy water that clung to my skin over every inch of my body.

"The perfect woman," he muttered. "A dirty mind in a clean body."

Finally we dried off, dressed, and headed out to Sam's ship. But first he maneuvered the little scooter along the length of my asteroid.

"Doesn't seem to be much more done than the last time I was here," he said, almost accusingly.

I was glad we were in the space suits and he could not see me blush. I remained silent.

As we moved away from "The Rememberer," Sam told me, "The lawyers aren't having much luck with the arbitration board." In the earphones of my helmet his voice sounded suddenly tired, almost defeated.

"I didn't think they would."

"The board's gonna hand down its decision in two weeks. If they decide against you, there's no appeal."

"And they will decide against me, won't they?"

He tried to make his voice brighter. "Well, the lawyers are doing their damnedest. But if trickery and deceit won't work, maybe I can bribe a couple of board members."

"Don't you dare! You'll go to jail."

He laughed.

As we came up to Sam's transport ship, I saw its name stenciled in huge letters beneath the insect-eye canopy of the command module: *Klaus Heiss.*

"Important economist," Sam answered my question. "Back fifty years or so. The first man to suggest free enterprise in space."

"I thought that writers had suggested that long before spaceflight even began," I said as we approached the ship's airlock.

Sam's voice sounded mildly impatient in my earphones. "Writers are one thing. Heiss went out and raised money, got things started. For real."

Klaus Heiss was fitted out more handsomely than *Adam Smith*, even though it seemed no larger. The dining lounge was more luxurious, and apparently the crew ate elsewhere. There were four of us for dinner: Sam and myself, and the two "nut cases," as he had called them.

Morton McGuire and T. Kagashima did not seem insane to me. Perhaps naive. Certainly enthusiastic.

"It's the greatest idea since the invention of writing!" McGuire blurted as we sat around the dining lounge table.

He was speaking about their idea of painting the ionosphere with advertisements.

McGuire was a huge mass of flesh, bulging in every direction, straining the metal snaps of his bilious green coveralls. He looked like a balloon that had been overfilled to the point of bursting. He proudly told me that he was known as "Mountain McGuire," from his days as a college football player. He had gone from college into advertising, gaining poundage every passing day. Living on Earth, he could not be classified as an agravitic endomorph. He was simply fat. Extremely so.

"I'm just a growing boy," he said happily as he jammed fistfuls of food into his mouth.

The other one, Kagashima, was almost as lean as I myself. Quiet, too, although his oriental eyes frequently flashed with suppressed mirth. No one seemed to know what Kagashima's first name was. When I asked what the "T" stood for he merely smiled enigmatically and said, "Just call me Kagashima, it will be easier for you." He spoke English very well, no great surprise since he was born and raised in Denver, USA.

Kagashima was an electronics wizard. McGuire, an

advertising executive. Between them they had cooked up the idea of using electron guns to create glowing pictures in the ionosphere.

"Just imagine it," McGuire beamed, his chubby hands held up as if framing a camera shot. "It's twilight. The first stars are coming out. You look up and—POW!—there's a huge red-and-white sign covering the sky from horizon to horizon: *Drink Coke!*"

I wanted to vomit.

But Sam encouraged him. "Like skywriting, when planes used to spell out words with smoke."

"Real skywriting!" McGuire enthused.

Kagashima smiled and nodded.

"Is it legal," I asked, "to write advertising slogans across the sky?"

McGuire snapped a ferocious look at me. "There's no laws against it! The lawyers can't take the damned *sky* away from us, for God's sake! The sky belongs to everyone."

I glanced at Sam. "The lawyers seem to be taking my asteroid away from me."

His smile was odd, like the smile a hunter would have on his face as he saw his prey coming into range of his gun.

"Possession is nine tenths of the law," Sam muttered.

"Who possesses the sky?" Kagashima asked, with that oriental ambiguity that passes for wisdom.

"We do!" snapped McGuire.

Sam merely smiled like a cat eyeing a fat canary.

At Sam's insistence I spent the night hours aboard his ship. His quarters were much more luxurious than mine, and since practically all space operations kept Greenwich Mean Time, there was no problem of differing clocks.

His cabin was much more than an alcove off the command module. It was small, but a real compartment, with a zipper hammock for sleeping and a completely enclosed shower stall that jetted water from all directions. We used the shower, but not the hammock. We finally fell asleep locked weightlessly in each other's embrace and woke up when we gently bumped into the compartment's bulkhead, many hours later.

"We've got to talk," Sam said as we were dressing.

I smiled at him. "That means you talk and I listen, no?"

"No. Well, maybe I do most of the talking. But you've got to make some decisions, kiddo."

"Decisions? About what?"

"About your asteroid. And the next few years of your life."

He did not say that I had to make a decision about us. I barely noticed that fact at the time. I should have paid more attention.

Glancing at the digital clock set into the bulkhead next to his hammock, Sam told me, "In about half an hour I'm going to be conversing with the Right Reverend Virtue T. Dabney, spiritual leader of the Moralist Sect. Their chief, their head honcho, sitteth at the right hand of You-Know-Who. The Boss."

"The head of the Moralists?"

"Right."

"He's calling you? About my asteroid?"

Sam's grin was full of teeth. "Nope. About his worms. We're carrying another load of 'em out to his Eden on this trip."

"Why would the head of the Moralists call you about worms?"

"Seems that the worms have become afflicted by a rare and strange disease," Sam said, the grin turning delightfully evil, "and the hauling contract the Moralists signed with me now contains a clause that says I'm not responsible for their health."

I was hanging in midair, literally and mentally. "What's that got to do with me?"

Drifting over so close that our noses were practically touching, Sam asked in a whisper, "Would you be willing to paint the world's first advertisement on the ionosphere? An advertisement for the Moralists?"

"Never!"

"Even if it means that they'll let you keep the asteroid?"

Ah, the emotions that surged through my heart! I felt
anger, and hope, and disgust, even fear. But mostly anger.

"Sam, that's despicable! It's a desecration! To turn the
sky into an advertising poster . . ."

Sam was grinning, but he was serious about this.
"Now don't climb up on a high horse, kid . . ."

"And do it for the Moralists?" My temper was boiling
over now. "The people who want to take my asteroid away
from me and destroy the memory of my own people? You
want me to help *them*?"

"Okay, okay! Don't pop your cork over it," Sam said,
taking me gently by the wrist. "I'm just asking you to think
about it. You don't have to do it if you don't want to."

Completely bewildered, I allowed Sam to lead me up
to the ship's command module. The same two husband-
and-wife engineers were there at their consoles, just as
blond and even more bloated than they had been the last
time I had seen them, it seemed to me. They greeted me
with smiles of recognition.

Sam asked them to leave and they wafted out through
the main hatch like a pair of hot-air balloons. On their way
to the galley, no doubt.

We drifted over to the comm console. No one needs
chairs in zero gravity. We simply hung there, my arms
floating up to about chest-height, as they would in a swimming pool, while Sam worked the console to make contact
with the Moralist Sect headquarters back on Earth.

It took more than a half hour for Sam to get Rev.
Dabney on his screen. A small army of neatly scrubbed,
earnest, glittering-eyed young men appeared and tried to
deal with Sam. Instead, Sam dealt with them.

"Okay, if you want the worms to die, it's your seventy
million dollars, not mine," said Sam to the young lawyer.

To his superior, Sam spoke sweetly, "Your boss signed
the contract. All I'm doing is informing you of the problem, as specified in clause 22.1, section C."

To his boss, "All right! I'll dump the whole load right
here in the middle of nowhere and cut my losses. Is that
what you want?"

To Rev. Dabney's astonished assistant administrator,
"The lawsuit will tie you up for *years*, wiseass! You'll *never*

finish your Eden! The creditors will take it over and make a Disney World out of it!"

To the special assistant to the high pastor of the Moralist Sect, "This has gone beyond lawyers. It's even beyond the biologists' abilities! The damned worms are dying! They're withering away! What we need is a miracle!"

That, finally, brought the Right Rev. Virtue T. Dabney to the screen.

I instantly disliked the man. His face was largely hidden behind a dark beard and mustache. I suppose he thought it made him look like an Old Testament patriarch. To me he looked like a Conquistador; all he needed was a shining steel breastplate and helmet. He seemed to me perfectly capable of burning my people at the stake.

"Mr. Gunn," he said, smiling amiably. "How may I help you?"

Sam said lightly, "I've got another ten tons of worms for you, as per contract, but they're dying. I don't think any of 'em are gonna survive long enough to make it to your habitat."

It took more than a minute for the messages to get back and forth from Earth to the *Klaus Heiss*. Dabney spent the time with hands folded and head bowed prayerfully. Sam hung on to the hand grips of the comm console to keep himself from bobbing around weightlessly. I stayed out of range of the video and fidgeted with seething, smoldering nervous fury.

"The worms are dying, you say? What seems to be the matter? Your first shipment made it to Eden with no trouble at all, I believe."

"Right. But something's gone wrong with this load. Maybe we got bad worms to start with. Maybe there's a fault in the cargo containers' radiation shielding. The worms are dying." Sam reached into his hip pocket and pulled out a blackened, twisted, dried-out string of what must have once been an earthworm. "They're all going like this."

I watched intently for all the long seconds it took the transmission to reach Dabney's screen. When it did, his eyes went wide and his mouth dropped open.

"All of them? But how can this be?"

Sam shrugged elaborately. "Beats the hell out of me. My biologist is stymied, too. Maybe it's a sign from God that he doesn't want you to leave the Earth. I dunno."

Dabney's bearded face, when *that* line of Sam's finally hit him, went into even greater shock.

"I cannot believe the Lord would smite his faithful so. This is the work of evil."

"So what do we do about it?" Sam asked cheerfully. "My contract guarantees full payment for delivery. I'm not responsible for the condition of the cargo after your people inspected my cargo bay and okayed the shipment."

Sam blanked out the screen and turned to me. "Have you made up your mind, kiddo?"

"Made up my mind?"

"About the ads in the ionosphere."

"What do his dying worms have to do with me? Or with painting an advertisement on the ionosphere?"

"You'll see!" he promised. "Will you do it?"

"No! Never!"

"Even if it means saving your asteroid?"

I was too angry even to consider it. I turned my back to Sam and gritted my teeth with fury.

Sam sighed deeply, but when I whirled around to face him once more, he was grinning at me in that lopsided cunning way of his. Before I could say anything, he flicked on the screen again. Dabney's expression was crafty now. His eyes were narrowed, his lips pressed tight.

"What do you suggest as a solution to this problem, Mr. Gunn?"

"Damned if I know," said Sam. "Seems to me you need a miracle, Reverend."

He took special delight in Dabney's wince when that "damned" reached him.

"A miracle, you say," replied the Moralist leader. "And how do you think we might arrange a miracle?"

Sam chuckled. "Well—I don't know much about the way religions work, but I've heard that if somebody is willing to make a sacrifice, give up something that he really wants or even needs, then God rewards him. Something about casting bread upon the waters, I think."

I began to realize that there was nothing at all wrong with the Moralists' worms. Sam was merely holding them hostage. For me. He was risking lawsuits that could cost him everything he owned. For me.

Dabney's expression became even more squint-eyed than before. "You wouldn't be Jewish by any chance, would you, Mr. Gunn?"

Sam's grin widened to show lots of teeth. "You wouldn't be anti-Semitic, would you, Reverend?"

Their negotiation went on for the better part of three hours, with those agonizing long pauses in between each and every statement they made. After an hour of jockeying back and forth, Dabney finally suggested that he—and his Sect—might give up their claim to an asteroid that they wanted to use for building material.

"That might be just the sacrifice that will save the worms," Sam allowed.

More offers and counteroffers, more tiptoeing and verbal sparring. It was all very polite. And vicious. Dabney knew that there was nothing wrong with the worms. He also knew that Sam could open his cargo bay to vacuum for the rest of the trip to Eden, and the Moralists would receive ten tons of very dead and desiccated garbage.

Finally, "If my people make this enormous sacrifice, if we give up our claim to this asteroid that we so desperately need, what will you be willing to do for me . . . er, us?"

Sam rubbed his chin. "There's hundreds of asteroids in the Aten group, and more in the Apollos. They all cut across Earth's orbit. You can pick out a different one. It's no great sacrifice to give up this one little bitty piece of rock that you're claiming."

Dabney was looking down, as if at his desktop. Perhaps an aide was showing him lists of the asteroids available to help build his Eden.

"We picked that particular asteroid because it's orbit brings it the closest to Eden and therefore it is the easiest—and least expensive—for us to capture and use."

He held up a hand before Sam could reply, an indication of very fast reflexes on his part. "However, in the interests of charity and self-sacrifice, I am willing to give up that particular asteroid. I know that some Latin American woman has been carving figures on it. If I—that is, if *we* allow her to remain and give up our claim to the rock, what will you do for the Moralist Sect in return?"

Now Sam's smile returned like a cat slinking in through a door open merely the barest crack. I realized that he had known all along that Dabney would not give in unless he got something more out of the deal than merely the delivery of the worms he had already paid for. He wanted icing on his cake.

"Well now," Sam said slowly, "how about an advertisement for the Moralist Sect that glows in the sky and can be seen from New England to the Mississippi Valley?"

No! I screamed silently. Sam couldn't help them to do that! It would be sacrilegious.

But when the transmission finally reached Dabney, his shrewd eyes grew even craftier. "What are you talking about, Mr. Gunn?"

Sam described the concept of painting the ionosphere with electron guns. Dabney's eyes grew wider and greedier with each word.

Finally his bearded face broke into a benign smile. "Mr. Gunn, you were right. The Bible describes our situation perfectly. Cast thy bread upon the waters and it shall be returned unto you a thousandfold."

"Does that mean we've got a deal?" Sam asked flatly.

I pushed over toward him and banged the blank key hard enough to send me recoiling toward the overhead. Sam looked up at me. There was no surprise on his face. He looked as if he had expected me to fight him.

"You can't do this!" I said. "You're playing into his hands! You can't . . ."

"You want to stay on the asteroid or not?"

I stopped in midsentence and stared at him. Sam's eyes were flat gray, boring into me.

"This is the way business is done, kid," he said. "You want the asteroid. They want the asteroid. I make a threat they know is phony, but they pretend to consider it—as long as they get something they don't have now. What it boils down to is, you can stay on the asteroid if Holier

Than Thou gets to paint his advertisements across the ionosphere. That's the deal. Will you go for it or not?"

I couldn't speak. I was too furious, too confused, torn both ways and angry at Sam for putting me in this agony of indecision. I wanted to stay on the asteroid, yes, but not at the price of allowing the Moralists to deface the sky!

The message light on the screen began blinking. Sam touched the blank key again, and Dabney's face filled the screen once more, smiling an oily smile, the kind of unctuous happiness that a salesman shows when he's finally palmed off some shoddy goods at a shameful price.

"We have a deal, Mr. Gunn. We will rethink our options on acquiring that particular asteroid. Your, ah, friend"—he made a nasty smirk—"can stay and chip away at the rock to her heart's content. In return, you will help us to produce our ads in the ionosphere."

Sam glanced at me. I could negate the whole thing with merely a shake of my head. Instead, I nodded. And bit my lip so hard I tasted blood in my mouth.

Sam grinned at the display screen. "We've got a deal, Bishop."

"Reverend," corrected Dabney. Then he added, "And I presume our cargo of worms will arrive at Eden in a healthy condition?"

"That's up to you," said Sam, straight-faced. "And the power of prayer."

They chatted amiably for a few minutes more, a pair of con men congratulating each other. Each of them had what they wanted. I began to realize that Sam would make a considerable amount of money from producing the Moralists' ionospheric advertisements. My anger took a new turn. I could feel my face turning red, my cheeks burning with rage.

Sam finally ended his conversation with Rev. Dabney and turned off the comm console. It seemed to me that Dabney's bearded image remained on the screen even after it went dark and dead. It burned in my vision like the afterimage of an explosion.

Sam turned to me with a wide grin splitting his face. "Congratulations! You can stay on the asteroid."

"Congratulations yourself," I said, my voice trembling, barely under control. "You have put yourself into the advertising business. You should make a great deal of profit out of defacing the sky. I hope that makes you happy."

I stormed out of the bridge and headed for the locker where I had left my space suit. Yes, I could stay on my asteroid and finish my work. But my love affair with Sam Gunn was shattered completely.

He let the fat engineer fly me back to my quarters. Sam knew I was furious and it would be best for him to leave me alone.

But not for long. After four or five sleepless hours, bobbing around my darkened quarters like a cork tossed on a stormy sea, I saw the message light of my comm console flick bright red. I reached out and turned it on.

Sam's face appeared on the screen, a half-guilty boyish grin on his face. "Still mad at me?"

"No, not really." And I realized it was true even as I spoke the words. I was angry at Dabney and his smug Moralist power; angry at myself, mostly, for wanting to carve "The Rememberer" so much that I was willing to let them do whatever they wanted, so long as they left me alone.

"Good," said Sam. "Want me to bring some breakfast over to you?"

I shook my head. "I think not."

"Got to make a course change in another couple hours," he said. "So I can bring this can of worms to Eden."

"I know." He would be leaving me, and I could not blame him if he never returned. Still, it was impossible for me to allow him to come close to me. Not now. Not this soon after the deal he had struck. I knew he had done it for me, although I also knew he had his own reasons, as well.

"Listen—I can get somebody else to design the pictures for the Moralists. You don't have to do it."

He was trying to be kind to me, I knew. But my anger did not abate. "Who draws the pictures doesn't matter, Sam. It's the fact that the advertisements will be spread across the sky. For *them*. That disgusts me."

"I'm doing this for you, kid."

"And for the profits," I snapped. "Tell the whole truth."

"Yep, there's a pot full of money in it," Sam admitted. "You wouldn't have to depend on your university grant anymore."

"Never!" I spat.

He grinned at me. "That's my girl. I would've been disappointed if you agreed to it. But I had to ask, had to give you the first shot at the money."

Money. Art and money are always bound together, no matter what you do. The artist must eat. Must breathe. And that requires money.

But I stubbornly refused to give in to the temptation. I would *not* help that slithering Dabney to spread his advertising filth across the world's sky. Never.

Or so I thought.

Things happened so fast over the next few weeks that, to this day, I am not entirely certain how the chain of events began. Who did what to whom. I am only certain of one thing: Dabney had no intention of carrying out his part of the bargain he had struck with Sam, and he never did.

I was alone again, and missing Sam terribly. For three years I had lived in isolation without a tear or a regret. I had even relished the solitude, the freedom from the need to adjust my behavior to the expectations of others. Sam had burst into my life like a joyful energetic skyrocket, showering pretty sparks everywhere. And now that he was gone, I missed him. I feared I would never see him again, and I knew if he forgot me it would be my own fault.

Suddenly my sorrowing loneliness was shattered by the arrival of a team of two dozen propulsion engineers, with legal documents that stated they were empowered to move my asteroid to Eden, where it was to be broken up and used as structural material for the Moralists' habitat.

Without thinking twice I put in a frantic call for Sam. It turned out he was halfway around the Earth's orbit. He had delivered his worms to Eden and was now on his way back to the Moon to pick up electronics components for a new construction site at the L4 libration point.

There were no relay stations around Earth's orbit in those days. My call had to fight past the Sun's coronal interference. Sam's image, when he came onto my comm screen, was shimmering and flecked with pinpoint bursts of light, like an old hologram.

As soon as he said hello I unloaded my tale of woe in a single burst of unrelieved fury and fear.

"They're taking possession of the asteroid!" I finished. "I told you they couldn't be trusted!"

For once in his life Sam was silent and thoughtful. I watched his expression change from mild curiosity to shocked surprise and then to a jaw-clenched anger as my words reached him.

At last he said, "Don't go off the deep end. Give me a few hours to look into this. I'll call you back."

It took almost forty-eight hours. I was frantic, my emotions swinging like a pendulum between the desire to hide myself or run away altogether and the growing urge to take one of the high-powered lasers I used for rock carving and slice the propulsion team into bite-sized chunks of bloody dead meat.

I tried to reach Sam a thousand times during those maddening horrible hours of waiting. Always I got one of the crew members from his ship, or a staff person from his headquarters at the Earth View Hotel. Always they gave me the same message: "Sam's looking into the problem for you. He said he'll call you as soon as he gets everything straightened out."

When he finally did call me, I was exhausted and ready for a straitjacket.

"It doesn't look good," said his wavering, tight-lipped image. Without waiting for me to respond, Sam outlined the situation.

The Right Reverend Virtue T. Dabney (his T stood for Truthful, it turned out!) had screwed us both. The Moralists never withdrew their claim from the IAC's arbitration board, and the board had decided in their favor, as Dabney had expected. The Moralists had the right to take my asteroid and use it as construction material.

Worse still, Sam's cargo of worms had arrived at Eden in fine, slimy, wriggling earthwormy health. And even worse than that, Sam had signed the contract to produce the ionospheric advertisements for the Moralist Sect. The deal was set, as legal and legitimate as an act of the world congress.

"If I don't go through with the ads," Sam said, strangely morose, "the bastards can sue me for everything I've got. They'll wind up owning my hotel, my ships, even the clothes on my back."

"Isn't there *anything* we can do?" I pleaded to his image on my screen.

For long minutes he gave no response, as my words struggled across nearly three hundred million kilometers to reach him. I hung weightless before the screen, suspended in the middle of my shabby little compartment while outside I could *feel* the thumps and clangs of the propulsion team attaching their obscene rocket thrusters and nuclear engines to my asteroid. I felt like a woman surrounded by rapists, helpless and alone.

I stared so hard at Sam's image in my screen that my eyes began to water. And then I realized that I was crying.

At last, after a lifetime of agony, Sam's face broke into a sly grin. "Y'know, I saw a cartoon once, when I was a kid. It was in a girlie magazine."

I wanted to scream at him. What does this have to do with my problem? But he went on calmly, smiling crookedly at his reminiscence, knowing that any objections from me could not reach him for a quarter of an hour.

"It showed these two guys chained to the wall of a dungeon, ten feet off the floor. Chained hand and foot. Beards on them down to their kneecaps. Totally hopeless situation. And one of the guys"—Sam actually laughed!—"one of the guys has this big stupid grin on his face and he's saying, 'Now here's my plan.'"

I felt my lungs filling themselves with air, getting ready to shriek at his nonsense.

"Now, before you blow your top," Sam warned, "let me tell you two things: First, we're both in this together. Second—well . . . here's my plan."

He kept on speaking for the next hour and a half. I never got the chance to object or even get a word in.

That is how I came to paint the first picture in Earth's ionosphere.

Sam had expected me all along to draw the advertisements for him. He never planned to use another artist. "Why should some stranger make all that money?" was his attitude.

While the propulsion engineers fitted out my asteroid with their nuclear rocket systems and supply ships from the Moon towed huge spherical tanks of gaseous propellants, Sam relayed the Rev. Dabney's rough sketches of what the ionospheric advertisements should look like.

They were all photographs of Dabney himself, wrapped in pure white robes with heavenly clouds of gold behind him and just the hint of a halo adorning his saintly head.

I would have trashed them immediately if I had not been aware of Sam's plan.

The timing had to be perfect. The first ad was scheduled to be placed over the midwestern section of the United States, where it could be seen from roughly Ohio to Iowa. If everything went the way Mountain McGuire and T. Kagashima claimed it would, the picture would drift slowly westward as the day/night terminator crawled across the Earth's surface.

Sam himself came to visit me on the day that the first ad was to be produced. He was in the latest and largest of his cargo carriers, the *Laissez-Faire*, which he jokingly referred to as "The Lazy Fairy."

My asteroid was already on its way to Eden. The propulsion engineers had connected the last of their propellant tanks, turned on their systems, and left me alone to glide slowly, under the low but steady thrust of the nuclear rockets, to a rendezvous with Eden. They would return in a few days to make final course corrections and take me off the asteroid forever.

Sam looked absolutely impish when he stepped into my compartment. His grin was almost diabolic. My place was an even bigger mess than usual, what with the

sketches for the advertisements floating here and there
and all my other sketches and computer wafers hanging
weightlessly in midair.

"How can you ever find anything in here?" Sam
asked, glancing around.

I had remained at my drawing board, behind it actually. It formed something of a defensive shield for me. I
did not want to fling myself into Sam's arms, no matter
how much I really did want to do it. I couldn't let him
think that I was willing to be his lover again in return for
the help he was giving me. I couldn't let myself think that,
especially because it was very close to being true.

He gave no indication of expecting such a reward. He
merely eyed me mischievously and asked, "You really want
to go through with this?"

I did not hesitate an instant. "Yes!"

He took a deep breath. "Okay. I'm game if you are.
The lawyers have checked everything out. Let's do it."

I slid out from behind my drawing board and went to
the computer. Sam came up beside me and activated my
communications console. For the next half hour we were
all business, my checking my drawing and Sam connecting
with McGuire and Kagashima.

"I'm glad they attached the rockets and that other
junk to the end of the asteroid you haven't carved yet,"
Sam muttered as we worked. "Would've been a crime if
they had messed up the work you've already done."

I nodded curtly, not trusting myself to look into his
eyes. He was close enough to brush against my shoulder.
I could feel the warmth of his body next to me, even while
I sweated with cold apprehension.

Working together as a team linked across hundreds of
millions of kilometers, Sam, McGuire, Kagashima, and I
painted the first picture high in the ionosphere of Earth.
From my computer the design went forth to a set of electron guns on board the same orbiting station that housed
Sam's hotel. In the comm screen I saw the picture forming
across the flat midsection of North America.

The Virgin of the Andes.

I had no intention of spreading the pompous Dabney's
unctuous features across the sky. Not even the *Norte Amer-*

icanos deserved that. Instead I had drawn a picture from my heart, from my childhood memories of the crude paintings that adorned the whitewashed walls of my village church.

You must understand that it was years before I myself saw my creation in the way it was meant to be seen, from the ground. All I had to go on that day was the little screen of my comm system, and even there I was seeing the Virgin backward, like looking at a stained-glass window from outside the cathedral.

Everyone was caught by surprise. A few startled gringos tried to photograph the picture that suddenly appeared over their heads at sunset, but none of the photos showed the true size or scope or even the actual colors of my Virgin. The colors especially were impossible to capture, they were so pale and shimmering and subtly shifting each moment. By the time television stations realized what was happening and dispatched their mobile news units, the Virgin had disappeared into the darkness of night.

All of North America went into startled, shocked turmoil. Then the word spread all across the world.

Ionosphere paintings last only for those precious few minutes of twilight, of course. Once the Sun dips below the horizon, the delicate electrical effects that create the subtle colors quickly disappear, and the picture fades into nothingness.

Except that the *information* which created the picture is stored in a computer, *gracias a Dios*. Many years later, when it was safe for me to return to Earth, I allowed the university to paint my Virgin over the skies of my native land. I saw it at last the way it was meant to be seen. It was beautiful, more beautiful than anything I have ever done since.

But that was not to happen for many years. As Sam and I watched my Virgin fade into darkness he turned to me with a happy grin.

"Now," he said cheerfully, "the shit hits the fan."

And indeed it did. Virtually every lawyer in the solar system became involved in the suits, countersuits, and counter-countersuits. Dabney and his Moralists claimed that Sam had violated their contract. Sam claimed that the contract specifically gave him artistic license, and indeed those words were buried in one of the sub-sub-clauses on the next to last page of that thick legal document. The advertising industry was thunderstruck. Environmentalists from pole to pole screamed and went to court, which prompted art critics and the entire apparatus of "fine art"—the museums, magazines, charitable associations, social clubs, wealthy patrons, and even government agencies—to come to the defense of a lonely young artist that none of them had ever heard of before: Elverda Apacheta. Me!

Sam and I paid scant attention to the legal squabbles. We were sailing on my asteroid past the Moralists' half-finished Eden and out far beyond Earth's orbit. Sam's "Lazy Fairy" was crammed to its sizable capacity with propellants for the nuclear rockets attached to "The Rememberer." He jiggered the propulsion engineers' computer program so that my asteroid headed for deep space, out past even the orbit of Mars, out to the Belt where its brother and sister asteroids orbited by the millions.

When the Moralists' engineers tried to come out and intercept "their" runaway, Sam gleefully informed them: "This object is a derelict, under the definition stated in the IAC's regulations of space commerce. It is heading for deep space, and any attempt to intercept it or change its course will be regarded by the IAC and the world government as an act of piracy!"

By the time the Moralists' lawyers came to the conclusion that Sam was bluffing, we were moving fast enough and far enough so that Dabney decided it would not be worthwhile trying to recover my asteroid. "The Rememberer" sailed out to the Asteroid Belt, half a dozen propulsion engineers were fired by the Moralists (and immediately hired by S. Gunn Enterprises, Unlimited), and Sam and I spent more than a year together.

"And that is how I became famous." Elverda Apacheta smiled slightly, as if someone had paid her a compliment she did not deserve. "Even though I am a sculptress, I am known to the public for that one painting. Like Michelangelo and the Sistine ceiling."

Jade asked, "And Sam? You say he spent more than a year with you on your asteroid?"

Now the sculptress laughed, a rich throaty sound. "Yes, I know it sounds strange to imagine Sam staying in one place for two days on end, let alone three hundred and eighty. But he did. He stayed with me that long."

"That's . . . unusual."

"You must realize that half the solar system's lawyers were looking for Sam. It was a good time for him to be unavailable. Besides, he wanted to see the Asteroid Belt for himself. You may recall that he made and lost several fortunes out there."

"Yes, I know," said Jade.

Elverda Apacheta nodded slowly, remembering. "It was a stormy time, cooped up in my little workshop. We both had other demons driving us: Sam wanted to be the first entrepreneur to set up operations in the Asteroid Belt . . ."

"And he was," Jade murmured.

"Yes, he was. And I had my own work. My art."

"Which is admired and adored everywhere."

"Perhaps so," admitted the sculptress, "but still I receive requests to produce the Virgin of the Andes. No matter what I do, that painting will haunt me forever."

" 'The Rememberer' is the most popular work of art off-Earth. Every year thousands of people make the pilgrimage. Your people will never be forgotten."

"Perhaps more tourists would go to see it if it were in a lower orbit," the sculptress mused. "Sam worked it out so that it swung through the Asteroid Belt, returned to Earth's vicinity, and was captured into a high orbit, about twelve thousand kilometers up. He was afraid of bringing it closer; he said his calculations were not so exact and he feared bringing it so close that it would hit the Earth."

"Still, it's regarded as a holy shrine and one of the greatest works of art anywhere," Jade said.

"But it's rather difficult for people to get to." Elverda Apacheta's smooth brow knitted slightly in an anxious little frown. "I have asked the IAC to bring it closer, down to where the tourist hotels orbit, but they have not acted on my request as yet."

"You know how slow bureaucracies are," said Jade.

The sculptress sighed. "I only hope I live long enough for them to make their decision."

"Did the Moralists try to recapture your asteroid?"

"Oh, no. That was the beauty of Sam's scheme. By pushing 'The Rememberer' into such a high-velocity orbit, he made it too expensive for the Moralists to go chasing after us. They screamed and sued, but finally they settled on another one of the Aten group. More than one, I believe."

"And Sam left you while you were still coasting out in the Belt?"

With a sad smile, "Yes. We quarreled a lot, of course. It was not entirely a honeymoon trip. Finally, he detached his ship to investigate some of the smaller asteroids that we had discovered. He said he wanted to register a priority in their discovery. 'It's the only way I'll ever get my name in the history books,' he told me. That was the last I saw of him."

"No further contact at all?"

"Oh, we called each other. We spent hours talking. But he never came back to me." Elverda Apacheta looked away from Jade, toward the view of Earth in the lounge's lone window. "In a way I was almost glad of it. Sam was very intense, and so was I. We were not meant to stay together for very long."

Jade said nothing. For long moments the only sound in the lounge was the faint whisper of air coming through the ventilating ducts.

"The last time I spoke with him," Elverda Apacheta said, "he had a premonition of death."

Jade felt her entire body tense. "Really?"

"Oh, it was nothing dark and brooding. That was not Sam's nature. He merely asked me someday to do a statue of him exactly as I remembered him, without using a photograph or anything else for a model. Strictly from memory. He said he would like to have that as his monument once he was gone."

"His statue on the Moon."

The sculptress nodded. "Yes. I did it in glass. Lunar glass. Have you seen it?"

"It's beautiful!"

Elverda Apacheta laughed. "It does not look like Sam at all. He was not a tall, dauntless explorer with a jutting jaw and steely eyes. But it's the way he wanted to be, and in a strange sort of way, inside that funny little body of his, that is the way he really was. So that is the way I made his statue."

And she laughed. But the tears in her eyes were not from joy.

Jade found her own vision blurring. For the first time since she had found out the truth about her birth, she realized that Sam Gunn, her own father, would have loved her if he had only known she existed.

20

●-●-●-●-●-●-●-●-●-●-●-●-●-●-●-●-●-●-●-●

Titan

STANDING IN AN armored pressure suit on the shore of the
nitrogen sea, Jade aimed her rented camcorder at the huge
fat crescent of Saturn peeking through the clouds in the
hazy orange sky. The planet was striped like a faded beach
ball, its colors pale, almost delicate tones of yellow and
pink with whitish splotches here and there. The ring system looked like a scimitar-thin line crossing its bulging
middle, though the rings cast a wide solid shadow on Saturn's bulging disk.

"Dear Spence," Jade said into her helmet microphone. "As you can see, I've made it to Titan. And I truly
do wish you were here. It's eerie, strange and beautiful
and kind of scary."

The clouds scudded across the face of Saturn, blotting
it from view. The sky darkened, and the perpetual gloom
of Titan deepened. Jade turned slightly and focused the
camera on the nitrogen sea. It looked thick, almost oily.
Near the horizon a geyser pushed slowly skyward, a slow-
motion fountain of utterly cold liquid nitrogen.

"It only took two months to get here from Ceres on
the high-boost ship. It was expensive, but the university

runs a regularly scheduled service to the campus here. Titan's become *the* hub for studies of the outer solar system, although there are actually more people living and working in the Jupiter system. Which is natural, I suppose, since they discovered those squid things living in the Jovian sea."

Waves were lapping sluggishly against the rocks on which Jade stood. The whole nitrogen sea seemed to be heaving itself slowly, reluctantly toward her.

"Tidal shift," whispered a small voice in her helmet earphones. "Please return to base." She was being monitored by the Titan base's automated safety cameras, of course.

"The tide's starting to come in," Jade said. "With Saturn pulling it, the tide covers nearly a quarter of Titan's surface. Time for me to get back to the base"—she swung the camera around—"up on those cliffs. I don't know how much of it you can see in this murk, but it's pretty comfortable—for a short visit. Like a college dormitory, I guess."

She started walking toward the powered stairs that climbed up to the clifftop.

"I do wish you were here, Spence. Or I was there. I miss you. This will be the last interview for the Sam Gunn biography. I'll be coming back to Selene after this. It'll take six months, even at high boost, but I'm looking forward to getting back home. Please video me back as soon as you can."

Two months of enforced inactivity aboard the plasma torch ship that had brought her to Titan had given Jade plenty of time to think about Spence Johansen.

She wanted to end her videotape with "I love you," but found that she could not. I'm not sure of myself, she realized. I'm not sure of him. There'll be time enough for that when I get back, she told herself. Then she added ruefully, if Spence hasn't married again by then.

Solomon Goodman looked very young to be a famous professor and Nobel laureate. He's not much more than thirty, she told herself.

Unlike most of the other people she had interviewed,

Professor Goodman had no qualms about talking to her. He had immediately acceded to her request for an interview even before Jade had reached Ceres, and had personally set her up with a reservation aboard the plasma torch ship that had brought her out to Titan.

Now she sat in his office. What looked like a large picture window was actually a video screen, she realized. A beautifully clear image of Saturn showed on it, obviously taken from a satellite camera above Titan's perpetual cloud cover. Jade could see the mysterious spokes in Saturn's rings and the streaks of pale colors banding the planet's oblate body.

Goodman sat slouched in a pseudo-leather couch, his long legs stretched out, almost touching Jade's booted feet. She pictured him as a skinny, gangling student even though he was now getting pudgy, potbellied. His hair was still quite dark and thickly curled; his slightly puffy face could look quite pleasant when he smiled.

A robot had brought a tray of tea things and deposited them on the low table between the couch and the padded chair on which Jade was sitting.

"One of the perks of university life," Goodman said, almost defensively. "Real old English tea in the afternoon. I got into the habit when I was at Oxford. Really gives you a lift for the later part of the day."

Jade let him pour a cup of steaming tea for her, then added a bit of milk herself. The tea service was real china, brought in all the way from Earth. The Nobel prize brought its privileges, she thought.

"So what do you want to know about Sam?" Goodman asked, smiling at her. Jade noticed that he had large hands; they dwarfed the delicate cup and saucer he was holding.

"Well," Jade said, turning on the recorder in her belt, "You were the last person to see him alive, weren't you?"

His smile faded. He put the cup and saucer down on the tray in front of him.

Looking up at Jade with an almost guilty expression on his face, Goodman said, "I guess you could say that I killed Sam Gunn."

21

●■●■●■●■●■●■●■●■●■●■●■●

Einstein

GOODMAN LEANED EVEN deeper into the couch, head tilted back, eyes focused on something, someplace far beyond the ceiling of his office.

You can't pace the floor in zero gravity—he said, almost to himself. So Sam was flitting around the cramped circular control center of our ship like a crazed chipmunk, darting along madly, propelling himself by grabbing at handgrips, console knobs, viewport edges, anything that could give him a moment's purchase as he whirled by.

I was sweating over my instruments, but every nine seconds Sam whizzed past me like a demented monkey, jabbering, "It's gotta be there. It's *gotta* be there!"

"There's *something* out there," I yelled over my shoulder, annoyed with him. Angry at myself, really. It was my calculations that had put us into this fix.

The instruments were showing a definite gravitational flux, damned close to what I had calculated when I was still back on campus. But out here, well past the orbit of Pluto—farther than anybody had gone before—what I needed to see was a planet, a fat little world orbiting out in that darkness more than seven billion miles from Earth.

Planet X. The tenth planet. Astronomers had been searching for it since before Percival Lowell's time, but I had worked out *exactly* where it should be, me and the CalTech/MIT/Osaka-linked computers. And Sam Gunn had furnished the money and the ship to go out and find it.

Only, it wasn't there.

"It's gotta be there." Sam orbited past me again. "*Gotta* be."

The first time I met Sam, I thought he was nuts. Chunky little guy. Hair like a nest of rusted wire. Darting, probing eyes. Kind of shifty. The eyes of a politician, maybe, or a confidence man.

"Fly out there?" I had asked him. "Why not just rent time on an orbital telescope, or use the lunar observa . . ."

"To claim it, egghead!" Sam had snapped. "A whole planet. I want it."

He couldn't have been that dumb, I thought. He'd amassed several fortunes, and lost all but the latest one. To fly out beyond Pluto would cost every penny he had, and more.

"You can't claim a planet," I explained patiently. "International agreements from back in . . ."

"Puke on international agreements!" he shouted. "I'm not a national government. I'm S. Gunn Enterprises, Unlimited. And a whole planet's *gotta* be worth a fortune."

Sam had a reputation for shady schemes, but I couldn't for the life of me see how he planned to profit from claiming Planet X. Nor any reason for me to leave my home and job at the university to go out to the end of the solar system with him.

I didn't reckon on Sam's persuasiveness. He didn't have a silver tongue. Far from it. His language was more often crude, even obscene, than eloquent. But he was a nonstop needler, wheedler, pleader, seducer. In the language of my forefathers, he was a *nudge*. His tongue didn't have to be silver; it was heavy-duty, long-wearing, blister-proof, diamond-coated solid muscle.

So I found myself ducking through the hatch of a special ship he had commissioned. Only the two of us as crew; I was to do the navigating, Sam did everything else, including the cooking. Before I could ask myself why I was doing this, I was being flattened into the acceleration couch as we roared out into the wild black yonder.

But Planet X wasn't there.

Sam slowed down, puffing, until he was dangling right behind me, his feet half a meter off the floor. My softboots were locked in the foot restraints and still he barely came up to my height. He was wheezing, and I realized there was a lot of gray in his reddish hair. His face looked tired, old, eyes baggy and sad.

"Of all the eggheads in all the universities in all the solar systems," he groaned, "you've . . ."

Suddenly I realized what the instruments were telling me. I shouted, "It's a black hole!"

"And I'm the tooth fairy."

"No, really! It's not a planet at all. It's a black hole. Look!"

Sam snarled, "How in hell can I see something that's invisible by definition?"

With trembling fingers I pointed to the gravitational flux meters and the high-energy detectors. We even went over to the optical telescope and bumped our heads together like Laurel and Hardy, trying to squint through the eyepiece together.

Nothing to see. Except a faint violet glow, the last visible remains of the thin interplanetary gas that was being sucked into the black hole on a one-way trip to oblivion.

It really was a black hole! The final grave of a star that had collapsed, God knows how many eons ago. A black hole! Practically in our backyard! And I had discovered it! Visions of the Nobel Prize made me giddy.

Sam sprang straight to the communications console and started tapping frantically at its keyboard, muttering about how he could rent time to astronomers to study the only black hole close enough to Earth to see firsthand.

"It's worth a fuckin' fortune," he chortled, his fingers racing along the keys like a concert pianist trying to do Chopin's 'Minute Waltz' in thirty seconds. "A dozen fortunes!"

He filed his claim and even gave the black hole a name: Einstein. I grinned and nodded agreement with his choice.

It took nearly eleven hours for Sam's message to get to Earth, and another eleven for their reply to reach us. I spent the time studying Einstein while Sam proclaimed to the universe how he was going to build an orbiting hotel just outside Einstein's event horizon and invent a new pastime for the danger nuts.

"Space surfing! A jetpack on your back and good old Einstein in front of you. See how close you can skim to the event horizon without getting sucked in! It'll make billions!"

"Until somebody gets stretched into a bloody string of spaghetti," I said. "That grav field out there is *powerful,* and I think it fluctuates . . ."

"All the better," said Sam, clapping his hands like a kid in front of a Christmas tree. "Let a couple of the risk freaks kill themselves and all the others will come boiling out here like lemmings on migration."

I shook my head in wonder.

When the comm signal finally chimed I was still trying to dope out the basic parameters of our black hole. Yes, I was thinking of Einstein as ours; that's what being near Sam does to you.

His round little face went pugnacious the instant he saw the woman on the screen. I felt an entirely different reaction. She was beautiful, with thick platinum-blond hair and the kind of eyes that promised paradise.

But her voice was as cold as a robot's. "Mr. Gunn, we meet again. Your claim has been noted and filed with the Interplanetary Astronautical Council. In the meantime, I represent the creditors from your most recent bankruptcy. To date . . ."

She droned on while Sam's face went from angry red to ashy gray. This far from Earth, all messages were one-way. You can't hold a conversation with an eleven-hour wait between each transmission. The blonde went into infinite detail about how much money Sam owed, and to whom. Even though I was only half listening, I learned that our ship was not paid for, and my own university was suing Sam for taking my instrumentation without authorization!

Finally she smiled slightly and delivered the knockout.

"Now, Mr. Gunn—aside from all the above unpleasantness, it may interest you to realize that your claim to this alleged black hole is without merit or substance."

Sam made a growl from deep in his throat.

"International law dating back to 1967 prohibits claiming sovereignty to any body found in space . . ."

"I'm not claiming sovereignty," Sam snapped to the unhearing screen. "And this ain't a body, it's a black hole."

She serenely continued, ". . . although it is allowed to claim the *use* of a body found in space, I'm afraid that the law clearly states that you must establish an operational facility on the body in question before such a claim will be recognized by the Interplanetary Astronautical Council."

Sam snorted like a bull about to charge. Me, I thought about establishing an operational facility on the body attached to that incredibly beautiful face.

"So I'm afraid, my dear Mr. Gunn"—her smile widened to show dazzlingly perfect teeth—"that unless you establish an operational facility on your so-called black hole, your claim is worthless. And, oh, yes! One more thing—an automated ship is on its way to you, filled with robot lawyers who will have authorization to take possession of your ship and all its equipment, in the name of your creditors. Good-bye. Have a nice day."

The screen went blank.

Sam gave a screech that would make an ax-murderer shudder and flung himself at the dead screen. He bounced off and scooted weightlessly around the control center again, gibbering, jabbering, screaming insults and obscenities at the blonde, the IAC, the whole solar system in general, and all the lawyers on Earth in particular.

"I'll show 'em!" he raged. "I'll show 'em all!"

I stayed close to my instruments—actually, they were still the university's instruments, I guess.

After God knows how many orbits around the control center, screaming and raging, Sam propelled himself toward the hatch in the floor that led down to the equipment bay.

"They want an operational facility, they'll get an operational facility!"

I wrenched my feet free so fast I twisted an ankle and went diving after him.

"Sam, what the hell are you thinking of?"

He was already unlocking the hatch of our EVA scooter, a little one-man utility craft with a big bubble canopy and so many extensible arms it looked like a metal spider.

"I'm gonna pop an instrument pod down Einstein's throat. That's gonna be our operational facility."

"But it'll just disappear into the black hole!"

"So what?"

"It won't be an operational facility."

"How do you know what it'll be doing inside the event horizon? The gravity field will stretch out its signals, won't it?"

"Theoretically," I answered.

"Then we'll be getting signals from the probe for years, right? Even after it goes past the event horizon."

"I guess so. But that doesn't prove the probe will be operating inside the black hole, Sam."

"If the mother-humping lawyers want to prove that it's not working, let 'em jump into the black hole after it. And kiss my ass on the way down!"

I argued with him for more than an hour while he got the instrument pod together and revved up the EVA craft. What he wanted to do was *dangerous*. Maybe adventure freaks would like to skim around the event horizon of a black hole. Me, I don't feel really safe unless there's good California soil shaking beneath my feet.

But Sam would not be denied. Maybe he was a danger freak himself. Maybe he was desperate for the money he thought he could make. Maybe he just wanted to screw all the lawyers on Earth, especially that blonde.

He didn't even put on a pressure suit. He just clambered up into the cockpit of the EVA craft, slammed its hatch, and worked one of its spidery arms to pick up the instrument pod.

Reluctantly I went back to the control center to monitor Sam's mission.

"Stay well clear of the event horizon," I warned him

over the radio. "I don't know enough about Einstein to give you firm parameters . . ."

Sam was no fool. He listened to my instructions. He released the instruments well clear of the event horizon. But the pod just orbited around the faint violet haze that marked Einstein's position. It didn't go spiraling into it.

"Goddamned mother-humping no-good son of a lawyer!"

Sam jockeyed the EVA craft into a matching orbit and gave it a push inward. Not enough. Then another, swearing a blue streak every instant.

"That's close enough," I yelled into the microphone, sweating bullets. "The event horizon fluctuates, Sam. You mustn't . . ."

I swear the black hole reached out and grabbed him. The event horizon sort of burped and engulfed Sam's craft. I know it's impossible, but that's what happened.

"Hey!" he yelled. "Heyyyyyy!"

According to everything we knew about black holes up to that moment, Sam was being squeezed by Einstein's immense gravitational forces, torn apart, crushed, mashed, squashed, pulverized.

"What's going onnnn?" Sam's radio voice stretched out eerily, like in an echo chamber.

"What's going on?" I asked back.

"It's like sliding down a chuuute!"

"You're not being pulled apart?"

"Hell nooo! But I can't see anything. Like falling down an elevator shaaaft!"

Sam should have been crushed. But he wasn't. His radio messages were being stretched out, but apparently he himself was not. He was falling into the black hole on a one-way trip, swallowed alive.

I started to laugh. We had named the black hole exactly right. Inside the event horizon spacetime was being warped, all right. But Sam was now part of *that* continuum and to him, everything seemed normal. Our universe, the one we're in, would have seemed weirdly distorted to him if he could see it.

It had all been there in old Albert's equations, if we had only had the sense enough to realize it.

Sam Gunn, feisty, foul-mouthed, womanizing, fast-talking Sam Gunn, had discovered a shortcut to the stars, a spacetime warp that one day would allow us to get around the limits of speed-of-light travel. That black hole was not a dead-end route to oblivion; it was a spacetime warp that opened somewhere/somewhen else in the universe. Or maybe in another universe altogether.

But it was a *one-way* route.

Sam gave his life to his discovery. He was on a one-way trip to God knows where. Maybe there'd be kindly aliens at the other end of the warp to greet him and give him their version of the Nobel Prize.

I got the terrestrial Nobel, of course. And now I'm heading up an enormous team of scientists who're studying Einstein and trying to figure out how to put black hole warps to practical use.

And Sam? Who knows where he is?

But you can still hear him. Thanks to Einstein's time-stretching effects, you can hear Sam swearing and cussing every moment, all the way down that long, long slide to whatever's on the other side of the warp.

And according to Einstein (Albert), we'll be able to hear Sam yelling forever. Forever.

22

■·■·■·■·■·■·■·■·■·■·■·■·■·■·■·■·

Surprise, Surprise

JADE LEANED BACK in the yielding warmth of the form-shaping chair, suddenly weary and drained. She turned off the computer in her lap. The interview with Professor Goodman was on its way to Selene. The final interview. Her long trek after Sam Gunn's story was at last finished.

She felt as if she had been struggling all her life to reach the top of a mountain, and now that she had done it, there was nothing to see, nothing more to do. The challenge had been met, and now she was surrounded by emptiness. There was no feeling of triumph, or even accomplishment. She was merely tried and empty and alone on a pinnacle with nowhere else to go.

She leaned her head back into the chair's comforting warmth. The dormitory room that the university had given her was more luxurious than most of the hotels she had slept in. The chair adjusted itself to her body shape and temperature, enfolding her like a gently pulsating womb. How pleasant it would be, Jade thought, to just close my eyes and sleep—forever.

But the video window on the wall of the small room showed a view of Titan's spaceport out on the murky surface, and the sleek torch ship that had landed there only minutes earlier. The retractable dome was rising silently over it. Soon the ship would be disgorging its payload of passengers and cargo. In another two days it would start back toward the big scientific base in Mars orbit. And Jade would be on it, heading back toward Selene, toward the habitats crowding the Earth / Moon system, toward the world of her birth.

And what then? she asked herself. What then?

She drifted into an exhausted dreamless sleep. When the phone buzzed it startled her; her nerves jumped as if an emergency Klaxon were hooting.

The laptop had slipped to the thickly carpeted floor. Thinking idly that the university life had all sorts of unwritten perquisites, Jade picked up the tiny box and pressed its On switch.

Spence Johansen's grinning face filled the little screen.

"Hello there," he said.

Jade waited for him to go on, knowing that this was either a tape or a call from the Earth / Moon area, hours distant even at the lightspeed of video communications.

"Hey, Jade, say something! I'm here. On Titan. Up in the flight lounge. Surprised?"

She nearly dropped the computer again.

"Spence? You're here? It's really you?"

"Sure, I just arrived."

"I'll be right up!"

Jade tossed the computer onto her bed and dashed for the door, all fatigue forgotten, all the weariness melted away. By the time she tore through the corridors and rode the power stairs up to the flight lounge, Spence already had a pair of tall frosted drinks sitting on the bar, waiting for her.

She threw herself into his arms. Their long passionate kiss drew admiring stares and a few low whistles from the other new arrivals and regulars in the lounge.

"Whatever . . . how did you . . . why . . . ?" Jade had a million questions bubbling within her.

Johansen smiled, almost sheepishly. "Ol' Jefferson got kind of boring after you went away. I missed you, Jade. Missed you a lot."

"So much that you came all the way out here?"

He shrugged.

She perched on the bar stool next to his, ignoring the drink standing before her, all her attention on this man who had traveled across half the solar system. To be with her.

"I missed you, too, Spence."

"Did you?"

"Enormously." She suddenly grinned maliciously. "Considering where we are, I might say *titanically*."

Spence Johansen threw his head back and laughed a genuine, hearty, full-throated laugh. And Jade knew that she loved him.

She took his big hand in her little one and tugged him off the bar stool. "Come on," she said. "There's so much I've got to tell you. Come on to my room where we can be alone together."

Without another word, Spence allowed the elfin little woman to lead him away.

There is no natural day/night cycle on Titan. Ten times farther from the Sun than Earth is, Saturn's major moon is always in gloomy twilight, at best. Usually its murky, clouded atmosphere even blots out the pale light from Saturn itself.

The university base kept Greenwich Mean Time. The lights in the windowless base's corridors and public areas dimmed at 2000 hours and went down to a "night" equivalent at 2200, then came up to "morning" at 0700.

Jade and Spence had no way of knowing the time. He had purposely put his shaving kit in front of the dorm room's digital clock, so that from the bed they could not see it. The only light in the room was from the video window, which they had set on views of the nitrogen sea up on the surface: shadowy, muted, almost formless.

Jade told Spence about all her discoveries, and the pain that they brought. He seemed utterly surprised when she explained that she was probably Sam Gunn's daughter.

"Talk about Kismet," he whispered low. "For both of us."

"If Sam were alive he could give the bride away," Jade said.

"And then be my best man." Spence chuckled softly in the shadows. "Just like him to turn the ordinary rules upside-down."

They made love again, languidly, unhurriedly. They slept and then made love once more. And talked. Talked of the past, of the wondrous ways that lives can intertwine, of the surprise and sheer luck—good or bad—that can determine a person's fate. Talked of the pain one person can inflict on another without even knowing it. Talked of the happiness that can be had when two people click just right, as they had done.

Suddenly a new question popped into Jade's mind. "How many children do you have?" she asked. "Am I going to be a stepmother?"

In the darkened room she could barely see him shake his head. "Never stayed married long enough to have kids. But now . . ." His voice drifted into silence.

"I want babies. Lots of them."

"Me, too," he said. "At least two."

"A boy and a girl."

"Right."

"And then maybe two more."

He laughed softly. "Maybe we ought to have twins."

"That would be more efficient, wouldn't it."

"Want a big wedding? The main chapel at Selene and all the trimmings?"

Jade shook her head. "I never even thought about it. No, I don't think I know enough people to invite."

"My parents are gone, but we could ask your adoptive mother to come up."

"No!" Jade snapped. "She abandoned me. I haven't seen her for seventeen years. Let it stay that way."

"But she's the only kin you have."

She peered at the video window, the murky gloom of the nitrogen sea. "I have family. Lots of family. Monica Bianco and Zach Bonner and Felix Sanchez. Frederick Mohammed Malone. Rick Darling. Elverda Apacheta. The owner of the Pelican Bar. They're my family. They'd come to Selene for my wedding, if I asked them to."

Spence said, "And here I thought you were an orphan."

"Not anymore," Jade answered, surprised at the real-

ity of it. I'm not alone, she told herself. I have friends all
across the solar system now. And a man who loves me.

"I'm pretty old for you," Spence said in the darkness.
"Hell, if Sam really is your father, I'm a year or two older
than he is."

"Would you be embarrassed to have a wife young
enough to be your daughter?" she asked, half teasing, half
fearful of his answer.

"Embarrassed? Hell no! Every guy my age will eat
his heart out with envy the minute he meets you."

Jade laughed, relieved.

"But there's you to think about," he said, turning toward her in the bed. "How're you going to feel, tied to an
old fart like me when you're so young? There's plenty of
stories about old men with young wives . . ."

"Old stories," Jade quickly said. "Stories from ancient
times. You're as young and vigorous as Sir Lancelot was,
and you'll stay that way for another thirty or forty years, at
least, thanks to modern medicine."

He propped himself on one elbow and, with his other
hand, traced a finger from her lips to her chin, down her
throat and the length of her body. Jade felt her skin tingle
at his touch.

"Well," he said, quite seriously, "I'm sure going to keep
abreast of all the research going on in the field of aging."

Jade burst out laughing and grabbed for him. They
made love again and then drifted back to sleep.

It was the phone buzzer that awoke Jade. She blinked
once, twice, coming out of the fog, suddenly panicked that
she had been dreaming. Then she felt the warmth of
Spence's body next to hers and heard him snoring softly,
almost like the purr of a contented cat.

Smiling, she groped in the dark for the oblong box
that controlled the video window. Without turning on any
lights she pecked at the keys until the scene of the nitrogen sea was replaced by bold yellow lettering:

URGENT CALL FROM PROF. GOODMAN

Jade had to turn on her bedside lamp to see the control wand well enough to tap out the command that put

Goodman on the video window without activating the wall camera that would let him see her.

Spence stirred groggily. "Whassamatter?"

"I don't know," she said.

Goodman was apparently in the communications center, hunched over a technician who was sitting at one of the consoles. Display screens covered the wall behind him, no two of them showing the same picture.

The professor was scowling fiercely. Or was his expression one of fear? Or even utter surprise, shock? Jade could not tell.

"Professor Goodman? This is Jade."

"Oh!" He jumped back slightly, as if pricked by a hot needle. "There's no video."

"I know. You have an urgent message for me?"

He bobbed his head up and down so hard that a lock of his curly hair flopped in front of his eyes. Brushing it back, he broke into a strange, toothy smile that just might have been a grimace of pain.

"It just came in ... from the automated station at Einstein ..."

"Einstein? The black hole?"

"Yes. No video, of course. But—well, listen for yourself."

A long, low bass note, throbbing slightly, like the last distant echo of faraway thunder or the rumble of a torch ship's engines.

Spence sat up in the bed beside Jade. "What the hell is that?" he whispered.

"What is it?" Jade asked Goodman's image on the video screen.

The professor looked startled all over again. "Oh! Excuse me. In my haste I activated the raw data tape. Here—here's the same message, but time-compressed and computer-enhanced."

"... you wouldn't believe what these guys can do! It's fantastic!"

Sam Gunn's voice!

Jade felt her heart clutch in her chest. "What is that?" she blurted.

"It's Sam!" Goodman almost yelled. "Sam! He's on his way back! He's coming out of the black hole!"

"That's impossible," Spence said, his voice hollow.

"I know! But he's doing it," Professor Goodman answered, oblivious to the fact that he was now speaking to a man's voice.

"He's alive?" Jade asked.

"Yes! Yes!" Goodman seemed ecstatic. "He found aliens on the other side of the black hole. An intelligent extraterrestrial species! They've provided him with the means to come back through the spacetime warp!"

"*Sacre dieu,*" Jade breathed.

"He's alive and coming back to us." Goodman was almost capering around the comm center now. "He's discovered intelligent extraterrestrial life. It's a miracle. Two miracles! Miraculous, the whole thing is miraculous!"

"The time distortion," Jade asked. "How long will it take before Sam is back with us?"

Goodman sobered, but only slightly. "We're working on that. Trying to get a Doppler fix on the raw data. It's only a rough estimate, but from what we've got now I'd say that Sam will pop out of the event horizon in another twenty to twenty-five years."

"Years?" Spence gasped.

"He's been gone for more than fifteen," Goodman said. Then he fell to musing. "Maybe there's a symmetry here. Maybe it'll take him exactly as long to return as it did to go through the other way. Still, it'll be fifteen years, at least. Unless . . ."

Jade turned to Spence and clutched him by the shoulders. "He's alive! Sam's alive!"

"And on his way back. The little SOB is coming back to us."

"And he's met intelligent aliens."

"Holy cow," said Spence, fervently.

Two days later Jade and Spence stood at the observation bay of the torch ship as it sped away from Titan, heading back toward civilization and the Earth / Moon system.

Holding one arm protectively around the tiny young woman he loved, Johansen pointed with his free hand.

"There's Jupiter, the big bright one. And Mars, the smaller red star, down to your left."

Jade nestled into the crook of his arm, rested her head against his chest. "And Earth? Can we see Earth?"

"Yep. Kind of faint at this distance, but it still looks distinctly blue. See it, out there to the left of Jupiter."

Jade saw the distant blue speck and knew that her mother lay buried there. And there was another woman on Earth, Jade realized, still alive. But for how long? The one thing she had learned in the past year or so was that life surges along, always changing, whether you want it to or not. Nothing remains the same.

"Spence?" she asked, turning to look up into his face. "Would you mind if we went down to Earth? Just for a few days."

"Earth? I thought you couldn't . . ."

"I can wear an exoskeleton for a few days. And attach myself to a heart pump."

"But why?"

"My adoptive mother lives in Quebec. I want to see her. I want to tell her that I understand why she had to leave me."

"I thought you hated her."

"I thought so, too. Maybe I did. But I don't anymore. I can't. Not anymore."

He gazed down into her lovely green eyes, knowing that he could not deny her anything.

"Couldn't you speak with her on a video link?' It's just as good, almost."

Jade shook her head gently. "No. This has to be in person. For real. Flesh to flesh."

He shrugged. "I might need an exoskeleton myself. Been a long time since I faced a full gee."

The ship was accelerating at just under one-sixth gravity. They had weeks of leisure ahead of them. Solar News was planning an elaborate special series on Sam Gunn, now that the news of his return had broken. Raki had promised Jade that she would narrate the entire series and be the on-camera star. Her career was assured, even though she had carefully withheld the information that she was probably Sam Gunn's daughter.

"Will you go out to the black hole for the show?" Spence asked.

"No," said Jade. "We can tape that with the remote cameras already on station at Einstein and patch me into the scene. There's not much to see, really. No point going out there until Sam's about to emerge, and he won't be coming out for another fifteen or twenty years."

"But he's on his way back."

"I wonder if he's aged? Maybe I'll be his age when he comes out."

Spence let a little grin show in his face.

"It's so like Sam," Jade went on. "He has the whole solar system in a commotion. Intelligent alien life! All these years the astronomers have been searching and Sam's the one to find them."

Spence made a sound that might have been a barely suppressed laugh.

Jade took no notice of it. "The scientists, the politicians, the *military*—they're all in an uproar. To say nothing of the world's religious leaders."

Spence made no reply.

"Well," Jade said with a sigh, "at least we have fifteen or twenty years to get ready for it."

"Maybe," Spence said at last.

She looked sharply at him. "What do you mean?"

"I don't know for sure," he replied. "But there's a strange flavor to all this."

Jade knit her brows.

"I mean," said Spence, "Sam disappears while a ship-load of lawyers are on their way to strip him naked. Then fifteen years later he pops up again claiming he's met intelligent extraterrestrial creatures."

"You don't think . . . !"

"Before we left Titan I used the university library access system to look up the status of all the lawsuits filed against Sam. The statute of limitations runs out on the last one next year."

"But the signals from the black hole!"

"He's Sam Gunn, honey. He's been hiding out *someplace* for the past fifteen years. Maybe he really did fall into a black hole." Spence pulled her tighter and gazed out at the wide starry universe. "I wouldn't put any money on it, though."

She smiled up at him. "And you claim to be his friend."

"I knew Sam pretty well. I wouldn't put *anything* past him."

"He couldn't have! It just isn't possible."

Spence grinned and looked out at the stars again. "He's Sam Gunn, honey. Unlimited."

ABOUT THE AUTHOR

BEN BOVA is a writer of science and science fiction and is past president of the Science fiction and Fantasy Writers of America. He and his wife live in Connecticut and Florida.